MW01139565

MURDER IN PITIGLIANO

MURDER
IN
PITIGLIANO

CAMILLA
TRINCHIERI

Published by
Soho Press, Inc.
227 W 17th Street
New York, NY 10011
www.sohopress.com

Library of Congress Cataloging-in-Publication Data

Names: Trinchieri, Camilla, author.
Title: Murder in Pitigliano / Camilla Trinchieri.
Description: New York, NY : Soho Crime, 2025. | Series: The Tuscan mysteries ; 5
Identifiers: LCCN 2024057732

ISBN 978-1-64129-695-3
eISBN 978-1-64129-696-0

Subjects: LCGFT: Detective and mystery fiction. | Novels.
Classification: LCC PS3553.R435 M873 2025 | DDC 813/.54—dc23/eng/20241230
LC record available at https://lccn.loc.gov/2024057732

Interior design by Janine Agro, Soho Press, Inc.

Printed in the United States of America

10 9 8 7 6 5 4 3 2 1

EU Responsible Person (for authorities only)
eucomply OÜ
Pärnu mnt 139b-14
11317 Tallinn, Estonia
hello@eucompliancepartner.com
www.eucompliancepartner.com

In memory of Dr. Barbara Lane,
the very best of friends

CAST OF CHARACTERS

(in order of appearance)

Nico Doyle: American ex–homicide detective now living in Gravigna

Gogol: Nico's Dante-quoting breakfast friend

Nelli Corsi: Nico's artist girlfriend

OneWag: Nico's adopted dog, also known as Rocco

Cilia Bianconi: a little girl seeking help

Livia Granchi: Cilia's mother, new to Gravigna

Gustavo: a pensioner and town meddler

Sandro Ventini: co-owner of Bar All'Angolo

Enrico: owner of the town's salumeria and bakery

Jimmy Lando: cornetto baker, co-owner of Bar All'Angolo and Sandro's husband

Luciana: Enrico's wife and owner of the flower shop

Ugo: the Coop's produce buyer

Salvatore Perillo: maresciallo of the Greve Carabinieri Station

Ivana Perillo: Perillo's wife and successful career woman

Stella Morelli: grammar school teacher and Daniele's girlfriend

Tilde Morelli: Stella's mother and chef at the Sotto Il Fico restaurant

Rita Doyle: Nico's deceased wife and Tilde's cousin

Daniele Donato: Perillo's Venetian brigadiere and right-hand man

Enzo Morelli: Tilde's husband and Stella's father

Elvira Morelli: Enzo's mother and owner of Sotto Il Fico

Vince: Perillo's food-loving brigadiere

Renzino: dog-fearing bar waiter

Saverio Bianconi: Cilia's father, now a runaway

Angela Rossi: concerned Pitigliano native

Giancarlo Lenzi: Saverio's business partner and murder victim

Signora Ferruzzi: deceased owner of an apartment and a knit shop in Gravigna

Annamaria Lenzi: Giancarlo Lenzi's wife

Mimmo Lenzi: Annamaria's thirteen-year-old son

Eddi Lenzi: Mimmo's nineteen-year-old brother

Matteo Necchi: Giancarlo Lenzi's cousin and manager of a Pitigliano winery

Debora Costa: retired psychotherapist and one of the few Jews still living in Pitigliano

Maria Grazia Bertini: Latin professor living in Orvieto

Alida la Rossa: Livia's ill-reputed mother

Laura Benati: manager of Hotel Bella Vista and Nelli's good friend

Riccardo Cerani: the possible new chef at Hotel Bella Vista

Mariella: waitress at Caffè Degli Archi in Pitigliano

Alba: Ivana's boss and majority owner of Cantuccini d'Alba, SRL

Stefano Granchi: Livia's estranged husband

Paolo Fulci: Livia's neighbor

Tino Parucci: owner of the electronics shop Giancarlo Lenzi took over

Fausto Parucci: Tino's son and Mimmo's classmate

Susanna Necchi: Matteo's beautiful, estranged wife

Leo: Angela Rossi's young nephew

Bianca: Eddi's ex-girlfriend

MURDER IN PITIGLIANO

ONE

Gravigna, a small town in the Chianti hills of Tuscany
A Wednesday morning in November

B ar All'Angolo was busier than usual.
Outside the cold morning was darkening. The light rain was ready to turn into the forecast all-day downpour. Workers quickly downed Jimmy's espressos to give them an extra boost for the long day ahead. Grade school students knocked against each other's loaded backpacks and umbrellas while reaching for the ciambellas and cornetti Sandro, the co-owner of the café, handed out when he wasn't behind the cash register. Parents urged them to hurry. The high school students had already gone to take the bus for Greve. Nico and Gogol were having their usual breakfast by the French window. Nelli had already left for the Querciabella vineyard. With so many feet shuffling across the café floor, OneWag had chosen to lie down under Nico's chair.

"Want some?" a small voice asked from behind Nico. Nico turned around to see a little girl kneeling on the floor offering OneWag a piece of her chocolate-filled cornetto.

"Please don't give him that," Nico said gently. "Chocolate is very bad for dogs."

"I know that." With her face hidden by a mass of red curls, the girl quickly put the piece in her mouth. OneWag sniffed her hand.

"Cilia, get off the floor!" ordered a woman, slamming her coffee cup down on the near counter. Dressed in jeans and a green down coat, she had the same red curls down to her shoulders. "Floors are dirty, dogs are dirty and they bite. Why don't you ever listen to me?"

"Do not let your fear defeat her," Gogol announced.

"My dog doesn't bite," Nico added, wondering why any mother would ever place fear in a child's heart. He had heard Italian women tell their children, "If you're not good, the boogeyman will get you." It made him angry.

Cilia gave OneWag an awkward hug and quickly stood up to face her mother, who was marching over on heeled boots. "He looked hungry, Mamma."

Cilia's mother, a tired-looking woman somewhere in her late thirties, grabbed Cilia's hand and addressed Nico and his Dante-quoting friend. "You'll have to excuse me. Nice and mean dogs all look the same to me. That goes for men too. Come, Cilia." She pulled her daughter's arm. "You'll be late for school."

The little girl tugged her hand away and ran out of the café. Her mother shook her head in exasperation and followed her out.

"I've never seen them before, have you?" Nico asked the old man now chewing on the salame crostino meant for Nico.

"The little girl grieves with purpose; the mother grieves with anger," Gogol mumbled. "My words."

I like your words best, Nico wanted to say, but for fear of insulting Gogol's idol, he bit into his second whole wheat cornetto instead. It was still warm. "Why do you say they're grieving?"

"Can you not feel it?"

"It was clear the mother was not in a good mood. The child seemed all right."

"Rocco holds the truth," Gogol said.

"What?"

"The little one slipped something under his collar."

"She did?"

Gogol answered with a slow blink.

Nico looked down. "Come out, buddy." OneWag had slid between Nico's feet to nudge Gogol's leg for a treat.

"Let me see." Nico slapped his thigh lightly to call the dog just as the old man lowered his arm, his fingers dangling a bare crostino. OneWag gently took the bread and lay down to eat.

A cold sweep of wet air made Nico look up.

"Maremma maiala!"[1] Gustavo swore as he quickly closed the café door.

As the dog chewed, a small roll of paper dropped to the floor.

"Buongiorno, Gustavo," Sandro said from behind the cash register.

Gustavo took off his fedora and shook it free of water, revealing a full head of white hair. He wore a heavy gray coat with the countless scarves his wife knit for him. He saw Nico and raised his hand. "Buon di', amico."

"Buongiorno," Nico answered. Gustavo was one of the four pensioners Perillo liked to call the Bench Boys. He was somewhere in his eighties and often grumpy.

"A cappuccino and a ciambella," Gustavo called out to Jimmy at the far end of the room as he made his way to Nico's table. He loosened his scarves. "No sitting on benches today." The friends spent their days sitting in the main piazza just outside the café.

"'The dense air to water changed,'" Gogol quoted.

"Well said." Gustavo pulled out a chair and sat down with a thump.

"Do you know a little girl named Cilia?" Nico asked. Gustavo was the town historian of past, present and future.

---

1 A Tuscan curse meaning "Maremma pig." Maremma is a region of Tuscany.

"Ah, la piccola[2] found you. I'm glad."

"She found my dog." Nico slapped his knee again. "Come here, OneWag."

Now licking a paw, the dog paid no attention. Gogol leaned down with a loud sigh, picked up the small rolled-up piece of paper lying next to OneWag and held it up.

Gustavo took it from him. "I see writing was easier for her. What does it say? She seemed most anxious to find you. You must read it."

"If you give it to me, I will."

"Ah, forgive." Gustavo reluctantly dropped the note in Nico's hand. He quickly unrolled it.

Elp mio babbo pleese. He not do

Nico put the note in his shirt pocket.

Gustavo stretched out his neck over the table. "What does it say? Why does she want a detective?"

Nico gave Gustavo an apologetic grin. "Maybe it's the dog she is interested in. Don't you think?"

"Ah, that's a good one. I don't think."

"How would she know I was once a detective?"

"Not once. Still a detective. Everyone knows who you are. And if anyone has a question, they ask Gustavo."

"She's not from here, is she?"

"No. My wife spotted her mother—you can't miss the fiery hair—at our Coop. She's the new cashier. The salumeria was my wife's next stop, and according to Enrico . . . Have you had one of his olive loaves?" Gustavo closed his eyes. "Manna from Heaven."

"I agree. According to Enrico what?"

"Signora Livia and la piccola moved into the apartment next door nine days ago. Yesterday—"

---

2 The little one.

"'Yesterday,'" Gogol interrupted, earning a frown from Gustavo, "'upon all sides, the sun shot forth the day.'"

"So it did," Gustavo conceded through tight teeth as the rain lashed against the French windows in front of their table. "Yesterday la piccola walked up to my bench and introduced herself. *'My name is Cecilia but everyone calls me Cilia. Who are you?'* After I gave her my name and asked her where she was from—" Gustavo turned away suddenly to glare at Sandro, who was facing a line of customers waiting to pay. "Time is not on my side anymore, young man. When will you bring me my cappuccino and ciambella? I'll be eighty-nine next week."

Nico stood up and walked to the far counter.

"Gustavo, you were eighty-nine last week," Sandro said, grinning as he took money and gave out change. "It didn't work then either. You can see that Jimmy and I are busy. You'll have to come get your own breakfast. Besides, you're only eighty-four."

Nico picked up the tray Jimmy had prepared, walked it back to the table and sat down.

"Now here's a true friend," Gustavo loudly declared after taking a long drink of cappuccino. He now had foam whiskers.

"Where is she from?" Nico asked.

"Instead of answering me, she asked if it was true that you were a detective from America. When I said it was, she wanted to know how to find you. I told her to look for a big man with a cowboy walk and fluffy dog called Rocco. I also told her when she would find you here." Gustavo bit off a large piece of ciambella, showering the floor with sugar. OneWag started licking.

Cowboy walk? Nico picked up cornetto crumbs on his plate with his index finger. He'd never even met a horse. He'd ask Nelli. "You didn't ask her why?"

"I did. Her answer: '*I will tell Nico.*' She also wouldn't give me her last name. Something is off-kilter with mother and

daughter. That's what my nose says." Gustavo had one prominent enough to make any Roman statue proud.

"'There is no greater pain than remembering a happy time
when in misery,'" Gogol quoted.

"True enough," Gustavo admitted. "I am, however, not in
misery. Only annoyed I do not know anything about them, not
even their last name. La piccola chose me to ask her question,
which makes it hard to leave her be." He stood up and wrapped
the blue scarf around his neck. "My first love had hair as red
as Cilia's and her mother's." He wound the green scarf over the
blue one. "That could explain everything. Don't tell my wife.
Arrivederci, I go and pay."

"Breakfast is on me," Nico said, standing up.

"For la piccola?"

"For her and your first love."

"Ah! I was only twelve, but it was a great one. I am in your debt.
I hope I have not brought you trouble. We have had a peaceful
fall. See you again when the sun shines forth." Gustavo shrugged
on his coat, donned his wet hat and strode out into the rain.

"It is the child who is in misery," Gogol said after the door
closed on Gustavo's back.

"I hope not. She's too young for misery."

"It can come at birth."

Nico stood and picked up his umbrella. Born not knowing
who his father was, mercilessly bullied growing up, losing his
mother at fourteen, Gogol had had his share of misery. He had
buried his head in Dante's *La Divina Commedia*, Italy's equivalent of Shakespeare in the English world. Gogol remembered
every word and would quote the Florentine poet every chance
he got. Dante's travels through Hell, then Purgatory were perhaps a voyage Gogol was familiar with; Heaven the ultimate
goal for a man who never missed a Sunday Mass. "It's time to
start my day. Ciao, Gogol. See you tomorrow."

"If I live."

"Make sure you do." He waved to Sandro and Jimmy. "A domani."[3]

Sandro nodded. Jimmy gave him a thumbs-up. There was no need to pay. Sensible Nelli had convinced him to open an account. Now he paid monthly. "Come on, buddy."

OneWag crouched between Gogol's legs, head between his paws. He hated getting wet.

Nico shook his head. "To think you used to live on the streets." He bent down and picked the dog up. Tucking OneWag under his arm, Nico walked to the door, managed to open his umbrella without dropping the dog and walked out.

A gust of rain slapped his face. "Maremma maiala!" Nico exclaimed. Whatever that meant, it sounded right. OneWag tucked his snout in Nico's jacket. Nico splashed toward Luciana's flower shop two doors down. The metal shutter was still down. Nico tightened his hold on the dog and ran across the piazza to his Fiat 500.

In the car he managed to take off his sneakers and socks despite the tight space. OneWag's towel dried his feet. A dry OneWag watched him from the back seat with what Nico interpreted as a snickering look. "I deserve that, buddy." One sneaker had a nice long split on the sole. The other, two small ones. He'd known they were there but had been too lazy to drive to Greve to buy new ones. Buying online wasn't an option with his feet.

Nico sat back and reread the note Cilia had left him: *Elp mio babbo pleese. He not do*

She'd been too shy to ask for help or give him the note directly. Or was she afraid her mother would spot her talking to him? Something had stopped her from finishing what she had planned to write. Her mother was working the cash register at

___
3 Till tomorrow.

the Coop right now. What would he say to her? *Hi, your daughter asked me to help her father. Do you know why?* He couldn't. It could get Cilia in trouble. He also needed a last name.

He parked the car next to the Coop, picked up a grocery bag from the back seat and got out. OneWag tried to hide under the front seat.

"Relax. You're not allowed in." Nico shut the door. Thanks to the threat of more rain he didn't have to worry OneWag would start tearing the seat cover. The dog had made it clear from the start of their friendship that being left behind was a punishable affront to his street dog freedom.

Livia was sitting at the cashier counter just left of the Coop entrance, wearing a spring green sweater, her red curls tied on top of her head with a rubber band. She was busy with a customer and did not see him. Nico picked up a basket and walked along the three aisles buying onions, eggs, porcini mushrooms, a box of Carnaroli rice, a six-pack of Panna water, chicken broth cubes, a couple of boxes of De Cecco spaghetti, butter from the Alps and several cans of anchovies. He hoped Livia wouldn't add up his groceries with the speed of the cashier she'd replaced.

"Buongiorno, Signora." Nico dropped the six-pack of water on the counter. He was going to take his time unloading. Luckily no one was behind him. "I hope Cilia got to school on time."

She gave him a quick sullen glance. "Barely."

Nico took in her intense blue eyes and the spread of pale freckles across her cheeks. Pursed lips. No makeup. *Add a smile and Livia would be attractive*, Nico thought.

"She wanted to stay with your dog."

"He's a good, clean dog and fully vaccinated. He's also very sweet."

"If you say so." She looked up at him with weary eyes, waiting for Nico to continue emptying his basket.

"I believe you are new in town," Nico said, adding the

anchovy cans to the counter. "I moved here four and a half years ago. I found the Gravignesi are very nice people."

Livia reached into his basket, picked up a spaghetti box and ran it through the reader. "I'm sure they are."

Nico took half a step back. She held out her hand. He played dumb and shook it. "It's a pleasure, Signora. Nico Doyle. What is your name?"

Livia took her hand back, her eyes aimed at his basket. "Are you going to pay for those or put them back?"

"Oh, I'm sorry." He emptied the basket on the counter. "I'm holding you up." He made a point of looking behind him. "No one there."

Livia tugged at a stray curl at the back of her neck. She looked embarrassed. "Sorry. I got nervous. I was told speed was important." She finished running the items through the reader. He packed everything except the six-pack of water in his grocery bag. Livia gave him back his credit card.

"Thank you. What's your name?"

She stared at him, the blue of her eyes seeming to grow darker.

"I'm as harmless as my dog," Nico said in a soft voice he had sometimes used with suspects. "Maybe not as sweet."

A hint of a smile showed up in her eyes. "Livia." She handed back his credit card and receipt. Her wedding ring finger was bare.

"Livia what?"

"Just Livia."

"Grazie, Livia and arrivederci. Let me know if Cilia wants to play with Rocco. You can find me at Bar All'Angolo having breakfast every morning except Sunday."

Livia sprayed some alcohol on the counter and wiped it clean. Nico picked up the heavy six-pack and walked out.

The Coop produce guy was standing under the entrance awning smoking a cigarette, wearing jeans and a red sweater with unraveling cuffs. "Ehi, Nico." An apron with green vegetable stains covered his ample stomach.

"Ciao, Ugo. When are you going to have those tiny yellow potatoes again? They were pure butter."

"When I can find them. The new cashier turn you down too? Three times I asked her out. The movies? No. A pizza? No. A ride on my brand-new motorbike? No." Ugo took a long drag of his cigarette. "Her loss."

"All I asked her for was her last name."

"Granchi. I took a peek at her identity card when she was applying for the job. Those freckles stir my heart." Ugo winked at Nico.

Nico ignored the implication. "Where is she from?"

"Don't know and don't care."

"Ciao, Ugo."

"See you. You just wait. The fourth time, she'll say yes."

"Good luck. Find those potatoes."

Walking back to the car, Nico called Perillo.

"Ehi, Nico, nice to hear from you. Are you staying dry?"

"As dry as the Arno. I have a question."

"Mine first. Are you still not working Sunday lunches?"

"After a great but exhausting summer and early fall season, Tilde initiated a new schedule. Sotto Il Fico serves dinner only, Thursday through Saturday. I work only when she gets a full house."

"Full pay?"

"None of your business." He was going to be paid by the evening. He would have happily worked for free. "All my Sunday lunches are free for now."

"Good news. Ivana wants to invite you and Nelli for one of her after-Mass meals that can send you to Heaven and hold you there for the week. Not this Sunday. The next one. It will be our anniversary."

"How many will it be?"

"None of your business."

"Okay. We're even. That's wonderful, but after all your complaining about feeding yourself, I thought Ivana was too busy with her Cantuccini d'Alba work to celebrate."

"Alba is a religious boss. There is no baking and packaging i Cantuccini di Alba on the day of the Good Lord. I give thanks to her every seventh day. What goes with you?"

Nico quickly told him about Cilia's meeting with Gustavo, her incomplete note, her mother's name. "Ugo saw the last name on her identity card. Do you know anything about them or can you find out?"

"Where did they live before coming here?"

"I don't know."

"The father's name?"

"I'm assuming Granchi."

"So you want me to find a goldfish in the ocean."

"I guess." Cilia's note had pierced something in his heart.

"Maybe Cilia's problem is unfortunately common. '*He not do*' what? Cheat on Mamma? Either the father left and the mother and the little girl want him back, or the mother wants nothing to do with him, but the girl wants him back."

"Why seek out a detective?"

"Maybe little girls watch too much television and want to play out a make-believe drama with a real-life detective. All the more fun if he's American."

"You're cynical."

"No, I look at the possibilities of what you have told me. You, bless your American heart, are a romantic. Why don't you just ask the girl why she needs your help?"

Nico let out a silent breath. Sometimes Perillo could be irritating. "Of course I plan to ask her, Perillo, but she's in school right now." He was glad he couldn't talk to her right away. If

Gogol's assessment of both mother and child was correct, he needed to tread lightly. "Knowing something about them before approaching Cilia would help."

"I have annoyed you."

"Yes, you have."

"My apologies. I see you have taken this note very seriously."

"She's a little girl asking for help. She deserves to be listened to." He and Rita had not been blessed with children. It had left them wanting. "Thanks for the invitation. I'll check with Nelli and let you know. Ciao." He clicked off and walked back to the car.

When he opened the car door, a curled-up OneWag acknowledged Nico by opening one eye. Nico pushed him off the driver's seat, got in and drove to Salita della Chiesa, a steep uphill street that led first to the salumeria, the grammar school, then to Sotto Il Fico and the church of Sant'Agnese. He was lucky to find a parking spot halfway up the incline.

"We're good to go, buddy." Nico got out of the car. "Rain's let up. Come on. Out we go." OneWag jumped to the back seat and got busy gnawing at a paw.

"Come on, buddy, we're off to Enrico's." OneWag looked up with head tilted left, his *for real?* expression.

Nico raised his hand as if taking an oath. The dog jumped out and ran. By the time Nico reached him, OneWag was wiggling his body in anticipation in front of Enrico's closed door.

Nico opened the salumeria's door and stepped inside. "Buongiorno." He was glad to see there were no customers in the shop.

Behind the glass partition Enrico was cutting wedges from a wheel of Parmigiano-Reggiano the size of a go-cart wheel. "Buongiorno, Nico." He used a small hammer to help the knife pierce the hard crust. "I hope the downpour did not catch you."

"It did. I'm afraid I'm getting your floor wet. If you give me a rag, I'll clean up."

Enrico looked up in alarm. "Please no." He was a short, slight man with a pale face and a gentle, generous manner. "There will be more rain for sure and I hope many feet in my shop. Is Rocco outside?"

"Not even his fear of rain would keep him away."

"Rocco honors me. I have saved a few first slices of some of my salami. Finocchiona, Genova, Soppressata, Cacciatore. I had a big order yesterday." Enrico put his wedge and hammer down and picked up a small package. "I have removed the skin and the peppers." He handed Nico the treat and a piece of butcher paper over the glass partition. "Only a few at a time. We don't want to burden his liver."

"Three at the most," Nico reassured Enrico. Liver health was a big concern in Italy.

"If you are here for the restaurant bread, it will be here soon." Enrico picked up his knife again.

"Enzo ordered bread on a Wednesday?" During the tourist season, when Sotto Il Fico was hopping, one of Nico's duties was picking up the restaurant bread each day at eleven.

"Only a small amount. Enzo said he would pick it up himself."

"No, that's my job. I'll come back at eleven. Now I'm here to satisfy a curiosity." Nico extracted two thin slices from the package. "There was a little girl making friends with Rocco at the café while I was having breakfast. She was with her mother. I'd never seen them before." He stepped back and opened the door. OneWag sat up quickly.

"Here you go." Nico dropped the piece of butcher paper on the ground, lowered the slices on it and stepped back in. "Gustavo told me they're your new neighbors."

"Ah yes, in the Airbnb below us. Livia and Cilia. Is there a problem with them?"

"No problem at all. Cilia seems to be a very sweet girl. I

would like to reassure her mother that it's perfectly all right for
Cilia to play with Rocco."

"A sad child, I think. Luciana agrees and says Signora Livia
was rude to her. That may or may not be." Enrico went back to
tackling the parmesan wheel. "My wife takes offense very easily,
as you must know."

"I don't." Luciana provided him with lovely flowers for Rita's
grave and a big soft hug he wasn't always able to avoid.

"You are very fortunate then. You should talk to her. She is
knitting up stories about the signora. All from her imagination.
Luciana should have been a writer instead of a florist. She even
makes up stories for her plants." Enrico shook his head in resignation, then looked up. "Is there nothing I can give you today?"

Leaving the shop empty-handed would offend Enrico. "That
big piece you just cut off is tempting. I'll get it with the bread.
Ciao."

When Nico walked out of the salumeria, OneWag was
halfway down the street, jumping on a protesting Stella.

"Rocco, stop it," Stella cried out. "Yes, I love you too, but your
paws are wet!" She tried to push the dog away while greeting
Nico with a smile as he approached. "Ciao, Zio, tell him to
stop! I have to look decent for school." In September Stella had
left Florence and her job as a docent at the Opera del Duomo
Museum to come back home and teach art at the grammar
school. Homesickness and love had been the dual motivators of
the move, upsetting Tilde, her mother. Nico was delighted. He
considered Stella a beloved niece.

Nico snapped his fingers and with a *hands up* voice, com-
manded, "Down." OneWag obeyed. Stella's denim leggings were
now splotched with wet paw prints. She wore lace-up boots and
the long red leather jacket Nico had given her for Christmas.
Her long chestnut-brown hair was tied back in a ponytail. She'd
decorated her black cloth backpack with swirls of colored paint.

Nico and Stella kissed cheeks. "You look great."

Stella's startling green eyes smiled. "Thanks. Being happy does it."

"Some great genes help too." Tilde was good-looking and the deep green eyes came from a great grandmother. "Aren't you late?"

"On Wednesdays I don't have to go in until ten-thirty." Stella slipped her arm in Nico's. "Walk with me."

"Happy to." The school was just up a side street.

"Now that you're not at the restaurant every day," Stella said as they walked, "Mamma worries you're not concocting any new recipes. She depends on you now. You know that, don't you?"

"I depend on her." When he had decided to start a new life in Gravigna after burying his wife here, Rita's cousin Tilde had welcomed him with open arms. He found a home at the restaurant, volunteering to wait on tables and help in the kitchen. Last year, she promoted him to sous chef and even paid him, allowing him to indulge the cooking craving that appeared after moving to Italy. "I guess I'll have to come up with something soon to reassure her." Now in the offseason he usually ate at home with Nelli, cooking the light meals she preferred: sautéed chicken breasts, veal scallopine, branzino or orata when the weekly fish truck had it available. He didn't enjoy fish as much as meat or pasta, but she loved it and he loved her.

Nico stopped when he saw the school gate. "I met a little red-haired girl this morning. I've been told she's new to Gravigna and I—"

"You must mean Cilia Granchi. She joined my first-grade class two weeks ago."

"Yes, Cilia."

"Why are you asking about her?"

"She intrigues me." Until he spoke to Cilia, he didn't want to mention her note. "Do you know where she's from?"

"Her previous school was in Pitigliano."

"Is that in Tuscany?"

"Yes, on the southern border with Lazio. It's a walled cluster of medieval tufo houses on top of a ridge that became a haven for Jews escaping from Rome in the fifteenth century. It's still known as Little Jerusalem. It's a fascinating place and the white wine is delicious. You should go and visit."

"One day. What's your impression of Cilia?"

Stella studied Nico's face for a moment. "What's yours?"

"I wasn't with her very long. Her mother rushed her away. Sad maybe?" He hadn't gotten any impression of Cilia. Her request was sad.

"I'm sure she is. It must be awful to be yanked out of your school, plopped in a new school, a new town. Friends lost. She must be having a hard time. She sits quietly, always thanks me for even the slightest attention I give her. Doesn't want to participate in group drawings. I don't force her. She loves to draw though only with a pencil. She refuses to use color. I hope to find out why. It's very odd for her age."

"How old is she?"

"Eight in June. Ciao, Nico, if I keep talking I will be late." She quickly kissed his cheeks, scratched the top of OneWag's head and ran to the gate.

"I'll start thinking about recipes," Nico called out to her bouncing backpack.

He walked back to Salita della Chiesa with OneWag following and called Perillo. "Stella has Cilia in her art class. They're from Pitigliano."

"Ah, good. In order to restore our friendship, I will now ask my trusted brigadiere, our friend Daniele, to plunge into the ocean he calls the internet. If there is a goldfish to be found he will find it."

"Thank you. How about asking the Pitigliano carabinieri if they have any information?"

"I need more than a little girl's note to disturb them from their important duties."

Nico did a mental eye roll. "Perillo, what is with you this morning?"

"You have noticed." Perillo sounded pleased. "Yes, at first I was cynical. Now I have the pomposity of Nero. I am bored, Nico. My mind is sagging from the weight of empty thoughts. I am also getting old."

"Come on, you're not fifty yet."

"The threshold is a nose-length away. I miss our investigations. They had purpose. They gave me impetus. I think you also miss them. That is why you are giving this little girl's request so much importance."

"I guess I do miss finding out things, but not murder. I'll never miss murder. Cheer up, Perillo, and enjoy your forty-ninth year. I'm happy with my fifty-fourth." He didn't have the patience to be more helpful. If he even knew how.

"La Nelli?"

"What about her?"

"She still only visits?"

Ouch. "More and more. Ciao. Let me know if Dani finds anything." Nico clicked off. He'd brushed Perillo off. Perillo had hit back. Last year Nico had asked Nelli to live with him. Too impractical, she had claimed. His place was small and she liked to spend her free time at her studio. One day he hoped she'd change her mind.

THE RAIN STARTED UP again just as he reached Sotto Il Fico with Enrico's bread. OneWag slipped inside ahead of Nico and trotted down the room to Elvira's corner. This fall she had decided, "*because my heart is generous*," to let the dog sit in her corner, in wet or very cold weather. Nico thought it had more to do with her lonely heart.

"I didn't expect to see you," Enzo said, taking the small bag of bread from Nico. "Thank you."

"It's my job." Nico took off his jacket. He missed the hustle and bustle of restaurant work. "You're open tonight?"

"A favor for a wine dealer who gives us good discounts. My mother insisted. Only six people."

Elvira owned the restaurant. "Well, I'm glad I got here in time to miss this rain."

Enzo lifted a round of pane casalingo from the bag and inhaled the scent. "Don't worry. Wet bread is a Tuscan specialty. Tilde would have added tomatoes, red onion—"

"I was thinking about me, not the bread."

Enzo grinned. "So was I. Tilde's panzanella would have restored you and kept the cold bug away."

"For that you need chicken soup," Elvira called out from the other end of the room. "Come here, Nico."

"Bad day," Enzo whispered and pointed to the rain sliding down the glass of the front door. "Elvira's sciatica blooms with rain."

"Stop wasting time with my son, Nico. Rocco needs you."

"Coming." Nico walked past the five tables of the interior dining room. The terrace had sixteen.

Elvira was sitting in her armchair, pen in hand, the front-page crossword of *La Settimana Enigmistica* half filled. Her corrugated face held a sterner look than usual. OneWag was comfortably curled up on a small pillow that had suddenly appeared one winter day along with a water bowl. Nico had refrained from commenting. Enzo's mother, a widow for too many years, worked hard to hide a kind heart.

"Buongiorno, Elvira." Nico kissed her cheeks, an expected step before joining Tilde in the kitchen.

"Nothing good about it. Your face is wet and so is your dog. You need to dry him or he'll catch cold."

"I'll get a towel from the kitchen."

"What's in the kitchen stays in the kitchen. No dog hairs in my food or on my guests. There's a towel in the buffet drawer."

The only towel Nico found was a white linen one, embroidered with flowers. He showed it to Elvira. "This one?"

"It's old. Part of my dowry. Might as well put it to good use."

Nico bent down and started to rub OneWag's paws. The dog rolled over to show off a perfectly dry stomach.

"Nico, I need you!" came from the kitchen. It was Tilde's way of freeing him from her mother-in-law. Sometimes it was welcome, but despite Elvira's best efforts to be grating, he enjoyed her and was pretty sure she enjoyed him too. She at least liked his cooking, although always found something to critique.

Nico straightened himself up with the towel in his hand. "I'll get this washed."

Elvira reached over and grabbed it. "You'll lose it."

"Nicooo!"

Elvira waved him away. "Add some life to the potato soup. Hers tastes like liquid cement."

"Your clients clean their plates with that cement and ask for seconds so I won't touch it."

Elvira answered with a grunt.

When Nico strode into the kitchen, he was met by the always homey smell of sautéing onions. "Ciao, didn't know you were open tonight. What's my job?"

Tilde was standing in front of a big pile of boiled potatoes. Underneath her long white apron she was wearing plum-colored corduroy slacks and a gray sweater, her rich brown hair gathered under a green kerchief. "If you want to peel these—careful, they're still hot—I'll wash the spinach."

"Love getting my hands burned." Nico picked up a small knife. "What are you doing with the spinach?"

"Adding it to the soup and blending." She turned to look at

him. She had her daughter's beautiful small face, now softening. She was forty-three if Nico remembered correctly. "Anything new in your life?"

"Since yesterday?" When the restaurant was closed he checked in with a phone call.

Tilde stopped up the sink and filled it with cold water. "I didn't ask yesterday."

"No murders. If that's what you want to know."

Tilde plunged the spinach into the water and started swirling it around. "Glad to hear that. Anything else?"

"You mean with Nelli?" Nico knew that was exactly what she meant.

"She's okay, isn't she?"

"I haven't asked again, so nothing new."

"Your place is too small for a couple."

"Tilde," Nico warned. From the day he had taken Nelli out to dinner Tilde had rooted for them to get together. Sometimes she'd gone too far.

"I'm sorry. I worry about you."

"Don't. We're fine the way we are. We see each other practically every night. We're happy."

"Ah!" She unplugged the sink and watched the water drain. "Your nose is getting longer."

Nico's cell phone rang. Nico checked to see who it was. Perillo. He raised a finger at Tilde to say he needed a minute and hurried out to the terrace.

"Find anything?" He stood under the narrow awning; rain drops dripping onto his boots.

"Maybe. Dani's still looking. Why don't you come to the station now?"

"I'm giving Tilde a hand with tonight's dinner. What's the maybe?"

"Come on, Nico, what's the hurry? Do some cooking, have

lunch, then come and have coffee with me and Dani. I haven't seen your face in over three weeks."

"More like ten days." Nico wondered if Perillo's *maybe* was just a carrot. "I've been busy trying to clear out the ground floor—all those old broken wine barrels." He needed more space if . . . If.

"I'll add some Vin Santo and Alba's cantuccini if you like. Ivana insists they are the best."

"Coffee will be enough." He was trying to slim down this winter. Cooking every day during tourist season meant constant tastings. "Coffee and information, I hope."

"I hope too."

Nico went back to the kitchen to peel potatoes. "What else do you add to your soup?"

Tilde had wrapped the spinach in a large kitchen towel and was now squeezing it dry. "To my cement?"

"You overheard."

"She makes sure I do. To make her happy I will add a good amount of pepperoncino to her bowl."

"That's cruel."

"So is she."

TWO

The rain had stopped, and the clouds were disbanding. Before going to the carabinieri station in Greve, Nico made his way to the florist shop in the piazza. OneWag eagerly trotted ahead of Nico. Luciana was an old friend from his street days.

The florist looked up from rearranging the clutter of plants on the floor. She had a wide face, with friendly hazel eyes, and a chrysanthemum-like mass of thick henna-tinted curls. A green flowered wool kaftan covered her ample body.

"Ciao, Luciana, all is well?"

"As well as can be expected with this weather. I'd give you a hug but if I move my boots I might smash some pots and break my heart." Luciana reached her hand into a large ceramic jar on the shelf on her left. "I know what Rocco wants." She threw him a sugarless cookie; OneWag caught it on the fly. "What about you? After this amount of rain, I know that Rita's mums need replacing. I have gorgeous greenhouse peonies. Look over in the corner. They are just a tight pink fist, but when they open they are a burst of happiness. For Rita, I'm willing to part with them!"

"Thanks. I'll get them tomorrow. The sun's supposed to come out."

"It should have come out days ago. I'll hold just half a dozen.

They're pricey." Luciana dropped fists on her hips. "So? You didn't come here just to say hello. That would be a first."

"I'm sorry. You're closed when I'm here in the morning."

"Don't worry, I'm not holding it against you."

"I met your new neighbors this morning at the café." He hated having to fish for information, but asking direct questions in a small village would lead to suspicions and more questions. "Enrico mentioned you brought the little girl a plant. That was very nice of you."

"Of course it was. I should have saved myself the trouble. The mother has no manners. Ever since that apartment was turned into an Airbnb, I've stayed away from whoever stayed there. It used to belong to a very nice woman who had a wool shop. She died. It stayed blessedly empty for a couple of years. Now people come for one or two nights, a week at the most, playing loud music, arguing, leaving the garbage in the wrong place. I'm told the mother got a job at the Coop. To me that means she plans to stay awhile. I went down and introduced myself like any good neighbor would do with a small pot of purple anemones for the little girl. She's a sweet-looking child. I haven't heard her cry yet. Well, all I got out of her mother was a muttered *thank you*. I had to ask for their names. Livia and Cilia. No last name. That woman is hiding something, I tell you. What's your impression?"

"Cilia seems sweet. She liked Rocco. The mother was fine."

"Really?" Luciana found a narrow path between pots and stepped closer to a table cluttered with flowered plants. "Livia with no last name is anything but fine." She started picking off some dried petals. "If a man cheats, you kick him out and stay where you are. If a man hits you more than once, you leave. Livia and her child are now here, not in their home. That's their story." Luciana pressed her index finger against her stomach. "That's what this says. Those two are runaways. That's why they showed up here."

He shuddered as his memory released his mother's cries. His father was the one who left. "I hope you're wrong for both their sakes."

"You'll see. And keep a look out for her man. He'll come looking for his punching bag."

I'll stop him. Nico picked up a rose and smelled it. "There are other reasons people move away."

"Maybe. No perfume in those. Don't forget Rita's waiting for peonies tomorrow."

He felt a pang of guilt. With Nelli more fully in his life, he didn't visit Rita as often anymore. He put the rose back in the vase. "I won't. Ciao."

Luciana blew a kiss.

THE MARESCIALLO'S OFFICE DOOR was open when Nico arrived.

"Ehi, Nico." Perillo stood up from his behind his desk, met Nico halfway and gave him a pat on his back. Nico gave him half a hug and looked at the back of the room. "Ciao, Dani."

Daniele, standing in his usual spot by his computer, raised a hand in salute. His smile was wide and welcoming. "Rocco?"

"With Vince, where else." Vince, another one of Perillo's brigadieri, was always munching on something and willing to share. "Thanks for helping me." Dani was a great guy, good at his job, unfazed by Perillo's moods and best of all in love with Stella, who loved him back.

Nico walked over to sit in the "interview chair," an old wooden straight back chair directly in front of Perillo's desk. "Have you found anything?"

"Dani's found something that might be connected." Perillo lowered himself in his well-padded armchair and picked up the phone. "First some coffee."

"Not for me, thanks." Nico looked over at Dani who was rolling down his chair to sit with them.

"What else can I get you then?" Perillo asked.

"What I came for. Information."

Perillo put the handset back in the cradle. "You are still annoyed with me."

"No, I'm not. I'm sorry. Go ahead, order. A macchiato for me."

Perillo's disappointment turned into a big smile. "That is good news."

"Coffee is always good news for you."

Perillo gave Nico a quick worried glance and picked up the handset again. He called the bar directly and ordered a macchiato, a double espresso and apricot juice for Dani. Order done he settled back into his armchair, his eyes fixed on Nico. "You are no longer annoyed, but you are not your usual steady, strength-of-the-Rockies persona. The little girl's request weighs heavily on you."

"I talked to Luciana before coming here. Livia and Cilia moved into an apartment below Luciana and Enrico's, an Airbnb. Luciana thinks Livia is running away from an abusive relationship."

"I understand. That is a disturbing thought." Perillo knew Nico's father had been a drunk who enjoyed using his fists on his wife and son. "But perhaps Luciana is wrong. Dani, tell Nico what you found floating in the swamp of your computer."

Dani sat up straight. "I looked up Livia Granchi in the Pitigliano City Hall office and found her address. I then checked the registry office and found Cecilia Beatrice Bianconi, born May eleventh, eight years ago."

Behind the closed door, OneWag started barking. Daniele rushed to open the door. The young man from the bar next door stood frozen with eyes clenched shut. The tray holding their order trembled.

Seeing Daniele, OneWag stopped barking and strode into the room, tail held high. All was under control now.

"Come in, come in, Renzino," Perillo urged. "Rocco is as harmless as you are."

Renzino opened his eyes but stared straight ahead. "Sorry, Maresciallo. Dogs don't like me."

"Everyone likes you, Renzino."

Perillo swept some papers to one side of his desk. "Put the tray here. Right in front of me."

Now a twenty-year-old man, Renzino had been keeping Perillo supplied with coffee since he'd been a twelve-year-old boy. The diminutive had stuck. The fear of dogs also.

"Rocco knows you're a friend," Nico reassured him as he pushed his chair back to let Renzino lower the tray while the dog took long sniffs of the barman's sneakers.

"Signor Nico"—Renzino kept his eyes on the dog—"nice to see you."

Daniele, always mindful of other people's feelings, scooped up OneWag. The barman smiled his relief.

Perillo lifted his cup to his nose and inhaled deeply. "A perfume that brings instant clarity to the mind."

Two gulps and Perillo's cup was empty. "Thank you. Put it on the station tab."

"With a two-euro tip," Nico added and stirred his macchiato. Perillo narrowed his eyes. Daniele concentrated on drinking his apricot juice. Renzino hurried out.

"Tourists leave tips, Nico. You are no longer a tourist. The tip is included in the price."

"But doesn't show up on his salary."

Perillo pushed his cup away and sat back in his armchair. "Today you are difficult. Let's listen to Dani and see if that will smooth the sharp edges."

Daniele put his drink down. "I looked up Bianconi. There

are three living in Pitigliano. A Luca, a Saverio and a Giorgio, ages between nineteen and sixty-two." He lifted the sheet of paper from his lap. "Saverio Bianconi shares the same address as Livia Granchi and Cecilia Bianconi." He lowered the paper and looked at Nico with troubled eyes.

"What's wrong? You found him."

"If he is Cilia's babbo he will be hard to find," Perillo said.

"How so?"

Daniele looked at Perillo for permission to go on.

"Go ahead, tell him."

Daniele straightened his back. "Saverio Bianconi's name appeared in an article in a local paper, *Il Corriere di Grosseto*, on October twenty-sixth. I printed it out for you." Daniele reached for the sheet of paper he had left on the floor and handed it to Nico.

A MURDER IN PITIGLIANO

Early Sunday, October 20, Signora Angela Rossi was taking her usual morning walk when she noticed the metal gate and the front door of LenConi, the small electronics shop she passed every day, was open. Surprised that the store was doing business on a Sunday and knowing both owners, Signora Rossi stepped inside to say hello. The shop was empty, and everything seemed to be in order but being a concerned citizen Signora Rossi thought it best to call the carabinieri.

Pitigliano native, forty-one-year-old Giancarlo Lenzi, co-owner of the six-year-old LenConi with forty-one-year-old Saverio Bianconi, was found dead in the small office in the back of the salesroom in a sea of blood. A hammer was found next to the body.

Maresciallo dei Carabinieri Diego Fabbri is conducting the murder investigation and is seeking to interrogate

Signor Saverio Bianconi. At this printing, the victim's business partner, also a Pitigliano native, has not been found. If anyone has news of his whereabouts, please contact the Pitigliano Carabinieri Station.

"Murder instead of abuse," Perillo said. "Not much better."

Nico's heart tightened for Cilia. "Thank you, Dani." He held out the article.

Daniele took it. "I wish I had found better news for Cilia and her mother."

"Me too, Dani."

"What are you going to do?" Perillo asked.

"Cilia asked for help. I'll help if I can."

Perillo looked up at the ceiling. "Whoever's up there, please zap my friend with some sense." He looked back down at Nico. "Bianconi took himself off to wherever, which means he either killed his business partner or aided the killing of his business partner. Bringing him home to be arrested is not going to get you a gold star from Cilia."

"If he is guilty. If he isn't, the Pitigliano carabinieri will handle the problem."

Perillo twirled a hand in the air. "Assuming. Assuming. We are spinning air. Nico, no more of this. Find Cilia. Better, find Livia. If you are going to get involved, the mother needs to know."

Nico stood up. "I agree." But how to do it without Cilia getting into trouble over the note? Maybe Nelli could help. She was staying over tonight. "Ciao and thanks. I'll let you know."

NELLI POURED HERSELF A glass of the 2018 Querciabella Chianti she had brought over. "Pinot Grigio for you?"

"Yes, please." Nico was standing by the stove, wiping porcini mushrooms clean with a damp cloth. Olive oil was heating in a wide sauté pan.

Nelli took the Pinot Grigio bottle out of the refrigerator. She had come directly from work, wearing black suede ankle boots, a pair of jean leggings that flattered her thin figure and a pearl-gray knit top that matched the color of her long braid. "Mushroom risotto begs for red wine, not white."

"White for my first glass. Then I switch. It's an old habit."

"I've noticed. I'm guessing Rita liked Pinot Grigio."

Nico turned around. Nelli was standing by the table he'd already set for dinner, pouring him the glass of wine he had always shared with Rita. She smiled up at him.

"You don't mind?"

"No. It's a sweet tribute." Nelli walked Nico's glass over to him and raised her own. "To love past and present." They clinked glasses and drank. Nico gave Nelli a hug before turning back to the kitchen counter.

Nelli settled down in the one armchair of the room that served as living room, dining room and kitchen. OneWag hopped up next to her, resting his head on her thigh. "Tell me about the bind you're in," she said.

Nico stirred some olive oil into the pan and turned on the gas. As he told Nelli about Cilia's request and what Daniele uncovered, he sliced the mushrooms, sautéed them until they were golden, took a few more sips of Pinot Grigio, added minced garlic and parsley to the pan, then added the rest of the wine. He stirred for a minute or two, then spooned the cooked mushrooms into a bowl. "The girl's father may have killed his business partner, but in her note she started to write '*He not do.*' I take that to mean she doesn't believe her father killed his business partner."

"What child would?"

"I agree." Nico circled some olive oil in the sauté pan and added the sliced onion. "Does her mother know she wrote that note? If she doesn't, shouldn't she know? What if Cilia wants to keep the note a secret?" Nico lowered the flame on the back burner. The chicken broth he'd made with broth cubes was boiling.

"If you want to help the girl, her mother needs to know."

"What if the mother says it's none of my business?"

"You have to respect that. It is a very private matter. You are a complete stranger to both of them."

"So what should I do? The one thing I know is that I can't turn Cilia down. No child asking for help should ever be turned down."

"Was it that bad for you?"

"That's in the past. Cilia is now."

Nelli watched Nico's profile, the strong nose and chin, the still-full head of graying hair, the softened jowls, the intensity of his attention to his dish, the silly I LOVE TUSCANY apron that covered his spreading middle. She wanted to run over and throw her arms around his waist and tell him how much he was loved by so many.

Nelli stayed seated with OneWag now the beneficiary of her need to soothe. She didn't think Nico would welcome her gesture. He was a man who treasured his strength. A stubborn man with wounds in his heart he worked hard to hide. A good man. The best.

Nico threw two fistfuls of Carnaroli rice into the pan with the onions and stirred. "That note isn't a child's whim. For some reason I know that. Whatever help she needs I want to give it to her."

Nelli got up and filled a glass on the table with her Querciabella wine. "Cilia is very young, but she's obviously smart." She walked over to the stove and held out the glass to Nico. "How did she know you're a detective?"

"Oh, thank you. I have no idea." Nico took the glass while adding a ladle full of broth to the rice.

"Tell her you can't help her unless she tells her mother. I believe she'll listen."

"I hope so." He kept stirring.

"Don't hope. Believe." Nelli leaned her head against his back for a moment. "What can I do? Prepare a salad?"

"Ingredients washed and ready in the fridge."

"Good." Nelli let go of him. "I'll assemble and dress."

"You can also help me with Cilia. Don't rush off to work tomorrow morning. If you're with me Livia Granchi might find me more simpatico."

Nelli clamped her arms around his waist. "I might get jealous."

"Don't be. By the way, do I walk like a cowboy?"

"Cowboys are sexy."

Nico turned around and wrapped his arms around her. They kissed.

The rice thirsted for more broth.

THREE

Gogol, Nico and Nelli were enjoying breakfast at Bar All'Angolo in the early light of the sun coming through the French doors and spilling onto their table. Yesterday's downpour had somehow cleaned the sky. "It is a good day," Gogol decreed and bit into his lard crostino. Sergio the butcher had been in a generous mood this morning and had offered Gogol four crostini instead of the usual two. He was now on his third. A good day but not a sharing one, Nico noted.

"A good day," Nelli repeated, "followed perhaps by indigestion." She was on her second espresso.

Nico had finished his cornetti and Americano and was watching the café door. It kept opening, bringing in customers, letting them out.

Another swath of spring air entered the café. OneWag stood up and went to greet Cilia with one wag of his tail.

"Ciao, Rocco." Cilia bent down and hugged the dog's head.

Her mother swung Cilia's backpack over one shoulder with an exasperated sigh. "Now you're going to have to wash your hands again."

Cilia shook her red curls. "He's clean, Mamma."

"Buongiorno, Signora Livia," Nico said with a welcoming

smile. "Rocco is pristine today." The dog had joined Nico in the shower after Nico's run. Nelli added her "Buongiorno."

With a nod in response, Livia paid Sandro and walked down to the end of the counter to order from Jimmy. "Come, Cilia. We have to hurry."

Nelli pushed her chair back and stood up. "Anyone else want something?"

"Thanks," Nico said, catching on.

Gogol clasped Nelli's arm. "'Set lies aside,'" he said. "'A mother merits the truth.'"

"Yes, she does," Nelli said, "and Cilia too." Gogol released his hold.

Nico watched as Nelli, wearing last night's outfit, greeted the bar customers she knew as she made her way to Jimmy manning the espresso machine at the far end of the bar. She inserted herself next to Cilia's mother, said something to her.

Nico looked over at Cilia, who was now rubbing OneWag's stomach. "Ciao, Cilia, come talk to me."

She walked over to the table with a determined look on her small face. "You will help?"

"I want to."

"Babbo didn't hurt Giancarlo. He was just angry. Mamma gets angry sometimes too. He ran away because he's scared." She turned her head to look for her mother. Nelli was talking to her. "We ran away."

A smart little girl. "To help you I need to talk to your mother about Babbo. Does she know you wrote to me?"

Cilia shook her head. "She's scared."

"Are you scared?"

She lifted her blue eyes and pierced him with a stare, as if assessing whether she had been wrong in trusting him. After a few beats she said, "No. You?"

"If you're not, neither am I." Her eyes smiled briefly. "But you need to tell Mamma you asked for my help. Once you tell her, call me or ask Mamma to call." Nico wrote his phone number down on his paper napkin and slipped it into the pocket of her down jacket. "Agreed?"

Cilia nodded.

"Now go have your breakfast with Mamma."

"I already ate mine." She patted OneWag's head. "Ciao, Rocco." The dog reached up and nuzzled her knee.

Nico watched as she made her slow way back to her mother. When she reached her, Livia quickly took Cilia's hand, said something to Nelli and on the way out, gave Nico a nod of acknowledgment. Cilia wiggled her fingers at him.

"Arrivederci," Nico called out.

"You have set a difficult task upon yourself," Gogol muttered.

"That's the way he likes it," Nelli said and sat back down.

Gogol raised his messy eyebrows at her. "You come empty-handed."

"I asked, you didn't answer. No ciambella, but at least information."

"Helpful?" Nico asked.

"She wanted to know if what she's heard was true."

"That I was a detective?"

"No. Was it true that you helped the local maresciallo solve many murders. I said it was true and added that they wouldn't have been solved without you."

"That's not true but thank you."

"Don't forget at Querciabella my job is to convince people to buy wine."

"How did she react to your pitch?"

"She didn't move away. How did Cilia react?"

"She listened."

"And her blue eyes grew gray with doubt," Gogol added.

"I wrote down my phone number," Nico said. "That's all I

can do for now." He clutched Nelli's hand. "Thanks for your help."

"Telling her I would trust you with my life should convince her." Standing up, Nelli gathered her bag and newspaper. "By the way, I mean that." She blew Nico a kiss. "Ciao, I'll talk to you later." She smoothed down Gogol's long white hair and kissed the top of his head. "Be well." She waved at Sandro and Jimmy. "Ciao. A domani."

"A domani," came back from both. OneWag walked her out.

Nico dumbly sat in his chair, his eyes, his mouth, his heart grinning with happiness.

"'His face was all aflame and there was so much happiness in his eyes,'" Gogol quoted as he lifted himself up with the strength of his arms, "'that I need leave it undescribed.' Tomorrow, Nico. If I live."

Nico kept his grin and stood up. "Yes, every tomorrow except Sundays. You'll live a long time."

"I already have."

Nico waved goodbye to the bar owners and walked out with Gogol. Out on the piazza, Nico whistled for OneWag, who popped out of Luciana's shop with a satisfied look on his face.

"Go. Do not hesitate," Gogol ordered. "The truth is waiting for you." He turned and made his slow way to the old Medici villa that had become an old age home.

Nico watched his old friend for a minute, then checked his watch. Perillo wouldn't be in the office for another ten minutes. He called Daniele.

"I'm counting on you and Perillo for support. I'm just letting you know before I talk to the boss."

"You will always have mine."

"Thank you, Daniele. Can you get all the details the Pitigliano Carabinieri has on Bianconi's partner's murder?"

"I'll try."

"Thanks." Nico hung up and walked into the florist shop with OneWag.

"Buongiorno, Nico, the sun shines today." Luciana opened her wide hand-knit shawl and hugged him with it. He tried to relax. She pulled back and studied his face. "You look worried and tired." She picked up the peonies she had saved for him, dried the stems, then wrapped the flowers in shiny green paper. "Have a nice chat with Rita. It will make you feel better."

Nico took the flowers from her and felt a flash of guilt. "I'm sure it will." In the first two years after his move to Gravigna, his visits to Rita's grave had consoled and bolstered him each time. Now it was Nelli who helped him when he needed it. His visits to Rita were still made with love, but they had become less essential. Sometimes he worried that Rita was fading from his mind. He had to concentrate to hear her voice, her gurgling laugh. It made him sad.

"Go. She's waiting for you. I'll add the cost to your account. Rocco's treats are on me." Luciana looked down at the seated dog, his eyes meeting hers. "No more, sweetheart. I get to eat some too."

ONEWAG SETTLED DOWN AT his usual spot next to Rita's grave while Nico threw out last week's rain-soaked chrysanthemums, changed the water and arranged the peonies. He walked back to the grave and placed the flowers on the beaten-down grass. His mind searched for a memory to share with Rita. There had been so many happy ones, but today what came up was sitting in the doctor's office, holding hands, the words *There can be no children, I'm sorry* ringing in his ears, understanding the meaning only hours later. Rita lifting her chin, thanking the doctor as if he'd said the opposite.

Nico stepped closer, rested his hand on the marble tomb and silently shared what he knew of Cilia's story.

On the way to the produce shop, Nico called Perillo.

"Povera piccola," Perillo said before Nico had a chance to speak. "This will be a hard one to carry with her."

"Let's not convict Bianconi before we know the facts."

"Fear is burden enough. Daniele is eager to help. I will also if you need me."

"I appreciate that. Thanks."

Perillo's *Eh* came with a long exhale. Nico sensed him smiling. "After all, the three of us are, caro Nico, in the business of finding justice. No murder should go unpunished. I am surprised, now that Daniele has provided us with the facts of the situation, that Maresciallo—what was his name, Dani?"

Nico heard a faint "Diego Fabbri."

"Maresciallo Fabbri has not made himself present. Once the fugitive's partner and child moved to Gravigna, I would think Fabbri would want to apprise me of the unfortunate situation. Saverio Bianconi could be nearby. I will call the Pitigliano station. It is best not to mention your interest. I will let you know."

Perillo clicked off.

"FINALLY A DECENT POTATO soup." Elvira was folding napkins. "You did well."

Nico lowered the bag of vegetables and kissed her cheeks. "I had nothing to do with it."

"A man's modesty is always false," Elvira decreed.

"You think?"

"I know."

Nico walked into the kitchen. "Buongiorno, chef."

Tilde looked up from slicing a boneless, skinless chicken breast. Today's head scarf was hot pink, bringing out the color to her cheeks. "Ciao. What are you doing here?"

Nico dropped the bag of vegetables on the far counter, his

workplace. "I know I'm off, but I feel like trying out a vegetable torte Rita used to make. Do you mind? I won't be in your way."

Tilde gave Nico a quick glance. His face looked pinched. "You know I don't mind. We always need new ideas."

"Congratulations." He lowered his voice. "She liked the soup. You didn't burn her mouth off."

"I need to keep peace. I fried some thin salami slices in the microwave, crumbled them up, tossed them in, added only a moderate sprinkle of pepperoncino. I said it was your idea."

"Thanks, but why not take credit?"

"Elvira would have found something wrong with it." Tilde picked up another chicken breast and cut it horizontally.

Nico spread out the cabbage, spinach, leeks, onion, the slices of pancetta. "You have eggs, right?"

"Plenty."

Nico picked up a santoku knife and started slicing, the edge of the blade hitting hard against the wooden board.

Too hard, Tilde thought. She turned to look at Nico. He was bent over, his shoulders hunched. During all the times they had cooked together, she had never seen him tense up while preparing a dish. He loved the process too much.

"Anything new in your life?" Tilde asked.

"You asked yesterday. Nelli and I are still fine."

"Good. I'm happy for you."

Nico went over to the sink, put the stopper in and filled it with water. "For a while, how Nelli and I were getting along was all you worried about." He tossed the cabbage in and swished it around. The shoulders stayed hunched.

Tilde laughed. "Forgive me, but you were being obtuse then. Stella mentioned you asked about her new art student yesterday."

Nico swished harder. He didn't want to talk about Cilia. "I did. Sweet little girl. She's new here and made friends with OneWag at Bar All'Angolo."

Tilde recognized the tone. A tone Nico used when he was investigating a murder. It precluded any sharing of information. Well, she would give him some, useful or not.

Tilde took a large kitchen towel from a drawer. "Stella told me Cilia came here with her mother from Pitigliano. The mother must have had a very good reason to come here to take a child out of school in the middle of the year. Enrico told me the girl and her mother moved into the apartment below his." She couldn't tell if Nico was listening or not. That kept her going.

"It used to belong to Signora Ferruzzi, who owned a knitting shop my mother loved. I often did my homework there while Mamma knitted and kept the old woman company. I was told to be very nice to the signora because her only daughter had run away, and she had no one else. I was in middle school when she died. The shop closed. The apartment stayed empty. Luciana and Enrico moved in upstairs a few years ago. Whoever owns it now turned it into an Airbnb."

Nico lifted the sliced cabbage from the sink. "How old do you think the daughter would be now?"

Tilde quickly wrapped the dripping mass in the kitchen towel and held it over the sink. "Somewhere in her fifties, I would guess. Too old to be Cilia's mother if that's what you're thinking."

Nico shook his head. "I don't know what I'm thinking." He had wondered if Cilia's mother had any connection to Gravigna.

"You're upset. It has something to do with that little girl and you are here to cook food that will give you comfort. Now take your wet bundle out on the terrace, hold it tight and swing your arm like a propeller about to take flight."

"At your orders, chef."

THE OFFICE PHONE RANG. Perillo put down his pre-lunch espresso and picked up. Dino announced, "Maresciallo Fabbri returning your call. He barks."

Perillo pushed back his armchair, put his feet on the desk and with a mellifluous voice said, "Buongiorno, Maresciallo, it is a pleasure to meet you even if only by phone. Thank you for taking the time to call me back."

"Yes, at the moment there is much to take care of in Pitigliano, as you obviously know." Fabbri's voice was very deep and loud. "What is your interest in the Giancarlo Lenzi murder?"

"The victim's business partner, Saverio Bianconi, I believe is still missing. Is that so?"

"I am perfectly aware Livia Granchi and Bianconi's daughter have moved with her mother to Gravigna, a town under your jurisdiction if that is why you called. We will not make an appearance in your jurisdiction if that is your concern."

"Bianconi is still missing then."

"He has been spotted in Lugano. We will be bringing him in very soon."

"He is your main suspect?"

A scoffing laugh came through the phone. "Bianconi is our murderer. There is no need to investigate any further. One evening in front of three witnesses he attacks his business partner with a fist that sends the poor man to the ground, yells, '*You will pay*,' and walks off. Thirty-eight hours later Giancarlo Lenzi is lying in the back room of their store, dead from a blow to the head and Bianconi is gone."

Perillo heard a creaking noise, as if Fabbri had shifted in his chair. "Listen, Maresciallo Perillo, out of the necessary respect for a colleague, I have answered your questions." His voice lowered to a soft growl. "I realize you and your men have solved a few murders in the past few years. Success is invigorating. Favorable press even more so. I can therefore understand your interest in my murder case. I do not, however, need any advice from you. The carabinieri of Pitigliano solve their own problems."

"As we do in Greve. The child and the mother leaving Piti- gliano and coming to Gravigna has made me curious. I would feel more comfortable knowing the facts of the case."

"To do what with them?"

What a blowfish! A real puffer. "It would allow me to respond to Signora Bianconi."

"Granchi. They are not married. She has come to you?"

"No, Cecilia, the child, has." He wasn't lying. Nico was part of his team.

Fabbri blew out air. "Poor thing. What can you possibly tell her? The facts aren't going to help. Her father will be going away for a long time."

"There's not even an air-thin possibility Bianconi is innocent?"

"Not a fart's chance," Fabbri barked. "Good luck explaining that to his daughter. Remember, please, we solve our own murders."

"You were quick with this one."

"Faster than you've ever been." The line went dead.

Perillo turned to look back at Daniele, who thanks to the volume of Fabbri's voice, had heard most of his side of the con- versation. "It would give me a great pleasure to prove Fabbri wrong."

"They must have filed a detailed report of the case," Daniele said.

"You can get it?"

Daniele nodded with a smile in his eyes. "The carabinieri are one unit."

Perillo didn't know if that meant one station was allowed to stick its virtual nose in the affairs of another station or whether Daniele would have to use his internet spying talents. Which- ever it was, he said, "Indeed we are."

NICO WAS IN TILDE'S kitchen adding the beaten eggs to the cooled sautéed vegetables and pancetta when his phone rang.

Without glancing at the number, he swiped with one finger. "One minute please." He quickly mixed in the eggs, slipped the small casserole dish in the already hot oven, closed the door and picked up his phone. "Sorry, my hands were tied."

"Am I speaking to Signor Doyle?" a woman's voice asked.

"Yes, Nico Doyle." He walked out of the kitchen.

"I'm Cilia's mother. I would like to meet with you."

Good for Nelli and Cilia. They'd both delivered. "I'd be happy to." He walked out onto the terrace. "When and where?"

"This afternoon, possibly away from curious eyes?"

"Come to where I work, the restaurant Sotto Il Fico." He gave her the address. "The owners are friends of mine. I vouch for them. Four o'clock?"

She accepted, but warned Nico she was bringing Cilia who would want the dog.

"Rocco is already here." He was fast asleep in his winter rest spot behind Elvira's armchair.

Nico walked back into the kitchen and told Tilde about the meeting. "She wants privacy and I didn't want to make her come all the way to my house. Do you mind?"

"I see. Privacy with a detective. I don't mind because I love you and I know whatever the problem is, you'll help that little girl. I won't ask to know more. For now."

"Thanks. You're the best."

"Toss the flattery and give me a taste of your vegetable casserole when it is done. Thanks to you and Elvira, I could use some comfort food too."

LIVIA AND CILIA WALKED into Sotto Il Fico exactly at four o'clock. She had exchanged the jeans and sweatshirt she'd worn in the morning for flannel slacks and an intricately knit turquoise and green sweater underneath her open down jacket. Her red curls were tied in a puffy ponytail. Cilia was wearing sage-green sweatpants and a sweatshirt, a pink flower barrette failing to hold her curls in place.

Nico stood up. He'd been waiting for them at the corner table. "Buonasera, Signora. Ciao, Cilia."

"Welcome to the best restaurant in town," Enzo said from behind the bar. He took his role as host too seriously to join Tilde in the kitchen as Nico had suggested. "Signora, may I offer you an espresso and a hot chocolate for the signorina?"

Livia shook her head.

Cilia looked up at Enzo with regret in her eyes. "No, thank you. Chocolate is bad for me and dogs." She turned to Nico who was now standing next to her. "Is Rocco here?"

"He's waiting for you." OneWag was still asleep on his pillow in the alcove. Elvira had gone home to nap, as always. Nico whistled.

Tilde's voice sailed down the room. "Enzo, I need help!"

Enzo raised his hands in surrender. "I'm needed," he said with a grin.

Nico's phone rang. He quickly picked it up, saw it was Perillo's number and stepped away. "I can't talk right now."

"Dani got the Pitigliano case report for you."

"Good news. I'll come by in an hour or so."

"If we're not here we're next door."

"I'll follow the coffee smell. Ciao." He pocketed the phone and walked back to Livia. Enzo was still talking.

"Do come and have dinner here one night. Friends of Nico's get a big discount."

"Now!" came from the kitchen.

"Coming. Nice to meet you." Enzo rushed off just as OneWag appeared from behind the alcove, stretching out one leg after another.

"Rocco," Cilia called out with a timid voice.

The dog greeted her with his one wag. Livia lifted the collar

of Cilia's down coat and pulled it off her. She took a plush teddy
bear out of her bag. "Here's Dormiglione. Go and have fun."

Cilia grabbed the toy and ran to OneWag. Nico watched
Livia's tired, pale face soften as she watched her daughter drop
down on the floor and give the dog a hug. That warmth and the
wan smile she gave Nico softened her features. Her deep blue
eyes flecked with black now studied him. She wore no makeup.

Nico wanted to say, "Trust me," but that phrase had been
misused by too many men. "Please sit down," he said instead,
pulling out the nearest chair.

Livia sat down. "Thank you for seeing me."

"There's no need for thanks. I'm here to listen."

A spurt of laughter came out of her mouth. "To be listened to
has become impossible. The Pitigliano Carabinieri think there
is no need to listen or inquire. They have all the answers. That's
why I asked to see you. To have you listen. You know about
murders, then you must know how things can look twisted, can
point the truth one way when the real truth is somewhere else."

"I do." There were countless innocent people in jail. "Go on."

"Maresciallo Fabbri and his men are convinced that Saverio
Bianconi, my partner and Cilia's father, murdered his childhood
friend and business partner after he discovered that Giancarlo
had been stealing from the business. That is what they believe,
what they insist on. A conviction sealed in concrete. Savi,
knowing this, fled. He insisted that running away was best for
us. I couldn't make him see reason." She tore off her jacket and
flung it on a nearby chair. "Running away was stupid. Stupid.
Stupid." Her face was now flush with emotion. "I know that.
So does anyone else with a brain between his ears." She let out
a long breath. "Savi is a sweet, good, loving and hardworking
man, but he never has been able to handle the negatives in life
well."

Nico glanced over at Cilia, hoping OneWag had all her

attention. She was busy putting the teddy bear in different posi-
tions, telling OneWag something about making too much noise.

Livia caught him looking. "Cilia is telling your dog the tale
of Dormiglione the bear, the lion and the mouse. I used to tell it
to her when she was younger. It's still one of her favorites. It's all
about trying to stop a bear from snoring so loudly. Sometimes I
worry she's refusing to grow up. Her babbo being gone has not
helped."

"You believe he is innocent."

"He is. I realize that Giancarlo's betrayal of their friendship
gives Savi a strong motive. Motive for anger, for disappointment, for punching him in the face, yes. Not for murder."

"Why not?"

"Because when I asked him, he looked me in the eyes and
said, '*I could not kill Giancarlo even if I wanted to. I don't have the
balls for it.*' I believed him. Still do."

*This is a woman in love speaking. A prosecutor would make
mincemeat of her belief.*

"Does Saverio have an alibi for the night that Giancarlo
died?"

"That Sunday night I tried to cheer up Savi by cooking his
favorite meal, beef stew with lemon. He managed to eat only a
few pieces. After dinner he put Cilia to bed and read to her until
she fell asleep. We went to bed early, maybe nine-thirty, quarter
of ten. When I woke up at six-thirty Savi was still asleep."

"You slept through the night?"

"Most of it. I was upset, tossed and turned for a bit. I fell
asleep around midnight after drinking my usual tranquilizer, a
glass of hot milk." She gave Nico a look. "You're thinking Savi
could have gone out while I slept, aren't you?"

"Yes," Nico said, surprised he was that transparent. "There is
that possibility."

"He could have, but he didn't." Livia shifted in her chair,

quickly eyed her daughter, who was still telling OneWag her story, then faced Nico again. "I know, Nico. What I believe won't help Savi. But at least you're not laughing at me. I got a big one from Fabbri. *'Women in love are worthless witnesses for the prosecution and the defense. They lie.'*

"It's not love that makes me believe him. Savi and I have been together for nine years. Knowing the man he is makes me believe. A man who wants to give his best to everyone without expecting the best in others. A man who came back from hitting Giancarlo, disgusted with himself, who the next morning called Giancarlo to apologize, saying that if Giancarlo had needed money so badly why hadn't he told him? Together they would have scraped up enough without stealing from anyone."

"What did Giancarlo say?"

"He hung up. I don't believe Saverio Bianconi is innocent. I know he is. That knowing is just there, as locked in concrete as Fabbri's belief in his guilt."

"Why did you leave Pitigliano?"

"To get away from the stares, the whispers. I've got big shoulders and wouldn't hesitate to tell them what they can do with their nasty thoughts, but I left for Cilia's sake. There's always someone ready to destroy a child's life."

Her bitter tone made Nico wonder what Livia's childhood had been like.

"I don't have much money," Livia said. "Our joint bank account has been blocked and—"

"You need a loan?" *What the hell? I don't have much either, but this woman and kid are having a really tough time.*

Livia's face softened into a smile. "I mean if you're willing to help Savi, I can't pay you a big sum."

"You want me to find Savi?"

Livia's "No!" was almost a shout.

Cilia turned to give her mother a questioning look.

Livia caught the look and let out an embarrassed laugh. "I'm sorry, honey. Sorry, Nico. Finding Savi is useless."

Does she know where he's hiding?

"I need you to find Giancarlo's killer first." Her voice was now low. "You found a few killers in Italy. You must have found many more in New York."

"Do you have an idea of who the killer might be?"

"I thought Giancarlo had caught a thief in the store, but the inventory was all still there and the money in the cash register tallied with the day's receipts. No one I know could have done this, and yet . . . Oh, forgive me. I'm tired of thinking, of asking myself, 'Who?' I don't know. Part of me doesn't want to know, but I have to find out to save Saverio. I don't know how. Will you help? Please. For Cilia's sake?"

"Killers get found by teamwork. Here, I have helped Maresciallo Perillo with his cases, but he and his men did most of the work. For Giancarlo's murder I would have to work alone. One maresciallo can't undermine a fellow maresciallo." *Why am I making excuses? Perillo and Dani would help in every way possible. They already have.*

"I understand," Livia said, reaching for Cilia's coat and her own. "Thank you for listening. Come, Cilia, time to go home."

Cilia stood up and waved at OneWag with the bear's arm.

"No, wait." Nico stood up. "I was trying to explain, to make you realize how difficult it will be to find the killer on my own. I was hesitating because—" *Why am I? Because she might be wrong?* "Well, as I said, the chances of succeeding aren't very good."

Livia hugged the coats against her chest, as if she were suddenly cold. "You speak like a man who is defeated before he has even started. That's not the idea of you that I got from your girlfriend."

"She flatters me, and I apologize." *I hope I won't regret this.*

Nico looked over at Cilia, her mass of red curls bent over OneWag. "Bianconi is a good father?"

"A very good father. They dote on each other."

"She's a lucky girl." He turned back to face Livia. "I will do my best to find the murderer."

Livia pressed fingers of one hand against her mouth. Her eyes teared. "Thank you," she said after a moment.

"Please understand that I may discover Saverio is—"

Livia thrust her hand in front of Nico's mouth. "You won't. Your fee?"

"I have no idea how much time and effort is involved. We'll figure it out when I'm done." Nico thought accepting money put a different spin on this deal, one he didn't like. Maybe he'd ask for a token amount, gas money, just enough not to make Livia feel she owed him eternal gratitude. Depending on the outcome. "I need you to make a list of names, addresses and phone numbers of all the people involved with Saverio and Giancarlo."

"I'll do that tonight."

"Let's talk again tomorrow. I need to know more about Giancarlo."

"I will tell you everything I know." Livia held up Cilia's coat.

"See, Mamma," Cilia said, as she slipped into it. "I was right."

"Yes, you were." Livia zipped her up. "Once she found out you were a detective, she had no doubts. You were going to help her babbo come home."

As Livia put on her own coat, Nico asked Cilia, "How did you find out that I was a detective?"

"I'm lucky. Babbo says it's because I was born under a crescent moon, and crescent moons grow big and light up the sky. I saw Rocco and you on the street outside school during recess. I tried to whistle to get Rocco to notice me." She wrinkled her nose. "My whistles stink. A boy saw me looking and told me

I should stay away from you because you're a detective from America and if I don't behave you could put me in prison."

"I'm glad he didn't scare you."

"I'm never scared because I'm lucky." Her mother gave her a look as the three of them walked to the door. "All right," Cilia conceded with a shrug. "I'm *almost* never scared. Besides, on television detectives send only bad people to prison," she said with the assurance of a grownup. "I'm not bad." She checked with her mother, who didn't react, before holding up her hand.

Nico high-fived it. "Right you are."

Cilia bent down and planted a kiss on OneWag's head. "Ciao, Rocco, see you tomorrow before school."

"He'll be there," Nico assured her and opened the door.

Livia stood there for a moment, then suddenly leaned forward, and kissed his cheek. "Thank you."

"Don't. I may find out you're wrong."

"You won't. I'll have the names tomorrow morning."

"I ACCEPTED THE JOB," Nico said, walking in with OneWag.

Perillo looked up from his desk. "That is not news." An empty espresso cup was in front of him. Daniele, sitting to one side of Perillo's desk, held a cup with what looked like hot chocolate dregs. Nico was glad they were in the office and not the bar where they could be overheard.

"Why isn't it?"

"Because you're as good as bread. You're going to try to find a murderer that will make that little girl smile again. If you don't, what can I say? We'll help Nelli pick up your pieces. As for la piccola, it will be up to Livia Granchi to find the magic glue."

Nico pulled out the interview chair and sat down. OneWag offered his back to Daniele, who happily scratched it. "Livia is adamant about her partner's innocence," Nico said.

"Some people are adamant fossil fuels don't contribute to climate change. What you believe most often depends on what's convenient."

"True enough, although Livia strikes me as a woman with her feet planted firmly on solid ground." Nico noticed his dog nudging Daniele. He snapped his fingers. "OneWag, come here and lie down." OneWag dropped down at Daniele's feet as if to let Nico know that two commands were one too many. Nico let it go and turned to Daniele. "Did you find anything helpful?"

"Yes." Daniele pulled his chair closer, took a notebook from under his arm and opened it on Perillo's desk. "I was able to get into the murder report and the statements by the few people Fabbri questioned. The hammer that killed Giancarlo Lenzi belonged to the Lenzis. Signora Lenzi recognized it because the wooden handle had a crack in it. Mimmo, their thirteen-year-old son, said he saw his father take it with him when he left for work the morning after he'd been punched by Saverio."

"That's the morning before Lenzi was killed?" Nico asked.

"Yes. In his statement Mimmo adds that he thinks his father took the hammer in case Saverio attacked him again."

"Did anyone else in the Lenzi household see Lenzi leave with the hammer?"

"No, Eddi, their older son, said he spent the night with his girlfriend and didn't get home until lunch time. Signora Lenzi was upstairs getting dressed and didn't see her husband leave."

"So, we only have Mimmo's word?" Nico asked.

"That's right."

Perillo nodded at Nico. "That's an opening."

"If someone in that household killed him. Who else lives in the apartment?"

"It's a house," Daniele said. "Only Lenzi, his wife and the two boys live there according to the report. A cleaning woman comes in three times a week. Monday, Wednesday and Friday. The hammer left the house on Saturday if Mimmo is telling the truth."

"Time of death?"

"Between twelve and two Sunday morning," Daniele said, "with the medical examiner leaning toward the earlier time. No defensive wounds. There was no sign of a physical fight. Lenzi was hit on the left side of his head with the pronged part of the hammer. The blow was strong enough to cut into his temple artery. He bled to death. Bianconi was called in a few hours after the discovery to see if anything had been stolen. He said no. He was asked to come to the station to make a statement. He said he needed to pick up his daughter from her catechism class first. Then he was gone."

"Does the report say why Lenzi was in the office at that time?"

"According to his wife's statement, he left their apartment right after dinner. Nine-thirty or shortly afterwards. He told her he had a lot of work to catch up on in the store's office. It looks like the catching up involved deleting the evidence. Bianconi had found more than three hundred fake invoices going back over two years that amounted to over two hundred thousand euros. Sixty-seven had been erased."

"It doesn't take long to delete sixty-seven invoices."

"Death interrupted him."

"How far is the store from the house?"

Daniele checked the report. "Twenty or so minutes. He walked. The house is in the medieval part of town, the store in the modern part."

"If he left the house at nine-thirty and he didn't die until midnight at the earliest, something else interrupted him. Maybe Lenzi didn't go to the store right away. Or if he did, he was doing something besides deleting."

"Having a long chat with his killer." Perillo's statement eyebrows shot up. "If Saverio is the killer, he could have come in to ask for an explanation. Lenzi makes excuses or refuses to explain. They argue verbally. A sudden rage takes hold of Saverio. He sees the hammer on the desk and strikes. The blood gushes out. No need to hit again. He walks away."

"Thank you, Maresciallo, but I've been hired to find a different killer."

With a slight shrug, Perillo said, "Works the same with another name."

"In the report, is there anything about Signora Lenzi and her husband's relationship?"

Daniele turned the page. "Maresciallo Fabbri asked two questions: '*Was your marriage a happy one?*' Her answer. '*As happy as riding a Ferris wheel can be. The view is beautiful, the ride thrilling but sometimes the mechanism jams and you sit at the bottom for a while.*' The maresciallo then asked, '*Where were you on the night your husband died?*'

"'*Oh, at the top. No worries at all.*' Fabbri must have made a face or a noise because she then understood. '*Oh, I'm sorry. Asleep. As I said, Giancarlo had gone to the office to catch up on work. When he called at eleven that he'd be very late, I took a sleeping pill and went to bed.*'"

"Interesting," Perillo said. "No worries at all but she has to take a pill to fall asleep?"

"Did his cell phone reveal anything that might help?" Nico asked.

Daniele ran a finger down his notes. "The phone was not found."

"Whoever killed him took it," Perillo piped in. "Obvious, I know." He didn't enjoy being on the sidelines. "I think that is positive news for you, Nico. What need would Bianconi have to steal his partner's phone?"

"Good point," Nico said, not knowing if it was or not.

Daniele picked up on the awkward moment. "The data on the store's computers was examined. Bianconi's was full of information about new products and how to fix things. Lenzi's computer held what was left of the fake invoices, some unremarkable business interactions and lots of information on some towns in the Dolomites—Cortina d'Ampezzo, Ortisei, Val di Funes. Signora Lenzi told Maresciallo Fabbri they were planning a Christmas vacation. The home computer was used only by the sons."

"Apart from Livia Granchi, who else was called in to make statements?"

"The four people who witnessed Bianconi assault Lenzi. Mimmo, Lenzi's thirteen-year-old son; Matteo Necchi, aged fifty-one; Paolo Fulci, aged fifty-four; and Debora Costa, aged ninety-one."

"What did they say?"

"Their statements are the same almost word for word. Lenzi was in front of his building, chatting with a man and a woman; another man was passing by with his dog when Bianconi turned the corner, walked over to Lenzi and waved some papers in his face, yelling, '*Fake invoices, that's how you honor our friendship. A thieving shit is what you are!*' Then he slammed a fist into his gut. Lenzi collapsed. Bianconi bent over him, said, '*You will pay,*' and walked off."

"You will pay for stealing?" Perillo asked no one in particular. "Or you will pay back the money you stole? That's what you have to find out, Nico."

"Even if Bianconi meant it as a threat in the heat of the moment, it doesn't mean he went through with it. Let me have a copy of the report, please."

Daniele gathered the four or five pages, clipped them together and handed them over. "I will keep a copy too."

"Thanks for finding this out for me." Nico folded the papers and put them in his deep jacket pocket. "Thank you, both." He stood up. Daniele did the same. OneWag scrambled up and scooted to the door. "I know you can't get involved with this murder," Nico said, "but can I count on you for advice?"

Perillo leaned back in his chair and spread out his arms. "Nico, what are you saying? Your case is our case." He shot a look up at Daniele. "How does it go, Dani?"

"'All for one, and one for all.'"

"Exactly. Dani and I will be silent partners."

"Thank you. It's not going to be easy."

"How will you approach the people you need to talk to? What will you say?"

"I will tell them a little girl asked me to help her find the truth."

Perillo got out of his chair and held out his hand. Nico took it. They shook. Perillo wished Nico luck with "In bocca al lupo."[4]

"Crepi il lupo,"[5] Nico answered.

Daniele walked him to the door. "I'm here if you need me to scout the internet."

"I'm counting on it. Ciao."

SOTTO IL FICO HAD no need for him that night, so after calling Nelli to find out when she was coming over, Nico got to the Greve Coop just before it closed, bought two chicken breasts, some potatoes and a lemon, then went home to cook dinner. While OneWag was eating his, Nico got both open wine bottles, poured himself a glass of Pinot Grigio and started peeling

---

4 In the mouth of the wolf.
5 Drop dead, wolf.

potatoes, cutting them into chunks and throwing them into the pot, which already held a cup of canned tomatoes, a chopped-up celery stalk and carrot. He added salt and pepper, a large piece of parmigiano rind and two liters of water. While it cooked gently, he cut the breasts in half and pounded the slices thin. The chicken piccata would have to wait until Nelli got home. In the meantime, after a few sips of his wine, he called Livia.

"Buonasera. It's Nico. Am I disturbing you?"

"Buonasera. No, we eat early. I have the names you wanted. You'll be at the café at seven-thirty tomorrow? School starts at eight and I don't want Cilia to be late."

"I'll be there. I want to ask—"

Livia's voice interrupted him. "Yes, Cilia, I'm sure Rocco will be there too. I'm sorry, Nico, Cilia was worried. You will bring him?"

"Rocco never misses a breakfast at Bar All'Angolo. How did Saverio find out Lenzi had stolen the money?"

"Giancarlo did the accounting and the buying. Savi was the salesman and the fixer when some item broke down. About a month ago Savi saw a paid invoice for half a dozen scanners he had never seen at the store. He searched for them, couldn't find them and spent a couple of nights in the back room poring over every invoice, comparing them to the stock and to what they had sold. The supplier confirmed the goods in those invoices had not been ordered. Giancarlo stole over two hundred thousand euros over a period of the past two and a half years."

Nico heard the key turning in the lock. "Thank you, Livia. I'll see you tomorrow."

Nelli walked in and took off her coat. Underneath she was wearing torn jeans and an oversize beige sweater decorated with moth holes and paint splatter. She held up her nose and sniffed like a wild cat catching a whiff of prey. "Hmm, your potato soup. Ciao." All Nico could smell was oil paint when he met her halfway and kissed her lightly. OneWag got between them, reaching for her knees. Nelli picked him up and studied Nico's face. She saw the determined look he got when he had taken on a job, be it a murder investigation or a difficult recipe. "You're going to help her, aren't you?"

"I'm going to try." He walked back to the stove and stirred the soup. "It took me a few minutes to decide, which I'm not proud of. I should have jumped at the chance to help. That little girl's world has been crushed."

"Do you have doubts about her babbo's innocence?"

"Doubts shouldn't stop me."

"Maybe you were scared of failing Cilia." Nelli started setting the table. She didn't want to think of the fallout if he did fail. Disappointing the child and her mother would put another hole in his heart.

He emptied his Pinot Grigio glass, always feeling a little guilty of paying tribute to his wife in Nelli's presence. "I guess. It's painful enough failing adults."

Nico had talked about his failures with her one night a few months back, sitting on the terrace after dinner listening to rain falling on the olive grove. A great deal of whisky had been consumed. He had not been able to win his father's love, had hurt his mother by being the cause of his father's abandonment, had not given Rita the child they both wanted. He had then failed in his job by breaking the law. She had tried hard to convince him those were regrets, not failures. His answer had been, *Whatever they are, I'm okay now.* She wasn't sure she believed him. In the morning, they had both woken up with a headache, and Nico had asked Nelli if she had wanted children. *Maybe if I had met a man like you years ago*, she had said. Now at forty-seven it was too late. She told him she had no regrets.

Shaking off the memory, Nico took out a canister of flour from a cabinet he'd installed next to the stove and spooned some on a plate. "How was your day?"

"Restful at the vineyard, frustrating at the studio. I have a new client."

"Congratulations." Nico tasted the soup, added salt.

"Maria Grazia Bertini wants me to paint her portrait, but she lives in Orvieto and wants me to use a photograph. I argued that to paint a good portrait I needed her to sit for me. It's the only way I can get a sense of who she is. A photograph is too flat. She's a retired teacher, but still helps some students with Latin so she doesn't want to come here, and I work five and a half days a week and can't go there."

"What about Sundays? I might have to give up a few of our Sundays to drive down to Pitigliano. I could drop you off in Orvieto."

"Sundays are out. She goes to Rome to visit her nephew. It's frustrating. I'm eager to paint her, she's eager to be painted."

Nico poured two glasses of the Panzanello red and handed one to Nelli. "I offer a guaranteed frustration remover and an idea. There's not that much to do at the vineyard in November and December that I know of, right?"

"It depends."

"Ask for some days off. I'll be going to Pitigliano during the weekdays too. It's only about forty-five minutes away from Orvieto. I could drive you there in the morning and pick you up in the afternoon."

Nelli tilted her lovely head at him. "Hmm, not a bad idea." They clinked glasses and drank. OneWag sauntered over to see what was going on.

Nelli looked down at the dog who was giving her an *anything for me?* look. "What about Rocco?"

Nico planted a kiss on Nelli's smooth forehead. "I'll take him along. I'll look less threatening."

"Good. I'll call Maria Grazia in the morning." Nelli sat down at the small round table. "Now please ladle out that soup. My stomach is protesting."

FOUR

Nico, Nelli and Gogol had finished their breakfasts when Cilia came running into Bar All'Angolo followed by Livia. She stopped at Nico and Gogol's table and knelt on the floor to hug OneWag.

Livia joined her daughter. "Cilia? Where are your manners? Buongiorno, Nico." She nodded at Nelli and Gogol. "Forgive her."

Nico stood up. "Buongiorno."

Gogol aimed his sagging blue eyes at Livia. "'It appeared her thoughts were turned elsewhere.' To love an animal shows a good heart if not good manners."

"Ciao, Nico," Cilia said finally as she stroked OneWag's long fur.

"Please join us, Livia," Nico said after introducing Gogol.

"No, thank you. We'll be late again. I just came in to give you this." Livia took out an envelope from her handbag and handed it to him.

"Thank you." Nico slipped the envelope into the inside pocket of his quilted jacket. "Why don't Rocco and I walk to school with you?"

"Yes, yes, yes!?" Cilia jumped up clapping. The sudden movement made OneWag retreat behind Nelli's legs.

"Shh, Cilia." Livia quickly glanced at Nelli and Gogol. "I don't want to take you away from your friends."

"I have to leave for work now," Nelli reassured Livia. "Gogol, I will walk you home."

"Always grateful, Nelli." Gogol pushed his hands against the table to lift himself up. Nico offered his arm. The old man slapped it away. "'What negligence, what standing still is this?' Go to the child and the mother 'so the unclear can become clear.'"

"You're always right, amico. I go." Nico gave Nelli a quick kiss as Gogol muttered his usual, "Tomorrow. If I live."

"You'll live. Ciao." Nico waved to Jimmy and Sandro and strode to the door where Cilia and Livia were waiting. OneWag dutifully followed.

CILIA KEPT RUNNING AHEAD then stopping to see if OneWag was following her. A wary OneWag was busy checking out the street smells. "It's too uphill for him to run," Nico explained, which was partly true. "And he'll get hot." The air was unusually warm, the sky bare of clouds.

"We're having a perfect Summer of San Martino Day," Livia said.

"Why does San Martino get the credit for this beautiful day?" Nico asked, remembering similar days he used to call Indian summer days, not realizing he was being offensive.

"Well, he was born on November eleventh, but legend has it—"

"Let me tell it. Let me!" Cilia ran back and stopped in front of Nico. "San Martino was walking on a very cold day. Well, Martino was walking. He wasn't a saint yet."

"You need to keep walking, Cilia," Livia said, taking her hand.

Cilia slipped in between Nico and her mother. "When Martino saw two poor beggars shaking with cold, he tore his beautiful, thick wool embroidered mantle in half and covered the men with each half. Suddenly the clouds all flew away, and the sun started shining like on a summer day. Now you know the story of l'estate di San Martino."

"Thank you for telling it to me," Nico said. "It's a lovely story."

"You're welcome. It's one of my favorite real ones." Cilia shook her hand free from Livia's and ran ahead.

Nico watched Cilia catch up with OneWag. "You have a very sweet daughter."

"Yes, I do. She's her father's daughter." Livia lowered her voice. "I've given you a list of all the people involved in our lives that I know of. I'm sure Giancarlo had friends I haven't met. His wife, well, you will find out for yourself."

"A difficult woman?"

"Indifferent of others, at least of me and Savi. I think she resented Savi and Giancarlo's friendship."

"What can you tell me about their friendship?"

"They got to know each other in lower school. Savi was a skinny runt of a kid—his words, not mine—and always had the right answer to the teacher's questions. Boys started beating up on him. Giancarlo, big and strong then and now, adopted Savi as his tuttofare."

"His lackey."

"Yes, which meant that Savi got left alone. Doing Giancarlo's homework was a small price to pay to be able to walk home unharmed."

"How did you feel about Giancarlo?"

She creased her forehead. "Does it matter?"

"The more I know the—"

"Mamma, Nico!" Cilia shouted. She had reached the school gate ten meters ahead. "The bell is ringing." She waved. "Ciao, ciao."

"Wait." Livia rushed up to her. "I need a hug." Cilia hugged her mother, then OneWag. She held her arms open waiting for Nico.

Nico reached her quickly and lifted her up with his hug. "Have fun!" He put Cilia down and watched her run across the playground until she disappeared into the school building.

"I feel a knot in my heart every time she disappears." Livia turned and started walking away. "Now I have to hurry; I'll be late at the Coop. I need this job."

Nico joined her. "I'll walk with you."

"I'd rather go alone." She picked up speed. "Talking slows me down."

Nico lengthened his stride to keep up with her. "When can we talk again?"

"You want to know about Giancarlo. What I think doesn't matter. Ask the people whose names I gave you. Please, go to Pitigliano. The answer is there. Ciao. Thank you."

Nico stopped. "Arrivederci, Livia." He waited with OneWag until she turned onto the street that would take her down to the Coop, then looked at his watch. The Coop didn't open for another twenty minutes. Yesterday Livia had agreed to tell him everything she knew about Giancarlo. Now he got the impression she was eager to avoid the subject.

What now? Nico stood on the street with OneWag, looking up at him with his *where to?* expression. Pitigliano was the obvious choice. Plunge in. Get the ball rolling. The game's afoot and whatever other cliché he couldn't come up with. He wasn't ready. He needed to study Livia's list, decide who to approach first. Would saying that he was trying to help Bianconi's little girl make people open up to him? Maybe some would. Others would brush him off. He needed to relax. Company would help.

At eight-thirty-five in the morning, Tilde would still be at home. Perillo and the Coop kept the same hours. Nico punched Daniele's number.

"Buongiorno, Dani, am I disturbing you?"

Daniele paused his computer game. "Not at all. I'm in the office waiting for the Capo. Everything good?"

"Yes. Livia gave me a list of people I should talk to. Will you have time to use your computer skills to look them up for me?"

"Absolutely. Take a photo of the list and message it to me."

"No, I prefer to stop by." He wanted company and Dani and Perillo were on this case with him.

Twenty-five minutes later Nico followed OneWag into Perillo's office. The dog headed straight for Daniele who started rubbing his back.

"Ciao, Nico," Perillo said from his desk. He was in civilian clothes—an open-collared checked green-and-white shirt under a forest green V-neck sweater. His desk covered the view of his slacks, but Nico knew Perillo always wore jeans. "Tell your dog that I am the maresciallo in this office."

"Dani gives him treats."

"Bribery is against the law."

Walking over from the back of the room, young, tall and thin Daniele cut the better figure in his jeans, blue shirt and navy V-neck sweater. OneWag watched Daniele drop a dog biscuit on his boss's desk.

Perillo ignored the biscuit. "Let's see this list."

Nico sat in the interview chair opposite Perillo. "I'd like to go over it with you first."

"Make copies, Dani," Perillo said.

Daniele took the list from Nico and left the room.

"Not a lot going on, is there?" Nico asked.

Perillo's dark eyebrows met in a frown. OneWag sat at his feet. "What makes you think that?"

"You said it. You're not in uniform and you're so bored you want attention from a dog."

"Rocco is not any dog. He is your estimable companion, who

discovered one murder and helped solve another. Besides I was joking to relieve the dispirited expression you had when you walked in. I made you smile."

This man can talk himself out of any situation. "Yes, you did," he said, but he had not smiled.

Daniele came back with Livia's list and two copies. He handed one to Perillo.

"Pull up a chair, Dani," Nico said in case Perillo was still annoyed over OneWag. "Nine people. First the victim's wife and her two sons."

"They'll be a waste of your time, Nico," Perillo said. "They will only confirm what Fabbri has told them. Saverio Bianconi is the murderer."

"I agree, but they might expand on who Giancarlo's friends were. Livia knows only three."

"Who do you plan to start with?" Perillo asked.

"Angela Rossi, the woman who called the carabinieri."

"Why her? She only saw an empty store."

"Because she knew the two men and set the investigation in motion."

"You are entering the fray on your tiptoes," Perillo said with a scold in his voice.

OneWag nudged Perillo's leg. He could smell the biscuit.

Perillo let one arm drop as he bent over the list of names. "I would start with the victim's wife, Annamaria Lenzi." One Wag sniffed his hand. "I've been thinking about your plan to tell the truth with these people. Some people will be moved and want to help Cilia. Others will ask what business it is of yours and brush you off. You're not even family."

"You want me to lie and say, 'I'm a New York homicide detective and I've been hired to find the real killer'?"

"It isn't a lie." OneWag dropped a paw on Perillo's leg. "Only a slight distortion."

"Tell them the truth about being an ex–homicide detective," Daniele offered.

"Or you could say you're a journalist." Perillo slid his forearm across the desk. As the biscuit dropped to the floor, he slid Livia's list over the empty spot. OneWag lunged. "You have come to write an article, possibly a book about this murder." Satisfied, Perillo sat back in his armchair. "People will happily open up if they think their name will appear in print."

"And also feed me exaggerations and lies."

"Isn't picking them out a detective's job?"

"I guess it is." Nico wondered if he could pull off pretending he was writing an article, What if someone asked him for writing credentials? He'd gotten a C in composition, and it had been given to him out of kindness. He'd been stung by his teacher's comment on his last paper, *You need to find your imagination.* He'd always been more comfortable with facts.

Nico turned to Daniele. "What do you think: Is it ethical to lie, to fool people for the greater good?"

Daniele wondered how Don Alfonso, the local parish priest, would answer. He had no idea, but Nico needed an answer. After a moment he said, "Telling them you are writing an article might give you more information than telling the truth."

A good compromise from his church-going friend, Nico thought. "Thank you, Dani."

Daniele, instantly regretting his words, held up his hand. "There is, however, the chance that having one's opinions appear in print might keep someone from speaking."

"Could be," Perillo agreed, "but that would tell you that person has something to hide."

"Which may have nothing to do with the murder." Nico stood up.

"Ehi," Perillo said. "Where are you going? What about the rest of the list?"

"You saw it. At this point they're just names. Thank you, both. If I want to find the truth, I think it's best I start by telling the truth."

Perillo rolled his eyes.

"I'll keep in touch," Nico said. "Come on, OneWag." With a quick glance at Daniele, Nico turned toward the door. "I'll find you a treat somewhere else."

After the door closed behind them, Perillo asked, "Did Nico just wink at you?"

"No, Maresciallo," Daniele answered, mentally crossing himself. Sometimes the greater good did justify lying.

AFTER GOING HOME TO put some order in the apartment and checking if he needed to buy anything, Nico drove back to Gravigna and parked the car in Don Alfonso's spot below the church, as he always did when he was working at the restaurant. OneWag jumped onto the passenger seat, ready to get out. Nico didn't move, suddenly wondering why he was here again. The restaurant didn't need him. Was he procrastinating? He did miss helping Tilde in the kitchen. It was a home away from home and he had lately complained of having too much time on his hands. Well, now he had a job to do. An urgent one.

Nico looked at his watch. Just past one. Pitigliano was at least a two-hour drive away. OneWag turned to look at Nico and barked in protest. "You're right, buddy. We'll go tomorrow."

Elvira and Enzo were sitting at the far end of the room when Nico and OneWag walked in. Three settings were on the table along with a carafe of water and a bottle of red. Enzo, wearing jeans and a blue sweatshirt, was slicing what Nico knew was last night's leftover bread. What they didn't finish today would end up in a panzanella tomorrow.

"Benvenuto," Enzo called out. "Come join us. Tilde, your

errant sous chef is here." OneWag had scooted between Nico's legs and scampered over to his new friend Elvira.

"The sun is out, Rocco," Elvira said, "but you may sit on your pillow anyway." Despite the mild day outside, she was wearing a long gray wool dress and a thick burgundy-and-gray cable-knit sweater. "Your dog looks hungry, Nico." Her tone held a tinge of reproach. "There are sugarless biscuits in the silverware drawer."

Nico bent down to give Enzo's mother her expected cheek kisses. "Thank you."

A loud "Wait!" came from the kitchen, followed by the enticing smell of garlic, tomatoes and rosemary. "Rocco deserves more than biscuits!" Tilde walked into the room wearing a red scarf on her head, a long white apron over a dark green wool dress, sleeves rolled up above the elbows. She was carrying a deep terra-cotta bowl. "He'll eat some of what we eat. Pappardelle with veal stew as sauce. Ciao, Nico." Still holding the bowl, she leaned over and kissed his cheeks. Her face was flushed from standing over the stove. "Happy to have you both for lunch."

"Happy to be here. I'll get a plate for me and Rocco."

"Use the tin one I use for his water," Elvira ordered, "and only put in some pasta. Veal is expensive."

Nico cut up a good fistful of pappardelle in OneWag's tin bowl and with the dog following, took it to the kitchen. He came back to the table with his plate and a fork and sat down. Tilde filled his plate and grated some parmigiano over it. "Thank you. I'm going to Pitigliano tomorrow for the first time. Any information you have on the place and its inhabitants would be very helpful."

"Why are you going?" Enzo asked as he speared a piece of veal and carefully wound a few strands of pasta over it.

"I'm looking into a murder that took place there a few months back. The wrong man may have been accused."

"It's a good thing that I don't need you here," Elvira said as she ate the veal pieces first. "Make sure you are being paid properly. The gas bill will add up."

"I'm not doing it for money."

Elvira put her fork down and aimed her sharp black eyes at Nico. "For what, then? Boredom relief?"

Enzo blurted out a shocked "Mamma!"

She ignored her son. "Nico, be wise. Work for free is not respected. If you are bored, do the crossword puzzle. You're not getting any younger. Solving crossword clues will keep your mind sharp."

"So will finding a murderer, I think," Enzo said, filling the wineglasses.

Elvira gave her son a sharp, cold look and ate another piece of veal.

Tilde ate in silence, thinking she should have added another sprinkle of pepperoncino to the meat sauce, while at the same time remembering Stella's new young student was from Pitigliano.

"One of the best white wines in Italy comes from Pitigliano," Elvira said. "The lady who made this sweater let me taste it when she took my measurements. Delicious. She had a nice yarn shop where the barber shop is now. Years ago this was."

"My mother loved going to her shop," Tilde said as she mixed the pasta and meat together. "What was the owner's name?"

"I forget. She began forgetting too. It got so bad she had to close the store. No one was willing to take over. I went to her funeral wearing this sweater."

"A nice homage to her," Enzo said.

Elvira twisted her fork around one long ribbon of pasta. "It was a cold day." The loaded fork went into her mouth.

Enzo gave Nico a *forgive her* smile. Nico smiled back. He'd grown to like Elvira.

"The pasta could use more salt," Elvira announced.

"Too much salt raises your blood pressure," Tilde said.

"My blood pressure is perfect."

"Mamma, it isn't," Enzo said.

Happy that there was no need for him to get involved, Nico continued to enjoy his perfectly salted dish.

"I think she had a daughter who ran away," Tilde said.

Elvira looked up with wide eyes. "Yes, she did. The girl just abandoned her mother. How could I forget? It was the talk of the town. Alida la Rossa! A tall girl with bright red curls she liked to toss from one cheek to the other. She was a few years younger than I was. I thought she was too pretty for her own good. One day, poof, she left a note and off she went. Children can be so cruel."

"Maybe she died," Enzo said.

Was there a connection to Livia, Nico wondered. Red hair wasn't that common in Tuscany. He swallowed before asking. "Where did she go?"

Elvira put her fork down and gave Nico one of her uncomprehending stares. "Why do you think I mentioned the yarn shop? You asked if I knew anything about Pitigliano and I'm telling you. I don't know if she went there right away but that's where Alida ended up. Not that the mother told me. When the shop was closing, everything was put on sale. Some of the home furniture too. I bought a small bedside table. In the drawer was a postcard addressed to the shop. *Stop worrying. I'm alive and happy*, it said. It wasn't signed but it had to be from Alida."

"When was it sent?" Nico asked.

"Years ago. I kept the postcard for a while. I liked the photo. The town, small buildings crowded together high on a tufa cliff, looked unreal. Maybe I thought Enzo's father would take me there sometime. He didn't. One spring cleaning it ended up in the trash." Elvira raised her wineglass to her mouth, suddenly put it back down and clapped her hands. "Bea!" A rare exultant expression was now on her face. "Beatrice. Alida's mother. Beatrice Ferruzzi. See, Enzo. I do remember everything. Tilde, look at the back of my collar. Bea always wrote her name on her knits."

Tilde lifted the sweater collar gingerly as if she were dealing with a flat-eared cat. "She stitched it on the label."

"Of course she did. What does it say?"

Tilde dropped the collar. "Fatto da[6] Bea."

"She made all the sweaters she sold. An excellent knitter. I would have ordered—" Elvira was interrupted by a bark from the kitchen. She picked up her wineglass again. "Rocco has finished his food, Nico. Let him back in. He knows where his pillow is."

Nico did as Elvira asked. OneWag gave him only half a tail wag as if to say, *you forgot me.* The tin bowl had been licked clean. OneWag dutifully settled on his pillow. When Nico came back into the dining room, Enzo was pouring his mother another half glass of wine.

"Poor Signora Beatrice, to lose a daughter like that. So sad." Elvira took a sip. "I was blessed with you."

Tilde quickly raised her full glass, afraid her mother-in-law would start expounding on how happy she had been when Enzo lived with her. "Let's wish Nico success with his new investigation."

Enzo lifted his glass. "To success."

"Yes," Elvira joined in, "and don't take too long. You might be needed here. There are a lot of birthdays and anniversaries coming up."

"I'll do my best." He missed being here more than he'd expected. "Do you need me tonight?"

"No, it's all done," Tilde said. "A birthday dinner for eight

---

6 Made by.

from Sicelle. I made the veal spezzatino yesterday so the meat would soak up the flavors. I made enough to add to our pasta today. They're bringing their own dessert."

"The sauce was the best part." Nico was doing la scarpetta,[7] soaking up what little meat sauce was left on his plate with a piece of yesterday's bread. "How clever of me to walk in at lunchtime."

"Come more often but only on Thursday, Friday and Saturday," Enzo said. "The rest of the week we eat at home. You're welcome there too."

"The meals here are better," Elvira said, "as they should be. Paying diners require more effort."

With a look of exasperation Tilde stood up and gathered the empty soup plates. "Maybe I'll start charging at home. Salad is next. Then pears and oranges for dessert."

Nico stood up. "I'll help." He picked up the pasta bowl and followed Tilde to the kitchen.

"That woman curdles the air we breathe," Tilde muttered as she dropped the plates in the sink.

"She's unhappy," Nico said softly so as not to be overheard.

"So she has to make me unhappy too?"

"Her put-downs make her feel in charge."

"Now you've added psychologist to your résumé?"

"I'm only trying to help."

"I know, I know, but one day—" Tilde slapped her hands down on the edge of the stone sink.

Nico put the pasta bowl down and gave Tilde a hug.

Tilde leaned her head against Nico's shoulder. "Thank you and I apologize. I should have developed the skin of a boar by now. La piccola Cilia is lucky to have you on her side."

"I hope she is."

---

7 Little shoe.

"I have no doubts. Come on, get the salad plates. I'll bring in the rest. Let's finish our lunch."

"With a smile, Tilde?"

"From one deaf ear to the other."

AFTER SPENDING THE AFTERNOON planting leeks, Tuscan kale and fennel in his vegetable garden, Nico washed up and changed into sweats. He and OneWag were on their own tonight. Nelli was having dinner with her friend Laura Benati at the Bella Vista Hotel and spending the night at her own place. He wasn't happy about Nelli not coming home after dinner, but the one time he'd asked her to move in with him, she had made it clear she valued her independence. Luckily, she did spend most of her evenings and nights with him.

Nico poured himself half a glass of Pinot Grigio and got dinner for OneWag. After both their heavy lunches, the dog was getting some boiled brown rice and shredded chicken meat wetted with the no-sodium chicken broth Nico made weekly. For himself he made scrambled eggs with a slice of Tuscan bread he salted and sautéed in olive oil. He sat down at the table and took his first bite. He heard a *bing* from his phone. If it was important whoever it was would have called. A text could wait.

Dinner over, OneWag settled on the sofa, Nico in his armchair. He read over Livia's list. With each name she had included who they were, what they did, address and telephone number. Nine people she thought knew something that would point to a different murderer. Would all nine talk to him? Nico wondered. How many was he going to anger, scare? How many would be eager to help? He'd find out soon enough. He added the names and phone numbers on his contact list adding who they were in the address line. His next step was getting off his rear end and going to Pitigliano. Tomorrow! Annamaria Lenzi was at the top of the list, followed by her two sons. Perillo was right. He should start with her, not Angela Rossi. Giancarlo's family deserved to be the first to know he was asking questions.

The phone rang. Nico picked up. "Buonasera, Livia. I was just going over the list you gave me."

"I wish I could have thought of more people involved with Giancarlo."

"More will come up. You talk to one person who will mention someone else. You follow up and that person mentions something interesting that sends you talking to another person. I'm going to Pitigliano tomorrow morning. I'm going to walk around and get a sense of the place first."

"It is a very special, beautiful town."

"When I come back, I will need to know more about Giancarlo. This morning you seemed reluctant to talk about him."

"I'm sorry I rushed off. Even having all the time on my hands I could wish for, Giancarlo is a difficult subject for me. He always has been."

"Why?"

"Giancarlo was good-looking, charming, caring, always ready to listen or help if you needed anything. Everyone admired him. Savi thought the man walked on water. I thought he was a little too perfect to be real. I will add that Savi accuses me of being afraid to trust people."

"You're trusting me."

"Thanks to Cilia. She is my weather vane."

"Thank Cilia for me then."

"I will. She's fast asleep in my bed with her bear. She won't sleep alone now and without her near me, I'm afraid to close my eyes." A short, dismissive laugh came over the phone. "I'm sorry, I shouldn't—what Cilia and I are feeling isn't important. I called to tell you—"

"It is important," Nico said, "and if talking about it helps,

I'm here to listen." After Rita died he couldn't bring himself to sleep in their big bed for over two months. The sofa ended up sending him to physical therapy and back to their bed. His back still twinged at times. The pain of loss was almost gone thanks to Nelli. The loss would always be there even though it now felt lighter. *Forgive me, Rita.*

"Thank you. I'll be fine," Livia said with a curt voice. "I called to let you know I told Annamaria I hired an American detective to find her husband's murderer."

Nico would have preferred being consulted first. "A retired detective with no license to investigate anything in Italy. You're correct on 'American.'"

"I'm hiring a brain with experience. Titles and pieces of paper don't matter."

"They do to me, Livia. From now on I'm a retired ex-homicide detective hoping to find the truth that will make an eight-year-old child and her mother happy again."

"As you wish, but are all you Americans so puntigliosi?"

The word *puntigliosi*—punctilious—made Nico laugh. "Oh, not at all, Livia. I laughed because it's a word my wife used whenever I got into one of my dot-the-*I*s, cross-the-*T*s moods." He did not add that those moods came whenever he was ill at ease. "How did Signora Lenzi react?"

"She understood, saying, '*I envy you can still hope the outcome will be different.*' She wanted to know how I found you so I told her. She's willing to meet you. She liked Savi, thought he was a good influence on Giancarlo."

"Does she work?"

"She's a pharmacist. Losing Giancarlo won't send her begging." She said this matter-of-factly, without a trace of envy.

Pharmacists in Italy had almost as much dispensing power as doctors and were revered.

"Can you and I meet tomorrow afternoon once I'm back

from Pitigliano? I want to know more about Giancarlo and Saverio's old friendship, who they were friends with, who not, and whatever else you can think of that might help."

OneWag jumped off the sofa and went to the front door, his head tilted to one side. Time to open the door.

"I don't know when I can see you," Livia said. "I work all day. Once I pick up Cilia at school at one-thirty she stays with me at the Coop. The manager has been very nice about it. I don't want her to hear me talk about her father and Sunday she'll be with me all day. I could call you tomorrow night after she's asleep."

"If that's the only way."

"I am sorry, but it is the only way."

A way he didn't like. He needed to see Livia's face. It allowed him to read what emotion lay behind the words. Tomorrow was Saturday and he'd thought of having dinner at Sotto Il Fico with Nelli. Tilde had accused him of keeping Nelli all to himself. *If only that were true.*

"She's usually asleep by eight. Say hello to Pitigliano for me. I miss home. Ciao."

"Buonanotte, Livia." Nico clicked off the call. He couldn't help feeling Livia was hiding something.

OneWag started whimpering, wiggling his small body. Nico smiled as he heard a key turn in the lock. The door opened. OneWag jumped.

"Yes, yes, I love you too." Nelli bent over the dog, caressing him, her free arm holding up a package.

Nico watched from his armchair, a warm glow spreading across his chest. "You're a surprise."

"A pleasant one, I hope."

"Always."

Nelli tossed her black down coat onto the sofa. She had dressed up in a long-sleeved loose-fitting navy blue dress. Her long braid was twisted into a figure-eight bun at the nape of

her neck. She had added a touch of lipstick and gray eyeshadow
that brought out the blue of her eyes. Her cheeks were flushed
from the cold. Looking at her, Nico thought she could have just
walked out of a painting in the Uffizi.

"You look lovely."

"Thank you, but you say that even when I'm wearing jeans
and a shirt splattered with paint."

"You look especially lovely tonight. Better?"

"Much. The hotel is closing at the end of the weekend until
April. To honor the four guests who hadn't left with all the other
tourists, Laura treated them to a special end-of-season dinner."
Nelli dropped the package on the table, sat down and gave
OneWag a hug.

Nico, who had counted on a kiss and a hug of his own, joined
her. "What was on the menu?"

Nelli caressed her flat stomach. "Too much food. The usual
antipasto, risotto with the last of the porcini mushrooms, bis-
tecca alla Fiorentina with small roasted potatoes and broccolini.
I told Laura you were looking into a murder in Pitigliano—don't
worry, I gave no details—and she introduced me to Riccardo,
the chef she was testing out tonight. She wants to hire a new
chef for next season. He's been working at La Dogana in Sorano,
which is very close to Pitigliano. Laura asked him if he knew
about a murder that took place in Pitigliano. He knew a lot about
it. You should talk to him."

"The murder was reported in the local paper. I'm sure everyone
in the area knows about it." The back of his hand grazed Nelli's
package. It was cold. "What's in here? Ice cream?" Dessert hadn't
been part of his dinner.

"A semifreddo made of chocolate-covered panna cotta.
A present from Laura and Riccardo. Judging from how they
looked at each other, I think Laura and Riccardo like each other
very much."

"That's good news. She deserves a ton of love." Nico unwrapped the paper. "Shall we share?"

"No, thanks." Nelli sat back, opened the table drawer, got out a small spoon and gave it to Nico. "I had mine with Laura." She got up.

"You're not leaving, are you?"

"While you enjoy your present, I will get ready for bed."

"Music to my ears."

"And if I'm not asleep by the time you join me, I may tell you why you should talk to Riccardo."

NELLI WAS SLEEPING WHEN Nico got to bed. The next morning she was still sleeping when he went off for his run. She was gone by the time he came back. Riccardo could wait.

FIVE

Tilde had told him to approach Pitigliano from the south. It added some kilometers to the drive, but she insisted the extra time was worth it.

Nico had been driving in his Fiat 500 for two and a half hours through sunlit low-lying land when the road started climbing. Ahead was a sharp curve. Nico slowed. On the other side of a wide ravine, Pitigliano rose above a vast rugged outcrop of volcanic tufa looking like an apparition straight out of a medieval fairytale.

At the curve he swung into a wide rock ledge that housed a small church and got out of the car. OneWag scrambled after him, but the sight of a ginger cat sleeping in a sunny spot at the very edge of the ledge stopped him. Nico walked a few feet down the road with his eyes scanning the length of the old town, taking in the tight jagged cluster of stone buildings with their terra-cotta roofs, the church tower, what looked like an aqueduct, the thick vegetation in the ravine below. He wasn't the only one mesmerized by the view. Many others lined the road taking photographs.

How many murders had the town witnessed through the centuries, Nico wondered. Countless, probably. He only needed to worry about the most recent one, although he found it hard to reconcile ugliness with the beauty he was staring at. *A sight that will sear itself in your mind*, Tilde had said.

Nico took one last look and walked back to the open car. OneWag was now sitting in the driver's seat, his gaze still aimed at the sleeping cat. Seeing Nico, he wagged once as if in relief.

"Get in the back, buddy. It's time to get to work."

ONCE ON TOP OF the thousand-foot-high outcrop, Nico turned left, away from the old quarter, and entered the modern part of Pitigliano. He had called ahead and gotten directions. He drove to the very end of the street, passing shops and balconied buildings painted in various shades of yellow and orange.

The road ended at a large grassy sunlit field with debris thrown here and there. He let OneWag out to do his business on the grass while he took in the metal fence surrounding this carabinieri station with its four-story barracks and large parking lot. In comparison, Perillo's station in Greve looked like a doll's house.

Fence or no fence, Nico knew he wasn't going to be welcome here. "Come on, buddy, in the car. I can't take you with me this time."

OneWag checked a few different smells before ambling back, jumping onto the driver's seat and circling several times before finally settling down.

"I'll be right back." Nico held out half a beef stick. OneWag turned away.

"As you wish." Nico dropped the stick on the seat, shut the car door and walked to the gate.

Telling the voice on the intercom that he was an American detective investigating the Lenzi murder got Nico inside the station in two minutes. To be received by Maresciallo Fabbri took ten minutes more.

Diego Fabbri was standing in front of a metal desk, dressed

in his black winter uniform, arms crossed. A thin man in his late forties, with dark gelled hair hugging his scalp, narrow eyes and sunken cheeks. The only fullness in his face came from his lips.

Nico took a step inside the room. "Buongiorno, Maresciallo. A pleasure to meet you." As he spoke he took in the room. One end of the long room held a half-empty bookcase, in front of which sat a rigid two-seater sofa, a glass coffee table and two equally rigid armchairs. At the other end two windows overlooked the grass field. The walls were bare.

Fabbri caught Nico's eyes wandering. "I find that the guilty more easily make mistakes when comfortably seated on a sofa with a cup of coffee or water waiting for them." The maresciallo turned around and sat behind his desk. He pointed at the two neat stacks of papers in front of him. "I am a very busy man, Signor Doyle, but I am willing to give you a few minutes. I know who you are due to the help you have given Maresciallo Perillo with his many murders. If you are here to offer your American expertise, you have wasted your trip. I require no help with my murder. The case has already been solved."

Had there been a chair in front of Fabbri's desk Nico would have sat down without waiting for an invitation. He stayed standing. "I wanted to introduce myself to you before voices reached you that an American speaking accented Italian was going around asking questions about the Lenzi murder."

"And why are you doing that?"

"Maresciallo Perillo is not involved. I've been hired by someone who doesn't believe Saverio Bianconi is guilty."

"And who would that be? If you tell me it's Livia Granchi, I will have a hearty laugh at your expense."

"Saverio's daughter, Cilia, asked for my help."

"And she will pay with what? Her little bear? An ice cream cone?"

"Her happiness."

"Ah, the American soft heart, which seems to be disappearing from what I read in the papers. I wish you buona fortuna."[8] Fabbri lifted the top sheet from the stack on his right and started reading.

"I want you also to know that should I find Lenzi's murderer, it will be your discovery, not mine."

Fabbri looked up for an instant, a flicker of pleasure in his eyes, then continued reading the sheet of paper he held in his hand.

"Arrivederci, Maresciallo."

Fabbri nodded his goodbye.

Sitting in his car, watching OneWag chew the beef stick with relish, Nico thought of Fabbri's comment about having a laugh at his expense. He needed to ask Livia what it meant.

Nico drove back down through the modern section of the old town and parked the car at the edge of the historic district. With OneWag pulling on his leash, Nico walked through a small piazza with a staircase leading to the bottom of the ravine. The archway of a wide medieval building took him to city hall and the information office. *A map might be useful*, Nico thought, but he preferred to discover a place by getting lost. He trusted OneWag to lead him back to the car.

Nico followed his dog along an arched aqueduct built by the Medici according to the plaque, past the massive fortress-like Palazzo Orsini—now a museum—and into a long, elegant piazza flanked by large holm oak trees.

OneWag pulled Nico to the nearest tree, sniffed, left a short signature and moved on. Facing two streets leading away from the elegant piazza, Nico chose the straighter one. Via Roma was narrow and long. They passed a few shops, quite a few catering

---

8 Good luck.

to tourists, reached the cathedral, continued walking through a maze of narrower short streets crowded with dark stone houses, stone staircases leading to the entrance doors. This was the medieval heart of the town. The only sounds came from the dog's excited pants and Nico's shoes hitting the stone pavement worn down by centuries of footsteps. Nico chose a staircase flanked by cyclamen pots to sit down and let the wonder he was feeling in this new out-of-time world dissipate. He had a very modern murder to solve. He took out his phone, checked the list Livia had given him and clicked a number.

A woman's voice said, "Pronto?"

"Signora Lenzi?"

"Yes?"

Nico introduced himself. "I hope I'm not disturbing you." It was past noon.

"No, I was waiting for your call. Where are you?"

"In Pitigliano."

"The best place to be. It is otherworldly, is it not?"

Her friendly tone surprised him. "It is a long step back in time. I feel very much an intruder here."

"Not just you. The modern world does not belong here. But you have come because Livia has engaged you to investigate my husband's murder."

"It was her daughter who first asked me to help."

"Cilia is a smart little girl. Why don't I meet you in half an hour?"

"That would be great." He hadn't expected to get an appointment today. He'd brought OneWag along. "At your home?" Her quick no stopped him from mentioning the dog. Too bad. Seeing how the Lenzi family lived and what they surrounded themselves with would have given him a sense of who they were. "Where would you like to meet?"

"In Piazza della Repubblica. If you haven't seen it yet, you must." He said nothing. "It's lovely. Just ask anyone to direct you. You can have lunch while we talk. Go to Caffè Degli Archi. How will I know you?"

"I'll be the man in a baseball cap, jeans, green sweater and gray sneakers."

"Like most Italian men."

"With a dog."

"I'll be there at one."

IT WAS ANOTHER MILD day. Nico sat outside drinking a Coke Zero and admiring the view of the lush valley below while OneWag lapped from the plastic bowl a kind waitress had brought out. The sound of heels hitting the stone pavement made Nico and the dog look up. A sturdily built woman of medium height was walking past one of the two baroque marble fountains placed near each end of the long piazza. She wore a stylish charcoal-gray pantsuit. A pearl-gray shawl hung from one shoulder. Her outfit and assured walk conveyed efficiency.

She noticed Nico looking and nodded as if to say, *Yes it's me.*

As Annamaria Lenzi approached, Nico stood up and pulled out a wicker and metal armchair for her.

Annamaria said, "Buongiorno" and sat. Nico was relieved to see she had a pleasant, open face. Next to Annamaria's name Livia had written her age and her job. She was five years older than her forty-one-year-old husband.

Nico sat back down. "Buongiorno. Thank you for seeing me."

"Your dog is not what I expected, Signor Doyle."

"How so?"

She was observing OneWag sniffing her black ankle boots with wet whiskers. "He is too small and sweet-looking for a detective's pet."

"Ex-detective. I didn't have him back in New York."

"Ah," she said, her perfectly groomed eyebrows lifting, "you are retired. That makes more sense."

"You expected a German shepherd?"

"At least something fiercer, macho."

Nico laughed. "The dog goes along with my car, a 2015 flaming-red Fiat 500." The smile he hoped for didn't come. "Thank you for agreeing to talk to me. It's very kind of you."

"It has nothing to do with kindness. If there is a truth that is different from the one Maresciallo Fabbri believes, my sons have a right to know."

"Don't you?"

"My husband is dead. That is the truth I know. Are you hungry?"

His stomach had been moaning for a while. "I wouldn't mind eating something."

"Their antipasto tagliere is good and large enough to share and I also suggest a glass of Pitigliano white."

"You know best, Signora."

"I wish I did." A rueful smile appeared on her face, then quickly vanished. The kind waitress approached. Annamaria ordered. As soon as the waitress was gone, she asked, "Who are the others on Livia's list?"

"I'm not sure Livia would want me to share that information."

"I can probably guess. First, my two sons. I have told them not to speak to you. Answering questions about their father's death would be too painful. And useless. What can they know that could point to another suspect? Before the shock of their father's death, their waking hours were consumed by study, the internet, seeing friends, and for Eddi, my oldest, commuting to the Liceo Scientifico in Orvieto and spending time with a sweet girl he is too sad to see now. Cross my sons off your list. They will not speak to you."

"I understand," Nico said with regret. In his work back in the States, he had discovered that children and teenagers were good at picking up the odd sentence or expression, the unusual behavior. They hadn't reached complacency yet.

"Debora Costa is certainly on the list," Annamaria said as the waitress placed two glasses of white wine on the metal table. "Grazie, Mariella." She picked up the glass and took a sip. "She lives in the building across from us. She was a good friend of Saverio's family. They are all gone now. Debora saw Saverio hit my husband and was very shaken by it. She is one of the few Jews that still live here. She is very old and looks frail, but do not be taken in. She has an indomitable spirit. Do not believe everything she says." She looked at Nico holding the wineglass in his hand. "Taste it."

Nico did. A smooth, gentle taste not dissimilar to the Pinot Grigio Rita had loved. "It's very good."

"Pitigliano is famous for it." Mariella lowered the large round wooden tagliere on the small table. It was covered with the usual Tuscan salumi and cheeses.

"What is this?" Nico asked, pointing an unusual-looking brown schiacciata.

"Ciaccia con i friccioli," Mariella said and walked away.

"We are close to the border with Lazio," Annamaria explained, "so the Tuscan schiacciata becomes a focaccia in Lazio. Here it becomes ciaccia. The friccioli are pancetta previously sautéed and added to the oiled dough."

Nico picked up a piece and bit into it. He chewed slowly. Crisp salted bread embedded with crackling pork. *What could be better?*

"Go ahead, Signor Doyle. Ask your questions while we eat. I must be back at the pharmacy at three."

"You haven't taken time off?"

Annamaria picked up a piece of parmigiano. "Medical

matters don't take holidays and I welcome being busy now. The boys have their schoolwork and soccer."

Nico sat back. He couldn't eat and think at the same time. "Do you believe Saverio killed your husband?"

"From what I know of Saverio, I find it hard to picture him murdering my husband. He adored Giancarlo, believed he was the best of men. He told me countless times."

Odd. Why did he feel the need to tell her? Nico wondered. *Was he reassuring her or himself?*

Annamaria continued. "But people change. One doesn't notice at first, but then something happens. It can even be a small something and the change is revealed."

"Saverio changed?"

"The first thing you need to know is that my children's father did not steal a cent from Saverio or from anyone else."

"I was told he had proof."

"The carabinieri have proof that the electronics company did not invoice products that weren't requested. That is all. What need would my husband have to steal from his own business?"

What need indeed? Nico asked himself as he bit into the ciaccia.

"If he needed money, all he had to do was withdraw it from our healthy bank account." Annamaria spoke calmly.

With conviction, Nico thought. Maybe Maresciallo Fabbri had chosen not to mention that her husband was deleting the false invoices from his computer before he died. Nico's telling her now would only antagonize her.

"Saverio is the one who fabricated those invoices, Signor Doyle."

"I was told your husband oversaw the business end. He paid the bills."

"Yes, of course. Saverio would never have been able to steal any money. I think he just wanted to shame my husband in front of witnesses."

"Why would he do that?"

"As I said before, people change. My husband enjoyed inviting Saverio and Livia over for dinner often. They came at least once every two weeks. The evenings were pleasant enough, especially when the weather allowed us to eat on our small terrace. The men enjoyed themselves. Livia and I come from different backgrounds and so had little to say to each other.

"In August, after we came back from Forte dei Marmi, where we spend our holidays every year, there were no more dinners with them. I didn't wonder why. I was only too pleased to spend my evenings with just my husband and the boys. It was Mimmo, my thirteen-year-old, who one night asked why Livia and Saverio didn't come over anymore. He liked to play computer games with Saverio. Giancarlo said something about Cilia needing special attention. I could tell he was lying. When we were alone, I repeated Mimmo's question. My husband told me Saverio was being difficult, resentful of anything he said. He was making my husband's work life difficult."

"Signor Lenzi stopped inviting Saverio over?"

"No, he kept inviting them, but Saverio always came up with an excuse."

"Did your husband know the reason Saverio was being difficult?"

"I asked but he didn't want to talk about it. The rift between them upset him."

Or he didn't want to tell her, thought Nico. If the men were such good friends, Giancarlo would have had at least an inkling.

"I told my husband Saverio's behavior had nothing to do

with him. It was obvious Saverio and Livia weren't getting along anymore. Maybe Livia was leaving him for someone else. She is much stronger than Saverio, and her mother, now dead I believe, didn't have a stellar reputation. The last time they came to dinner, the expression on Livia's face was as stiff as the starched collars on my husband's shirts. She barely spoke and Saverio ate almost nothing. Something had certainly changed between them."

Nico put down the glass he'd been sipping discreetly while he listened. "Signora Lenzi, forgive me but I don't understand. Why would love problems make Saverio want to shame his best friend and then kill him?"

"I'm not saying Saverio killed my husband. I'm saying my husband did not steal. Since he did not, only Saverio could have faked the invoices."

She keeps saying *my husband*, Nico noticed. As if she needed reassurance on his status. "No one else worked in the store?"

"Giulia Favelli, my part-time housekeeper, went to clean on Monday mornings when the store was closed. I'm sure she's not on Livia's list."

She wasn't. "I would like to talk to her."

"Giulia wouldn't be of any help. A good cleaner but has mattress stuffing for brains." Annamaria looked at her Apple watch. "Don't worry about the bill. I have an open account here."

"Thank you, but I prefer to pay." He had to stay neutral. Accepting favors, even very small ones, could alter perceptions.

"As you wish, although for so little you wouldn't be in any way beholden." Annamaria picked up her briefcase from the chair next to hers. "There is one recurring question that creeps up on me at night." She finished her glass of wine. "Did the failure of Saverio's personal life make him so angry and resentful of my husband's happy marriage he killed him in an outburst of jealousy?" She put the glass down on the table. "I see from your expression that you find that far-fetched."

"A little."

"My husband oversaw every situation they were in since they were children. Saverio was the one who told me that when I first met him. He claimed he was happy to stand in Giancarlo's shadow. I found it sad for him, but I understood. Giancarlo did enjoy being the general."

She didn't sound resentful, Nico noticed. She must have known how to hold her own.

"My job, not unlike yours, requires me to be diligent and find solutions. My husband's murder is not solvable by me, but in bed at night I find myself asking him, as if he were still next to me, *'Did Saverio kill you? Was he so crazed by the fear of losing Livia, he lashed out at you?'*"

"In my experience, when couples are breaking up, it's the one who wants to leave who gets killed, not the best friend."

"But then who, Signor Doyle? Can you answer who?"

Her voice was so devoid of feeling she could have been asking who was going to win the Sanremo song festival. "With your help, I hope to."

"I have none to offer. The only name I come up with is Saverio, which seconds later I reject only to again ask an empty pillow next to me in bed at night, *'Was it Saverio who killed you?'*"

"Your husband was a strong, charismatic figure. Inadvertently or not, he must have put others in his shadow."

"No, only Saverio was in his shadow because that's where Saverio wanted to be." She rose from her chair.

Nico stood up. "Thank you for seeing me."

"I'm sure I only confused you, but don't dismiss all my assumptions. Arrivederci, Signor Doyle. Go and see Debora.

She knows half the town and maybe can send you in a more hopeful direction. Don't call today. It's the Sabbath. She won't answer."

Nico sat back down and started eating what was left on the tagliere while OneWag slept under the seat. His phone rang. He quickly swallowed and answered.

"Ciao, Nico," Nelli said. "Where are you?"

"In a beautiful piazza, overlooking . . ." A boy in jeans and a striped T-shirt seemed to be staring at him from behind the fountain. Nico looked down at what he was wearing. Jeans, sneakers, a thin old down jacket he should toss. Nothing odd or eye-catching.

"Ah, Pitigliano," Nelli exclaimed. "You're back in the sixteenth century."

Nico stared back. The boy turned away.

"Lovely, isn't it?" Nelli said.

"It is," Nico said. "So why should I talk to Riccardo?" The boy turned back; his eyes again fixed on Nico. Small, chubby, in his early teens. Nico returned the boy's stare with a smile.

"Are you going back to Pitigliano tomorrow?"

"I hope so. I need to set up some appointments first." Annamaria Lenzi had piqued his interest in Debora Costa. He would call her after sundown. "You want to come with me?"

"I'm going to Orvieto. Maria Grazia agreed to stay home tomorrow so I can start on her portrait."

"Great news. I'll drive you even if I don't have to come here. Now tell me about Riccardo."

"Giancarlo Lenzi very often ate at his restaurant. He didn't mention Lenzi's wife so I asked, '*Alone?*'"

Half a minute of silence followed. The boy, head lowered, fidgeted with his phone.

"Still there?" Nico asked Nelli.

"I'm creating suspense."

"I'm holding my breath."

Could that boy be Mimmo, the Lenzis' thirteen-year-old son? Nico wondered as he asked, "What did Riccardo answer to '*alone*'?"

"He glanced at Laura, eyebrows raised—he's quite good-looking, by the way."

"Uh huh." *Could be Lenzi's youngest son. Livia had written: "shy, sweet boy. Doesn't get the attention he deserves."*

"Mimmo!" Nico called out.

The boy looked up with a startled face and ran away.

Bull's-eye! At fifty-four it was pointless to run after a thirteen-year-old.

"Who is Mimmo?" Nelli asked.

"Sorry for interrupting. I'll tell you later. Go on."

"Laura explained to Riccardo that the detective investigating the murder was a good friend of mine and hers. Riccardo in turn explained he didn't like to talk about the patrons of the restaurant where he still worked but, not taking his eyes off Laura, admitted Lenzi never ate alone."

"And now you think Riccardo might know the people he ate with, maybe people who aren't on Livia's list?"

"Yes. He's told Laura he wants this job and he's obviously smitten by her. I think he'll tell you what he knows."

If anything. "Okay. I'll talk to him. Thanks. Are you coming home or are we meeting directly at Sotto Il Fico?"

"I'm home now, my place. I'll meet you at Sotto at eight."

Nico shut off the phone. *My place, Your place. Why couldn't it be our place?*

AT SOTTO IL FICO only three of the five tables the inside room held were occupied with Italians of varied ages. Nico did not recognize any of them. He handed Enzo two bottles of wine. "Bianco di Pitigliano DOC for you and Tilde."

Enzo gave Nico and Nelli a hug. "Thank you!" The bottles disappeared under the bar. Enzo led them to a corner table. OneWag dutifully headed to Elvira's alcove, where a pillow was waiting for him.

"Another murder for you, I hear," Enzo said in a low voice as he pulled out a chair for Nelli, who was dressed in flannel slacks and a thick-knit purple sweater that reached her knees.

"Not tonight." Nico sat facing Nelli, his back to the room.

"Good." Enzo straightened up and patted down his white shirt. "I am Enzo. I will be your waiter tonight. That is how you say it in America, a man from Chicago told me."

"Not in any place I went to. Where's Alba?" Nico asked. Despite the success of her cantuccini business, she would not stop waitressing for Tilde.

"She's presenting at a food festival in Perugia."

"Good for her. Mamma Elvira?"

"She is at home, feet up, watching television and texting me every ten minutes to ask if any more people have come in. Two more will make her happy. I won't mention it's the two of you."

"Why not? I'm paying."

"She'll like that, but Tilde won't." Enzo paused as if thinking. "No, you can't pay. You are staff and you brought two bottles of wine."

"Only during the tourist season and the wine is a present. Tilde doesn't have to know." Nico reached into his pocket and took out his wallet. "Here's my credit card."

"If she finds out I am rat food."

"Make sure she doesn't. Mamma Elvira does the accounting, doesn't she?"

"Yes."

"No problem then."

Enzo took the card Nico held out and slipped the card in the back pocket of his slacks. "The menu is in front of you."

Nico picked up a sheet of paper and recognized Stella's neat handwriting.

"For red we have Antinori, Querciabella, Ferriello and Panzanello or the house wine. If you want white, I have to check."

In the heart of Chianti no one drank white. His Pinot Grigio tribute to Rita he drank only at home. Nico looked over at Nelli. "Your choice."

"I work for Querciabella, but Panzanello Riserva is my favorite."

"That's what we'll have then." It was a great wine, but out of loyalty to his vintner landlord who owned the Ferri Winery, he would have chosen the Ferriello.

Nelli and Nico took their time over a dinner of spinach soup, fricassee of chicken with roasted potatoes and the chantarelle mushrooms Tilde had frozen in September, at the height of their season. Now Nico was watching Nelli plunder the pile of fried ricotta tortelli covered in powdered sugar while he debated whether to bring up the my-place, your-place conundrum. *Where to start?*

Nico poured himself the last of the wine. "I don't know if you've noticed the ground floor room of the farmhouse is almost empty. I got Aldo to remove the old barrels he stored in there without my rent getting raised."

"Yes, I saw that. It will be a nice space once it's cleaned and repainted. It will need a proper floor. Those uneven stones are just asking to be tripped on. I'm glad you are making more room for yourself. Upstairs is very small and you're a big man."

"Well, I was thinking—"

His cell phone rang. Livia. He needed to answer.

"Am I disturbing you?" she asked in a hushed voice.

Very much so.

Nelli looked up, powdered sugar covering her chin. Sprinkles of it decorated her. Nico mouthed *Livia*.

"Cilia is asleep?" Nico asked.

"Yes, she is. Can we talk now?"

"Give me a minute." Nico got up and popped a tortello in his mouth, knowing there would be none left when he came back. He walked out on the terrace with his phone against his chest while he chewed and swallowed. OneWag followed him out. "Annamaria Lenzi met with me today."

"Did she have any helpful information?"

"It seems Saverio started being difficult with Lenzi late in the summer. He stopped accepting the weekly invitations to dinner." With the phone to his ear, Nico tried to hug himself. The temperature had dropped considerably. The patch of sky he could see had turned into a tar-black vault with sporadic pinpricks of light. The moon was somewhere else. "Annamaria thinks Saverio was upset because you were breaking up with him. Is that true?"

"I finally told Savi I hated those dinners. Annamaria was always showing off her good taste, her perfect home, her cooking mastery. She made me feel small. I come from a single runaway mother who kept making bad choices."

"Your mother kept you. That was a good choice." Nico felt something warm fall on his shoulders. He turned around to see Nelli close the terrace door behind OneWag.

"She kept me in food and when no man was around, sometimes even love. Annamaria is wrong. I wasn't breaking up with Saverio."

Nico slipped his jacket on. "Do you know why Saverio was giving Lenzi a hard time?"

"Well, we don't know if that's true, do we? Maybe it was Annamaria who was making life difficult for Giancarlo."

"Why would she? Was he playing around?"

"I don't know. Ask his widow, not that she'd tell you."

"You never witnessed any unpleasantness between them?"

"Or pleasantness. She's very reserved so it's hard to tell if she's happy or not. Giancarlo loved an audience and played the star of the evening. The last night we had dinner at their home was different though. Giancarlo was dressing his salad and spilled a few drops of olive oil on the rug. Annamaria snapped, accusing him of doing it on purpose to spite her. Savi and I exchanged looks and left as soon as we could."

"Saverio never spoke to you about Lenzi's marriage?"

"Savi was tight-lipped about everything and anyone. I wasn't interested in knowing anything about them anyway. I know I sound as if I dislike them. I simply have nothing in common with them. I have envied Annamaria's poise. Now I admire her. She's put up a marble front, not a crack in it. I'd be howling in anger."

Anger can come before pain. Nico remembered he had wanted to punch the doctor who gave Rita the cancer diagnosis. When she'd died thirteen months later, he'd shut down. "What do you think is behind that front?"

"Maybe her blood runs cold."

"Do you think she's capable of murdering her husband?"

"Most women should be capable, given how we've been treated, but we're usually the ones that get killed. I got lucky with Savi. I hear Cilia muttering. I better go."

"I need you to answer one more question. Why would Maresciallo Fabbri have a good laugh at my expense if you hired me to find Lenzi's killer?"

"Well, I did hire you and he'll laugh at his own expense when you prove him wrong about Saverio."

"Livia, I hope you haven't kept anything from me."

"I have, but it has nothing to do with Lenzi's murder."

A distant *mamma* came over the phone.

"I have to go. Cilia's calling me."

"Buonanotte." Nico slipped the phone in his jacket pocket and walked back into the warm room. "Thanks for the jacket," he said as he sat down. OneWag was curled back up on his pillow.

"It's the least I could do," Nelli said as she guiltily looked at the dessert plate with its thin spread of powdered sugar pockmarked by thumbprints. The fried bundles of ricotta-stuffed dough were gone. "How did it go with Livia?"

"I'm not sure. I think she's holding something back."

"If she is, you'll find out."

Nico leaned forward with elbows on the table. "I want to get back to the room I'm clearing out. I thought—"

Nelli reached over and squeezed his hand. "Please, amore. Not now."

Stung, Nico sat up straight, elbows by his side. Was he boring her or had she understood what he was leading up to?

"Buonasera, amici. Thank you for the wine." Tilde picked up a chair from the nearest table and joined them. Her face was still flushed from the heat of the kitchen. Her long apron covered most of a dark green knit dress. She had gathered her long hair under an orange scarf. "What's the verdict on a meal cooked without Nico in the kitchen?"

"Ciao, Tilde." Nelli blew her a kiss. "A wonderful dinner."

"Good to hear. Don't look so glum, Nico. I miss you and your cooking, but not enough people are eating out now. I want to be open for dinner only on Fridays and Saturdays. No more Thursdays. Last night we had one couple who ate a full meal and two men who had a plate of bruschetta and a carafe of house wine. Of course, Elvira said no to cutting out Thursday."

"Tilde, I'll come in and help you," Nico said. "Keep you company." When Nelli stayed at her place, usually three times a week, his place had begun to feel abandoned. "Your company as payment."

"You worked for free for a long time. No more. Would you like some dessert wine with Alba's cantuccini?"

Nelli shook her head. "No more room. Thank you."

"None for me," Nico said.

Tilde locked arms with Nico. "You should make eating dinner at Sotto Il Fico a Saturday night ritual. Give your cooking a rest."

Nico stole a glance at Nelli. "I don't cook when I'm alone."

Tilde tightened her grip, letting him know she understood. Nico took her hand in his. Tilde had cheered when he had finally allowed himself to love Nelli, had suffered for him when Nelli pulled back. And now he was confused. Maybe he needed to talk to Tilde, ask for her advice. Falling in love with Rita had been easy. After eight months of dating, he said he loved her, she said she loved him back. They got engaged. Four months later they married and were happy until cancer took her away. Loving Nelli was complicated.

"Come on, you two," Tilde said. "Help me fill up the room. Bring Cilia and her mother. It might cheer them up to have dinner served to them. Stella worries about her pupil."

"Stella has a big heart."

"So do you." Tilde gave Nelli a pointed look. Nelli acknowledged it with a guilty smile.

Tilde unlocked hands with Nico and stood up. "Now get out of here so we can clean up. Dinner is on the house."

A big *grazie* came from Nelli and Nico. The three of them kissed and buonanotted each other. OneWag uncurled himself from the pillow and stretched.

"See you soon, I hope," Enzo said as Nelli and Nico stopped to say goodbye. He shook hands with Nico and muttered, "I signed your name." The credit card exchanged hands; Nico, Nelli and OneWag walked out the front door.

As they strolled down the hill to the car, Nelli wrapped one arm around his waist and dropped her head on his shoulder. "We're happy together, aren't we?"

"Yes, we are," Nico admitted. Their living arrangements discussion could wait for another night. Debora Costa he would call tomorrow.

SIX

"Jimmy, Sandro, buongiorno," Nico said, walking into Bar All'Angolo with Nelli and OneWag at ten Sunday morning.

"Buona Domenica a tutti." Nelli directed her *to all* at the three customers standing at the bar.

Jimmy, manning the espresso machine, raised a hand in greeting with a surprised look on his face. "This is new."

Nico headed straight to the pastry display to check on the whole wheat cornetti. Were they plain or with orange marmalade? He'd take whatever was available, but the orange marmalade ones were true bliss.

OneWag, his nose on high alert, began his usual tour of the tile floor for sugary tidbits.

From his post behind the cash register, Sandro twirled the small gold hoop hanging from his left ear. "Your presence on a Sunday? What happened? Nico burnt the coffee?"

"Never!" Nico said, his head bent over the glass counter.

"Then Gogol is coming!"

"He is not." From the beginning of Nico's life in Gravigna, his breakfasts at Bar All'Angolo had been shared with the old man. Gogol's constant Dante quotes had brought up warm memories of Dante-loving Rita. On Sunday Gogol went to Mass. Nico breakfasted at home and now, most often, happily with Nelli.

"It's a workday for us, Sandro." Nelli held up the paint-splat-tered smock she was going to wear over gray corduroy slacks and a sky blue open-collared sweater. She wanted to make a good first impression on her client. "I am going to Orvieto to paint a portrait."

Sandro clapped. "Good news."

"What will it be today then?" Jimmy asked her. "Something special to celebrate?"

"Just a cappuccino." Nelli sat down at their usual table. It was another San Martino summer day, and the sun, now just over the low buildings across the piazza, dropped a ribbon of warm light through the glass of the French doors.

The three men at the bar drank their coffees, said goodbye and left.

Jimmy looked over at Nico who was still trying to spot the orange marmalade cornetti. "I just took those out of the oven."

Nico grinned. "Three this time, please, and an Americano."

"When are you going to start drinking an Italiano?" Jimmy asked as he clamped the first cornetto and dropped it on the plate.

"One inch by one inch of pitch-black coffee?" Nico watched Jimmy pick up the second cornetto. "Grazie, no. I prefer to keep my stomach lining intact."

Sandro laughed. "What work is our resident detective doing today?"

Nelli folded the smock and pushed it into her bag. Her por-table easel and paint bag were in the trunk of the car. "He's driving me to Orvieto."

"La bella Orvieto!" Sandro exclaimed. "Jimmy and I got engaged in front of Saint Patrick's Well!"

"We wrote a love note to each other," Jimmy added, drop-ping the third cornetto on Nico's plate, "and dropped it down in Saint Patrick's Well. Fifty-three meters. That is how deep it is." Jimmy went back to the espresso machine. "You can climb down."

"What is the connection to Saint Patrick?" Nico asked.

A sound made OneWag raise his head.

"An odd one," Sandro said. "The well was compared to Saint Patrick's entrance-to-hell cave in Ireland."

Nelli turned her head to the voice coming from the open door. "Ah, ciao!"

Perillo strode farther into the room in his rumpled jeans, red polo shirt and his beloved leather jacket. OneWag scampered over in greeting and sniffed the old suede ankle boots Perillo refused to replace. They smelled of stale cigarettes.

"Buongiorno, Maresciallo!" Sandro said. "This is a Sunday full of welcome surprises."

Salvatore Perillo didn't return the smile.

"Ciao!" Nico called out, realizing he should have called Perillo last night. Keep him informed. His thoughts had been with Nelli. "Great to see you."

"You are welcome unless there's been another murder," Sandro added.

"Thousands all over the world, I'm sure. Today not here." Perillo raised two fingers to signal a double expresso.

Nico walked back to the table with his plate of cornetti. "Sit down with us."

Perillo hesitated with a petulant look on his face. "Don't want to interrupt anything."

Nico looked up in surprise. "Please sit down, Perillo." He bit into his first cornetto. Three bites and it was gone.

Nelli patted the chair seat next to her. "It is always wonderful to see you."

Perillo sat with a nod. "You too."

Nelli ventured a guess. "Did Ivana go with Alba to the Perugia Food Fair?"

"Yes, selling those damn cantuccini!" He raised his hand, as if in surrender. "I know. I know. I should be proud of her. I am, I really am, but if I never see another cantuccino, I will die a happy man."

"You miss her," Nelli said.

"Yes, I do."

"And her cooking," Nico added, knowing his friend's heart was reached by way of his stomach. He attacked his second cornetto with a hunger that came from being happy. Happy for having spent the evening and night with Nelli, for the time they'd have together on the drive to Orvieto. He was also looking forward to entering deeper into the Lenzi investigation in Pitigliano. Debora Costa, one of the names on Livia's list, was willing to see him today.

"Daniele was with Stella?" Nelli asked.

"Every chance he gets."

"I'm sorry you didn't tell us you were by yourself. You could have joined us at Sotto Il Fico last night."

"I ate here in the piazza. At Gino's. His bean and pasta soup is better than Ivana's, but do not tell her. Nico, I thought you would call. How was Pitigliano?"

Nico waited until Sandro had served them their coffees.

A group of cyclists wearing their skintight shorts and shirts came in.

"I met Annamaria," he said with a lowered voice. "I'm meeting a neighbor today."

Perillo sighed. "Ivana is coming back tomorrow."

Nico glanced at Nelli.

She picked up in a flash. "Join us for dinner tonight then."

"My place," Nico said. "No need to bring anything."

Perillo acknowledged the invitation with a grateful nod and drank down his double espresso. "I will bring the wine."

"I've got that."

"Then I will bring Ivana's untouched chocolate crostata."

"That I can't resist. Are you sure she won't mind?"

"It is my consolation prize for her absence."

Nelli looked at her cell phone and stood up. "Nico, I think we better go."

Nico checked his watch. "You're right." He stood up and laid a hand on Perillo's shoulder. "I'll call you when I get back." Nelli picked up her smock. OneWag made for the open door.

"A domani," Nico called out to Sandro and Jimmy, now busy with the cyclists.

"Ciao and grazie," was Nelli's goodbye. OneWag, being a lucky dog, headed for Nelli's car. Debora Costa had said yes to Nico *and* his dog.

THEY WERE ON THE autostrada for almost an hour before Nelli broke the silence. "You are upset with me, aren't you?"

"You drive too fast," Nico said, picking an easy objection. They were in Nelli's five-year-old Citroën, a car far bigger and more comfortable than Nico's Fiat 500. OneWag was happily curled up between Nico's feet.

Nelli gave Nico a quick sideways glance. His Easter Island statue look confirmed he was upset. She slowed down to the speed limit of a hundred and thirty kilometers per hour. "I do not want to be late."

Five minutes went by. "I love you, Nico. I know you want more from me. All of me maybe. I cannot give you that. I need to feel free. I am sorry if that is not enough. You have seventy-five percent of me. I need to keep that twenty-five percent for me and my work."

"I'm greedy, I guess." Nico's feet shifted. OneWag sat up and looked at Nico.

"No, you are not. Rita probably gave you a hundred percent of herself."

"No. She carved out her own space in our marriage." But they were together every night. He missed that. Maybe he wasn't greedy, just needy. Rita's death and his forced retirement had taken a lot out of him. He was older too. *Come on, Nico. Shape up.*

After a few minutes had gone by, Nico put his hand on Nelli's thigh. "I want you to know that despite my grumblings, I know that I'm damn lucky you're in my life at all." He looked at the wide, straight band of road ahead. "I thank you for that seventy-five percent that you give me. That is far more than I deserve. I love you and I will now stop being greedy." After all, he reasoned, he wasn't giving Nelli a hundred percent. Rita still had part of him.

"Thank you, Nico, for understanding."

OneWag curled back down.

Nico retrieved his hand. "Slow down now. That sign says the Orvieto turnoff is coming up in two kilometers."

She slowed down even though she had plenty of time.

DEBORA COSTA LIVED DEEP in old town, in a narrow cul-de-sac just left of the Chiesa di San Rocco, the oldest church in Pitigliano. Nico and OneWag climbed fifteen sagging stone steps to reach the heavily carved door. A silver mezuzah was nailed at an angle on the right side of the stone doorway. The door opened before Nico could use the knocker.

A short thin woman dressed in black tights and a long patterned knit dress scanned Nico with dark deep-set eyes. She held a cane in one hand and could not have been more than five feet tall. She had a pale wrinkled face with assertively high cheekbones and a strong jawline cupped by short doll-like white curls.

"Buongiorno, Signora Costa," Nico said, returning her scan with a smile. OneWag, suddenly shy, stayed by Nico's side. "I'm Nico Doyle. You kindly agreed to see me."

"Indeed I did and kindness has nothing to do with it. Justice does." She leaned down and held her hand out for OneWag to sniff. The dog obliged. She smelled powdery. "And who are you?" she asked, running her hand down his soft furry ear.

"OneWag in English, Rocco in Italian."

She straightened up. "He is a clever one if he answers to both. Come in, come in." She walked quickly away from the door, her back held surprisingly straight, her cane barely touching the floor. According to Livia, she was ninety-one years old. "Lock the door behind you, please."

Nico and OneWag followed her down a short, narrow ochre-colored corridor lined with faded photographs.

"You are both welcome in my family home."

Nico stepped into a large square living room crowded with heavy antique furniture, differently shaped armchairs, two sofas that didn't match and various Persian rugs that overlapped in places. Every surface was covered with old framed photographs, porcelain bowls, vases of different sizes holding desiccated flowers or branches. The fireplace was filled with books. Warmth came from two large radiators under the windows. On a piano bench sat a stack of worn photo albums. There was no piano. Nico felt as if he'd walked into an attic or storage room. A perfectly dusted one though.

Catching him looking, Debora said, "Yes, the room is overstuffed, but every object holds some of the history of my family, at least for the past two hundred years. Sit where you want, Signor Doyle. I will get you a coffee."

"No need, thank you. I'm fine."

She tilted her head, as if she'd heard an unusual noise. "In this country we offer coffee when someone comes to visit. If you don't want it, I hope you won't mind if I offer it to myself?"

"Of course not."

"In the United States they probably offer you a drink, no matter the time."

"Before dinner maybe."

The wrinkles on her cheeks deepened with her smile. "I know. The cocktail hour seen in so many films, although probably not as popular today. I was testing your taking-offense meter. From what I read Americans have recently become very thin-skinned."

"I hope I passed."

"You did for now." She walked toward an arched doorway. "The blue armchair has the best springs."

"Where will you sit?"

"In the one that has no springs. Make yourself comfortable. I'll bring you a glass of water, needed or not. OneWag, come with me." She pronounced his name perfectly.

The dog followed, his nose telling him a kitchen wasn't far away.

Nico found his way to one of the two small curtainless windows cut into a foot-deep wall. Debora's house was on the northern edge of the town. The house overlooked a deep ravine covered with a thick spread of deep green and yellowing trees.

"I am lucky to have a beautiful view, small medieval windows notwithstanding."

Nico turned around. Debora was holding a tray with her coffee and Nico's glass of water.

"Pitigliano sits above the meeting point of three river valleys. That explains the lushness of the vegetation and why the Etruscans settled here. The area is rich with their tombs." Nico took the tray from her and looked for a place to put it down.

"Thank you. The piano bench will do. It was also an important prehistoric site. I could tell you much more, but you are not here for a history lesson."

As Nico put down the tray next to the stack of photo albums, OneWag dropped a rawhide bone at his feet with one wag of his tail.

"I assumed you wouldn't mind." Debora handed Nico a small plate holding a cut glass goblet filled with water. "I also gave him water."

"I take it you used to have a dog?"

"Always. My last one was sweet enough to keep me company for seventeen years. I have now reached the age where I must do without. My knees rebel against the stairs. I am unfortunately allergic to cats. Please sit." She pointed to the small blue armchair.

Nico obeyed. OneWag dropped down on one of the rugs and started chewing his bone. Debora picked up a pillow from a sofa, dropped it on a hard chair and sat down. "Now you can begin." She crossed her hands on her lap.

"Livia said you are a psychologist."

"Yes. I practiced in Orvieto and retired twelve years ago. My seventy-nine-year-old brain was still efficient, but I got tired of the commute. Now tell me about you. I promise not to psychoanalyze you. I will keep my opinions to myself."

Nico gave her a short summary of his adult life.

"I'm sorry you lost your wife. I was too absorbed in my work to marry or have a live-in partner. A faithful dog was all I needed here and at the studio. Now to answer what surely will be your first question. Saverio Bianconi is as innocent of wrongdoing as a newborn baby. I have known him since he was born. Our two families have been friends since the war. Sadly, only Saverio and I are left."

"How do you know he's innocent?"

"Forty-nine years of studying people's psyches tells me he is. Saverio is incapable of murder."

"He knocked down his best friend in front of witnesses."

"Yes, he did. I was surprised, I admit that." She closed her eyes.

"You were present."

"Yes. It was an unpleasant scene. Saverio came to me shortly afterward with a cauldron of mixed emotions. He was shocked by his action, ashamed of it and totally bewildered by Giancarlo's theft. I sat him down in the chair you are sitting in now. He started talking about the respect and awe he'd always had for Giancarlo. It's important to understand that Saverio is a quiet man, introspective, gentle. Giancarlo was the opposite. Together they completed each other.

"Saverio spoke to me through tears. I gave him a brandy. He drank it slowly and apologized. '*What should I do now?*' he asked. I suggested he call Giancarlo and ask to meet. Saverio needed to understand Giancarlo's actions and Giancarlo needed to explain."

"Did he call?"

"Yes, the next morning. Saverio sounded incredibly relieved when he phoned to tell me." She smiled at the thought. "He is such an innocent soul."

"Why relieved?" Nico asked. Livia had told him Giancarlo had hung up on Saverio.

"Giancarlo agreed to see him, saying he would explain the false invoices, that Saverio would understand and forgive. They were going to meet at Beppe's Bar, just around the corner from the store the next morning."

"By then Giancarlo was dead."

"Yes."

"Do you know where Saverio is now?"

Debora touched the small Star of David she wore around her neck. "I do not."

Her gesture jolted a very old memory back into Nico's mind. His mother used to touch the crucifix she wore around her neck when answering questions. Seven or eight years old, he'd asked her why she did it. *Jesus comforts me.* Not understanding why only some questions made her uncomfortable, he convinced himself she was asking forgiveness for answering with a lie.

"If you knew," Nico asked, "would you tell him to give himself up?"

Debora sat up, her back stiff. "That is a difficult question for a Jew who had to hide with her family while the Nazis raked through these villages looking for us."

"I apologize." He wanted to kick himself.

"No need. You are only trying to find the truth of this sad story."

"Did Pitigliano have many Jews living here then?"

"We first came in the fifteenth century. More came in the sixteenth, when the pope decreed we had to live in ghettos, allowing us only to sell used clothes. A subsequent pope expelled us from the Papal States. The ruling Orsini family welcomed us. When the Medicis took over, we had to live in a ghetto again, and the men were required to wear red hats and the women had a red mark on their sleeve. If you want to know more, you should go to Via Zuccarelli to visit our synagogue, the museum and the small ghetto we were forced to live in. Once Italy became unified in 1861, we were granted equal rights and many left for bigger towns like Florence. By the time the Nazis came, only about sixty of us still lived here. We were hidden and fed, but the Nazis still managed to send twenty-two of us to the camps. Now less than a handful of us remain."

"Why did you stay?"

"Pitigliano welcomed my ancestors when no one else did. This house holds their history. It is home. Now to answer your previous question, I do not know if it would be best for Saverio to came back. He is convinced his disappearance is best for Cilia and Livia. A frightened man does not reason well. I understand his fear only too well. Maresciallo Fabbri is limited in his thinking."

"What can you tell me about Giancarlo and his family?"

"A troubled, unhappy family even before Giancarlo's death."

"You know the family well, then."

"Annamaria grew up in the building next to mine. Giancarlo across the street in the house they live in now. My bedroom window faces their house and I confess my bad knees have turned me into a window watcher. Our street is narrow and last summer Mimmo, her youngest son, and I started talking to each other from our windows. Annamaria put a stop to our 'too public' chitchats, so Mimmo started coming over. In the summer I made lemonade for him, now he gets hot chocolate."

"Do you have a picture of him?"

"I asked him for one. As you can see, I surround myself with the photos of the people I love. Mimmo took one with his phone and sent it to me. As often happens I have no idea where my phone is at the moment. I have no landline. If you don't mind."

Nico took out his phone.

"Thank you." She gave him her number.

A series of loud trumpet blasts came from somewhere far behind her. OneWag looked up from his wet, gnawed rawhide bone. Whatever hunting dog gene he had inherited sent him scrambling across the room, under chairs, tables, between two bureaus. He stopped in front of the open drawer of a small desk. He barked once.

Nico had followed him and picked up the phone. "Here it is."

Debora showed her delight by clapping. "How wonderful of OneWag to find it. Thank you." She patted OneWag's head as he lay back down at her feet to chew on his bone. "The ringtone is irritatingly loud but I'm forever leaving it somewhere so trumpet blasts are necessary. I also don't always remember to put on my hearing aid." She took the phone from Nico and paged through the photos. "Here he is. Isn't that smile heartwarming?"

Nico looked at the photo she held up. The boy smiling at him now was the same boy he had seen at the café in Piazza della Repubblica. "A sweet smile."

"He's a sweet, loving boy. He is my Sabbath goy. Comes in before school on Saturday to turn on the lights."

Nico handed back the phone. "What about the rest of the family? You said they are sad, troubled."

"You want to know if I think Annamaria or her older son are capable of killing Giancarlo?"

"To start with. Also who else could have a motive to kill Giancarlo."

"Or send Saverio to jail for the rest of his life?"

"That seems far-fetched to me."

"Perhaps but not to be forgotten. Let me start with the victim. Giancarlo Lenzi grew up with adoring parents, easy money and good looks. He was the pearl in the oyster. I confess I found his exaggerated self-confidence and his ensnaring charm irritating."

"And Annamaria?"

"She was Giancarlo's backbone and his bridle."

"He needed reining in?"

"I see Annamaria as a woman only comfortable when wearing a tight corset. She believes in rules, in decorum. She is strict with her children, too much so, at least with Mimmo. Giancarlo grew up with no rules, a vast ego and little sense of decorum. Adoring parents, good looks and easy money don't always help a child grow up. I think Annamaria, who loved him very much, felt she needed to watch over him. She's the one who came up with the idea of Giancarlo and Saverio going into business together. I don't think Giancarlo knew much about electronics, but Saverio had been selling them in Orvieto and playing guru to us grayheads who are bewildered by the virtual world. Maybe she hoped Saverio's quiet manner would act as some sort of restraint."

"Did it work?"

"Annamaria seemed pleased. Giancarlo took over the money end, Saverio the rest. The store was successful."

"What can you tell me about Edoardo?"

"Eddi is a handsome nineteen-year-old with his mother's patrician airs but lacking his father's charm. Annamaria has always favored him, which has led to some loud disagreements with his father I had the misfortune to witness more than once."

"Father and son did not get along, then."

"Giancarlo found himself suddenly being disobeyed, even confronted, not by a boy, but by an impetuous young man protected by his mother. Jealousy, awareness of time passing, loss of power—they are not pleasant feelings. Giancarlo released them by shouting. Eddi shouted back. If Eddi was going to bludgeon his father with a hammer, I think he would have done it only in the heat of the moment, during one of their fights."

"Why do you think Giancarlo started stealing?"

"Gambling debts? Another woman? A modern apartment in the new town? Take your pick."

"He wanted to leave Annamaria?"

"I don't know. I do know he thought the old town was for the old and poor. He hated the tourists peering in every corner, taking photographs, the attention given to the town's Jewish history. *'Enough with the old stuff!'* he declared to my face. I just shook my old head. He immediately apologized. *'I didn't mean you. Mimmo loves you.'* I had nothing to say."

"Could he have been blackmailed?"

"You ask questions I cannot answer one way or the other." Debora picked up her cane. "After years of listening and choosing my words with extreme care, my mouth has sprung a leak today, spouting one declarative sentence after another. Liberating, but guilt-inducing, nonetheless. I believe what I told you, but I am certain your past work has taught you not to count on only one person's opinion of the truth."

"It has."

"Good. Now it is time for me to restock my energy. Giulia has left me a lovely potato, spinach, and onion frittata."

"You have been of great help, thank you. Is Giulia by any chance Giulia Favelli?"

"Yes. I share her with Annamaria. She's a young, patient soul and a passable cook. The frittata is big enough for two. I hope you will join me. I have a good Pitigliano white I look forward to sharing with you. I am too old to drink alone."

"Gladly. Thank you." Nico stood and held out his arm to help her stand, but she was already on her feet.

She chuckled. "Thank you for wanting to help but I have been a hiker all my life, and a jogger years before it was fashionable. Only my knees scold me for it now. Follow me. Drop the bone, OneWag. I have some poached chicken for you."

NICO STEPPED OUT OF Debora Costa's building and bent down to leash OneWag. The dog protested by shaking his head repeatedly. A leash was an insult to his street-dog chops. "Stop it. You don't know this place; the people don't know you." OneWag lowered his head in resignation. Leash clipped on, Nico straightened up and they headed back up the main street. The old town of Pitigliano was made up of three narrow main streets from which short, narrower streets and arched alleys branched out like the legs of a centipede. Nico was counting on OneWag's nose to lead him back to his car at the other end of the old town. The dog pulled hard on the leash, his usual comeuppance. As they approached yet another corner, OneWag suddenly sat down. Nico stopped.

A boy stepped out onto Via Roma, the same boy Nico had seen yesterday in Piazza Repubblica, and on Debora's cell phone.

Nico waited with a smile on his face. Mimmo lowered his head to look at OneWag. He had his mother's round face and the same pale brown hair neatly cut. He was dressed in blue slacks, a puffy kelly green down jacket and expensive-looking brown leather sneakers. *Church wear*, Nico thought.

"Ciao, Mimmo. I'm Nico."

Mimmo held out a hand for OneWag to sniff. "What's his name?"

"Rocco." He leaned down and undid the leash. "Go ahead, pet him. He's very friendly."

As OneWag stretched to sniff the outstretched hand, Mimmo took it back and lifted his eyes to peer at Nico. "Mamma won't let me have a dog and I'm not allowed to talk to you."

"She's worried I'll upset you."

Mimmo shook his head. "She knows Savi didn't kill Babbo. She's afraid I'll tell you who did, but I won't. I can't."

"Why can't you?"

"I just can't."

"Are you sure you know who it is?"

Mimmo looked up with large tea-colored eyes and slowly nodded. "Is it true you are a detective from New York?"

"I was."

"Fico." The Italian word for *cool*. Suddenly aware that OneWag was sniffing his sneakers, Mimmo stepped back.

"He won't bite. Do you like Saverio?"

Mimmo nodded vigorously. "We played Master Chess. I was getting really good at it."

"Don't you want him to play with you again?"

"Yes, but I can't tell you anything else. You find out." He ran back down the alley he'd come from. OneWag ran after him. Nico whistled and the dog stopped. So did Mimmo as he was about to turn a corner. "Ask Eddi," he yelled and disappeared.

Eddi, Mimmo's older brother. He very much wanted to talk

to Eddi, but how to reach him without his mother knowing and without making the loss of his father worse for him?

A wind had swept up while he was talking to Mimmo. Nico realized he was cold. "Come on, buddy, you look cold too. Let's go find a warm place for a cup of hot chocolate and a yummy treat for you."

The word treat sent OneWag running back while Nico's phone rang.

"Hi, Nelli, you're done for the day?"

"Far from it. That's why I called. Maria Grazia invited me to stay over so I can work late and get an early start in the morning."

Nico's shoulders sagged. Now that today's work was done, he was looking forward to the ride back with her, sharing their day, then their evening, their night. "What about clothes? A toothbrush?"

"Don't worry," Nelli said with a laughing voice. "Maria Grazia has a new toothbrush for me. I'll wash and blow dry my underwear. My painting clothes will survive. So will you."

Nico let out a purposefully loud sigh. "If you think so." Nico snapped his fingers at OneWag who was testing his freedom up and down the street, sniffing at every protruding stone on his way. The dog kept going.

Nico pressed the phone against his chest and raised his voice. "OneWag, get over here!" Mouth to phone again he said, "I'll miss you."

"I will too. A big hug to you. I'll call you in the morning. Ciao."

"Hug back." Nico clicked off. OneWag was now sitting at his feet, panting, looking very pleased with himself. "Wish I felt the same," Nico muttered and snapped the leash back on.

NICO LIFTED HIS VEGETABLE garden spinach from the water in the sink and dropped it in the colander to drain.

He fed OneWag next, then poured himself a glass of Pinot Grigio. He had a dinner for three to cook. On the drive back, Perillo had called to say that Daniele was coming to share some "eye-popping" information about the Lenzi murder. Being the usual teaser, Perillo had refused to elaborate.

For Sunday dinner Nico had originally planned on one of Nelli's favorite meals: roasted pork loin, sautéed potatoes and spinach, with pears and apples for dessert. It was a meal Perillo would have enjoyed too, but Dani was a vegetarian. He decided to serve spaghetti with caramelized onions and spinach he'd picked from the garden sautéed in garlic and olive oil and topped with fried breadcrumbs.

Before starting, Nico checked the refrigerator. Good, he had pancetta. He'd dice it and sauté it separately to add to his and Perillo's pasta.

OneWag gave a last lick to his empty bowl and made his way to Nico's armchair, his new favorite spot for a nap. Nico took a first sip of his wine, unhooked the I LOVE TUSCANY apron Rita had given him years ago and wrapped it around his expanding waist. He peeled a garlic clove and finely chopped it. Back in the States he'd have used three cloves. Italian garlic was much stronger.

A car horn honked as he was thinly slicing his first onion. OneWag ran to the door. Nico looked at his watch. They were half an hour early.

"I brought gelato!" Perillo announced as he climbed up to the open door with Daniele. They were both dressed in jeans and pullovers of different blues.

"Buonasera, Nico," Daniele said. "I hope you don't mind we're so early."

OneWag greeted Daniele with a wag and a hopeful look.

Daniele bent down to give OneWag a back rub as consolation. "I couldn't find anything for you. The stores are closed."

Perillo handed Nico a Styrofoam package. "Quick in the freezer. Salted caramel, chocolate, coffee, pistachio, and Dani insisted on lemon sorbet."

"Thanks. What happened to Ivana's chocolate crostata?"

"She called an hour ago and said she couldn't wait to get home tomorrow and watch me eat her crostata. So I unwrapped it and put it back untouched."

OneWag had left Daniele and was now sniffing Perillo's shoes. He licked a fat drop of chocolate.

Perillo looked down. "Bravo, Rocco. Clean up my sin."

Nico had to remove the ice tray to make the package fit in his small freezer. "Sit down. Wine and glasses are on the bench. Help yourselves."

Perillo looked at the sturdy backless wooden bench sitting in front of the sofa. "That's new."

"One of Nelli's finds. She thought I should have a coffee table."

"She's adjusting your place to her liking. That's a good sign." Perillo knew Nico wanted Nelli to move in.

"I don't think so. She's too much a free spirit. I guess that's the artist's way." Nico plucked a large onion from another Nelli addition: a wicker basket hanging from under a kitchen cabinet. "She's staying over with her new client tonight in Orvieto to get more work done on the portrait. Her painting is what really matters to her. Now, while I work on your dinner, I'm ready to have my eyes popped."

Perillo sat in Nico's armchair and crossed his arms in front of his chest. "I received an interesting phone call just before coming here from Maresciallo Fabbri. He wanted to know if I had sent you to Pitigliano."

Nico peeled the onion. "He was going to find out I was sniffing around asking questions, so I thought it best to introduce myself."

"I was caught off guard."

"I'm sorry." Nico started slicing the onion. "I was going to tell you tonight."

"Fabbri also wanted to know if in my experience, you kept your word. What did you promise him?"

"That I would tell him whatever I discovered so he could act on it. It would be far better if Pitigliano were in your jurisdiction—"

"Certainly far better. There would be justice." Perillo drank some wine, momentarily appeased.

An impatient Daniele looked at his maresciallo, who was now sitting in Nico's armchair with his glass of wine.

Perillo shook his head and turned to Nico. "So was the old psychologist any help?"

Perillo loved to stall. Nico took a sip of needed patience with his Pinot Grigio. "Debora Costa has known Saverio since he was a child and claims he's incapable of murder."

"That's reassuring," Perillo said, pouring more wine in his glass.

Eager to share his news, Daniele felt restless. He walked over to the table, opened a table drawer, took out place mats and started setting the table.

"Thanks, Dani," Nico said as he finished slicing. "You know where everything is. Annamaria has some doubt about Saverio killing her husband but can't contemplate her husband stealing money from his own business. She thinks Saverio faked the invoices to get back at her husband for some reason. According to her they weren't getting along anymore but doesn't know why."

"You believe her?" Perillo asked.

"Livia said something about it and during lunch I asked Debora if she knew anything. About a month before the murder, Saverio seemed very upset during one of his visits.

When she prodded, he shut up." Nico turned on the gas underneath a wide cast-iron pan, wet it with two swirls of his landlord's olive oil and tossed in the onion slices. "The onions have to caramelize which takes a while." He lowered the flame. "On the street I ran into Mimmo, Lenzi's thirteen-year-old son. He'd seen me talk to his mother yesterday. He announced Saverio didn't kill his father, that he knew who did, but couldn't tell me."

"Do you think he does know?" Perillo asked.

Daniele picked three napkins from a second drawer. "He would want to see his father's killer punished, no?"

Assuming he loved his father, Nico thought. "He might just be defending Saverio. They're computer game pals."

"Or he is just giving himself importance," Perillo suggested.

Nico finished his Pinot Grigio and set the glass down in the sink. "I'm going to keep an eye on the onions and, Maresciallo Salvatore Perillo permitting, listen to what Brigadiere Daniele Donato has discovered. Sit down, Dani. Setting the table can wait."

Daniele went back to sit on the sofa. Eager and proud of what he'd found out, he didn't wait for Perillo's okay. "I was looking up the Pitigliano residents and their addresses, making a list of who lived near the LenConi store in case you wanted to talk to them. I came across a Stefano Granchi, the only other Granchi. Maybe a relative, I thought. I typed in both their names. Stefano and Livia married sixteen years ago. There is no record of a divorce."

"Interesting."

"Important," Perillo corrected.

"Yes, that too. Thank you, Dani." Nico lifted a fistful of spinach and squeezed hard. Green water dripped down his wrist.

With a peevish voice Perillo asked, "Did Livia at least put

her husband's name on the list?" He wished he also had information to give.

"No." Nico pulled his phone out of his back pocket.

"Unbelievable!" Perillo filled his wineglass again. "I would tell her to find another detective to lie to."

"An omission. Not a lie." Nico clicked Livia's number.

She picked up after the second ring. "Buonasera, Nico. Cilia was just asking me when she can play with Rocco again."

"Tomorrow morning Rocco will walk her up to school"—Nico spoke in a low voice, trying to control his anger—"and then you and I need to have a serious conversation."

"You've found out something?" Her voice trembled. "Tell me. What?"

"Cilia is still awake, and I have guests right now. We'll talk in the morning. A domani." Nico went back to stirring the onions and spinach.

"She won't sleep tonight," Daniele said with a touch of disapproval in his voice. He was rubbing OneWag's stomach.

"She made me angry."

Perillo added, "Food comes first. I think the pasta water is bubbling."

Daniele pushed OneWag gently off his lap and sat closer to the edge of the sofa. "The maresciallo was curious as to why Livia came here instead of going to a bigger town."

"That is true!" Perillo exclaimed. How clever of Dani to bring that up. He didn't remember mentioning it. "I did think it would have been easier for her to get lost in a town like Siena which also has more job opportunities. Even Greve-in-Chianti would have made more sense. I am not trying to disparage your new home, Nico, but Gravigna is not the place to come to if you want privacy. You burp, the town knows about it."

Nico turned away from the stove to look at Dani's eager

face. His body leaning forward, elbows propped on his knees, as if ready to take off. "You acted on that curiosity?"

Daniele gave Perillo a quick look. "The maresciallo said we needed to help you."

Perillo squared his shoulders. "I did indeed." That he did remember. "One for all, all for one."

"I now had Livia's maiden name and looked her up on the town birth registry," Daniele said. "Livia Beatrice Ferruzzi, born February third, 1990, mother Alida Giacinta Ferruzzi, father unknown."

"She must be Beatrice Ferrruzzi's granddaughter. That explains why she chose to come to Gravigna." Nico told Perillo and Daniele about the knit shop owner whose daughter, Alida, had run away to Pitigliano years ago. "Tilde remembers going to that shop with her mother." He threw a fistful of large salt crystals in the boiling water, raised the flame and covered the pot. "Any more interesting news?"

Daniele let his now happier boss answer.

"I should hope that's enough for now. The water is bubbling. Throw in the pasta. Dani and I are hungry."

"It is more than enough. Thank you, both." Nico lowered the spaghetti into the pot and put the lid back halfway. Daniele was setting the table.

Perillo filled Nico's empty wineglass on the bench with some Panzanello red. "Here, sit. You've got a four-minute wait before you stir and then another four before you check."

"Thanks." Nico took the glass and stayed by the pot. The spaghetti needed the occasional stir. "With Livia's husband entering the picture, maybe Debora Costa's theory that Giancarlo was killed to get Saverio blamed shouldn't be written off."

"Possible," Perillo said. "He hears about Saverio punching Giancarlo and the 'You will pay' threat and sees a chance to get rid of his wife's lover without risking being a suspect."

Daniele put down bowls and added a jug of water to the table. Drinking wine made him sleepy. He was hoping to meet Stella after dinner if it wasn't too late for her. "Stefano Granchi is on Tinder."

Perillo widened his eyes at his brigadiere. "You are on Tinder?"

Daniele blushed. He'd quit over a year ago thanks to Stella. "No. A friend of Stella's is on the site and looked for me. He's also on Metic and Badoo." He pulled out a chair and sat down. The table was now set. "Stefano's bio is the same for all three. The photos are different."

"So maybe he doesn't want his wife back." Perillo joined Daniele at the table and looked at his watch. "It's time."

Nico lifted a spaghetti strand with a long fork, tasted it. "Two more minutes at least."

Perillo puffed out air. "Americans do not know al dente."

"My mother was Italian and so was my wife. I used thicker spaghetti." It was a necessary lie, Nico thought. Tonight his proud friend was having a hard time. Daniele had taken over the evening with all his information. "What does Stefano's bio say?"

"He is thirty-eight years old, now lives in Sorano, owns Granchi Elettrica that services all the neighboring towns, according to the website. I wrote down the address and telephone number for you. He likes to go hunting and taking long walks in the countryside. He loves to cook, enjoys good wine and good friends, but hopes to find a good-hearted woman to share the best that life has to offer."

"Well done, Dani." Nico added half a cup of pasta water to the sauce.

"Bravo." Perillo gave Daniele's back an enthusiastic slap. "You must admit, Nico, I do know how to choose my brigadieri."

"You certainly do, Perillo." Nico drained the spaghetti, tossed it in the pan, stirred and let everything cook for a minute. "Okay, si mangia." He turned off the flame, lifted the pan off the flame and started serving. "Buon appetito!"

From the sofa, OneWag lifted a sleepy head and sniffed. Vegetables! He dropped back into his dream.

SEVEN

Monday morning, under a washed-out blue sky, Livia, Cilia, Nico and OneWag reached the school gate ten minutes before the bell. "Cilia, I need you to do me a favor," Nico said.

Cilia kicked the small red ball she had brought with her at OneWag. "What?"

"Could you say goodbye to Rocco and your mother now and go to your classroom?"

OneWag dropped the ball at Cilia's feet. She kicked it farther. "The bell has not rung."

"I know. That's why it's a favor."

She watched OneWag bring the ball back to her. "You want to talk to Mamma about Babbo and you do not want me to hear."

"I do want to talk to your mother, but about other people. Not Babbo."

Cilia took a moment to answer, as if deciding whether she believed him or not. "All right." She reached up and met her mother halfway for a hug. "You too." She hugged Nico's knees before he could reach her. "Tell Rocco he can keep the ball." She ran across the schoolyard and entered the building, this time without stopping to wave goodbye.

Livia waited until Cilia had disappeared to face Nico. "All

right, let's have this serious conversation." Worry was in her eyes. "You have bad news. You're quitting?"

"No. I'll walk you to the Coop." They crossed the street and entered an unpaved downhill road that flanked a small park. "Why didn't you tell me you are married?"

"Because Stefano has nothing to do with Giancarlo or Saverio. I married him when I was scared I was turning into my mother. I was seventeen and needed someone to steady me."

"Alida Ferruzzi is your mother."

Livia stopped abruptly. "Silly me!" She slapped her thigh. "I thought I could keep my mother out of this. Why, I do not know. I did hire a detective. So now you know why I chose Gravigna as our shelter. I'm living in the apartment my mother inherited from her mother. I did not know my grandmother even existed until my mother transferred the deed to me. I regret I never met her. She might have been nice."

"Where's your mother now?"

"She took off after I married Stefano, probably following some new lover." There was no bitterness in her voice, just a resigned calm.

Nico's anger dissipated. He recognized the pain of having a bad parent. "Maybe she left because she didn't have to worry about you anymore."

"That is a sweet thought. She never did worry. Whatever man was in her life was more important. Besides she was too young to be a mother. She had me when she was fifteen. I am the reason she left Gravigna. I always felt she blamed me for it." Livia waved a hand over her face as if shooing away a mosquito. "I left Stefano after two years."

"Why didn't you divorce?"

"His family are strict Catholics. His mother fought hard to stop Stefano from marrying the daughter of the 'town slut.' We got married in the church, which meant no divorce."

"Was Saverio the cause of your breakup?"

Livia shook her head, her red curls slapping against her cheeks. "No! I met Savi years later. On my twenty-fifth birthday, in fact." A smile lit her face. "I was celebrating it in Siena with a girlfriend. We walked into this electronics store to charge our phones. Savi was behind the counter and recognized my friend. He had gone to school with her brother in Pitigliano. That's how we met. He started driving down to see me on his days off. Then he got a job at the old electronics shop in Pitigliano to be near me. That is before Giancarlo bought it and modernized it."

They took the stairs that led down to the Coop. At the sight of the gray nondescript building that held the Gravigna supermarket and pharmacy, Livia started rushing down the stairs. "I am going to be late!"

Nico and OneWag kept up. "Why did your marriage break up?"

"I got tired of Stefano always watching over me, afraid I was going to turn into the 'town slut' he thought my mother was."

They reached the front door just as the manager was opening it. Livia let out a breathy laugh. "Buongiorno. I made it."

The manager responded with a nod and went inside.

"Is the friend who recognized Saverio in Orvieto someone I should talk to?" Nico asked as she was halfway in.

She stopped. Her eyes narrowed. "No. We lost touch."

"I'll need to talk to Stefano."

"He will only tell you what a bitch I am."

"I need his number."

Ugo, the produce man, bumped shoulders with Nico and smirked at Livia. "Woman of my dreams, are you going to let me in?"

Livia walked inside, letting the door slam into him.

Ugo turned his smirk toward Nico. "Aggression is a sure sign of love."

"That's bullshit," Nico exclaimed in English. The insult was more satisfying in his own language even if Ugo hadn't under-stood. "Livia è un'amica[9]," he added, hoping the jerk would take it as a hint to leave her alone. Ugo lifted a shoulder and disap-peared into the Coop.

"Time to go, buddy," Nico told OneWag, who was following a scent along the wall of the building. "We've got a big day ahead of us." They walked back up the stairs. In three hours he was meeting with Paolo Fulci, Livia's apartment neighbor who had witnessed Saverio punching Lenzi. Fulci welcomed dogs in his home.

AFTER AN HOUR ON the autostrada, Nico stopped for gas. Clouds had moved in, darkening the sky, giving the day a bleak, cold look. Getting back in Nelli's car, his phone pinged. Nico swiped it open. Livia had sent a text with Stefano's phone number. She'd added, MY MOTHER WASN'T A SLUT. SHE JUST FELL IN AND OUT OF LOVE TOO QUICKLY.

FULCI'S APARTMENT WAS IN the modern section of town, on the same street as the LenConi Electronics store. As Nico swung into the street, he checked his watch. He was early for Fulci. Even though the store would be closed, he was curious to take a look. The civic numbers were hard to spot. He'd find both addresses by walking.

Nico drove past the hospital and parked. As he and One Wag got out of the car, a white fluffball came flying toward them, barking its throat dry. OneWag barked back, with Nico holding tight on his leash.

A voice yelled, "Cippi, stop! Stop!" The voice became a man running toward them. "Pick him up. Cippi won't bite."

---

9 is a friend

"OneWag, sit," Nico ordered. OneWag stopped barking and sat. "Good boy."

The fluffball stopped at Nico's feet. Still barking.

The owner, a small, gray-haired man who looked to be somewhere in his sixties, stopped to catch his breath. "I apologize. My dog is crazy, but harmless."

Except for splitting eardrums, Nico thought.

"Cippi is asking to be picked up."

Nico swept up the fluffball with one arm and held him tight against his chest. "Shut up, Cippi!" The dog obeyed, then licked his hand.

Seeing the lick, OneWag swallowed a growl and pulled on his leash to sniff the dog owner's sneakers. Mothballs!

"You spoke in English." The man tucked his wide patterned tie into the closed double-breasted suit jacket he barely fit into. The pants needed ironing. "Can I presume you are Signor Doyle?"

Nico took a step forward. "Nico Doyle."

"Paolo Fulci. Paolo to Livia and Cilia and I hope also to you." A friendly, puffy-cheeked face smiled at Nico.

"All right, Nico and Paolo it is." They shook hands.

Fulci bent down to scratch behind OneWag's ear. "And you are Rocco. Cilia has told me all about you."

"Thank you for taking the time off from work."

Fulci straightened up. "Come. My home is just a few blocks farther up." They started walking. OneWag for once was not pulling on the detested leash but keeping one eye on the white fluffball tucked in Nico's arm. "I have accrued many vacation days since my wife died six years ago."

"I'm sorry to hear she died."

They passed a row of shops. "That is kind of you. My job at city hall consists mostly of shuffling papers from one room to another. Vacation day or no vacation day, I will not be missed."

That statement didn't seem to evoke any sadness or regret in Fulci. Maybe he was not an ambitious man.

"My home is modest, but I hope welcoming. You can let Cippi down now. Your friendship is sealed. He's a rescue I brought home last Christmas as a present to myself."

"And to him."

"Yes. I hope he's happy with me. Still hungry for attention, he has not learned his manners yet."

Nico put the dog down on the sidewalk. "Attention is scarce in a shelter filled with other needy dogs." Cippi scampered ahead.

"Of course. I had not thought of that. I have never been one to seek attention. I find it embarrassing. I much prefer to give it, preferably to animals and books." Fulci stopped in front of a small plain three-story building that badly needed a new coat of yellow paint. "Here we are." While Livia's neighbor searched for his keys, Nico looked up. There were no balconies. A few planters holding empty terra-cotta pots hung from the street-facing windows.

Cippi led the way up two flights of stairs. Fulci opened the door to a small entranceway whose only piece of furniture was a cast-iron tree on which he hung Nico's down jacket, OneWag's leash and his own suit jacket, revealing a multicolored hand-knit vest that gave him a happier air. He hooked his house keys to a bronze hook in the form of a bird. Following Cippi, Fulci and a curious OneWag down a short corridor, Nico walked into a small living room with two lace-curtained windows facing the next building across the street.

Fulci turned on a couple of standing lamps. Bookcases filled with books and bric-a-brac covered two facing walls. Scattered over the furniture was an assortment of books, magazines and loose newspaper pages. On the tile floor was a large rug with many colors too faded to identify.

"The apartment is small, but it was enough for me and my wife. And now for me and Cippi." He cleared an end sofa seat with a sweep of his arm. "As you can see, I am not a neat man. I am an avid reader and rereader and like to have everything within arm's length. Please sit. Would you like a coffee?"

Nico sat down in the one empty space. "No, thank you." Cippi jumped up next to him. OneWag was too busy identifying scents to notice.

Fulci gathered a pile of papers from the one armchair, dropped them on the floor and sat down. "I have been very worried about Saverio." He clasped his hands against his chest. "Now I feel great relief that Livia has asked you to make sense of this terrible murder."

"How long have you known Saverio and Livia?"

"I met Livia fifteen years ago or so. She had just started working in the panificio where my wife bought our bread. On Saturdays I took over the shopping with orders to let only Livia pick our loaf. I found a very nice, unhappy nineteen-year-old with a knack for picking the freshest and tastiest loaf. When the family renting the apartment across the hall was moving out, I told Livia. She was leaving her husband and was looking for a place to live. I helped negotiate the price with the landlord. She moved in fourteen years ago."

"You became good friends."

"Yes. I do not want you to think there is anything inappropriate in our friendship."

"Why would I think that?"

"You are making inquiries. There are always people ready to find dirt where there is none. I have only wanted to help." His cheeks rose with a smile. "Cilia considers me her zio."

Nico believed him. Fulci emanated kindness. "What can you tell me about Saverio Bianconi?"

"When Livia told me she was falling in love with a man who

was then working at Tino Parucci's electronics store, I went to see what sort of man he was. Parucci is the man you should speak to." His face puckered with indignation. "Lenzi stole the store from him! He found out that Parucci owed the landlord a few months' back rent and swooped in, paid what was owed and agreed to a higher rent. Five months later, Parucci was out on the street. Lenzi fancied up the store with a big sign in front, put in computers people can use by the hour. Even added two printers and hired Saverio to run the technical stuff."

"Parucci is on Livia's list." Nico had made an appointment with him for late tomorrow morning. He had seemed eager to talk to him.

"That is reassuring. The first time I saw Saverio, I introduced myself and explained I was a friend of Livia's. I must say I was surprised he knew all about me." He looked pleased now. "He told me he was happy Livia had such a good friend. I liked him instantly and a few months later when he moved in with her, I was relieved. There was no need to worry about her anymore."

"Why did you worry? Livia strikes me as a very competent woman."

Fulci swept up his dog as if he needed to feel his warmth. "Livia had a frightful childhood, followed by an unhappy marriage. She deserved happiness and Saverio gave that to her. Cilia was a gift to them both." He rubbed his chin over Cippi's head. "And to me. My marriage did not bring children." There was no sadness in his voice.

OneWag, scent tour over, sat down at Nico's feet, eyes aimed at Cippi. Nico reached down and rewarded him with an ear scratch. "From what you know of Saverio do you think he killed his best friend?"

"A difficult question." Fulci let go of his dog and clasped his hands in front of his mouth. "I have thought at length about what you ask." He closed his eyes. "Guilty? Not guilty? My mind sways from one to the other." He lowered his hands. "My heart says no. Which one is correct? I am afraid I don't have an answer. Lenzi's betrayal had to be incredibly painful, overwhelming. The kind of pain that can destroy rational thought, I would think." Fulci's face and voice were filled with great feeling, as if the pain were his own.

This man knows betrayal, Nico thought.

"I was passing by with Cippi when Saverio struck Lenzi to the pavement. That act of violence gave him no satisfaction, no release. You could see that on his face. He shouted, '*You will pay!*' and Lenzi laughed. Did you know he laughed?"

"I did not."

"Saverio is a quiet, sensitive man. Lenzi could have made him feel as if he'd been spit on. He rushed off and I followed him. I wanted to calm him down, help him. He wouldn't stop, but I saw the tears running down his face."

"What do you think Saverio meant by '*You will pay*'?"

"He was demanding the stolen money back. It was not a threat. I heard it as a conviction, an assurance that Saverio expected Lenzi to pay back the money he had stolen. To reach the point of wanting to kill Lenzi, I think Saverio would have needed time for his pain or anger—whatever you want to call it—to fester, grow, become uncontrollable. Saverio is not a man of action. From what I have heard from Livia, Lenzi was the roiling motor of the pair. Saverio was his calming agent."

"Faced with trouble, Saverio ran. That's action."

"No. That is desperation." Fulci stroked his dog's back. "As I said, in my heart, I do not believe Saverio killed Lenzi."

"What can you tell me about Lenzi?"

"Very little. I have only encountered him at the store. He would acknowledge my presence, if at all, with a nod and walk away. I found that surprising for a store owner, but Lenzi's marriage elevated him to patrician status in this town. Annamaria

Baldi's family claims a distant relationship to the branch of the Orsinis who ruled over Pitigliano before the Medicis established the Grand Duchy of Tuscany. According to what I have read, the Pitigliano Orsini branch became extinct in the middle of the seventeenth century." He raised his hand. "Let them have their illusions. Pitigliano is a small town. We know each other. I believe the general consensus of the humbler inhabitants of this town—shopkeepers, manual laborers, people like myself—is that Lenzi had charm but far more arrogance. A harsh judgment, harsher now that he can no longer prove us wrong."

"Why steal money?"

"Independence. Pocket money he doesn't have to account for to his wife."

"Any gossip about women in his life?"

"That is a question best answered by Livia. Gossip is more of interest to women than men. If there is prurient gossip about Lenzi, she is in a better position to know than I am." An alarm went off somewhere in the crowded room. "Ah, a reminder to feed myself."

Nico stole a look at his watch. It was exactly one o'clock.

"When I am in the depths of a book I easily forget," Fulci explained. "The clock is my poor substitute for a wife who enjoyed adding kilos to me. A big pot of potato and pasta soup is waiting for me. That and a glass of Chianti red will take the chill off the day." He gave Nico a hopeful smile. "It would make me happy to share them with you if you don't mind eating in the kitchen."

Nico was hungry. "Thank you. The kitchen is the best dining room there is."

As they made their way to the kitchen with the dogs, Nico's cell phone rang. He looked quickly. Nelli. "Forgive me, Paolo. I need to take this call."

"Go ahead. The kitchen is just behind that door. Take your time. I will warm the soup and set the table."

Nico stepped farther back into the room. OneWag stayed with him. "Ciao. Everything okay?"

"Ciao. You don't have to pick me up this afternoon. Maria Grazia is driving me back."

"Why, what's wrong?"

"Everything is fine." There was a tremor in her voice.

"Did something happen?"

"Nothing, Nico. I am tired. If I kept working, I would have just pushed paint around. I will see you tonight."

"No, I'll come get you. I'll reschedule my meeting with Necchi. Wait for me."

"I'm already on the autostrada. I'm sorry. I did not want to stop your work. I'm fine, Nico. Really, I am. I will pick up prosciutto and cheese from Enrico for dinner. Ciao. See you at home." She clicked off.

Home was a first. Had she called his place home any other time, he would have been glowing with pleasure. Now he was worried. Something had happened to make her stop painting.

"Nico," Fulci called from the kitchen. "La minestra è pronta."[10]

"Arrivo!"[11]

BEFORE MAKING HIS WAY to the vineyard that Lenzi's cousin, Matteo Necchi, managed a few kilometers from town, Nico called Nelli's good friend, Laura.

"Nico, ciao, it's been weeks." She sounded happy to hear from him. "How is your murder investigation going? Nelli told

---

10 The soup is ready.
11 Coming.

me about the little girl who asked you to help her babbo. Heart-breaking."

"I just started. Look, I need a favor."

"Just ask."

"Nelli is on her way back to Gravigna. She should be home in two hours. Could you give her call and see how she is without mentioning me?"

"Did you have a fight?"

"No. She had planned to paint all day, but now the woman who commissioned the portrait is driving her back. Something must have happened. I'm worried, but I have an appointment with the victim's cousin in twenty minutes."

"I'll call right away."

"No, she might not want to talk in front of the woman."

"You think the woman fired her?"

"I hope not. She said she was just tired. Just see if she's all right."

"I will, although knowing how intense Nelli is about her work, she probably painted halfway through the night. I'll call to make a date for the four of us to have dinner. I want you to meet Riccardo. I just hired him as the hotel's chef. You'll like him."

"Thanks, Laura."

"No thanks needed. I'll let you know. Ciao."

A short balding man with a large round face and matching nose was walking to the car just as Nico parked behind a small white building. He was wearing thick boots, jeans and a thick black down jacket that looked like it would have kept him warm in a blizzard. "Welcome to Cantina Carrucci, Signor Doyle." He pronounced it *doll*.

Nico got out. "Call me Nico."

"Then I am Matteo." They shook hands. OneWag jumped out of the car and sniffed Necchi's boots.

"Your dog doesn't wander off, does he?"

"He'll stay by my side, but if you prefer, I can leave him in the car."

Hearing *macchina*, OneWag dropped down, his whole body stretched out as if rooting himself to the ground.

Necchi noticed and chuckled. "You can stay with us but no digging holes under the vines. Come, Nico and dog, follow me. If it is not too cold for you, I have set up a small wine tasting under our magnificent oak tree, believed to have been planted by the great condottiere Niccolò Orsini. If that is true, it is six hundred years old. If not, it is still magnificent."

"I'll be fine," Nico said. The temperature was at least fifty.

Necchi led Nico down an earth-beaten path flanked by descending rows of vines, leaves curling and beginning to lose their summer green. "Deprived of their luscious grapes," Necchi said, "the vines look naked and sad, I find. We did our last harvest early this year because of the heat."

The path turned and medieval Pitigliano appeared in the not-far distance. The view of the medieval town high up on a rugged outcrop of volcanic tufa stopped Nico from moving just as it had the first time he caught sight of the town.

Necchi stopped too. "Yes, a picture-perfect view, but it's a dead town. Thankfully it brings tourists, which is good for the wine trade." He resumed walking. Nico kept pace.

"Pitigliano seems very much alive to me."

"You don't live here. I wanted to leave years ago, away from the small-minded, tightfisted Pitiglianesi who feed off everyone else's failures." There was oddly no resentment in his voice, only in the words he'd chosen.

"What stopped you from leaving?"

"Lack of money and an idiot's hope that the sun would rise."

"And it didn't for you?"

"Let us say only halfway. I have to consider myself lucky. I love my work among these vines, making sure the grapes fatten and turn into good wine. I have been managing this place for the past eight years now. I have Giancarlo to thank for that."

"He got you the job?"

"He knew the owner. Here we are."

They walked into a grassy opening almost entirely covered by a gigantic yellow-and-green-leafed oak tree. A square wooden table and two chairs stood under the outer edge of the tree. A pitcher of water, two bottles of wine, a glass and a small bowl of taralli waited on the table.

"Please sit down, Nico. I have my two top wines waiting for you. Then we talk."

"Can we talk first? I am expecting some news that could mean I need to go home right away."

"Then I suggest we talk and taste at the same time."

"Good idea." He didn't want even a sip of wine, but he needed to keep Necchi happy if he was to get any information out of him. Nico sat down. A wary OneWag sat at his feet.

Necchi uncorked the first bottle. "Giancarlo and I were cousins, only a year apart in age. Our mothers lived two streets away from each other, near Palazzo Orsini." He poured an inch of white wine in the glass and handed it to Nico. "They were very close and Giancarlo and I also got close. Two brothers, really." He blinked and a hand went to his chest. "Giancarlo's death has left a hole in my heart."

"How did you find out?"

"Eddi, my nephew, called me at home late that morning. '*Your cousin's dead,*' he said in his usual matter-of-fact tone. He hung up before I could ask to speak to Annamaria."

"Did you call back?"

Necchi pressed his lips together, released them. "She did not pick up. Eddi called me back and screamed in my ear, '*Leave us alone!*' He was clearly in shock. He is only nineteen." Necchi looked down at Nico's untouched glass. "Please, taste. This is the white that Pitigliano is famous for."

Nico took a sip. "It is very good."

Necchi smiled proudly, any sadness seemingly gone. "It brings spring to mind, does it not?"

To Nico it was light and refreshing. "That's a nice way of putting it." It made more sense than saying the wine gave off grapefruit and tart lemon notes with hints of fresh hay. "You must have been upset with Eddi. You had a right to know more."

"Yes, I did, but I understood. He had lost his father."

"What is Eddi like?"

"He is like the usual modern-day teenager. Self-involved, wants total freedom to do as he pleases. Annamaria likes to hold a tight rein on the family, but she spares Eddi. They are a mutual adoration society, which did not please my cousin. I think he was beginning to feel irrelevant. Giancarlo did always like to be the star."

"What about the younger child, Mimmo?"

"A sweet kid. He has been left on his own. Please, have another taste."

Nico obliged. "You and Giancarlo stayed close as grownups?"

Necchi took Nico's glass and tossed the rest of the wine on the grass, splashing some on OneWag. "We got married, which changed things. My wife had no patience with Annamaria's snobbery. I do not enjoy it either."

Livia had put Susanna Necchi on her list.

Necchi poured some water into the glass, swished it around and tossed it. Hearing the swishing, OneWag had moved under the table.

"We are now amicably separated." The second bottle got uncorked. "She moved to Sorano. We have no children." He poured an inch of the new wine. "Now taste this red and tell me what it evokes for you."

This is taking too long. Nico took a sip. This wine evoked nothing for him, but for the sake of moving this meeting along, he took a guess. "Autumn with a taste of oak."

Necchi sat back in his chair with a satisfied grin. "Exactly. Have a tarallo. It cleans the palate."

"Thank you, but no more wine for me. I was told Saverio and Giancarlo were close childhood friends. Were you also close to Saverio?"

"He tried to befriend me first. I found him boring. Too polite, humble, insecure. Giancarlo took him over. Saverio was very good at anything involving numbers. Giancarlo needed his help at school. Theirs wasn't a real friendship. Love him as I did, I must admit my cousin used people who were too weak to resist him. In Saverio, he found someone he could finally manipulate."

"Didn't that affect your relationship with your cousin?"

Necchi took Nico's glass and poured himself four inches of the red. He hadn't bothered rinsing it first.

This conversation is getting to him, Nico thought.

Necchi drank half the wine down. "Not in the least. Why should it? It had nothing to do with me."

"Do you think Saverio killed your cousin?"

"Yes, of course he did. I might have been tempted to kill Giancarlo myself if he had stolen from me. Not that he would have dared. I feel sorry for Saverio. He is a weak man. Running away proves it. When Giancarlo got the incredibly dumb idea of taking on Parucci's failing electronics store, I told Saverio not to go into business with Giancarlo. He was going to end up doing all the work. That's exactly what happened."

"Why do you think Giancarlo needed money?"

"I think he made some bad bets. Why else? Annamaria would have given him money if he needed it. Not for gambling though. Not a classy hobby especially if you lose."

"He didn't play around?"

Necchi raised the glass and, shaking his head, finished off the red wine. "Giancarlo made flirting a hobby, but he knew not to take it any further. I warned him once not to jeopardize his marriage." Necchi stared at the empty glass as if surprised it was empty. "His standing and the store's success had everything to do with his wife's family. Annamaria would have thrown him off the tufa cliff. No, he gambled." The glass came back down on the table. "On what is a mystery. I think Annamaria was worried. She came here in June, saying she needed to buy a case of white. It was the first time she came alone. I was not to say anything to Giancarlo. She said the case was a surprise gift. While I packed the bottles, she lightly dropped questions. Was Giancarlo spending a lot of time with me? Were we thinking of making some investments together? She said he had become moody. Did I know what was bothering him?

"I told her not to worry about him. Whatever was going on, my cousin would always land on his feet. I couldn't have been more wrong, could I? No more sunrises for him." Necchi stood up. "Is there anything else you need to know?"

"No. Thank you for your time." Nico got on his feet. "I'd like to buy two bottles of your spring wine and two of autumn."

"Make it three and three with a discount. Come along. I will bring them to your car."

"If something new comes up, I hope you won't mind my asking more questions."

"You are always welcome."

NICO STOPPED THE CAR as soon as he passed the gate of the winery and called Laura. "You didn't call."

"Nelli did not want me to. She told me to tell you she appreciates your concern, but she does not talk through intermediaries."

"You told her I sent you?"

"No, she guessed immediately. She sounded fine to me. Just needs some time to think."

"Does this have to do with the portrait?"

"Nico, whatever it is, she will tell you herself. She accepted my invitation for dinner at the hotel. Tonight. Riccardo is already in the kitchen making his magic. Eight o'clock. Ciao."

She hung up before he could say, "I'll bring the wine."

"What the hell is going on?" Nico asked himself as he released the brake, the knot in his stomach tightening.

NICO MADE THE TWO-AND-A-HALF-HOUR trip home in an hour and fifty minutes.

"Out here," Nelli called out as he opened the door. Hearing her voice, OneWag rushed out to the covered balcony, stretched up on his hind legs and covered her face with licks.

Hearing Nelli laugh, seeing her stretched out over two chairs, bundled up with a blanket, Nico felt the knot in his stomach loosen. Behind her daylight was sinking. The olive trees had become sharp silhouettes. "Ciao, Nelli. Can I join you?"

She turned her face toward him, the same beautiful face he now wanted to hold in his hands. "I hope you aren't mad at me." She pushed herself up on the chair so that OneWag had a lap to sit on.

"No, just worried. Can I get you anything?" He felt awkward, like a man on a first date, afraid to say the wrong thing. "I bought some Pitigliano white for you."

"Thanks, no. I have a cup of tea getting cold on the floor." She held out her arm. "Come sit with me." She lifted her legs off the second chair.

He dropped down in front of her.

She picked up the teacup and took a sip. "When something surprises me, I need to be on my own for a bit."

"What surprised you?"

"After working for a couple of hours late this morning, I took a walk to the cathedral to see the Luca Signorelli frescoes again. I was looking for inspiration. I am having a hard time capturing Maria Grazia's face. It reveals so little. As I walked back to her apartment, a man on a motorbike came down the street at high speed. As he passed me, he kicked out his leg, hitting me. I fell to the ground. He yelled something and kept going."

Nico felt that kick in his stomach. "Oh my God, amore. Are you in pain?"

"I'm sore. No blood. Just bruises. It was the ugliness of it that hurt. Now I am angry. I want to kick him back. Why would anyone lash out like that? Because I had no handbag he could steal? Because I am a woman?"

Nico took Nelli's hand and kissed it. "I'm so sorry. Did you get a look at him?"

"What does it matter? It is done. Over with."

"It matters to me."

Nelli's face softened with a smile. "You are sweet. I did not see his face, just a black helmet with a visor pulled down. I saw denim on the leg and a white sneaker. I was lucky he was not wearing boots. I'm saying '*he*,' but it could just as easily have been a woman."

"What did he yell at you?"

"If that scum wanted me to understand the words, that scum should have yelled them before kicking me. I was going to wait for you, but Maria Grazia got more upset than I was and insisted on taking me home. I have had my few hours of thumb-sucking. I am fine now. I apologize for not telling you right away. I hated when my parents worried over me, made a fuss. It made me feel powerless."

"I wasn't going to make a fuss."

"You did. You sent Laura."

"You're just not used to being loved."

"My parents loved me by sucking up all the oxygen in the room."

"Do I do that?"

"No, thank heaven." Nelli leaned over and kissed him lightly. OneWag nudged her elbow. She kissed him too.

"It was very nice of Maria Grazia to bring you back. It's a long drive."

"She packed a small suitcase and is now staying at my place until her portrait is done. I tried to change her mind; I am happier working in my studio. I am assuming you won't mind my sleeping here until she goes home. I should be done with the portrait in a week."

Forever would be better, he thought but didn't say. "You can stay as long as you want. She must be very upset by what happened to you."

"She kept saying it was her fault I was attacked."

"Why would she think that?"

"I asked her. She started mumbling something, then got flustered and went to her bedroom. Twenty minutes later she came back out with a small packed bag. She told me to gather my things. We were going to Gravigna. I would paint her in my studio because she was tired of sleeping with the smell of oil. On the drive here she explained that I wouldn't have been attacked if she had not insisted I come to her. She assumed I had an extra bed or sofa bed in my apartment. I told her I knew a wonderful man who would put me up." Nelli clasped Nico's neck and reached up to give him a long kiss. "You are indeed wonderful."

Nico would have liked to go on kissing, but she released him and settled back down. "Maria Grazia is a nice woman who has very recently had a facelift that has wiped away any expression. It does not make for an interesting portrait. I will have to concentrate on her eyes, which are not telling me a great deal yet. I am trying to get her to loosen up, talk about herself, bring some emotion into them. I end up doing all the talking. How did your interviews go?"

"Useful and enjoyable. I got fed lunch again by Livia's neighbor, this time a very good soup. I drank wine with Lenzi's cousin. It turns out that Livia is married to another man, something she didn't bother to tell me. I'm not sure I trust Livia Granchi, but that kid deserves all the help I can give her. Why don't you come in? It's too cold out here."

"I like to feel it on my face. The rest of me is warm. Rocco is making sure of that."

Nico went inside, took off his jacket, his shoes, helped himself to half a glass of red wine and sat down in his armchair. He started mulling over the day's conversations with Fulci and Necchi. He didn't get far. Nelli's incident took over. Only a sick person would get high from kicking a woman to the ground. Or someone delivering a message.

Nico walked back to the balcony. "What else do you know about Maria Grazia Bertini?"

"She's a fifty-five-year-old widow, recently retired, has enough means to live in a lovely apartment and is ecstatic over having her portrait painted. She wants it to join the rather ugly portraits of her mother-in-law and grandmother-in-law that have been hanging in her living room since she got married. Her husband didn't think she deserved a portrait of her own."

"Any children?"

"Her only living relative is a cousin. Why are you asking?"

"Portraits are costly and the cousin stands to inherit."

Nelli gave Nico a long, hard look, then she laughed. "Her cousin lives in Rome. He has plenty of money of his own, Maria Grazia has told me more than once. Besides what I am charging her will not deplete her coffers. Stop worrying. I will quickly get out of the way of approaching motorcycles. Now go do whatever you do at this hour, but please let me know when there are fifteen minutes left before leaving for dinner."

"Nelli, you'll be frozen by then." He wanted to pick her up, cradle her, rub her soreness away. "Come inside."

"I'm cooling my anger."

Nico closed the balcony door and walked to the bathroom. Maybe a long shower would wash away his frustrations along with the day's dirt.

NELLI AND NICO STOPPED as soon as they entered the sitting room Laura had led them to.

"Laura, this is lovely." Nelli gave her friend a hug.

"Very nice," Nico said, his mind reeling back to May and the painful meeting with the suspect of another murder in this room. This time the gathering would be a happy one. Lights flickered from glass-enclosed candles. The small marble fireplace was shooting up orange flames and crackling. A sofa and an armchair had been pushed back to allow room for the square dinner table covered with a white damask tablecloth. Four tall-backed upholstered chairs stood guard on each side of the table.

Laura, dressed in black velvet pants and a long white silk shirt, held out her arms. "Let me take your coats."

"We're friends, not hotel guests," Nelli protested. "We're dropping our coats in that armchair in the corner."

Nico held up a shopping bag. "I brought some red wine from Pitigliano. Like bringing marble to Carrara, but maybe you don't know it."

"Thank you." Laura looked at the label. "Oh, Riccardo was talking about this vineyard. He was going to bring me a bottle to taste next time he comes up. He thinks it would be a good wine to have for the hotel." She turned at the sound of creaking stairs, her body arcing toward the far door.

A tall, slender man wearing blue jeans and a chef's white jacket walked into the room holding a wooden cutting board.

"So good-looking," Nelli whispered.

"So are you," Nico whispered back. The silver knit top she was wearing over an ankle-length charcoal gray flannel skirt made her face glow.

"There you are," Laura said, the pleasure in her voice palpable. "Riccardo Cerani, the new chef."

"Not until the season opens in April," Riccardo said. "Tonight I am a man who has cooked a meal for his new friends." A smile spread across his handsome, sculpted face. "I have already had the pleasure of meeting Nelli and now you, Nico. Laura tells me you work for the competition."

"Not really. Sotto Il Fico is a small restaurant and I don't cook at your level."

"I was told you are very good. I was also told you are a detective. Nelli thinks I have information that will help you. I hope I do. We will talk later." He held up the cutting board in his hands. On it were three small plates with a thick tomato sauce strewn with waves of grated parmigiano covering a slice of something. "I apologize. I could not find a tray. The kitchen is still new to me." He wore his long dark hair in a tight knot at the nape of his neck.

"You should have called me." Laura took the cutting board from Riccardo and made room for it on the table.

"Please help yourselves to a slice of my eggplant torte as a starter while I open a bottle of wine."

Laura held out her hand to stop him. "Nico brought two bottles of red wine you wanted me to order."

"From Carruzzi's vineyard?"

"Yes." She showed him the bottle.

"Perfect. You will get to taste it and decide." He took the bottle Laura offered him, took out the thin corkscrew restaurant waiters used and with a few quick twists pulled out the cork. He passed it to Nico, who held it out to Laura.

She pushed his hand away. "I cannot tell anything by sniffing. Give me the wine."

Nico laughed with her. "Neither can I."

Riccardo poured the wine in four stemmed glasses.

Nelli grabbed the cork, held it to her nose and inhaled. "Good but would have been better in a couple of years. You two should learn to sniff. It is your sense of smell that allows you to taste fully."

While Nelli expressed her opinion, Riccardo pulled out the four chairs. "Shall we sit and enjoy food and wine to the best of our individual abilities?"

"Gladly," Nelli said.

They sat and clinked glasses. "Alla salute e agli amici nuovi."[12]

Four forks plunged into the eggplant torte slices.

"Delicious," Nico decreed. Laura and Nelli found their own complimentary words.

Nico forked another piece, this time holding it in his mouth, trying to detect what other ingredients were in the dish. *Onions for sure. Basil, parmigiano. A sprinkle of pepperoncino. Breadcrumbs. Salt and pepper. All of it held together by eggs.*

"Carruzzi is probably eager to sell his wine to get the vineyard to start earning what it merits. It was failing when he bought it five or more years ago."

Nico swallowed and started listening.

"He sold his trucking business and put a lot of money into modern machinery, promotion, new vines and whatever else was needed." Riccardo held his glass to the candlelight. "The wine was just as good before."

---

12 To health and good friends.

"Then why did it fail?" Nico asked.

"When you start a business, you must have enough capital to keep it going during the rough spots; the original owner ran out of money. He could not get a bank loan. It happens to a lot of restaurants. I have been tempted to start my own place, but each time the thought lifts its seductive face, wisdom prevails. Now I better go back to the kitchen to check on my Pesticcio sauce. No help needed."

FIFTEEN MINUTES LATER, FOUR heads were bent over terra-cotta bowls loaded with handmade malfatti enveloped in Riccardo's thick mushroom and sausage ragout. The only sound came from the occasional fork hitting the bowl.

After swallowing and waiting for the taste of the perfectly melded ingredients to fade, Nico complimented Riccardo and asked, "Who was the original owner of the Carruzzi vineyard?"

"Matteo Necchi. He's the manager now."

Nico put his fork down.

"He used to dine at La Dogana," Riccardo said, "where I was chef for the past ten years. I was one of the first restaurant buyers of his wines. Matteo hasn't stepped into the place since his wife left him and moved back to Sorano. He was desperate to keep NecchiVini going. At one point he even asked me to invest or loan him some money. I felt for him, but the salary of a small restaurant chef doesn't allow for generosity. NecchiVini became Vigna Carruzzi, his wife left him and now he manages what he once owned. It must be difficult."

"I hope doing something he loves is some consolation," Nelli said. "I have never eaten anything as delicious as this sauce."

"Thank you," Riccardo said. "It was a winner at La Dogana."

"Necchi is Giancarlo Lenzi's cousin," Nico said, the food forgotten.

"Yes, I know. Lenzi was also a patron of the restaurant. Ate a lot of dinners there with various friends."

"Women?" Nico felt a kick against his shoe telling him his timing was wrong.

Riccardo wiped his perfectly clean lips with a white damask napkin. "His wife of course. If you don't mind, Nico, I would prefer to answer your questions after dinner."

"Of course. Please forgive me." He was embarrassed and fought the urge to explain that he'd been with Necchi at the vineyard that very afternoon. He felt Nelli's eyes on him. He dug his fork back into the bowl and resumed eating.

After four big bites Nico wiped his mouth and declared, "Pesticcio alla Riccardo is indeed a winner. Good choice, Laura. With your new chef, you'll be turning people away."

Why was he overdoing it? The dish was very good, but hadn't he found it a bit too rich? That it would have been better served on spaghetti? No, he was being an asshole toward a tall, slender, good-looking man at least fifteen years younger, who could out-cook him any day.

I guess I'm jealous.

EIGHT

Perillo put his double espresso cup down. "We have information that might be helpful." He'd unexpectedly turned up with Daniele at Bar All'Angolo just after Nelli and Gogol had left. Nico had stayed, waiting for Livia and Cilia, hoping to walk Cilia to school again. They hadn't shown up.

"Good." Nico was glad for any help and the chance to discuss what he'd found out yesterday with his friends over a second breakfast. "Let's move over to that corner table." It was far from the counter. It was too cold to sit outside. They picked up their breakfasts and moved.

Nico sat down. "Come here, buddy. Enough licking." OneWag took a last look at the sugary crumbs lining the length of the floor below the counter and obeyed by sitting at Daniele's feet. Payback, Nico thought, then shifted his eyes to his friends' faces. "Go ahead but keep your voices low."

"My clever brigadiere has started following Eddi Lenzi's Twitter account."

"It's now called X," Daniele said. Perillo waved a hand in the air. "Whatever. You tell him, Dani."

"Eddi has over three thousand followers and posts mostly about soccer, motorcycles and 'the Parent' who bugs him about studying." Daniele consulted his notes. "In one post he wrote,

'*I have come to the conclusion the Parent even disapproves of my breathing.*' He got over eight hundred retweets."

"He's a kid blowing off steam," Nico said. "Debora Costa told me Eddi and his father didn't see eye to eye." He'd dealt with his own father by running to his school playground and batting his anger to the bleachers. It got him on the team without any questions asked.

"Very disrespectful steam," Perillo said. "Listen to what he wrote the day after Lenzi died."

Daniele read, "'*News bulletin: the Parent got himself killed during the night. Just info. Not a bid for pity.*' No retweets but over two thousand hearts. Three days later, he posted, '*Father murdered by his best friend and business partner now a fugitive thanks to our carabinieri. Fucking assholes!*' Then: '*Where the fuck are you, best friend? Have the guts to show up and own up.*' That's the last tweet."

"Thank the heavens," Perillo said.

"His mother probably stopped him." Nico leaned in. "Dani, is Saverio on X?"

"I have not found him. Eddi was easy. His username is @ elenza, a play on his own name. Lenza has a double meaning. A fishing line but also a quick-witted person who knows how to get out of trouble."

"I didn't know the second meaning," Nico said. "What about Instagram?"

"Just photos of him preening on his motorcycle or drinking and eating with his friends. Quite a few photos of a very pretty girl." For an instant Daniele clenched his eyes shut to stop himself from blushing. He was ashamed of having compared her looks to Stella's. Eddi's girl was prettier.

Noticing his brigadiere's discomfort Perillo said, "Dani showed me some of the photos. Eddi always has his arm around her, so I guess she's his girlfriend. And she is very pretty. No harm in noting it."

Daniele happily agreed with a nod. He hadn't blushed.

"I should talk to her too. She's Eddi's alibi."

Daniele looked at Nico, concern in his eyes. "You don't think?"

"It's always good to double-check."

"Eddi obviously has no doubts as to who killed his father." Perillo's loud sigh sounded more like a grunt. "I worry, Nico. I really do. What is that American expression you like to use when things go wrong for you? Having a frittata on your face?"

"Something like that."

"You may end up with one."

"It won't be the first time." Nico turned to Dani. "Is Mimmo on any social media?"

Daniele shook his head. "I couldn't find him anywhere."

"His mother probably doesn't allow it," Nico said.

Perillo leaned back in his chair. "How was yesterday?"

"Interesting."

"Light is peeking through the dark?"

"A little. I first met with Livia's apartment neighbor Paolo Fulci."

"He witnessed the fight," Daniele said after wiping off the milk foam whiskers cappuccinos always gave him.

Perillo shot an annoyed look at his brigadiere. "I do not need reminders, Daniele."

Daniele quickly drank more cappuccino, the cup not large enough to hide the color on his face. The maresciallo's memory had been a bit faulty lately. He blamed it on not eating a home-cooked lunch now that Ivana was working. He would not consider that aging brought consequences.

Nico allowed a peacemaking moment to pass by, picking up cornetto crumbs from his plate with his index finger. "He's a nice, lonely widower in his sixties."

"Paolo Fulci is sixty-three," Perillo said, with a reaffirming nod to Daniele. "According to his statement, the night of Lenzi's death Fulci took his dog out around ten o'clock and walked by the LenConi store twice. Both times the store was dark."

"Yes, he reiterated as much while we shared a very good pasta and potato soup."

"Is he a possible suspect?"

"He didn't try to hide his attachment to Livia and Saverio, and during lunch he told he how much he enjoys babysitting Cilia. He might in some way even feel responsible for them."

"He could be in love with Livia," Perillo suggested, "and saw Saverio's fight with Lenzi as an opportunity to get rid of the competition."

"No, he seemed genuinely happy Livia had found Saverio. He thinks she found a good man, although he didn't insist on Saverio being innocent. He does believe Saverio would have needed more time to build up enough anger to kill Lenzi. I'm not writing Fulci off the list of possible suspects, but right now I can't see him using a hammer on anything but a nail. The next man I spoke to yesterday is a more likely candidate."

Daniele and Perillo leaned over the table and whispered at the same time. "The cousin!" Nico nodded. "Necchi claims Lenzi's death left a hole in his heart and then he goes on to put him down. He has excellent reasons for it. He used to own a vineyard that then failed. He was forced to sell it when he couldn't get a bank loan."

"Which he would have gotten," Perillo said, "if his cousin had guaranteed the loan."

"Now Necchi manages the vineyard instead of owning it."

Daniele shook his hand as if he'd burned it. "Ai!"

"Ai, indeed. There's more. Necchi and his wife separated. Riccardo Cerani, Laura's new hotel chef, used to run the kitchen at a restaurant in Sorano frequented by Lenzi. A few years ago, Lenzi dined alone with Necchi's wife there quite a few times."

Perillo slapped his hand on the table. "That's it! Necchi loses a vineyard and a wife. You've got your man."

"Maybe."

"It could explain why Lenzi needed money," Daniele said. "He was going to start a new life with Necchi's wife."

"Livia put her on the list but doesn't know her cell phone number."

"I'll get it for you," Daniele said.

"Thanks. I didn't want to ask Necchi. She lives in Sorano. Here's something else to think about." Nico dropped his elbows on the table. "If Lenzi was going to bail out of his marriage, that puts Annamaria on the suspect list. From what I've heard of her, divorce or separation is not something she would tolerate. And now there's also Eddi, who is adored by his mother and fought with his father."

Daniele gave Nico a dumbfounded look. "But Eddi's screaming his anger at Saverio!"

"That could be a clever cover-up," Perillo suggested. "Think of the username he chose."

"I need to keep my mind open for now," Nico said. "I have more people to talk to. Today I'm seeing Tino Parucci, former owner of the LenConi store, then Stefano Granchi, Livia's ex-husband, and maybe Angela Rossi."

"The woman who called the police," Perillo said, still needing to show off what he remembered.

"Debora Costa texted me this morning, saying Angela Rossi wants to talk to me. She might have some helpful information."

"Rossi had nothing helpful to say in her statement to Maresciallo Fabbri."

"She might have remembered something," Daniele pointed out.

"I need to get going." Nico stood up and dropped a hand on Perillo's shoulder. "I need a favor I meant to ask for Sunday night."

Perillo slapped a hand against his chest with a crestfallen face. "Oh Nico, too late. Ivana's chocolate crostata is no more."

"That is indeed sad news but it's something else."

"Then it is done."

"See what you can find out about Maria Grazia Bertini. She's a retired teacher, lives in Orvieto. Nelli is painting her portrait."

Perillo beamed a smile. "Bravo, Nico. You are protecting your woman. I would do the same. I will relieve Dani of all his other duties."

"Thank you." Nico gathered his plate, cup, and saucer.

"We should go too." Perillo didn't budge. "Are you taking Nelli to Orvieto?"

"No, change of venue and cars. Nelli has to make wine deliveries this morning, which means she needs her car. I get to speed down the autostrada in my red tin can, and Maria Grazia Bertini has decided she wants her portrait done here." Nelli didn't want him to mention her motorcycle incident. "She's staying at Nelli's."

"You really need to get a new car," Perillo protested.

"I know. One day." Nico deposited his breakfast gatherings on the counter.

"Now," Perillo insisted.

Nico turned around to look at his friend. "Why? Do you have a car to sell?"

Perillo let a half-smile show. "Now that Ivana is bringing in some money, she wants a new car, and our Panda will not collapse on the autostrada."

Daniele turned his face to hide his grin.

"You have ridden in my car. There's plenty of room for your long legs, and it's only five years old. The price would be low. We are friends."

"We'll discuss cars another time. Thanks, Jimmy and Sandro. See you tomorrow."

"We're counting on it, Nico," Sandro said from behind the cash register. "Word is out that you are going to Pitigliano every day. That's a long drive. Why not stay there?"

"And give up Jimmy's cornetti? Never."

Sandro laughed. Jimmy bowed his head in thanks. Nico did mind the everyday back and forth, and he'd considered getting a room or asking Livia to let him stay in her apartment. It took him less than ten minutes to decide against it. Home was home and now Nelli was staying over until Maria Grazia went back to Orvieto. "Ciao to all."

"We want a report tonight," Perillo said as he raised his two fingers for another double espresso.

"Come on, buddy," Nico called out.

OneWag was already at the door, his whiskers white with powdered sugar.

NICO EASILY FOUND PARUCCI'S small hardware store at the beginning of Via Roma, the main street of the old town. There were several customers inside the store. Nico decided to wait outside. A display of tourist knickknacks on a small table next to the door caught his attention. He examined a foot-long grooved wooden roller used to cut sheets of pasta into various widths and debated buying it for Nelli as a joke. He put it back down. Her talent had nothing to do with cooking. She'd probably throw it at him.

Behind the rollers, another basket held a pile of rolled-up pastries, each packaged in cellophane and tied with a ribbon. The label read SFRATTO.[13] A printed note told the story of how, at the beginning of the seventeenth century, the Medicis became the new rulers. Not wanting Jews to have equal rights,

---

13 Evicted.

they served them eviction papers and forced them to live in a
ghetto next to the 1598 synagogue on Via Zuccarelli. A hundred
years later, the Jewish community had wanted to commemorate
that sad event with a pastry that recalled the eviction notice.
Nico picked up two sfratti, saw that only one customer was left
inside and walked into the small store with OneWag. Inside
every corner, every surface was crammed with hardware, pot-
tery, wooden bowls and taglieri. Many, like the pasta rollers and
sfratti outside, were there to appeal to tourists.

Odd, Nico thought, how neatness and order didn't seem to
be a Pitigliano trait. OneWag pulled hard on his leash trying
to smell the many boxes lining the walls. Behind the counter,
Tino Parucci looked up. He was a thin-faced man in his early
sixties with a high forehead, graying hair and a suspiciously dark
brown moustache and trim beard. He was wearing an old jean
jacket over a black turtleneck sweater. The night Lenzi was killed
he had told Maresciallo Fabbri he was alone at home, fast asleep.
His wife was in the hospital recovering from a hysterectomy. He
lived at the very end of the old town, which according to his
statement was a twenty-five-minute walk to Lenzi's store. Earlier, at a determined pace, it had taken Nico eighteen minutes.
If Parucci had gone to the store the night Lenzi was killed, no
one had reported seeing him.

"Buongiorno, Signor Doyle. I'll be with you in a moment.
You can unleash your dog. He can do no damage here."
Parucci wrapped a wrench in some newspaper and handed
the package and some change to his customer, who left with
a nod to Nico.

"Buongiorno." Nico freed OneWag, walked up to the counter
and showed the two sfratti to Parucci. "What do I owe you?"

Parucci told him. Nico paid. "How did you recognize me?"

"Your dog gave you away." A bare trace of a smile appeared
on his face. "My son came home from school yesterday and

announced that there's an American detective with a small fluffy dog going around asking questions about the Lenzi murder."

"How old is your son?"

"Thirteen. He goes to school with Mimmo Lenzi, a good boy. Not so his parents, which is why you are here, I suppose. I did not kill Mimmo's father, although what he did six years ago was despicable."

"What exactly happened?"

"Let me put up my TORNO IN VENTI[14] sign on the window, so we'll have some privacy." Parucci rummaged through a drawer and picked up some tape and a folded sign he ironed with the palm of his hand. "Here, you put it up. Just above the door handle. Then lower the shade."

Nico did as he was told. When he turned back Parucci had sat down. The counter now cut him off mid-chest. Nico looked for something he could sit on.

"You want to sit? I can get a stool from the back."

"No, I'm fine. Go on."

"Here's what happened. I was behind on my rent, just a couple of months, and Lenzi swooped in, paid the landlord what I owed and then offered him almost double the rent and took over my lease."

"Did you have a signed lease?"

"Sure. Made no difference."

"You could have taken your landlord to court."

"And wait three or four years for a solution?" Parucci crossed his arms on the counter. He seemed to sink farther down on his seat. "Plus a fight costs money I didn't have. I was angry, yes, ask anyone in town. Why my store?" The shopkeeper peered at Nico through his glasses as if he had an answer. "If he wanted to

---

14 Back in twenty.

get out from under his wife's heavy hand and make some money of his own, why didn't he go into the dress business? With his looks, women would have flocked to his store. He knew zero about electronics, still didn't when his brain got smashed. He had to snatch a school friend from a very good job in Orvieto to partner with him and run the store."

"You know Saverio?"

Parucci straightened his back. "Know him? I offered him a job about eight years ago, but I couldn't pay him what the Orvieto store offered. I had sometimes discussed new technology with Saverio. Being a lot younger, he caught on faster."

"Was LenConi successful?"

"They took over a successful store."

"If your store was successful, why did you fall behind in the rent?" Fabbri had not asked that question.

Parucci took off his glasses and massaged the top of his nose. He pulled out a handkerchief and started cleaning the lenses. "Do you really expect me to tell you?"

Nico didn't answer.

"You come here hoping to find proof that I killed Lenzi so that Saverio can come home and reunite with his happy family. Well, I did not kill him after he stole my store from under me, when it would have made sense, and I didn't kill him five years after the event. As I said, I was angry. Very angry. I let the whole town, old and new, know what a bucketful of diarrhea Lenzi was. I even confronted his wife at the pharmacy, asking her how she could stand the smell of him next to her." He pointed a finger at Nico. "Now that insult didn't even make her blink. She might as well have been a marble head plopped on a pedestal in some museum. It shut me up, that coldness. Made me feel like an idiot. Which is what I was, according to my wife. She was going to walk out if I didn't accept the facts, shut up, cool down and go back to being the man she had married. Well, I paid attention or maybe my rage was starting to disgust me. I even gave up gambling thanks to my signora, God bless her. At times, it pays to listen to women. You have your answers now. Please take the sign down."

Parucci swiped a finger across the cell phone on the counter. "Lunch time." He stood, picked up a bunch of keys hanging on a nail behind him and slipped his cell phone in his pocket. "I am closed until four."

Nico walked over to the door and took the sign down. The glass panes needed a good wipe. "Do you think Saverio killed Lenzi?"

Parucci took the sign from Nico and stuffed it back in the drawer. "All I am going to say is that whoever killed that man did this town a favor."

"Do you have any ideas as to who that whoever could be?"

"I read somewhere that most killings are family affairs." Parucci lifted the counter panel and came out into the selling area. "That's all I am going to say on that matter."

Nico suspected Parucci wouldn't welcome him here again and he had one more question. "Did Mimmo say anything to your son about his father's death?"

"If he did, he didn't tell me. You can ask him yourself. He is just behind the door you are blocking, waiting to walk home with me."

Nico stepped aside. Parucci opened the door to a plump short kid with a mass of curly dirty-blond hair piled on top of his head. OneWag sniffed his sneakers. He smelled potato chips. The boy looked down at the dog, then at Nico.

"How did it go?" Parucci asked the boy as he stepped out of the store and began to gather the baskets filled with merchandise.

"Nine." The boy continued to stare at Nico.

A *B+*, Nico translated in his head as he walked out onto the street.

Parucci showed his approval by a quick pat on his son's shoulder. "This is the man and dog Mimmo told you about." He carried baskets into the store.

The boy picked up the remaining ones, hooking them onto his arms.

"Ciao. I'm Nico. What's your name?"

Before the boy had a chance to answer, his father reappeared and relieved him of the baskets. "Hurry up and ask your question."

"Mimmo told you about me and my dog asking questions. I have one for you, if that's okay."

The boy stood taller. "Okay."

"Did Mimmo say anything else about what happened to his babbo?"

The boy's eyes shifted to his father.

"We're hungry." Parucci answered as he locked the shop.

The boy shrugged his shoulders forward. "Just that he's going to miss him and he likes your dog. I'm Fausto but everybody calls me Fau."

"Question time is over." Parucci grabbed Fausto's arm and started walking away quickly. "Buongiorno, Signor Doyle. Good luck with your search."

"Thank you and buon appetito," Nico called out to their backs.

One o'clock. He wasn't meeting Stefano Granchi until three at the café where he'd met Annamaria in Piazza della Repubblica. What the place had going for it was the view, but today it was too cold to sit outside. Besides he was in the mood for something more than café food. Something rich and reassuring.

"Come on, buddy." Nico started walking deeper into the old town. On his first walk through Pitigliano he had stopped in a piazza to look at the Cattedrale dei Santi Pietro e Paolo. He had only peeked in because he had OneWag with him, but a few meters beyond the cathedral, he'd been stopped by a small stone bear sitting atop a tall ornate pedestal overlooking the piazza. A cute bear, not in the least threatening. A bear was the symbol of the Orsini family. Orso—bear. Not just the bear, but also the sweet smell of roasting peppers had kept him and OneWag standing for a few minutes. Just beyond the bear was Hostaria del Ceccottino.

There were only half a dozen diners in the large, welcoming room. A smiling woman, the hostess or perhaps the owner, welcomed Nico and studied OneWag for almost a minute. Aware he was being examined, the dog sat, looking up at her with his long-lashed eyes, long ears drooping, his white paws resting next to each other. The perfect picture of innocence, Nico thought while trying to keep a straight face.

OneWag passed the test, and the woman led them to a small corner table away from the other diners. Sensing good behavior was required, the dog settled silently underneath the table. A menu appeared. Boar with hunter sauce was tempting. Hunter sauce meant a lot of tomato cooked with sautéed onion, celery, carrots, a clove or two of garlic, and red wine. With boar, they probably added dried porcini mushrooms. A hearty dish. Too hearty if he was going to keep his wits about him. He ordered nettle and ricotta stuffed tortelli in a browned butter sauce and a glass of Pitigliano white.

The luscious taste of the tortelli melting in his mouth made him feel a little bit better. His meeting with Parucci hadn't yielded anything useful. The man was still a strong suspect. He had motive, the means had been readily available in Lenzi's office and no alibi. But as Parucci pointed out, five years had gone by since Lenzi had cheated him out of his store. He admitted to being angry, even enraged. Does rage last that long? Could it lie dormant all those years? Was discovering Lenzi stealing from Saverio the match that relit the rage? Possible. But how to prove it?

Patience. He needed patience which seemed to be harder to find lately. Maybe Perillo was right. Maybe he was going to end up with a frittata on his face. Cilia would grow up without a father, one who loved her. A horrible thought.

Nico slipped a treat for OneWag under the table. The waiter brought his Americano. Nico slipped the small chocolate square that came with it in his mouth, took a sip of coffee and let the hot liquid soften it. Asked if Mimmo had said anything about his father's murder, Fausto looked at his father as if asking permission to speak. Had Mimmo said something important? Would he ever get a chance to talk to Eddi? Nico paid the bill and followed OneWag out of the restaurant. If not in a much better mood, he was at least full.

In front of the cathedral, a woman in a bright red coat took off her lace headscarf and waved at Nico with a relieved look on her wrinkled face. "Finally!"

He approached her.

"I've been looking for you all morning." She took his hand in both of her gloved hands and squeezed gently. She had a welcoming plump face, large dark popping eyes and lips painted as red as her coat. OneWag sniffed her lace-up shoes. She frowned at him but did not move.

Nico pulled the dog back. "Signora Rossi?"

She looked up with a triumphant smile. "Yes, Angela Rossi and your dog tells me you are Nico Doyle." Livia had written that she was in her late fifties, unmarried, and worked in a clothing shop in the new town.

"I am and this is Rocco. I was hoping to speak to you soon." She had gone from the first person to see to last on his list.

She straightened her back. "I was the one who called the carabinieri that terrible Sunday morning."

"I know. It's a pleasure to meet you."

"If I had not called them, poor Signor Lenzi would not have

been discovered for another twenty-four hours." She shivered, loosening from her bun a strand of blond hair too bright to be natural. "Well, I am pleased to meet you." She slipped it back in with gloved fingers. "I lit a candle to Saint Anthony for help in finding you. He delivered." She cocked her head at Nico. "He is the patron saint of lost things, you know."

"I do. My late wife invoked him often."

"Ah, she was Catholic," she said. "I never know with Americans if the saints have any meaning to them. You have so many religions. I am sorry you lost her. I have lost my cats and know how painful it is." She raised the synthetic fur collar of her coat. "It is cold today and the church is no place to discuss violent death although the saints it honors have suffered far too much of it. There's a nice café in Piazza della Repubblica with a lovely view over the gorge and the sweet Madonna delle Grazie church built as an ex-voto after a terrible plague, I forget the exact date. Centuries ago."

"It has indeed a lovely view." Nico cocked his elbow. She slipped her arm in his. They started walking down the main street. "It was from that church that I first saw Pitigliano. The view took my breath away."

"As it should." They walked past Parucci's shop. It was still closed.

"Why were you looking for me, Signora Rossi?"

"I paid Debora a visit yesterday. I like to go to her at least once a week, to see if she needs anything. It's an excuse really. In my free time I volunteer at the animal refuge center to look after the cats. I've been trying to convince Debora to adopt a kitten. She would find such joy having a furry thing to keep her company. She says she's allergic, which is nonsense. I am always covered in cat hair, and not a sneeze comes out of her." Angela lifted her free arm. Nico saw a spattering of long black hairs against the red of the coat. "Cosimo, my Persian. Debora told me you are trying to discover who really struck poor Signor Lenzi to death. An admirable quest. Also a difficult one since our maresciallo has made up his mind. Not a very enlightened mind, I'm afraid."

"You don't think Saverio is guilty?" They had reached the main piazza, and Angela steered him left to Caffè Degli Archi.

"First a cup of tea and a thick slice of their apple cake."

"I do have an appointment at three o'clock."

"I eat quickly."

As they walked into the café, the waitress who had served Nico and Annamaria on Saturday was behind the counter. "Good timing, Signora Angela," she said with a smile. "It just came out of the oven."

"Happy news, Mariella. A nice slice with tea and an extra slice of lemon."

"As always." Mariella turned to Nico. "And you, Signore?"

"An Americano, thank you."

The place had only three customers, but Angela led him to the farthest corner table near the kitchen. "Small town people have donkey ears."

They sat down, their backs to the room, the window they faced showing a small square of gray sky. OneWag pulled on his leash, eager to go on a sniffing jaunt. "Sit," Nico ordered in the no-nonsense tone the dog knew to obey.

Angela took off her gloves, slipped out of her coat and readjusted her purple sweater. "To answer your question. I witnessed Saverio's striking Signor Lenzi, heard those three words '*You will pay!*' Those words condemn him in the maresciallo's opinion and in many opinions, but I had a father who said terrible things when he was angry. He never meant them. He simply needed to unload whatever had gone wrong for him. Signor Bianconi has always been kind, polite, quiet. Sometimes quiet men make me uncomfortable. I always wonder what they are thinking behind

that calm façade. He does seem to be a good man. Good men do
not kill. Now I have a nephew who unfortunately has had a few
unpleasant run-ins with our carabinieri. There is no need to go
into details. They have given me enough pain."

"I'm sorry to hear that." *Where is this going,* Nico wondered.

Angela turned around to see if anyone was close. Satisfied
no one could overhear, she leaned in to Nico. She was wearing
a lavender scent. "I share this with you, Signor Doyle, only to
explain why Leo hasn't told the carabinieri what he saw that
night. He only told me last night when I mentioned over dinner
that an American detective was looking into Signor Lenzi's
murder." She sniffed and turned to look behind her.

Lying on the floor, OneWag did the same. The kitchen door
was open and Mariella, holding a tray, was walking toward them.

"Lovely," Angela said. "Thank you."

"You are welcome." Holding the tray with one hand, Mariella first lowered the hot drinks with the extra lemon and sugar
packets, then two plates, one with a large slice of apple cake, the
other with a sliver of cake. "Just for a taste, Signore," she said.
"It goes very well with coffee."

"Thank you," Nico said. It did look luscious, with dark caramelized apples on top and chunks of apples sitting in a deep
yellow dough that had to have some cornmeal in it.

Angela dropped the tea bag in the cup filled with hot water
and forked a big piece of cake. Nico tasted the cake, which was
even better than it looked, took a big sip of his Americano and
stole a glance at his watch.

Angela caught him and swallowed. "I'll enjoy this later." She
put her fork down.

"Thank you."

She looked behind her. The kitchen door was now closed.
The other customers had left. They were alone.

"The night Signor Lenzi was killed, Leo—"

"Forgive me, who is Leo?"

"Oh, my sister's youngest son. Leo went to a party some friends were throwing not too far from the LenConi store. He did not go by the store on his way to the party, but on the way home—he lives at the very end of that street—he saw Eddi walking out of his father's store."

"What time was it?" Lenzi was killed between midnight and 2 A.M., and it was probably on the earlier side according to the medical examiner.

"He does not know. Leo has sheepishly confessed he had smoked a lot of weed that night. Unfortunately, given his past scrapes, it was probably something stronger." She pinched a piece of cake and slipped it in her mouth. She gave Nico an apologetic smile. "Sugar mellows."

"How can he be sure it was Eddi?"

"I asked him the same thing. I got a lecture on how getting high sharpens the senses. He is certain it was Eddi. Does getting high sharpen the senses?"

"I've been told it does." After marijuana had made him sick, he'd stuck to alcohol to get a buzz.

Angela Rossi slipped another pinch of cake in her mouth. "Hmm, I will have to remember that when I get older. If Leo saw Eddi, it will help Saverio. For Debora, Saverio can do no wrong."

Nico heard the *ping* of a text coming through. "What did Leo see exactly?"

"He was walking on the other side of the street and saw someone walk out of the store. He stopped, thinking maybe it was a thief. Then the man walked under the streetlamp and Leo recognized Eddi. He didn't call out because he suspected Eddi had swiped something. Why else would he be at the store in the middle of the night?"

"I need to talk to Leo. It's important to know what time he saw Eddi."

"I asked Leo. He says he doesn't know what time it was. He wanted me to tell you he saw Eddi, but will not talk to you or anyone else."

"Because in the past he's gotten into trouble with the carabinieri?"

"That and the fact that Bianca, his new girlfriend, was Eddi's girlfriend until a month ago."

Ouch, Nico thought. That put Leo's story into question.

"Do you know his friends? If you don't, his parents must know. I need to talk to someone who knows what time Leo left the party."

"His friends are the ones who get him into trouble. He is careful not to let his parents know who they are."

"Look, I have to go." He took out his small notebook and jotted down his cell phone number. "Please ask Leo to call up his friends and ask what time he left the party. Let me know as soon as he finds out." Nico tore off the page and dropped it on the table in front of her. "Can you do that for me? It's important."

Angela stared at Nico with an open mouth. It took her a moment to say, "You cannot think Eddi killed his father!"

It wouldn't be the first time a child killed a parent, Nico thought but said, "He might have seen something he doesn't know is important."

Angela's face relaxed. "I see. I will ask Leo to call his friends." She pulled her cake plate closer and slipped Nico's note in her purse.

Nico thanked her.

"I will not forget, and I wish you success for Debora's sake."

Nico stood up. "Thank you. I hope to hear from you soon. If I don't, I'm afraid I'll pester you."

She looked pleased. "You will need my number."

"Livia gave it to me."

Angela nodded, with a pleased look on her face. "She showed good sense."

"Enjoy your cake. Arrivederci."

Angela smiled with a mouthful of cake. As OneWag licked up the crumbs that had fallen underneath the table, Nico checked his texts. Daniele had sent him Susanna Necchi's phone number. Floor clean, Nico paid and walked out with his dog.

NINE

Stefano had agreed to meet him in front of the Bastione di San Francesco on Via Santa Chiara, a street that marked the end of the historic district. It was a fifteen-minute walk past the Medici aqueduct, by the Orsini Museum, down through an archway that led to an elegant piazza and then up a road with deep recesses along one wall that were now used for storage.

A tall, thin man in jeans wearing a navy puffer and pale blue scarf stood in front of the bastion, pressing buttons on his phone.

Nico's phone vibrated in his pocket. He picked it up. "Pronto?"

"Stefano Granchi here. Are you coming?"

"I'm here."

Stefano looked up; Nico waved. They were about twenty feet from each other. Stefano slipped his phone in his back pocket and came forward with an embarrassed look on his face. "You are perfectly on time. I apologize. I am what my mother calls a punctuality freak. She says it in the most loving way as she is worse than I am." He held out his hand. "Piacere." They shook hands. OneWag sniffed his sneakers.

Stefano Granchi was handsome, suave-looking, Nico decided. Dark straight hair combed neatly away from his forehead, equally neat eyebrows, hazel eyes, a prominent straight nose, strong jaw and chin perfectly shaved. His down jacket and scarf looked expensive. His sneakers were made of smooth dark tan leather. Daniele had found out he was thirty-eight years old and owned Granchi Elettrica. The fact that his name had not appeared in the list of statements made to Fabbri meant he was not considered a possible suspect.

Nico smiled. "Thanks for seeing me."

"How could I not? I will do what I can to be of help to Livia. Are you afraid of heights?"

"No."

"Very good. I am a creature of habit. Every day, after lunch, I take a panoramic walk along the edge of old Pitigliano. It is not a long walk but very refreshing. Come."

At the far edge of the old fortification, Nico stopped. A long metal walkway ran along the ridge, hovering above a deep ravine.

"Are you afraid?" Stefano asked.

That a shove from you would make me meet my maker? "No. Surprised."

Stefano started walking on the passageway. Nothing swayed. Nico took four steps. The wooden slat flooring didn't budge. He looked down at OneWag. "What do you say, buddy?" The dog raised his tail and walked on. "Let's go, then."

They walked shoulder to shoulder with OneWag leading. Stefano hugged the rock side. "What is it you wish to know from me?"

Nico skimmed a hand along the railing, his eyes pointing straight ahead. "Are you still in love with your ex-wife?"

"Ah, you are abrupt."

"Time is important to you. Why waste it?"

Stefano slowed his walking as if thinking. Nico slowed too. A minute later Stefano turned to face Nico. "You think that if I am still in love with Livia, I might have taken the opportunity to dispense with Saverio by killing his partner and have Saverio go to jail for the rest of his life. Is that it?"

Out of precaution, Nico tightened his grip on the railing. "I hope you understand that I need to look into every possibility."

"No, I do not understand. Saverio killed his partner, probably in a rage beyond his control. I was never fooled by his meekness, his nice ways."

"You know him?"

"Same school, same small town, not that we hung out together. Lenzi called me in to do all the wiring for LenConi. Saverio was always hanging around, getting in the way. I had to tear all the old wiring out. How the previous owner got a light bulb to turn on in that place is beyond me. Now Lenzi, that is a man who had balls."

They started walking again. The passageway followed the deep inside curve of the rock. They passed an underground restaurant, the side facing them covered in glass. A waiter was setting up tables and waved.

Stefano waved back. "Great food. You should try it."

"Were you and Lenzi friends?"

"We had a work relationship. I enhanced the lighting in his home, started from scratch at the store. He hired me because I am the best electrician around."

"Why do you think Lenzi stole from his own store?"

"To take a long walk out of Pitigliano, is my guess. With or without a woman. Maybe the woman who cleans up the store and the house." Stefano grinned. "Makes it easy. She has a nice body and keeps her mouth shut from what I saw. She does not run his life like his wife does."

"Giulia Favelli."

"Yes. You should talk to her. Livia and Giulia used to be great friends, then something happened. No more Giulia from what I hear."

"What makes you think Lenzi was involved with another woman? Maybe he was being blackmailed or had run up gambling debts."

"I would have another woman if I were married to Annamaria. Livia let me breathe, did not pay surprise visits to my office. I loved her with all my heart." He lifted his index finger. "Loved, past tense, by the way."

Nico could see they were getting close to the end of the walkway. "Where were you the night Lenzi was killed?"

Stefano lengthened his stride. The walkway ended. Stepping onto firm ground, Nico found himself at the other end of Piazza della Repubblica. On one side a bar and restaurant and on the other side almost life-size bronze statues of a man and donkey.

"I can't cross you off the list until you answer," Nico said as Stefano unraveled the scarf he had wound around his neck before the walk.

"I do not know why you bother with a list of suspects. Saverio had two good reasons to kill Lenzi."

"Two?"

"Yes. I will wager Livia did not tell you Lenzi became her lover after she ditched me."

Nico didn't blink.

"Lenzi got stung in a bad way. Saverio came along and Lenzi did not want to let her go. He made Saverio a business partner to keep her close, that is what he told her. Livia came to me for advice." Stefano's face tightened. Then he chuckled. "I guess I should be flattered I was still good for something. Saverio was beside himself with happiness about the partnership, but she was worried Lenzi would expect her to keep him happy. She did not want to have anything to do with him anymore. I told her to stop feeling sorry for herself. '*Close your eyes and pretend Saverio is inside you,*' I said to her."

What a creep. "That must have been helpful."

"She deserved it."

"Where were you that night?"

Stefano rewound the scarf around his neck as if he needed the extra protection. "You asked if I am still in love with Livia. As I said, my love for her is in the past tense. I lust for her, that, yes. Very much so. No one makes love like she does and since she walked out on me, I have tried many women. Do I want her so badly I would kill Lenzi and get rid of that wet dishrag she partnered with? Well, you are the detective, you figure it out. Where was I the night Lenzi was killed? I slept at my parents' house. I do that sometimes to please my mother. If I was not in their house that night, they will always say I was." With another smart-ass grin Stefano then said, "Addio, Detective," and slipped into the bar.

OneWag started to follow, then stopped. Nico was leaning against the large sycamore tree next to the bar. The dog went over, sniffed the tree, the ground. After smelling the signatures of many dogs, he settled at Nico's feet.

Nico was looking at the view of a vast hill across the ravine with its thick blanket of trees. He needed to make sense of what he had just heard. If Stefano was telling the truth, he had not only strengthened the case against Saverio, but also against himself. What about Livia? If Lenzi was pressing her to have sex with him, could she have struck that hammer blow?

Nico called her. "We need to talk." He said it calmly. Showing his anger with her now was counterproductive.

"Oh, ciao. You have news?"

"Yes. News you didn't give me. I just met with Stefano. Now I understand what Fabbri meant by having a good laugh at my expense."

Livia responded with silence.

Nico looked at his watch. "I should be back in Gravigna by six o'clock. I'm coming over. Cilia can play with Rocco."

"It won't be a good time. Cilia has homework and I have to—"

"It's an excellent time. Unless you prefer I quit trying to clear Cilia's father." He was tempted to walk away except there was a very young heart involved.

"I do not like to be threatened."

"And I don't like to threaten. It's up to you."

"After nine o'clock. She will be asleep."

"I need the truth."

"I will give it to you."

"I hope so." Nico clicked off. "Come on, buddy. No use battering my head against a brick wall. Time to go home."

THAT MORNING NICO HAD parked his Fiat 500 in the first parking lot he found in the new town. It had been crowded. He'd only found a spot at the very end of the lot. Now the cars had thinned out. As Nico got closer, he saw that a note had been slipped behind his windshield wiper. He smiled remembering the time in Florence with Rita when, tired of finding a decent parking spot, he'd squeezed his rental car into a narrow space between two cars, leaving the rear sticking out. On their return, he found a note with the address of a driving school. This morning he'd had plenty of room to park correctly.

This time the note read: *Go back to America! You are not welcome here!*

Followed by a crude drawing of a hammer.

Both side mirrors had been smashed.

Nico got in the car and turned the key. To his great relief, the motor turned on. Next he checked the tires for punctures or slashes. They were firm.

He sat for a moment to consider what this meant. OneWag jumped up on his lap. Was this Eddi's anger, now aimed at him?

It had to be far more satisfying to know your anger is hitting home instead of floating on virtual clouds. Did Nico's investigating threaten him because he had been at the store the night Lenzi was killed? Father and son didn't get along. Had Eddi gone to the store to have it out with Babbo and walk away with Babbo still alive? Or in a rage lifted that convenient hammer and smashed it on Babbo's head and then walked away? Or was Babbo already dead? If so, Eddi kept it to himself.

Maybe this had nothing to do with Eddi. Had Nico rattled one of the people he'd interviewed or someone who didn't want to be interviewed?

Nico took out his phone and called the carabinieri station. He asked to speak to Maresciallo Fabbri.

"Buonasera," Fabbri said with his ear-shattering trombone voice. "Have you found your murderer?"

"No. Someone doesn't want me to." Nico told Fabbri about the note, the smashed side mirrors.

"I hope you are not thinking this station was in any way involved."

"No, I wanted you to know about it because why would someone threaten me if Saverio is the murderer?"

Fabbri scoffed. "What has happened to you is not a threat. I understand that it is upsetting, but it is only a foolish prank, someone having fun with a foreigner. Be careful driving home. Buonasera, Signor Doyle."

Nico looked at his now-silent phone.

Perillo had a different take. "This is good news for Cilia's babbo. It points to his innocence."

"I hope so." Nico quickly filled him in on what Stefano had told him.

Perillo let out a long whistle. "Holy heaven, what game is that woman playing?"

"I hope to find out soon."

"Can you make it home?"

"I'll be careful. Tell Ivana that if you give me a good price on the Panda you might have a sale."

Perillo whistled. "She will insist on a very good price. Let me know you are home in one piece."

"I will. Ciao."

He called Livia next. He was tired, upset and no longer sure he could handle Livia's omissions in a constructive way. "Ciao, Livia, I'm sorry. I need to postpone our talk until tomorrow. Meet me at Bar All'Angolo in the morning."

"I have to go to work."

"I am perfectly aware of that, Livia. And Cilia has to go to school. Rocco and I will, as before, walk with both of you and then with you alone. This is a request, not a threat."

"Like hell it isn't." She clicked off.

Well, maybe she was right. As he put the phone back in its holder, OneWag put a paw on his leg. "You're right, buddy. Home, it is." As Nico turned the motor on again he heard the *ping* of a message coming through on his phone. He pressed the icon and read:

HERE'S THE INFORMATION YOU ASKED FOR.

MARIA GRAZIA BERTINI, BORN IN ORVIETO IN 1963, ONLY DAUGHTER OF PROFESSOR FERDINANDO GIUSTINI AND MARIA . . .

Further down, two words—LICEO SCIENTIFICO—grabbed Nico's attention.

PROFESSORESSA BERTINI TAUGHT LATIN AT THE LICEO SCI-ENTIFICO IN ORVIETO FOR THIRTY-EIGHT YEARS. SHE RETIRED IN JUNE OF LAST YEAR BUT CONTINUES TO GIVE PRIVATE REME-DIAL LESSONS TO STUDENTS OF THE LICEO SCIENTIFICO.

LET ME KNOW IF THERE'S ANYTHING ELSE YOU NEED. DANI

Nico typed a quick GRAZIE, put the phone down and started the car. Dani had delivered good news. Latin was a must for every student at a science high school, which meant Maria

Grazia Bertini must have taught Eddi Lenzi. Maybe she could help him reach Eddi.

AFTER A VERY SLOW, careful drive that took too long, Nico got home just after seven o'clock. He kicked off his coat, washed his hands, fed a hungry OneWag, poured himself half an inch of whiskey and after a welcome sip, called Nelli.

"Hi, I'm home." He sat down in his armchair, legs stretched out on Nelli's bench. "How is your day going?"

"We just got home from the studio. It gets dark so soon I had to put in extra lights, which does wonders. Shadows give her a much more interesting face."

"Where is she?"

"In the shower. How did it go for you?"

"I need a new car."

"Yes, you do." Her laugh soothed him. "What made you finally come to that conclusion?"

"Someone smashed both side mirrors." A gasp came over the phone, then silence.

"Look, it meant I had a nasty drive home, but I'm here with OneWag, both of us in one piece. Whoever it was did me a favor."

"No, you're going to get hurt. I'm coming over with Maria Grazia. She needs to tell you what she told me just an hour ago."

"I'm all ears. I'll cook up the agnolotti dish I had planned for last night."

"Oh Nico, it's not about food."

"Well, I'm hungry. Whatever it is she needs to tell me will go down far better with food. Give me forty-five minutes." He hung up and texted Perillo.

Fifty minutes later the table was already set, the red wine uncorked. A terra-cotta bowl filled with taralli being eyed by OneWag sat on Nelli's bench. Nico had just finished mixing chopped fresh spinach, ricotta and grated parmigiano in a big bowl, grateful that his work in Sotto Il Fico's kitchen had taught him speed. Besides, cooking energized him. After a sip of his usual Pinot Grigio, he started filling a big pot with water as OneWag ran to the door and started yipping. Nico turned off the faucet, wiped his hand on his I LOVE TUSCANY apron and opened the door to the two women.

Nelli, keys in hand, gave Nico a quick hug as One Wag tried to climb up her leg. She scratched his head and introduced Nico to Maria Grazia.

"Welcome, Signora Bertini." Nico stepped back to let them in.

"Maria Grazia, please and thank you." They shook hands.

Nelli's portrait subject was a tall, sturdy woman dressed in wide forest green corduroy slacks and a matching green zip-up sweater under a tan wool coat. She had a smooth plain face, small gray-blue eyes and short straw blond hair she'd pinned behind her ears with two antique-looking silver combs.

While Nelli hung both their coats on the brass hooks next to the door, OneWag checked out the guest with his usual shoe sniffing.

"His name is Rocco. He's very sweet," Nelli said as she saw Maria Grazia step back. "Forgive his shoe fetish."

Maria Grazia managed a half smile.

Nico was back in the kitchen nook. "Please make yourself at home." He turned the faucet back on and filled the pot. "The meal will be a modest one. Just pasta and a salad, I'm afraid."

"And dessert." Nelli dropped a package on the kitchen counter. She was wearing skinny jeans and an old gray Yankees sweatshirt she'd borrowed last year, her long silver-gray braid hanging over one shoulder. "I got to Bar All'Angolo just as Sandro was locking up. Profiteroles." She put a hand on Nico's wrist. "Food can wait, Nico. Please sit down and listen to Maria Grazia."

Maria Grazia was sitting on the sofa with a straight back, arms folded. "I feel terrible about what happened to you. I should never have said anything, but when Nelli told me who you were, I got excited."

Nico turned off the burner and looked at Nelli.

"You carried my easel up to Maria Grazia's apartment on the second floor." Nelli joined Maria Grazia on the sofa. "When she opened the door, she saw your back running down the stairs and asked if I knew you."

"There have been so·many thefts in the neighborhood," Maria Grazia explained.

"I reassured her I knew you very well and because she seemed nervous, I added that she had nothing to fear. You'd been a detective in New York, and you were on your way to Pitigliano."

Maria Grazia's eyes smiled. "I got excited, you see, because I already knew that an American detective was looking into Signor Lenzi's murder."

Nico sat down on the closest table chair. "How did you know?"

"Signor Lenzi's son told me on Saturday. Eddi was one of my students at the Istituto and now that I'm retired, I have been helping him improve his Latin so he can get his degree in June. I teach Eddi three afternoons a week."

Not just one of many students then. "Do you know him well?"

"I have always preferred to keep a certain distance with my students. It makes it easier to grade them honestly. He is a very bright student, except in Latin, because he finds it boring and therefore a waste of his time. He refuses to acknowledge the importance of Latin in the pharmaceutical business. He gets along with most of his classmates, ones that come from privileged households like his. He's spoiled and somewhat arrogant but so many boys his age are nowadays."

"He must have canceled his lessons with you when his father was murdered."

"Only the Monday after his father was killed. He came punctually that Wednesday as if nothing had happened and rudely shrugged off my condolences. I understood and have guided him through the lessons as if all was well. We all have different ways of grieving."

While Maria Grazia spoke, Nico poured three glasses of red wine and walked two over to the women.

"Friday I couldn't get Eddi to concentrate." Maria Grazia took the offered glass with both hands, as if she was afraid to drop it. "Lovely, thank you. He said he was angry a detective was going to upset everyone all over again by asking questions they had already answered to the carabinieri. I thought he would have been pleased someone was trying to help Saverio. In the past I had the impression he liked Saverio. I said nothing about my own feelings regarding your investigation." Maria Grazia held the glass against her chest. "You see, I knew Saverio when he worked in the electronics store on Corso Cavour. He charged my students' phones and printed my class notes. He is not"—she shook her head with the *not*—"Signor Lenzi's killer. After forty-five minutes of wasting time, I sent Eddi home." She took a small sip.

"Yesterday after Nelli agreed to stay through Monday, I called Eddi to reschedule our afternoon class. He was annoyed and wanted to know why. I told him an artist was staying with me and then foolishly boasted that the detective he had told me about was the artist's friend and I was very relieved that someone was going to help Saverio." She put the glass down on Nelli's bench and sat back up, a strong emotion gripping her face. "It was a terrible mistake on my part."

Nico strained forward. "Why is that?"

"The words were barely out of my mouth when he yelled at me, using foul language, repeating '*Saverio killed my father!*

When I tried to calm him, he hung up." Maria Grazia picked up the wineglass and drank a long sip. "When Nelli told me what happened to her, I thought of Eddi. He has a few times gotten into trouble at school with his temper. And he does come here on a fancy motorcycle his mother gave him for his eighteenth birthday. I found it hard to believe it was Eddi, but the possibility made me nervous, nonetheless. I could see how upset she was and insisted on driving her home. I also suggested it would be easier for her to paint me in her studio." Maria Grazia looked over at Nelli. "You seemed relieved."

Nelli smiled. "I was."

Maria Grazia looked at Nico with crestfallen eyes. "After what happened to your car, I have no doubt it is Eddi's doing."

Nelli raised a hand. "No, wait. How would Eddi know that car was Nico's?"

"Thanks to me," Nico admitted. "When I met Eddi's mother on Saturday, she let me know she'd expected me to have a more macho dog." He stood up and went to the stove. "I added to her disappointed picture of me by telling her I drove a flaming-red 2015 Fiat 500." Nico turned on the burner and put the full pot on it.

Maria Grazia repeated, "I am so terribly sorry."

"Don't be. I really did need to get a bigger car."

Nelli shook her head. "Something doesn't make sense to me. Clearly Eddi is solidly convinced Saverio killed his father, but why act out with such anger at his teacher and then at us?"

Maria Grazia gave Nelli's arm a gentle touch as if to reassure her. "His world has been turned upside down. Eddi must be screaming inside. Now I think he's trying to hold on to the one certainty he believes he has—that Saverio is guilty."

Maybe, Nico thought. Or did Eddi have proof Saverio was not guilty, proof he didn't want found out? "I've heard father and son didn't get along."

"I know they had fights. Eddi would complain sometimes about his father making life impossible for him. Isn't that common between a man getting older and a son reaching adulthood?"

"Babbo getting jealous," Nelli commented as she refilled Nico's glass and her own. "I don't know about American families, but in Italy, Babbo loves his daughter and Mamma loves her son."

"I think that's international." Nico lifted the lid of the pot. The water was moving. He turned on a second burner very low under the pan with the browned butter. "We'll eat soon. Once the water boils, the agnolotti will only take three minutes at the most."

"I will pay for the damage to your car."

"Thank you, but no. I will, though, ask for a favor."

Maria Grazia leaned forward eagerly. "Yes, please ask."

He turned to face her. "Can you convince Eddi to meet with me?"

"How? He hates you. He might even attack you."

"I'm bigger and I've had training. Tell Eddi that I have a witness who saw him leave his father's store the night he was killed."

Nelli dropped down in Nico's chair. "Is that true?" Some of her wine had spilled on the Yankees sweatshirt.

Nico salted the pasta water and added a few spoonfuls of the hot water to the ricotta bowl to dilute the ricotta and soften the spinach.

"Did he kill his father?" Nelli rubbed her hand over the wet spot. "Please say he didn't."

"No," Maria Grazia said softly.

Nico turned his attention to Maria Grazia. "At this moment I have no idea who killed Giancarlo Lenzi, but I need to meet with Eddi." Nico threw in the agnolotti.

"I'll try," Maria Grazia said with little conviction. "He's

bright. I am afraid he might think it is a trick to make him pay for what he did to your car. Will you?"

"No. His world, as you said, has been turned upside down."

"Thank you," she said, clearly relieved. "I will do my best to persuade him you mean no harm."

"Thank *you*." Nico lifted the agnolotti with a spider spoon, dropped them into the bowl and gently mixed them with the ricotta sauce. "Now please come to the table."

TEN

With her mop of red curls pinned back with brightly colored clips to reveal all of her pale, frowning face, Cilia rushed into Bar All'Angolo ahead of her mother.

She spotted Nico, OneWag and the old man at their usual table. "You are here!" Her voice was full of surprise.

Nico spread out his arms. "Ciao, bella Cilia."

Her frown turned into a smile as she ran to give Nico a hug around his waist. He hugged her back.

"You came anyway."

"I was always going to come."

"Oh." She threw an angry look at her mother.

"I'm so happy to see you. Look, Rocco is too."

OneWag was looking up at Cilia with a wag of his tail.

Cilia dropped down on the floor, covered OneWag with kisses then looked back at her mother. Livia was ordering something from Sandro, her back to Nico's table. Cilia pulled on Nico's jacket and whispered, "I talked to Babbo last night."

Looking at her face, Gogol quoted, "'Such a smile was glowing in her eyes.'"

Cilia frowned at Gogol. "I did, I really did."

"Of course you did," Nico said. "We believe you."

"Your smile tells the truth," Gogol said.

Cilia looked behind her. Livia still had her back to the table, drinking something. "He wants to come home," she whispered. "When can he come home?"

The pleading eyes bore a hole in Nico's heart. "Not yet."

"When?"

"Soon."

"Soon when?"

"What are you two whispering about?" Livia asked as she walked toward them.

"I told Nico how Stella is teaching me to draw with colored pencils."

Her face reminded Nico of the cherubs he had seen in Madonna paintings. The picture of innocence. "Stella is a good friend of mine," he said as a distraction. "She knows a lot about art."

Livia shook her head. "You are quite the storyteller, Cilia."

"It's true!"

Livia held out her hand. "Come on, school is waiting."

Cilia strode past her mother. "Come on, Nico and Rocco, school is waiting."

Nico stood up. "Ciao, Gogol, see you tomorrow."

"If I live."

"You will. I'm counting on it." Nico waved to Sandro and Jimmy. "A domani."

The two men were too busy with other customers to answer.

THE SCHOOL BELL RANG. Cilia gave Nico and OneWag a quick hug and ran to join the other students entering the building.

Livia hugged herself despite the mild day. "She's angry with me now. I didn't want to see you, so I told her you weren't going to be at the café in the morning."

"You didn't want to see me because? I could finish the sentence, but I want to hear it from you."

"Because I hadn't told you about me and Giancarlo." She started walking at a fast pace. "I should have known Stefano would tell you, make me look like the slut his mother thinks I am. Well, I guess I was for those two weeks with Giancarlo. I'm not proud of them. Now you are angry with me too. I cannot blame you, but if I told you we had been lovers, you would have thought Savi did kill him and refused to help him."

Nico matched her stride. "Not if you'd told me the affair was over once Saverio entered the picture." OneWag ran ahead as if he knew their destination. "Was it over?"

Livia stopped and faced Nico. "Yes, but Giancarlo just could not accept that. He thought too much of himself. He insisted he had fallen in love with me, that only I could make him happy, that he would leave Annamaria for me, together we would leave Pitigliano, this tomb of a town, that he would leave the store to Savi as a consolation prize."

"You didn't believe him?"

She snorted. "He was singing this song to me while at the same time screwing his cousin's wife. No, I did not believe him. And even if he had been a decent man, I wanted no part of him anymore. I loved and love Savi." She resumed walking at a slower pace.

"How can you be sure Saverio didn't know Lenzi was putting pressure on you? Both you and Annamaria told me the partners weren't getting along anymore."

"Savi would have sat me down and asked me. If he knew Giancarlo was trying to get me in bed again, he would have offered to walk out of the partnership. Whatever was going on between them had nothing to do with me."

Nico did not share her confidence. "Saverio is coming across as an honest, upright man, and yet he runs away instead of facing whatever was coming his way. Did that surprise you? By the way, I hope you are using a burner phone, and he didn't tell you where he is."

"I am and he didn't. I did tell Cilia not to say anything about the call to anyone, not to her teacher, not to Luciana. If she was bursting to tell someone she could whisper it in Rocco's ear. I didn't realize that to her the dog and you are one. Savi running away? I was surprised but I think Debora Costa has something to do with it. Her family was hidden at Savi's grandparents' farm when the Nazis came to Pitigliano."

Nico was glad he now had another reason to get in touch with Debora. They had reached the park stairs that led to the Coop. He looked at his watch. Seven minutes to opening time. They started climbing down. "You have become friendly with Luciana?"

"Yes. Cilia was sitting in the Coop after school until I got off. Luciana took pity on her and offered to keep Cilia in her shop. She's nice, a bit overbearing maybe, determined to have Cilia draw every flower and plant in the shop. Cilia says she will try. I am happy that thanks to Stella she is using color again."

They had reached the bottom of the hill. Nico held her back with his arm on hers. "Livia, I don't want any more surprises."

"I do not have any."

"What about Giulia Favelli? She wasn't on your list. Why not? She cleans house for Annamaria, the store and Debora Costa. She could have interesting things to tell me."

"I didn't know she cleaned for them. We're not friends anymore."

"What happened?"

She shrugged. "I got involved with Savi. She got annoyed I didn't spend as much time with her."

The manager walked past them and opened the Coop door. Livia shuffled her feet. "I have to go. Are you getting any closer?"

"I've found some good motives for Lenzi's murder. The problem is finding proof."

"Please don't give up."

"I won't."

Livia rushed into the store. OneWag looked up at Nico with his *where to now?* expression.

LUCIANA WAS OPENING HER shop when Nico and OneWag walked back up to the main piazza. The dog lunged ahead to greet her.

Wrapped in a long, voluminous delphinium blue coat, the florist looked down at a wiggling dog. "Ah, there you are, disloyal mutt. You and your friend forgot the meaning of *tomorrow*."

"Buongiorno, Luciana."

She looked over at Nico approaching. "I don't know if it's a good day yet. I worry about Cilia."

"It's very nice of you to watch her in the afternoon."

"There's no need to watch that child. Poor thing, sitting in the Coop like a product for sale. I could not stand it." She flung open the door. "Come in, I need to talk to you."

OneWag scooted in first, then Luciana sideways because of her girth, Nico last. Luciana took off her coat and hung it on a wall hook. She was wearing a hand-knitted tunic sweater covered with big, embroidered flowers over wide black flannel pants. "Cilia sits by the window with a tray on her lap and draws my flowers. She doesn't say a word, just works one color then another. I have had to buy a ream of paper for her. Her drawings are very lifelike for someone so little. You should get your artist friend to look at them."

"Her name is Nelli, and you know it." Luciana would not forgive him for having a woman in his life after Rita.

"I forget names. Now for Rita I have pink, white, red roses, yellow chrysanthemums, and sunflowers. The peonies you put a week ago need to be tossed in the garbage bin."

"It was six days ago."

"Peonies don't last out in the cold." OneWag pawed her leg. Luciana looked down. "I suppose you can't blame the son for the father's misdeeds."

"What misdeeds?"

"Never mind." She reached into a ceramic jar on the shelf. "Here you are." The cookie she dropped fell right into One-Wag's open mouth. "So what will it be?"

He hadn't planned on visiting Rita today but it was useless to argue with Luciana. Besides, she made him feel guilty. "Sunflowers, thank you. I'll take them right over."

"Good." She lifted four sunflowers out of a big bucket, cut their stems shorter and wrapped them in shiny gift paper.

"You wanted to talk to me?" Nico reminded Luciana. He was eager to visit Rita and call Debora Costa. Nelli had left him her car to drive to Pitigliano.

"Yes." Luciana's furry pale eyebrows met. "Cilia's mother is being watched."

"What makes you think that?"

"On his way to work yesterday morning, Enrico saw a man sitting in a car parked across the street. When he came home for lunch, the man and the car were still there. Last night a different car and a different man were parked in the same spot. There were lots of other parking spots available. Enrico thinks the second car took over for the first one. He got curious, did an internet search on Pitigliano news and read about the murder. This morning the first man is back. I told Enrico to call the carabinieri." Luciana gave Nico the wrapped flowers. "That poor sweet child. To think her father is a murderer. What if he comes here?"

"He won't and he's not a murderer." He said it not fully believing Saverio was innocent.

"How do you know?"

"I'm a homicide detective, that's why." Bullshit, but he wasn't about to give her a lecture on innocent until proven guilty. "How much do I owe you for the flowers?"

She named a price, he paid.

"Oh, I'm so relieved. If you say he's not a murderer, then he's not." She came toward him with open arms. Nico stopped himself from stepping back. Her big breasts pressing against his chest embarrassed him, but hugging was second nature to her and she meant well. "I expect to see you next week, if not before. For a chat and a cookie for Rocco. Say hello to Rita for me."

"I will."

OneWag went ahead. The flowers in Nico's hands told the dog where they were going next. The cemetery was a fifteen-minute walk up the road next to Luciana's shop. On the way, Nico punched Perillo's cell phone.

"I am sorry, Nico. The maresciallo is on the office phone." Daniele was whispering. "He saw it was you and asked me to pick up."

Nico heard Perillo's voice pitched at higher than normal. "I consider it an insult to—" followed by muffled sounds. Daniele must have put his hand over the speaker.

"I apologize, Nico. I thought it best to leave the room." He was no longer whispering. "He is very angry."

"He's talking to Fabbri?"

"Yes. Maresciallo Fabbri is having Signora Livia watched with his men instead of asking us to do the watching as protocol dictates. The maresciallo had to call Pitigliano four times to get him on the phone."

"Why is she being watched all of a sudden?"

"I didn't hear our maresciallo ask that question yet."

"Tell Perillo I'll call again later. Wait, Dani. How are you? Everything fine?"

"Yes, Stella got her own apartment."

"Happy for both of you. Freedom at last."

Daniele laughed.

He was probably blushing too, Nico thought. "Give Stella a hug for me. Ciao."

"I will be more than happy to. Ciao."

A pale sun had appeared between gray clouds. OneWag was sitting up at his usual spot next to Rita's grave, ears at attention, his eyes focused on the path that led to the entrance gate. When Nico finally walked up, the dog relaxed and lay down on the grass that edged the grave.

Nico threw the very sad-looking peonies out, changed the water and arranged the sunflowers in the vase while his mind told Rita that Luciana said hello. He stood for a moment, hands clasped in front of him, looking at the small, enameled photo of a young, smiling Rita taken at their wedding, a picture she had picked when she knew she had little time left. "You're still in my heart, Rita," he said out loud, leaned over and kissed her photo.

NELLI HAD A CONVENIENT cell phone holder in her car. As soon as he reached the autostrada he lowered the volume on the phone and called Perillo.

"I'm sure you want to fill me in on all the Neapolitan insults you hurled at Fabbri, but try to hold on to your temper for a minute. Why is Livia being watched now? What has changed?"

"They are desperate. Fabbri admitted it after I calmed down. He's got our nemesis Substitute Prosecutor Della Langhe demanding results. Fabbri continues to insist Saverio is guilty of the murder, but he hasn't been found."

"Why didn't Fabbri ask you to take care of watching Livia?"

"Because he's a cap 'e cazzo."

A dickhead, Nico translated in his head.

"If my men catch Saverio, I would get some of the credit. That turd does not share. Are you sure Saverio is innocent?"

"There's no tangible evidence that he killed Lenzi unless Fabbri is keeping it hidden."

"No. A guy like Fabbri would be screaming it from the rooftops. He is that hungry for attention. Listen, you better get your New York homicide detective action going a little faster."

"I don't need you to tell me that."

"Okay, okay, sorry."

"I'm sorry. You hit a nerve."

"I know you are doing the best you can. Good news now. Ivana is on her way to Florence to buy us a brand-new red Panda, offering to pay for it. Can you believe it? My Ivanina making enough money to buy a car? New car, not used. I am so proud of her."

And probably relieved, Nico thought. Perillo was careful with money. "Good news, indeed." Aldo, his landlord, was going to find replacement side mirrors for the Fiat 500. With new ones, the car still had some value.

"She'll find out what they would give her for our Panda, and if the price is right for you, it is yours."

"Thanks. Ciao. My exit is coming up soon and I better start paying attention."

"Who is it today?"

"Debora Costa to start with." He clicked off. The exit sign was just ahead.

WITH THE HELP OF her cane, Debora led Nico and OneWag to her small, crowded living room. "Have you had lunch?"

"I have, thank you." He'd gotten to Pitigliano a little after one. Not wanting to barge in on Debora at lunchtime, he'd grabbed a mortadella and provolone sandwich at the small Coop he'd passed on his first visit to the old town. As he ate, he'd followed OneWag, zigzagging through the narrow streets, trying to imagine what life was like in its heyday under the Orsinis and then the Medicis. Surely busier streets, more noise, more color, more stench, more hardships for the workers. At two-fifteen, with the sun now covered by a blanket of gray clouds, he had knocked on Debora's door.

"A coffee, then. I will happily have another myself."

A welcome offer. The room was chilly. "Thank you." Debora had dropped his down jacket and OneWag's leash on a bench in the entrance. "Can I make it for you? I've become a proficient espresso maker."

Debora chuckled and wrapped her wool shawl more tightly around her shoulders. She was wearing a long dark wool dress that reached her ankles and made her look like she belonged to a previous century. "I am certain your coffee is excellent, but it's quicker with a Nespresso. I'll be right back. Sit in the blue armchair. It has the best springs."

She had told him that last time. "Yes, I will. Thank you." He would wait in case she needed help.

Leaving the room, she used her cane to point to a bowl of water on the floor under the archway. "For you, OneWag, whether you need it or not." OneWag ignored the bowl and followed her.

Nico let his eyes wander. The winter light from the windows was enhanced by three lamps perched on various pieces of furniture, giving the room a soft golden glow. To add more warmth to the room, a small electric heater burned in front of the hard-backed chair she had sat in last time.

"I was hoping you would visit again." Debora came in pushing a walker, followed by a satisfied-looking OneWag. The tray with the coffee cups and sugar bowl sat on the seat of the walker.

"I had every intention of visiting again even if I didn't need your knowledge."

"Good. Saverio bought this walker as a Hanukkah gift last year. As I don't consider myself needing anything more than a sturdy cane, I'm afraid my pride won over gratitude." She lowered her tall thin frame down gently on the hardback chair, the walker pushed to one side. "Clever Saverio quickly explained he thought I could use it to ferry things from one place to another. It is indeed very useful. Now help yourself, have your coffee and tell me what knowledge of mine you need."

Nico took his cup, sat in the blue armchair and sipped a very strong espresso, which meant he would have what the Italians called una notte in bianco. A white night. No sleep.

"I was hoping you would pave the way for me to speak with Giulia Favelli."

"Since she is the maid and Lenzi's store cleaner, you think she might know something that will help your investigation?"

"Yes."

"How is the investigation going?"

"Slowly. Several people have good motives for killing Lenzi. It appears he was not a nice man."

"He was not." She drank her espresso with two sips, then tilted her head at Nico. "You could have asked for Giulia's number by phone or text."

"I wanted to talk to you. You know the people involved. I feel somewhat on uneven ground in this case. I'm not used to working alone."

"I understand. On television shows there's always a team behind the protagonist." She smiled. "I am happy to be of help."

"I would like to start with knowing more about your relationship to Saverio."

"Why is that important?"

"Livia thinks you encouraged Saverio to run away, and I suspect you know where he is."

She leaned down and handed OneWag a treat. "Sweet boy," she said.

She was hiding her face. "I'm not asking you to tell me where he is," Nico said. "I just want to know more about him."

She sat up, her expression neutral. *An essential expression for a therapist*, Nico thought.

"You want to know more about Saverio because your belief in his innocence is wavering."

"Yes. Some information has come up that gives him another motive for ending Lenzi's life."

"Livia's affair with Giancarlo when she left her husband ended when she met Saverio."

"That's what Livia says."

"That is what Saverio said, but you don't believe Livia."

"I want to for Cilia's sake, but not telling me about the affair when she hired me tells me she's not trustworthy."

"I can see that. Did her husband tell you?"

"Yes. You know Stefano?"

"Yes."

The curtness of her answer made Nico wonder if Stefano had once been a client. "He also told me that Lenzi was in love with Livia. He supposedly partnered with his old friend Saverio to get close to her again and could have asked for certain favors from Livia to keep her man on the job."

She put her cup down. "I am not surprised. Too many men think that marriage is no impediment to their sexual freedom. I have heard rumors that Giancarlo broke up his cousin's marriage. His being in love with Livia is new to me. I didn't think he was capable of loving anyone besides himself, but from what I know of Stefano, he is not a man to lie."

"Annamaria must have known her husband was unfaithful."

"If she wanted to know. When it comes to their men, women are very good at suppressing what is too painful."

"What if she did know?"

"Many Italian women accept infidelity in silence for the children's sake. Apart from the children I do not think Annamaria's pride would permit her to end the marriage. It has also always been clear to me that she was very much in love with Giancarlo."

"What if he was preparing to leave her, even leave Pitigliano? That would explain his needing money."

Debora looked down at the palm of her hand as if it had information for her. Nico watched her mull over his question. After a long moment she put her hand down on her thigh and turned her dark eyes on him. "She would not kill him under any circumstance. That is what I think."

"What about Eddi? He's very close to his mother and didn't get along with Babbo."

"Giancarlo mistreated his eldest son. I have found that is often the case with a middle-aged man and his oldest son. Jealousy, competitiveness, the son testing his strength and at the same time yearning to be loved back. Eddi does have a temper, and there might have been a time when he would have been tempted to give Babbo a good punch in the stomach, but no more than that. I know he loved his father."

"He's talked to you?"

Debora answered with an apologetic smile.

"I see. Confidential information." No telling her then about the incident with Nelli or his car, which he was pretty sure was Eddi's doing. "Last time I was here, I met Mimmo on the street. He told me Saverio didn't kill his father. When I asked him how he knew that he said to ask Eddi."

"He would say that. Saverio has given Mimmo a great deal of attention, and as for Eddi, Mimmo thinks his big brother knows everything." She rested her head against the back rail of the chair and closed her eyes.

"I'm tiring you."

"No." She fingered the small Star of David hanging from her frail neck. "You were going to start our conversation by asking me about Saverio."

"Yes, I'm sorry. There are too many questions in my head."

"You do not understand why an innocent man of Saverio's integrity would run away instead of standing strong."

"Yes. He doesn't strike me as a coward."

Debora looked down at the floor where OneWag had curled himself up on the overhanging skirt of her dress. "Will your dog mind if I pick him up and put him in my lap?"

"Not at all. You've fed him so you're a friend. He'll keep you warm."

Debora leaned down and lifted OneWag. With a quick look at Nico, the dog let Debora settle him on her lap. She kissed his head. "What a good boy you are." She watched him make two turns on her bony thighs, bunch up the dress with his paw, then curl up in her lap.

"The idea came to me as soon as I heard Giancarlo had been murdered." Head down, she slowly caressed the dog's long white and orange fur. "Running away had and has saved so many people. We ran in the dark. I remember my legs kicking back and forth as hard as they could. *Faster, faster* I kept screaming in my head." She spoke in a low, calm voice as if reading a bedtime story. "And then I heard the shots. Two. I didn't stop."

She raised her head to look at Nico. "I owe Saverio's grandparents my life and my mother's. During the war, my father was in the mountains with the other resistance fighters of the area. Mamma and I had avoided attention as Jews thanks to no one pointing the finger at us. When the Nazis overtook Italy after the armistice was signed in September 1943, we had to disappear. Saverio's grandparents hid us on their farm for months. Then someone warned them that the farm next to theirs was being searched. We grabbed what little we had and ran.

"I convinced Saverio to run. I knew that Fabbri, with his petty mind, would arrest him and do nothing to investigate whether he was guilty or not. Saverio would end up spending the rest of his life in prison. I promised him I would keep him safe. He worried about Livia and Cilia. I gave him my burner phone. Told Livia to get out of here and get herself a burner. I am happy that she listened and that she found you."

"How old were you in 1943?"

"Ten."

"You mentioned hearing two shots."

Her hand stopped caressing. "In my hurry to run away, I left my notebook in the barn where we slept. On one page I asked a question over and over again. *Why is it bad to be a Jew?* An officer found it and shot Nonno Nando and his dog. It was market day in town. That's what saved Nonna Gina and Saverio's father. They were selling at the market in town."

"Did your father come home?"

"Yes, thanks to God, he did after the Allies took over." Her face glowed for an instant. "He found us here back in our home. I think we cried of happiness for a week."

"You are a very brave woman."

"We all were. Jews, resistance fighters, the men forced to fight a war they didn't believe in, the wives, mothers and fathers, the children. Who are you meeting next?"

"Susanna Necchi."

"A necessary choice. Susanna was very close to Giancarlo for a while. I think you will find her engaging, very likable and beautiful. Be cautious, Nico."

"I try to be."

She set her eyes on Nico's face with a slight smile. "Listen to me giving advice to a New York detective. My hubris sometimes astounds me."

"I welcome your advice."

"You are kind." Debora reached into the pocket of her dress, careful not to disturb a fast-asleep OneWag. "Let me give you Giulia's phone number. Now I am tired."

NICO WALKED DOWN UNDER the archway into Piazza Petruccioli, considered the gateway to the historical center of Pitigliano. The end of the L-shaped piazza led to two roads, one that rose to the modern town. The second one descended to the valley, the road he took every time he came here, always stopping by the same little church to absorb the view of Pitigliano spread out on top of the tufa ridge. He was early for his meeting with Susanna Necchi. Nico had hoped to see her in Sorano, where she lived since separating from Lenzi's cousin Matteo. He had read that the town was almost as beautiful as Pitigliano. Susanna had said, "Not here. Pitigliano," in a friendly voice when he had called her yesterday. "I came to Sorano to get away from anything that had to do with my husband and Giancarlo. I'll meet you tomorrow, Wednesday at four, in Piazza Petruccioli. You can treat me to a Prosecco."

Nico lifted OneWag up on the thick rock ledge. It was a mild day. The sun sat low in the clear sky, dropping a warm light on the thick vegetation below and on the ridge on the other side. The deep green was pocked here and there with yellow and brown spots; the Madonna delle Grazie rested on its own ledge. Nico wondered if this meeting might get him closer to a solution.

"It gets boring after a while."

Holding OneWag tight against his chest, Nico turned around. "I don't think this view would ever bore me."

"You haven't lived here all your life."

Caught off guard by the woman's beauty, Nico stared. High cheekbones, light olive skin, large thick-lashed dark eyes, full naked lips, her face framed by long dark hair cascading over her shoulders. She couldn't have been older than her mid-thirties.

"I'm sorry." Nico leaned over to put OneWag back on the

pavement. "You surprised me." OneWag sniffed her suede boots and the heavy leather bag that hung from one hand.

A light laugh was followed by "Susanna Necchi." She did not extend her hand. "Matteo said to look for a tall handsome man with a fluffy white-and-orange dog and here you are."

"Thank you for meeting me."

A small head toss. "Matteo made me curious. Your visit made him nervous. I'm surprised he realized what a perfect suspect he makes."

She got the put-down in early, Nico thought. "Where would you like to go for a Prosecco?"

Susanna tightened one of the multicolored shawls she was wrapped in. "I thought the restaurant at the end of the piazza would be open. It isn't. Are you cold?"

"Not at all." He was wearing his down jacket unzipped.

"Let's stay here, then, since you like the view so much." She put the leather bag on the ledge and lifted herself up next to the bag, her legs dangling, her back to the view.

"That's dangerous," Nico said.

Susanna narrowed her eyes. "Only if you push me. You don't want to push me, do you?"

Nico was reminded of a cat purring. He stepped away from her and leaned a hip against the ledge.

"There's a good wine store just before the Arch so I bought a bottle of Prosecco." She extracted an open bottle from her bag and handed it to Nico. Next came two plastic flutes, one in each hand. "You pour."

Nico did so slowly to control the foam, twisted the top back on and rested the bottle on the pavement.

Susanna clinked plastic against Nico's flute. "To Giancarlo, who did not deserve to die."

Nico took a small sip, watching her empty her flute. "Do you think Saverio killed him?" he asked as she lowered the flute.

"It seems so. Why run if you are innocent?" She thought for a moment, a finger weaving in and out of a shawl fringe. "I don't know him well. I met him first at a dinner Giancarlo and Annamaria gave. That was after Matteo declared he would have nothing to do with them again. I went hoping to convince Giancarlo to help us save the vineyard. The four of us used to have such good times together." She raised her flute.

Nico refilled it. *Interesting*, he thought. Her husband had claimed Susanna didn't like Annamaria.

"As you know from Matteo, I did not succeed." She drank down the wine and put the flute on the ledge between them. "I didn't stop trying. I would visit Giancarlo at the store and bring my laptop, saying it was not working. Saverio understood the excuse right away. I would slip into Giancarlo's office and beg." Susanna crossed her arms under the layers of shawls, her torso bent forward.

Nico put the bottle down on the pavement. "Are you too cold?"

"No, I am angry. Now you are going to think I murdered Giancarlo because he shafted us."

"Did you?"

Susanna sat up and turned her body to offer Nico her face. "No, I got over that fiasco by leaving Matteo and the wine business."

Her beautiful face was relaxed, Nico noticed. There was no emotion in her words.

"Not nice of me, but I had enough of Matteo putting all the blame on Giancarlo for his own stupidity. I married a man who was not cut out to own a vineyard. You need brains and balls." She crossed her legs, revealing black leather slacks. "I tried to help. With a little charm and good looks, I got people to buy, but I knew nothing about how to fill those bottles with good wine. Since my separation I manage the spa at the Thermal

Baths in Sorano, a perfect job for me. We recently celebrated our third anniversary. I love working there.

"It was clear to me Saverio loved his job. He has brains, but he never struck me as a strong man. I guess maybe he ran because he was scared. Livia must be furious. How could he do that? Just abandon her."

"Maybe he thought disappearing was best for her and Cilia."

"No. If you love someone, you don't do that. He was thinking of himself like most men." She lifted her chin up. "Are you selfish, Nico Doyle?"

He looked back at her sunlit beauty with what he hoped was a stony face. "Whether I am or not is of no consequence to you."

"Too bad." She turned away. "Matteo turned out to be selfish. I thought he was madly in love with me. That is what he claimed. I quickly discovered I was only an acquisition he could show off. *'Look what ugly little Matteo caught!'* He especially loved to rub it in to Giancarlo, wanted me to wear sexy clothes whenever we had dinner together. I played along. Why not? Matteo had money until he didn't."

"What was your relationship to Giancarlo like?"

"Ah, you have heard the rumors. This is getting very personal, but I don't care. Yes, it is true. We had a fling. It started with me asking him to help us. He started saying he needed to think about it while kissing me, touching my breasts. I played along, then I started to like his hands on me and more. Matteo does not have Giancarlo's touch. I stopped caring about saving the vineyard."

"Did your husband know about your affair with Giancarlo?"

"He was clueless."

Why do adulterers always think that? Nico wondered.

"It only lasted a couple of months."

"Why only two?"

"I started to feel cheap, used, the way Matteo made me feel

when he showed me off. It's an ugly feeling. I told Giancarlo it was over."

"Was he upset?"

She threw her head back. "Nooo, we laughed. It was just sex, not love. I think he was relieved because Annamaria had started asking too many questions about his late work hours." Susanna picked up the empty flute. "Come on, let's finish the bottle."

"You have to drive home."

"Twelve minutes. That's all. Don't be a spoilsport."

He filled her flute and poured one inch in his. His drive home was much longer. "One last question before we toast again."

"If you're asking me if I think Matteo killed Giancarlo, I don't see him doing it, no matter how many reasons he has to hate him." She took a long sip. "He does not have the backbone or the energy to hate enough to kill."

"That wasn't the question."

"Oh." She frowned as if annoyed. "What then?"

"Where were you the night Giancarlo was murdered?"

Susanna threw her head back and laughed. "What an idiot I am. That's always the first question." She grew serious and leaned forward until her face was two inches from his. He could smell her flowery perfume. "The night my ex-lover died I was in my new home in Sorano, fast asleep, regretfully all by myself. What do you want to toast to now? To finding the murderer or to me for answering your questions?"

He raised his flute. "Why not to both?"

They clinked plastic, drank. "It has been a real pleasure, Nico Doyle." Susanna slid off the ledge and strode off, the loose ends of her shawls flowing behind her.

THAT NIGHT DINNER WAS at Nelli's. She lived on top of the hill behind the church, in a building next to what was left of the castle that had been a defense post for Florence during the thirteenth-century wars between Florence and Siena. It was no grander than Nico's place, about the same size, with thick walls, a small one-bedroom with a window facing a remaining castle wall. The main room's windows faced the tower, but she had brightened the room with her colorful paintings.

He had a spent a handful of nights with her in the apartment, but eating there was an interesting first for Nico. Nelli didn't like to cook. Meals together had always been at his home or out. Maria Grazia had insisted on cooking an Umbrian meal before going back to Orvieto in the morning.

"Giving you both a taste of my region is the least I can do after what Eddi's done." Maria Grazia was standing behind a waist-high wall that separated the two-meter-deep kitchen from the living/dining room. She was wearing one of Nelli's color-fully stained painting aprons. Nelli, her long braid twisted into a large knot on the back of her neck, was next to her, getting the dishes from a cabinet. She'd refused Nico's help.

"As his teacher I somehow feel responsible for his terrible behavior." Maria Grazia lifted the lid of Nelli's dented pot, releasing a rich, tangy aroma of tomatoes, garlic, rosemary and something Nico couldn't place. OneWag, who had followed Nelli into the kitchen, held his nose in the air. Meat!

Nico brought a stool over from a corner and sat down in front of the table where Nelli did her drawings. "It wasn't your fault but thank you." Nelli had only two chairs. "I know nothing about Umbrian cuisine." He hadn't registered that Orvieto was in Umbria.

"We'll start with pasta alla Norcina, my husband's favorite. It's a specialty of Norcia. Maybe you know the town by its Latin name, Nursia. I read that is how the English call the town, which seems a bit snobbish to me."

Nico fingered the two bottles of wine he'd brought. "Red or white with the pasta?"

"Red."

He was anxious to find out if she'd talked to Eddi, but knew he needed to wait. Food was always a welcome distraction. "What are the ingredients?"

"Penne. Not the smooth kind. You want the sauce to adhere. Onion, a clove of garlic, broken-up sausage, sheep ricotta and parmigiano. Very simple. Then pollo alla cacciatora, a dish you can find everywhere in Italy, but every region has a different version of it. Ours adds a few capers and anchovies."

"Ah, that explains the tang."

"And lemon."

"Sounds wonderful."

Nelli slipped out of the kitchen with napkins, cutlery and plates clasped against her chest. Nico stood to help. She shook her head. "Maria Grazia, please forgive Nico. He loves hearing about food, but I know he's holding his breath for news about Eddi."

Nico gave Nelli a grateful smile and sat back down.

"Oh, sorry." She stirred the smaller pot. "I did talk to him, said what you asked me to say. I don't think he even blinked. He calmly stated you are lying to trick him into meeting you. He was in bed with his girlfriend when his father was killed. That is what he told Maresciallo Fabbri, and the girlfriend confirmed it."

She could have been fast asleep, Nico thought, *or lied*. "She broke up with him soon after that night."

Nelli looked up from setting the table with her mismatched plates. "What a terrible thing to do! He'd just lost his father."

Maria Grazia threw two scoopfuls of sheep ricotta into a small pot. "That surprises me. Eddi came with her a few times, hoping I would check a few passages of her translation of Seneca's *De Ira*. An interesting essay to pick given the anger Eddi has shown lately. If she broke up with him at such a bad moment, there must be a good reason. She was very sweet, polite. Very grateful for the few suggestions I made. Her translation was almost impeccable."

"So that's it," Nico said, regret in his voice.

"No, I reminded him that you were a New York City detective with a lot of experience, and if you lied, it showed how very anxious you were to meet him. Was he not curious to know why? '*You are obviously very important to him.*' After a couple of beats, he said he would let me know and hung up."

"That was clever of you."

"Young people so often hunger to count, to be important. I will talk to him again, mention what happened to your car. He might just feel guilty."

Nico hoped so. "The portrait is finished then?"

"Almost," Nelli said.

"Can I see it?"

"Nelli will not even let me see it." Maria Grazia threw the penne into the boiling water. "Now, please, I would enjoy a glass of your red wine."

Nelli handed him a glass. Nico poured the wine he'd bought from Lenzi's cousin. "Autumn with a taste of oak from the Carucci Vineyard." He filled two more glasses.

The three of them toasted. "Alla salute!"

ELEVEN

The next morning Nico was sitting with Perillo and Daniele in a corner of the small café bar near the carabinieri station in Greve, filling them in on yesterday's Pitigliano visit. Only two customers were still having coffee at the counter. OneWag was resting at Nico's feet after having cleaned the floor of sugar crumbs. It was past nine o'clock. The early morning coffee rush was over.

"I thanked Debora for telling me her story and for answering all my questions," Nico said. "She said I could thank her by finding the real culprit."

Perillo put his espresso cup upside down in its saucer, a signal to himself not to order a third espresso. "I cannot begin to envision being hunted down like a wild animal."

"Hunted and killed," Nico added.

Perillo turned to Daniele, who had just stopped himself from making the sign of the cross. "That's right, Dani. Where was your God, then? Eh? Sunday at Mass, ask him. If he comes up with a believable answer, let me know."

Daniele's face paled. "I pray that it never happen again," Daniele said. "Not to anyone."

"Let's hope," Nico said, knowing that hope was useless. His job had showed him how much hate could exist in only one person. Hate multiplied was overpowering, uncontrollable.

Perillo raised two crossed fingers. "I also hope Debora does not end up regretting convincing Saverio to run away."

"She will not," Daniele said, color coming back to his cheeks. "Nico will find the real murderer." He looked at Nico across the table. "Who else did you see?"

Nico told them about running into Angela Rossi and finding out Leo, her nephew, had seen Eddi in front of the LenConi store the night Lenzi was killed.

Perillo let out a whistle. "Patricide! It would explain his ranting about Saverio's guilt on social media."

"And his damaging your car," Daniele added.

"Maybe." Nico pushed his half-finished Americano away from him. The coffee at Bar All'Angolo was much better. "I still have to find out at what time Leo saw Eddi at the store."

"Whether he saw his father dead or alive?"

"That's right, Dani."

Perillo popped a piece of his half-eaten pastry in his mouth. "And Necchi's wife? Did you get anything useful from her?"

"She's very beautiful, flirted with me. I don't know if she always acts that way with men or if she was trying to distract me. She had an affair with Lenzi, says she got bored and ended it. She doesn't think much of her husband but doesn't think he has the balls to kill his cousin. She has no alibi."

"What about Lenzi's housekeeper?" Perillo asked. "When are you seeing her?"

"I called her on the way home last night, hoping to see her today."

"And?"

"'*Ah, finally!*' was her first comment after I explained who I was. She said she felt snubbed."

"She is eager to see you." The rest of the pastry went into Perillo's mouth.

Nico smiled. "Eager only if I pay for her time. She claimed she gets paid fifty euros an hour. I said I would check with Annamaria Lenzi. She quickly changed her rate to thirty an hour. Still high, but I accepted."

"What did you hope to find out from her?" Daniele asked.

"She cleans the Lenzi household and the store. I'm hoping she's witnessed or overheard things that might help."

Perillo was frowning in disapproval. "Thirty euros an hour? You are being robbed."

"I doubt she has even an hour of information."

"She will drown your ears with a cascade of nonsense if not downright lies just to keep the clock ticking. Fabbri did not bother to interview her."

Perillo's negativity didn't surprise Nico, but he found himself saying, "Since when do you respect how Fabbri has handled this case?"

Perillo's face sagged. "You are right. I do not. But I am worried about you. I do not trust Livia."

"I'm seeing her during her lunch break today. I want to find out more about her relationship with Lenzi."

Perillo shook his head. "For all you know, she could be the one who used that hammer."

Daniele jumped in. "She would have a good motive if Lenzi forced her to have sex with him."

Perillo reached out and touched Daniele's arm. "Thank you, Dani, for backing me up. I know you do not believe that and maybe I do not either." He sat back and dropped his hands on his knees. "All is quiet at the station which should please me, but instead it makes me feel useless. I am becoming a crotchety old man."

"Crotchety or not," Nico said, "fifty is not old and you will never be useless." Perillo's bad mood was perfectly understandable. He was used to being the top dog. He had to resent that the man he'd convinced to help him with previous murders now worked on one out of his jurisdiction. Ivana was busy with her Alba's Cantuccini job. Daniele had Stella to fill his thoughts. "I depend on your opinion and your friendship, Perillo. Capito?"[15]

Keeping his head low, Perillo nodded.

"I do too, Maresciallo," Daniele said in a burst of enthusiasm.

Perillo slowly raised his large dark eyes at his brigadiere. "From you it is expected. I am your boss."

Expecting friendship from a junior officer was a bit much, Nico thought but did not say. Daniele's response was the usual blush.

Nico stood up. "See you two tonight." Stella was giving a housewarming party at her new apartment. "What should I bring, Dani?"

Daniele clasped his hands together as if in prayer. "Please, nothing. Even Tilde is not allowed to bring anything. Stella wants the party to be all her own doing."

Perillo nodded slowly in approval. "A proud woman."

Daniele beamed a lovesick smile.

"WHERE ARE WE GOING?" Livia asked as they left the Coop with OneWag.

"Where do you usually eat?" Nico asked.

She crossed the street to look out on the Golden Valley now covered with vineyards instead of wheat fields. It was another mild day. A few clouds dropped puffy flat shadows on the land, adding curves to the linear pattern of the vineyards. "I park here instead of in the parking lot so I can look out. It is such a gentle

---

15 Understood?

view. I love how far the eye can wander here. In Pitigliano I'm surrounded by tufa ridges. Beautiful green covered ones mostly but sometimes I feel hemmed in." She ran a hand through her red curls. "Or maybe the view has nothing to do with it." She turned to Nico with a smile on her face. A first. "The Coop salumiere makes me a sandwich and I eat it at home." The Coop didn't reopen until four.

"How about Da Gino up in the piazza for something warm?"

"That would be a nice change, but I'm not walking up all those park stairs. My car or yours?"

"Yours. Mine is kaput." The 500 was still in the shop; Ivana's new car hadn't been delivered to the car dealer yet and Nelli had needed her car to get to work. He had said nothing to Livia about the damage to his Fiat 500. She had enough to worry about.

"Cilia made something for Rocco," Livia said as soon as all three were in her old metallic-blue Fiat Punto. "Look in the glove compartment. A foil package." She drove out of the parking lot and up the steep hill that led to the main piazza and Da Gino. A gray Citroën pulled out and followed. "There's cretino[16] number two. He has the day shift. You know Fabbri sent two men to watch me?"

"So I've heard."

"You could have told me."

"You probably knew before I did."

"Yes, thanks to Luciana."

As soon as Nico opened the compartment OneWag stretched up, both paws on Nico's knees, and sniffed. "Get down!" Nico held the package away from the dog. "What is it?"

"Homemade treats made by Cilia with a little help from her

---

16 Idiot.

mother. Carrots, zucchini, an egg, yogurt, whole wheat flour. Very healthy and easy. She found the recipe on the internet."

"How sweet of her. Thank her and thank you." He opened the package and held out a large wobbly shaped biscuit. OneWag gently took it from his hand and dropped back down.

"Cilia is sweet, generous, stubborn, bright," Livia said over the sound of crunching. "And so much happier after talking to Babbo."

"You smiled today."

"Did I?"

"Yes."

Livia swung into the piazza and parked at the far end. "His phone calls have helped lift some of my gloom. I am hoping you have good news."

They got out of the car as the gray Citroën was looking to park. There were no spaces left. OneWag jumped out with the uneaten biscuit between his teeth. "I only have more questions," Nico said, "and I need you to answer them honestly."

They walked across the piazza. "I have not lied to you," Livia said.

"You've omitted information."

"I am not used to baring my life. I do not like it when others do it either. Stefano wanted to know every thought in my head, loved to jabber about whatever popped in his head. I wanted to tape his mouth shut. Saverio is a quiet man. He's happy with a quiet woman."

Nico raised a hand to Gustavo and his bench friends. All three were covered in heavy wool from head to toe.

"Ciao, Nico." Gustavo raised his cap. "Buongiorno, Signora. La piccola Cilia, how is she?"

Livia stopped, turned her head. "She's in school."

"How is she," Gustavo tapped his heart, "here?"

Livia's face tightened. "Doing her best." She hurried toward the restaurant.

"Do not worry," Gustavo called out to her back. "Nico will make you both happy."

OneWag dropped Cilia's biscuit behind Gustavo's bench and followed Nico, who led Livia to the back of the restaurant. Customers preferred to sit in the light that came from the large picture window next to the front door, so the back area was empty.

Enzo's daughter brought a menu. They both ordered pasta e fagioli. Enzo made the best pasta and beans soup Nico had ever tasted, even better than Ivana's. No wine for either of them. It would only slow up the questions and answers.

Livia picked up a breadstick. "What is it you need to know?"

"Your relationship with Lenzi after you got together with Saverio."

"There was no sex if that is what you're asking."

"What made you stop seeing Lenzi?"

"I met Savi, fell in love and told Giancarlo our little secret get-togethers were over."

"How did he react?"

"He did not believe me. A natural reaction for a vain man, I think."

"What did Lenzi do before he started the electronics store?"

"He did the accounts for Annamaria's pharmacy."

"When did he offer Saverio a partnership in the store, before you broke up with him or after?"

"After." It took Livia a moment to catch on. "You think I was the reason?"

"Could be. Saverio was living and working in a successful electronics store in Orvieto, then he falls in love with you. Lenzi wants you to stay close and gets the idea of starting an electronics store with his old best friend Saverio."

"Maybe." She played with a breadstick. "He kept saying he was in love with me. I did not believe him—and didn't care. If he really was, what does it change?"

"Did he ever pressure you to give in or grope you, kiss you?"

"He tried, but I never told Savi. It never happened when he was around." The breadstick snapped. "You are not trying to—"

Gino's daughter lowered the bowls of pasta e fagioli in front of them, added a swirl of olive oil on each and a good dusting of Parmigiano-Reggiano.

"Grazie." Nico waited until she was gone. "I'm not looking for a motive for Saverio. He has one already. There are other people who might be jealous or angry."

She dipped her spoon in the thick soup, stirred and ate. "Buono! You mean Annamaria?"

"And Susanna Necchi. She had an affair with him."

"That is why I put her on the list. Have you talked to her?"

"Yes." Nico joined her in eating. "Did you confide in anyone about Lenzi making passes at you?"

"No, but one evening this summer Giancarlo was waiting for me when I came out of the panetteria where I worked. He pushed me against the wall, put his hand between my legs. I kicked him in the groin and he stumbled away. Unfortunately, Paolo, my neighbor, was coming toward me with Cilia. Luckily, she was playing with Cippi and didn't see anything." She went back to the soup.

"But Paolo did."

"He pretended he didn't, but I could see he was upset. He walked me home with Cilia and insisted on staying with us until Savi walked in."

"Does Paolo always pick you up at work with Cilia?"

"Whenever Cilia is bored with the game she is playing. Paolo's job at city hall ends at two-thirty and he's been babysitting Cilia weekday afternoons since she was six months old. He is a blessing."

"You're very close?"

They spoke between hurried spoonfuls of pasta e fagioli.

"Close in an old-fashioned, respectful way. Paolo keeps a certain distance, always fearful of intruding, but I can depend on him for anything that has to do with Cilia. She calls him Zio Paolo and now that we are here, they talk on the phone almost every night. She knows she must not mention Babbo calling."

"Good." Nico ate the last of the soup. "I need to talk to Saverio."

Livia looked up, the full spoon halfway to her mouth. "Why?"

"Because Giancarlo and Saverio were good friends from way back, because they worked together, because he will know things about Giancarlo that no one else knows. I need help, Livia. I have too many people with motive and not an ounce of proof against a single one."

"Savi calls me. He won't give me his number."

"Next time you talk, set up a time in the evening and I'll come over. I'll bring Rocco for Cilia."

Instead of answering, Livia scraped her bowl clean.

"Please, Livia. For Cilia's sake."

She answered with a slow nod. Then, "Thank you for lunch."

"You're welcome."

ON THE DRIVE TO Livia's apartment there was no sign of the gray Citroën. As they reached her building, Nico's phone rang. He didn't recognize the number. "Nico Doyle."

"Ah, buongiorno. I am Angela Rossi."

"Buongiorno. You have news for me?"

"Yes. Where are you?"

"In Gravigna."

"Ah, what a shame."

"Can't you tell me over the phone?"

"Well, yes, I can tell you what my nephew found out, but I have someone with me with information she is not convinced she should tell you. You can convince her."

"I can be in Pitigliano tomorrow."

Livia parked and opened the door. The motor was still running. "You're wasting time. Take my car now, Nico. Go!" She jumped out and ran to her building.

"Signora Rossi, I can be there in two hours."

"That is driving too fast. In two and a half hours or thereabouts, you will find us at Mariella's café. Don't worry if you are late. I will keep Bianca happy with hot chocolate and cake."

"What did your nephew tell you?"

"I will tell you when you are here. First drive safely."

As Nico drove up the hill to hit Route 222, the gray Citroën passed him on the way down. Nico waved. The Citroën screeched to a halt. Nico kept going, without bothering to check his rearview mirror.

ANGELA ROSSI RAISED HER hand when Nico walked into the café. She was sitting at a window table next to a young woman.

Nico approached the table. "I hope you haven't been waiting too long." He'd been delayed. Just before reaching the ticket booth for the autostrada, he had spotted the gray Citroën following him. Remembering how he'd hated that job the few times he'd been stuck with it, he'd pulled over, gotten out of the car to show the poor man he'd made a mistake. With car horns blaring, the Citroën did an illegal U-turn and was off back to Gravigna. He took advantage of his stop by calling Giulia Favelli, hoping she'd see him after Angela Rossi. She kept him on the phone with a million excuses as to why she couldn't see him today. They made a date for the next day, Friday. In Gravigna.

Angela's red lips widened into smile. Her matching red coat was draped over her shoulders. "I am happy you drove sensibly. I saved you a slice of Mariella's cake."

"Thank you." Nico sat down facing the two women and extended his hand to the young woman, who couldn't have been twenty yet. She was clearly nervous. "Ciao. Nico Doyle and this is Rocco." He hoped his having a dog would reassure her.

She pressed her lips together, glanced at OneWag checking out her sneakers. She was blandly pretty, with long light-brown hair, the ends dyed purple. She was wearing jeans with striped leg warmers and a short sheepskin jacket that matched her eyes—the color of barely steeped tea.

Angela gave the woman's hand an encouraging pat. "Bianca was Eddi's girlfriend until a few weeks ago."

OneWag sniffed her sneakers. Bianca tucked her feet underneath the chair.

Okay, Nico thought, *the dog didn't help.* "Now you're with Leo?"

Bianca shrugged. "We're friends."

"And you told him something," Angela prompted.

Bianca tossed her hair from one shoulder to the next, a scowl on her face. "I don't know why Leo told you. It was private!"

"Leo is a good lad. He understood it was important."

"No, he's just jealous of Eddi." Bianca looked as if she might cry.

Angela scoffed. "Why should he be? Bianca, you're not reasoning. Nico already knows that Leo saw Eddi at his father's store that night." She turned to face Nico. "Leo's friends told him he left the party a few minutes before three-thirty."

Lenzi was dead by then. "How can they be so sure?"

"Because a few minutes later the upstairs neighbors paid a visit saying either everybody went home, or they were going to call the carabinieri. The party broke up right after that." Angela nudged Bianca with her elbow. "Go on, tell him."

Bianca widened her eyes at Nico. "Is Eddi going to get into trouble?"

"At three-thirty his father was already dead," Nico said.

Bianca's eyebrows met. "Oh, that's good, isn't it?"

"For Eddi, yes." *Unless he visited his father earlier, hit him, panicked, then went back to check if he was dead.* "What did you tell Leo?"

"Eddi made me lie to the maresciallo about being with him that night."

"You weren't with him at all?"

"I thought I was going to spend the night with him. His mother has let him take over the space in the back of the house where they used to store stuff they didn't need. A lot of the medieval houses have these storage spaces. Eddi made it really comfortable with electricity and all."

Nico hoped the *and all* included a bathroom. "Go on."

"I met him at the entrance after I had dinner with my parents. They were really happy I was with Eddi because his family is so prominent. I didn't care. I just liked being with him. He was fun until he wasn't."

Angela reached out her fork and quietly picked at the slice of cake she had reserved for Nico.

"What happened that night?" Nico asked.

Bianca rubbed her nose. "He was all nerves, in a bad mood. I might as well not have been there for all the attention I got. His parents had been fighting. It was happening a lot, according to Eddi. He couldn't stand it, always wants Mamma to be happy. It's like he's in love with her. We drank some, smoked some, but it didn't help. I finally got annoyed and went home. Next morning, he calls and tells me his father is dead and I have to say we spent the whole night together."

"You didn't ask why?"

"Yeah, I did. He said he didn't want his mother to worry about his whereabouts." Bianca's eyebrows shot up. "Like she could ever think her golden boy had done something wrong, like kill his father!" Her face relaxed. "I guess he was really upset. I played along because I know he didn't kill his father."

"How do you know?"

"I just do. I mean more than once, when I was in their house, I caught him watching his father with this adoring, hungry look on his face. Your dog probably looks at you like that when he wants you to pet him." She picked up her backpack from the floor and woke up OneWag. He'd been leaning on it. "Oh, sorry. So now you know I lied, but I'm glad I did. Eddi's an okay guy when things are good. I need to get home now."

"Thank you for telling me," Nico said.

Angela clasped Bianca's arm. "Grazie, cara, grazie. Leo is so lucky. You are wonderful."

Bianca stood up, shook her arm free. She was halfway out the door when she turned around and strode back with an angry face. "If you try to pin his father's murder on Eddi, I'll deny everything!" Without waiting for an answer, she walked out.

Angela picked up her fork again and pulled Nico's plate closer to her. "Leo never has liked them too bright, but she's sweet."

Nico didn't comment. He was annoyed with Signora Angela Rossi. She wasn't very nice, and she'd made him drive for over two hours for no good reason. He watched her attack the plate. It didn't take long. "Why did you insist Bianca admit she'd lied to Maresciallo Fabbri? Thanks to Leo, we already knew Eddi hadn't spent the whole night with her."

She put her fork on the empty plate. With a paper napkin she carefully cleaned her lips without smudging the red lipstick. "I was worried that Leo dating Eddi's ex-girlfriend could make you doubt he's telling the truth. Now I know you believe him."

She had a point. Nico stood up. "It's also time for me to go home." He picked up the check.

Angela's eyes brightened. "Oh, how kind of you." OneWag stretched.

"My pleasure. Arrivederci." He paid at the counter and walked out with his dog.

WHEN NELLI, NICO AND OneWag walked in, Stella spread out her arms with a radiant face. "Benvenuti!"

They hugged and kissed Stella. OneWag wiggled in greeting. "I'll take your coats," Daniele said. "They'll be in the bedroom." Curious, Nelli followed him into a small room with a queen-size bed that only left room for a nightstand and a chair. Another "Welcome" from Stella took them back into the living room.

Her family had walked in.

"What possessed you?" Elvira managed to say between heaving breaths. Stella's apartment was a third-floor walk-up in an old building overlooking the cemetery.

Stella hugged her grandmother. "Nonna, on a teacher's salary I can't afford an elevator building."

"Not the stairs! The dead! So close. They could haunt you."

"Now, Mamma, you know that's not true." Enzo took his mother's elbow and steered her to the two-seater sofa, the only furniture in the room besides a round table laden with colorful crostini and paper cups.

Stella took the cups of Prosecco Daniele had quickly poured and gave one to Elvira. "I am not afraid of ghosts, Nonna."

"Well, I am. I have heard stories. Many stories."

Stella sat next to her. "Tell me."

Elvira unbuttoned her coat. "I cannot remember right now. I am too upset. And you should know better than to wear jeans and a scruffy sweater to your own party. Tilde should have taught you how to dress properly."

Stella shut her up by flinging her arms around her again. "Oh, Nonna, I love you!"

While Stella coddled her grandmother, Tilde, Nico and Nelli kissed cheeks. "She's upset her home is no longer Stella's love nest," Tilde said, "and naturally, everything is my fault."

"What about you?" Nelli asked. "Won't you miss not having Stella at home?"

Tilde pressed her lips together before saying, "Deeply, but I am proud of Stella. She did this on her own. We offered to help. '*No, it's time to be an adult*,' she said. She is right and I will eventually get used to having a grown-up daughter without feeling old."

Nelli squeezed Tilde's hand. "You cannot afford to feel old running a restaurant."

"I miss having Nico in the kitchen with me."

"Tilde, I told you," Nico said, "anytime you need me, just call."

"I do not need you during the winter, but I still miss you. It is more fun when we try to outdo each other. Have you had time to come up with a new recipe?"

"No." Once Pitigliano was over, he was going to experiment with Maria Grazia's Umbrian chicken cacciatore dish. If it was ever over.

Laura walked into the apartment with a terra-cotta vase holding two amaryllis buds pushing out of the soil. Perillo and Ivana were right behind her. "Luciana promised the flowers would be red. I know, I was not supposed to bring anything."

Ivana held up a tin box of Alba's cantuccini and a bottle of Vin Santo. "No one told me."

Stella kissed the new arrivals. "Thank you. I love it all."

Perillo whispered to Nico. "News?"

"Some. Not now."

Tilde took the vase and put it on the table with the food and wine. "Flowers are always welcome."

Stella added Ivana's gift to the table, then picked up the amaryllis plant and placed it on the floor below the only window. "Scusa, Mamma, not next to the food."

Nico noticed Tilde exchange glances with Nelli. Boundaries were being set.

"When?" Perillo asked Nico. Ivana tugged Perillo's sleeve. "You're being rude."

"Tomorrow." Nico joined Nelli, who was helping Daniele distribute paper cups filled with Prosecco.

Enzo raised his. "To my beautiful daughter. I wish you happiness here." His voice broke.

"Not with the dead next door," Elvira piped in.

Enzo raised his cup higher. "Please remember you will always have a home with us."

Stella hugged him. "Babbo, I know that. Everyone, please eat. It took me all afternoon to put this together. I wanted to make a few cicchetti Veneziani to celebrate Dani, but they all seem to have meat or fish."

"I thought we were here to celebrate your new apartment." This time Perillo got an elbow poke from Ivana.

Stella's face broke out into a wide smile. "Yes, we are." She turned to look at everyone in the room. "Dani has a lot to do with my setting off on my own. I know his job as a carabiniere does not permit him to move in with me." Dani, standing just behind Stella, was turning purple. "And if we want to get married, we have to wait until he turns twenty-six."

"Be thankful," Perillo interrupted. "I had to wait until I was twenty-seven."

Elvira, still seated on the couch, raised her arm. "At my house you had clean sheets every time."

A frustrated look crossed over Stella's face. "Nonna, you were wonderful, and I cannot thank you enough for letting Dani and me be together in your home."

Elvira accepted the thanks with a grunt and a nod.

"What I am trying to explain is that, yes, having my own apartment makes intimacy much easier." Stella took Dani's hand and pulled him next to her. "I love this man. He loves me back. Feeling that has made me want to create a home. Now it's mostly for myself. One day, it will be with him. I probably would have eventually done this without Dani being in my life, but I did it now thanks to him."

With tears in her eyes, Tilde crossed the room and hugged her daughter. "And I thought I had raised a feminist." Enzo joined in the hugging.

"What about us?" Nico asked. It became a noisy hug fest for a few minutes. OneWag retreated to sit on the sofa with Nonna.

Nonna gave her guest a pat on his paw. "You are a sensible dog."

An hour or so later, Enzo took Nonna home. Nelli offered to help clean up. Tilde shooed her way. As soon as the door closed on Nelli and Nico's back, Tilde picked up two empty cups.

Stella took them from her. "Thank you, Mamma. Dani and I can manage."

A small gasp escaped Tilde's mouth. She tried to cover it up with a smile. "Of course. Enzo will be waiting for me."

Stella saw the pained expression on her mother's face and hugged her. "I'm sorry, Mamma."

Tilde took her daughter's face in her two hands. "Don't be." She kissed Stella's forehead. "It is life in the right direction. Ciao, bella mia. Dani." She kissed his cheeks, then with a laugh in her voice, said, "Don't stay up too late, Stella. You have school tomorrow." Stella and Dani laughed with her.

NELLI WRAPPED HER ARM in Nico's as they walked back to the car. OneWag, knowing the destination, had gone ahead. "They looked so happy."

"They are."

"They're young."

Nico stopped. "What do you mean by that?"

"Just that. They are twenty-three years old."

"Do you think it's easier to be happy at that age?"

"They are full of hope."

"At fifty-four I am still full of hope," Nico said. "Aren't you?"

"Yes. I hope my portrait of Maria Grazia will be a fine one, but that's because experience has told me there is a good chance it will be fine. You hope you will solve the Saverio case, but you also know you are good at solving cases. For Stella and Daniele, it's all new. They don't have experience to back them up. Scary."

"And exhilarating."

"That too."

"Are you envying their youth?"

"No, I was miserable at that age. I am worried about us."

Nico went cold. "Go on."

"You want me to live with you."

"I do, but I have accepted the fact that you don't want to."

Nelli dropped her head on his shoulder. They continued walking. "I want you to be happy."

"I am happy, just greedy."

"And I am stubborn."

Nico put his arm around her waist. "We'll manage."

Managing was a poor substitute for fulfillment, Nelli thought. Nico deserved happiness. She was more than stubborn. She was selfish. Wanted everything her way. Why was that? There had been a few lovers in her life, but she had never lived with any of them. None had lasted more than a couple of years, and the decision to part had been mostly theirs. *You don't pay enough attention to me. Your thoughts are always elsewhere.* At least Nico had made it clear he didn't want her to get involved with his detective work and he knew she was hopeless in the kitchen. What he wanted was proof she loved him. Moving in with him would be that proof.

She did love him.

WITH TILDE GONE, THE table cleared, the dishwasher running and the floor swept, Dani and Stella sat down on the sofa, holding hands.

"No hesitations?" Dani asked.

"About you, none. And you?"

"None."

"Why did you ask?"

"You went to Florence and studied hard to get an art degree. You got a job in a great museum right away. I worry that you could regret giving that up. Now you teach kids how to draw."

"I'm sure there will be times when I'll wonder what my career would have been like. I think that's natural. But I came back not only because of you. I love this town. I missed being here and"—she slapped Dani's thigh—"I don't only teach kids how to draw. I open their eyes, and, I hope, their hearts to the beauty that surrounds us in nature and art. Lecture over. Let's go to bed."

"Whatever you wish," Dani replied happily.

TWELVE

The next morning no clouds were in the sky. Nico had his usual breakfast with Nelli and Gogol at Bar All'Angolo and then, with OneWag tucked under his arm, took the bus to Greve and picked up a white Ford Fiesta rental. Back in Gravigna, he parked the car behind the butcher shop and walked to the main piazza where he was to meet Giulia Favelli in half an hour.

"Salve, Nico," a bundled-in-scarves Gustavo called out from on his bench. "Is there music in your ears, amico?"

"Not yet." Sitting next to the old man was a full-figured woman wrapped in a knit coat bordered with fake fur, with a fuzzy pink hat on her head. She had her eyes closed and held her face up to catch the sun.

"I have been satisfying this young woman's curiosity about our resident detective. I told her only the good things."

"Thank you and buongiorno." OneWag had reached the bench first and was busy sniffing the woman's boots. He smelled bleach.

Nico approached Gustavo and his new bench mate. "Signora Favelli?"

She slowly lowered her face. Wide, black-lined amber eyes looked up at Nico. She wore no other makeup.

Nico extended a hand. She shook it with her fingertips. Nico was surprised by the very long pink nails. "It's Signorina and Giulia."

"Glad to meet you, Giulia." He hoped she wasn't upset. Tilde had told him that women over thirty were usually referred to as Signora. "I'm Nico."

"Who else?" She noticed OneWag getting a scratching from Gustavo. "Oh carino! Can I pet him?"

"He'd love it."

"Rocco is with me now," Gustavo grumbled.

"Of course." Giulia gave Nico a raised-eyebrow look. "Here I am. What do you want to know from me?"

"I thought we could go to the café and talk."

The black eyebrows descended into a frown. "But it is such a beautiful day. Why can't we stay here?"

"If you wish. We can go over to the other bench."

Gustavo flung an errant scarf back across his shoulder and straightened up. "No worries. I am leaving. I have no interest in detective chatter and Signorina Giulia, you can now pet Rocco as long as you like. You may get fleas."

"Gustavo!" Nico protested. "He has no fleas."

With a chuckle, Gustavo lifted himself off the bench and tilted his hat at Giulia. "Signorina, the detective always knows best. I bid you good day."

Giulia grinned. "Ciao e grazie."

Gustavo ambled in the direction of home. Nico sat down next to Giulia. "What did he tell you?"

She picked up OneWag and put him on her lap. He sniffed at her face. So many different new smells. He ventured a lick on her chin. Giulia laughed. "Yes, I love you too, Rocco." She held him in a hug. "Il vecchio[17] thinks you are a good, honest gentleman and a healthy addition to the town. He instructed me to answer all your questions with honesty."

OneWag squirmed, and she soon put him back on the ground.

"He seems very worried about Cilia," Giulia said, watching OneWag wander off. "I met her only once when Saverio brought her to the store early. She looks like such a sweet little thing. How is she doing? She must be so unhappy."

"You'll have to ask Livia. Are you going to see each other?"

"Il vecchio told me she works at the Coop."

"Il vecchio has a name: Gustavo."

"Well, he is old. When I'm done with you, I'll pop in the Coop and surprise her."

"Is that the best idea?"

"Better than Livia hanging up on me. Listen, first thing I want you to know is I don't want you to pay me for my time. I was just testing how serious you were about helping Saverio. Go ahead, ask what you want. Who knows, I might lead you straight to the real killer."

"You think Saverio is innocent."

"I think it, but I don't know it. Livia hired you thinking she knows. Only Saverio knows."

"And the real killer. What happened between you and Livia?"

Giulia wrapped her arms around her waist. "We were close since lower school. She was different. I got curious, a little envious of what I thought was her *don't give a damn* attitude. She kept to herself during break, let the other kids call her 'figlia di puttana'[18] and 'bastarda,' asking her if she knew who her father was. One time I joined them." Giulia's leg started

---

17 Old man.
18 Daughter of a whore.

swinging. "I insulted her to get a reaction. I wanted her to put up a fight, insult us back." She shook a hand in the air. "Madonna mia, I've kicked boys in the crotch for rolling their eyes at me. Livia paid no attention to the insults. She kept reading her book or working on her homework. The next day I sat next to her at lunch and apologized. That's how we became friends.

"We stayed close even after she got married. We were different, me always opening my mouth, Livia always careful, but we usually saw things in the same way. That started changing when she left Stefano. I thought she was making a big mistake and told her. The man adored her. Still does, I think. It was so dumb of her. She was safe with Stefano. Livia was always worried about turning into her poor mother who had the worst luck with men, and what does my best friend do? She walks out on a good man and then lets Giancarlo get into her panties. You know they had an affair, don't you?"

"Yes, I do."

"'*What is a married man going to get you?*' I asked her. Some fun and excitement maybe, a trinket or two but then? He gets bored or the wife finds out." Her hands did a dance as she spoke. "How do you get your dignity back from there? '*I've been there,*' I told her. '*Don't do it. Stick with what is solid.*' She told me to mind my own affairs. After that we didn't see each other for a bit."

"Do you know how long her affair with Giancarlo lasted?"

"Yes, we were still more or less friends. Two months or so, I think. On her birthday we went to Orvieto and ran into Saverio, a friend of my brother's. I guess lightning struck and zapped Giancarlo out. Once Saverio moved back here and in with Livia I was shut out. She had no use for me anymore."

"Were you angry?"

She bobbed her head a few times before answering. "Angry, disappointed, sad. All of that. Then you get over it. I was going to call her after Saverio ran off, but I was afraid she would think

I was gloating. And maybe just a little ugly part of myself was thinking *serves you right*. I should thank you for giving me the excuse to come here and face her." Giulia looked up at the sky. A spool of clouds was taking its time crossing over the sun. She pulled her coat tighter. "A cup of tea would be nice."

"Good idea," Nico said. His rear end had gotten cold from the bench. "We only have to cross the piazza. And if you're hungry, Jimmy, one of the owners, bakes schiacciatine that he stuffs with what the morning inspires."

Giulia stood up with a gleam in her eye. "I had to skip my cornetto this morning." They started crossing the piazza. "I didn't know how long it would take me to get here."

Before entering Bar All'Angolo, Nico whistled. The florist's door opened and OneWag ran out to join them. Luciana put her hennaed head out the door. She held up a finger. "Nico, please, give me a minute. It is important."

Nico noticed her worried expression. "I'll be right there, Luciana."

"Could not stay away, eh?" Sandro joked when Nico walked in with Giulia and OneWag.

"The sun disappeared. Giulia, meet Stefano and Jimmy, the two men who get me started in the morning."

Giulia nodded her greeting. Stefano raised a hand as he rang up an order.

"Benvenuta," Jimmy said from the far end of the counter. He was polishing his huge espresso machine.

Nico steered Giulia to a table in the far corner. "Order what you like. I'll be right back."

LUCIANA SAT HERSELF DOWN on a stool as soon as Nico and OneWag walked into the shop. "Thank you for coming, Nico. I have been looking out for you all morning." Luciana refused to use cell phones, convinced they would give her brain cancer.

"What's wrong?"

"Cilia. A few days ago she was happily drawing flowers. Yesterday the whole time she was with me, she sat staring at nothing. She has every reason to be upset, but she was doing so well before. I tried everything. Offered her cookies, showed her different flowers to draw, sang her the songs my mother used to sing to me. They made her cry. She kept repeating she wants to go home. Not home here. Pitigliano. I don't know how to help her."

"Did you tell Livia?"

"I tried last night when I brought Cilia home. She was surprised for a second, then acted as though she did not believe me. Shooed me away with '*Thank you so much. I am very grateful.*' She is so grateful she has never invited me in." Luciana's hand fluttered to her mouth, chagrin all over her face. "Please forgive me. I am being unkind. I cannot even begin to imagine what she is going through. And poor little Cilia. She is a rosebud wanting to bloom."

"You have been wonderful, Luciana. Livia has told me how grateful she is. I'll talk to Livia and see what more we can do to help them."

"Please do. I so want Cilia to be happy."

"So do I. Ciao, I have someone waiting for me."

Luciana's eyes lit up with her usual curiosity. "A new friend?"

"No. I will talk to you later."

BACK IN THE CAFÉ Nico saw that Giulia had not ordered anything. "What inspiration did the morning bring today?" he asked Jimmy.

"I have no more wheat cornetti, but if you want a stuzzichino,[19]

---

19 Snack.

I have schiacciatine with smoked salmon over stracciatella, tuna with artichokes and the usual prosciutto."

Giulia chose the salmon sandwich with tea, Nico his usual Americano. He waited for Giulia to take a few sips before asking, "How long have you worked for the Lenzi household?"

"Ah!" She wiped her mouth with the miniscule paper napkin the café offered. "You want me to share the household dirt with you."

"Is there dirt?"

"Enough to plant a tree, I would bet. Not that I know much. Annamaria's family goes back to the Middle Ages. Mud Ages, I called it when I had to study that stuff in school. Annamaria hired me five years ago after sniffing me up and down and all over just like your dog's doing now to the floor. I guess she wanted to make sure I was clean. She told me I should thank Saverio for guaranteeing my honesty. I like to think it was Livia. Saverio and Giancarlo had just opened LenConi." She slipped out of her coat and sat back. "The honesty guarantee did not work when Annamaria's sapphire pin went missing. Who else but the cleaning lady? I kept my job, thanks to Giancarlo. He used his usual charm to convince Annamaria she had lost the pin."

"You were on good terms with Giancarlo?"

"He found me useful. I kept my mouth shut. He did surprise me when he came so strongly to my defense. He had to work hard to convince Annamaria that I didn't take her dumb pin. Made me wonder if he had hocked it. Annamaria kept a tight grip on the family purse strings. His stealing money from the business did not surprise me. Sometimes he would ask me to lend him twenty or thirty, even fifty euros. He always paid me back quickly.

"Now the Lenzi dirt I know is the usual one. Husband who has an equal opportunity pecker, a wife who is too in love and too proud to kick him out and let the world know she made a mistake. One kid angry and rude, the other one a kitten you want to pick up and take home. I'm not being disrespectful by telling you any of this if it's going to help you clear Saverio. We were together for a while before he moved to Orvieto. Nothing earth-shattering." She shut her eyes for two seconds. "Wrong. I loved him, and, yes, I was jealous when he went for Livia. Maybe that's why she shut me out."

"You are answering a question I didn't ask."

"I know. Something about you makes me want to be honest with you and I guess with myself. It's funny the things you hide when it hurts."

Did it hurt enough to seek revenge? Nico wondered. "How often did you clean the office?"

"Two hours Monday morning was the established time. I had the keys. I was called back at least two or three more times a week to find the stapler or the invoice that needed to be paid or whatever Giancarlo couldn't find. I guess his mother never taught him to put things back in their place. I didn't mind. I like putting things in order. You should see the smudges the customers leave on the glass counter. They must wipe their hands on it. With a clean surface, all is good in the world." She twisted her mouth to one side. "I know, crazy. Well, that's how it makes me feel for a little bit. The more I clean the more it lasts.

"Maybe sometimes I went in just to say hello. Saverio always had a smile ready for me. When we were still in school—he was two years ahead of me—we both liked to walk home using the walkway. I pretended to be frightened to hold on to him." She looked up at Nico with a shy smile. "Silly girl stuff. Have you walked it?"

"Once. My dog ran ahead fearlessly. I held on to the banister."

"For me the view lifts my heart and stops it at the same time. Livia and I liked to run after each other up and down the passarella, screaming and laughing, no fear at all. That was before her mother jumped from there."

Livia had given him the impression her mother was still alive somewhere. "When was this?"

"We were both seventeen. The school principal called her into her office and told her. When she came back to class you wouldn't have known anything had happened. When I asked why she was called to the principal's office, she only said, '*My mother is dead.*' I found out it was suicide when I got home. The news spread quickly. She married Stefano six or eight months later. After her mother died, I kept wondering if she had been watching us run down the passarella, worried Livia might fall. Livia was pretty much on her own growing up and I guess I wanted to think her mother did care, just wasn't able to show it."

"Thank you for telling me." It helped explain why Livia hadn't been completely open with him. She must have formed the habit as a survival skill.

Giulia bit into the smoked salmon schiacciatina and chewed. Her eyes widened. "Mmm." She raised a thumb in approval and took the second and last bite. "That was good. I saw you and your dog in Piazza Petruccioli talking to Susanna Necchi the other day. I guess you know about her and Giancarlo."

"They were lovers for a couple of months."

"Is that what she told you?"

"It's not true?"

"She's off by a few years. Since shortly after the opening of LenConi. Beautiful women can get away with lying. I'm not being resentful." She ran a hand over her face. "Well, I guess I am. She is very beautiful, but also a bitch. Best you accept what I say about her with caution."

"How is she a bitch?"

"She tried to get me fired. She didn't want me to have the keys to the store. It meant I could walk in any time. I guess she was afraid I would rat to her husband. Not that he would have done anything about it. From what I hear, Signor Necchi is a limp man. At least she had the good sense not to offer me money. I would have thrown it back at her face. They liked to meet in Giancarlo's office with its two-seater pull-out sofa. I changed the sheets once a week."

"I'm surprised. I heard that Giancarlo was in love with Livia."

"In love? I never thought he had any love left over for anyone but himself." She let out a closed-mouth breath. "I don't know why I'm surprised. Stefano and Saverio are in love with her, why not Giancarlo?"

Have you not been loved? Nico wanted to ask her. "Did you ever run into Livia in the store?"

"The store was closed on Monday mornings, but she used to come in with Saverio, who claimed he had something to take care of. I think he was worried I would mess up one of his fancy gadgets, but that's just me being paranoid. Livia and I exchanged hellos, how are you? Fine. Fine. Kiss kiss. Giancarlo would walk in later, Livia would leave and I would go back to cleaning. She stopped coming in after a few months, at least when I was there."

"Why do you think she stopped?"

Giulia pointed a finger at her chest. "Not because of me. I'm not that paranoid. I saw Giancarlo look at her, undressing her with his eyes, touching her arm or her hand when he said something to her. I knew he had wandering fingers. They'd wandered on me a few times. I didn't give him the satisfaction of noticing. Livia did notice. Her face told me she did not appreciate it."

"Did Saverio notice?"

"I thought men in love could be just as blind as women. At least for a while."

"What do you mean?"

"This summer Saverio asked me if I thought Giancarlo and

Livia were having an affair. I told him not even in a dream. I lashed out that if he thought Livia was cheating on him, he did not even have the palest idea of who she was, that he did not deserve her."

"What did you think?"

"I believed what I was saying, but I went and asked Livia anyway without mentioning Saverio. She turned to stone. '*You think like mother like daughter? Never!*' and stomped away. I should have known better. I guess I was still angry with her for pushing me away. I ran after her and apologized. She shrugged a shoulder at me and kept going. We haven't run into each other since."

"And now you want to surprise her?"

"I want to hug her and tell her how sorry I am for her and Saverio and Cilia. The only way I can do that is to surprise her."

"It is not the best way."

"Then you come with me. Tell her I'm answering all your questions."

Helping to restore a friendship was not part of the job, Nico thought, but if he could help, it would be a good thing. "I'll come with you, but I won't stay." He had a sandwich lunch date with Perillo and Daniele.

"Oh, grazie." Giulia leaped up and hugged him. "Grazie." OneWag started barking.

Nico freed himself and swooped up the dog with his arm. "Buddy, shush."

Giulia stretched out her arm and stroked the dog's long soft fur. "I wasn't going to hurt Nico." With head pulled back, OneWag didn't look convinced.

"Let's go back to Susanna Necchi." Nico put OneWag down. The dog stayed by his feet. "Do you know if her affair with Giancarlo had ended before he died?"

"It pays to be nosy, doesn't it?"

"When there's a murder involved, it can be helpful."

"Do you think I can have another schiacciatina?"

"Sure. Which kind?"

"I have never had tuna with artichokes."

Nico walked over to Jimmy at the far end.

"Give her two." Jimmy plated the schiacciatine. "If she doesn't like my tuna chopped with marinated artichokes, tomorrow's breakfast is paid for. And here are some plain schiacciata for Rocco. I like the way he looks out for Nelli's man."

"Come on, Jimmy, she was just thanking me."

"That's how it starts."

Nico frowned. Jimmy laughed. "Just a joke, Nico. You have been looking very serious these past mornings. Trust yourself. You will find the real killer."

"You know?"

"All of Gravigna knows what you are doing for la piccola. Gustavo is telling everyone." He handed Nico the filled plate. "Now go back to work. Nelli will not know from me."

Nico shook his head, took the plate and made his way back to the table. OneWag leapt up and caught the treat Nico tossed him. Giulia thanked him, tasted Jimmy's combination, and declared it *squisito* in a voice loud enough for Jimmy to hear.

His *grazie* came back just as loud.

One more bite and Giulia's first tuna and artichoke schiacciatina was gone. "Now back to dirt that might help you. Sometime before the store closed for two weeks this past August, I noticed the sheets on the office sofa were not used and the thong Susanna forgot the week before was still there. I had washed it, slipped it in an office envelope, left it on the sheet, and folded the bed. The sofa looked innocent again, not that Annamaria was ever going to walk into that store. She was against the idea of Giancarlo opening a business of his own from the beginning. While I was doing my job at that house—"

She sat back and eyed the second schiacciatina. "Now wouldn't you think someone with her family money would leave that damp, thick-walled building with three floors of worn stone stairs for a home surrounded by windows, a balcony and an elevator? That's what Giancarlo wanted. I heard more than one argument, in voices pitched low that carried more in that old moldy house than if they had yelled. She was proud to live in her family home, it held history, important history. Debora too. And she can barely get down the stairs to the front door! Madness!" She picked up the second schiacciatina.

Nico nudged her with, "You were saying that Annamaria was opposed to the store."

"You can bet on it. I work hard cleaning. I put my whole body into it, but my ears stay open. I had just started working for them. They argued, she saying he should use his money to invest in his cousin's vineyard, he saying that was putting money in the garbage. He was tired of working for her father, he wanted freedom. '*Freedom from what?*' she would yell back at him. Freedom from feeling grateful all the time, freedom to stand on his own ideas. '*I will never set foot in that store,*' she said once. I did not hear his answer." Giulia looked at the small sandwich in her hand. After two bites it was gone. She gave Nico a sheepish smile. "Where was I?"

"The sheet in the office was clean and Susanna's thong was still where you left it."

"The clean sheet and the thong stayed there for two weeks. I thought Susanna had gone on vacation. A few days before Ferragosto the store closed for two weeks. The Lenzis went off to Porto Ercole with the boys as they have for the six years I have worked for them. The only work I did during that time was cleaning, shopping and making lunch for Signora Costa."

"I've enjoyed your very good frittata."

Giulia's black-lined eyes brightened. "You have? I like

working for her. She is always so grateful. Saverio got me the job. He adores her and trusts me to take good care of her. I appreciate that."

"What happened when the Lenzis came back from vacation?"

"They came back on a Saturday. Annamaria texted me to stock the refrigerator with milk and fresh fruit that morning. Monday morning I went to check on the store before it reopened. The sheet and the envelope with the thong were gone."

"The affair with Susanna was over?"

"I thought they had found a different place to meet. One morning, two or three weeks later, she is standing in front of the store, all smiles, and asks me to let her in. I explain I am not allowed to let anyone in if Giancarlo or Saverio are not there even if she did have an appointment like she claimed. I told her he would be there soon.

"She asked me to call him, but whatever is going on between them, I didn't want to be part of it. I did enough by changing their love sheet every week. I told her to call him herself. She offered me a fifty-euro note. That pays for two and a half hours of scrubbing. The phone call took me two minutes."

"Giancarlo came?"

"Twenty minutes later with a smile on his face. He kissed her cheeks and they walked off together."

"Do you believe Susanna was telling the truth about having an appointment with Giancarlo?"

"I clean the Lenzi house four mornings a week. On those mornings Giancarlo stays in bed until nine, has breakfast by himself and doesn't leave the house before ten. He stopped showing up at the store on Monday mornings once Livia stopped coming." She chewed on her finger for a few seconds. "I guess you heard right. He was in love with her."

"In the arguments you overheard between Annamaria and Giancarlo, did Susanna's name ever come up?"

"It did not."

"Thank you, Giulia." Nico looked at his watch. It was twelve-forty-five. "The Coop will close in a few minutes. I'll take you down there."

At the entrance to the supermarket, Nico said, "Let me tell her you're here first. I'll let her know how helpful you've been. It might take a few minutes." He wanted to ask about Cilia first.

A now-tight-faced Giulia mouthed a *thank you.*

Livia was sitting at the cashier station near the entrance, counting the money in her drawer. She glanced at Nico and held up a finger. Counting done, she wrote out the sum on a sheet of stamped paper, wound it around the money and stood up. "Sorry, Nico. I always lose count. If you are here, you have news or Luciana talked to you."

"Both."

"Ah. I'll be right back." Livia hurried to the back of the store and handed the money to the manager. Nico met her halfway. "News first," she said.

"No. Cilia first."

"I don't know what happened. She was so happy after hearing . . ." She looked over her shoulder. Six feet behind her, Ugo, the produce man, was adding small boxes of grape tomatoes to the depleted stock.

Hearing Babbo's voice brought back the need to hug him, to have everything be all right again. "Chocolate brings joy," Nico said, "but when it's gone you want more."

"I know, I know." Livia picked up her coat from her chair and slipped into it. "Now she wants to go home. She says she misses Zio Paolo and Cippi. I told her I would take her home for the day on Sunday, but she wants to go now." She made her way to the entrance.

Nico stepped in front of her. "I can take her for the day

tomorrow." He was hoping to connect with Susanna Necchi. "Missing a day of school won't hurt her."

"Would you? Paolo offered to come pick her up and bring her back, but I know she would love to go with you and Rocco."

"Done. Bring Cilia to the café tomorrow morning and I'll take her home."

"Sei un angelo!"[20] Livia threw her arms around him. This time OneWag didn't bark. He was outside with Giulia.

Nico stepped back. "I hope you won't be upset, but—"

"You have news."

"I have just had a long talk with your friend Giulia, and she has been very helpful. She is now standing outside, waiting to see you."

Livia's hand shot up to her mouth. Her eyes questioned Nico.

Nico took her elbow in his hand and escorted her to the door. "She is being a friend, Livia. That's all." He opened the door. Livia took a few steps out and stopped. A few feet away, Giulia smiled and didn't move. Nico let the door close behind him. "Ciao, Giulia, thanks again. Livia, we'll see each other in the morning. Come on, buddy, let's get out of the way."

Halfway up the steps of the park behind the Coop, Nico stopped to look back. Livia and Giulia were sitting together in Livia's car, heads huddled together. Behind them the driver of the gray Citroën had his face deep into an open newspaper.

"I REFUSE A SANDWICH lunch," Perillo announced as soon as Nico walked into his office. He picked up his worn suede jacket. "Come on, we're going upstairs to have a proper meal in my kitchen. Dani's putting the water on. I hope he has the good sense not to salt it right away."

---

20 You're an angel.

Nico gave Perillo a military salute. "And a buongiorno to you, Maresciallo."

Perillo walked past him to the hallway. "A hungry man loses his manners. Ciao, Nico. You have good news?"

"Interesting news." Nico and OneWag followed Perillo up the back stairs of the station. His apartment was on the third floor, what the Italians consider the second floor.

Taking the stairs was a first. "Did the elevator break down?"

"No, I need the exercise. You run every morning so this is nothing to you."

Perillo stopped on the second-floor landing to catch his breath. OneWag panted.

"If this kills me, tell Ivana I was doing it for her."

Nico gave Perillo a gentle push on his back. "Forza! Just one more."

Perillo opened the door to a short hallway. OneWag scampered into the kitchen, a bright white square room. In the center a round table, covered in a floral oilcloth, was already set for three. The only window, curtained with white lace, faced the small park directly across the station. A uniformed Dani was keeping guard over the pot of water on the burner.

"Salve, Dani," Nico said.

Dani's *buongiorno* came with a smile. "Maresciallo, I think the water is about to boil."

"Lower the flame. I need to make the sauce." Perillo unhooked an apron with a picture of the bay of Naples on it and tied it over his jeans. "You did not salt it, did you?"

"I did not know how much salt."

"For us a big fistful but only once it boils. The sauce will only take a moment." Perillo put a wide saucepan on the stove, dripped a big tablespoon of butter into it. Next he picked up a large knife and an onion. "Dani, open that can of tomatoes, please."

"What should I do?" Nico asked, happy to be in this welcoming room. He had shared a few of Ivana's famous never-ending Sunday meals here.

"You sit, talk and grate some pecorino." Perillo quickly peeled the onion and started chopping. "There's a big wedge in the refrigerator along with a package of prosciutto, which I need. An open bottle of red is on the door. Nothing fancy but satisfying. Help yourself." He reached up and brought two glasses out of a cabinet. "Pour me one too. Dani?"

"Grazie, no. I would fall asleep."

Nico poured Perillo a glass of red, handed over the prosciutto and took the grater off the wall. "I met Bianca, Eddi's ex-girlfriend. She lied to Fabbri about being with Eddi during that night." He started grating on a paper towel.

"And Eddi was seen at the store that night." Perillo was now chopping the prosciutto. "You've got your killer."

Nico held up his hand. "Wait. I've found out that Angela Rossi's nephew couldn't have seen Eddi at the store any earlier than three-thirty that morning. Lenzi was dead by then."

Perillo used the flat end of the knife to squash three garlic cloves. "Could it not be that Eddi struck his father's head with the sharp end of the hammer, saw the blood gushing out, ran out in a panic. At three-thirty or thereabouts, he goes back to see if his papi is dead or alive?" He turned on the gas under a large saucepan.

"It could be," Nico admitted, although he had a different scenario in his mind.

"That explains why he did not call the carabinieri," Dani said.

Nico watched Perillo add the onion to the melting butter. What he needed was to find Eddi, hear what he had to say to defend himself. Lies often led to the truth. He inhaled the enticing smell coming from the cooking onions and the pecorino he was grating. "I spoke to Giulia Favelli this morning.

She came to Gravigna to see Livia. They used to be friends. I think she wants to patch things up between them."

Perillo stirred the onions. "Was Giulia helpful?" He tossed in the prosciutto and picked a bunch of basil leaves from the plant in the window next to the stove.

"But Daniele," Nico started to say. Perillo interrupted him.

"Do not worry, Nico. I know Brigadiere Donato is a vegetarian. His maccheroni will be swaddled in butter and cheese."

"Swaddled? That's a fancy word."

"Neapolitans are poetic. Just listen to our songs. Now tell us about Giulia."

"She told me Saverio asked her if Lenzi and Livia were having an affair. Giulia knew Lenzi wanted Livia, but she gave Saverio a hard time for thinking it was possible. It does mean Saverio had noticed Lenzi eyeing Livia."

Perillo retrieved a package of pasta from a metal cabinet. "This is not good news."

"I agree. Giulia also revealed, if she's telling the truth, and I think she is, that Susanna Necchi lied about how long she and Lenzi had an affair."

"Does it matter?" Perillo threw in the smashed garlic cloves. "Dani, raise the flame under the water pot, please."

Nico answered, "I want to know what she's covering up by lying."

"If he dumped her, vanity." Perillo dropped the whole can of tomatoes into the saucepan. The splash made Daniele jump back. Perillo looked down at his green sweater. No sign of tomato. "Sorry, Dani."

"No worries," Daniele said. His blue uniform jacket was now splotched with red.

"The water is boiling, Maresciallo. One fistful?"

"A full one. I am throwing in the whole box." Perillo added salt and pepper to the sauce. Stirred some more. "I want leftovers for tomorrow's lunch." He watched in disbelief as Dani dug a spoon into the salt bowl and poured the thick grains into his cupped fist. "Take the plunge, Dani. Dig in with your hand."

Daniele threw the first fistful of salt in the water. "I was taught it's not hygienic."

Perillo shook his head in disbelief. "It is going into boiling water!"

Daniele ignored his boss and filled his fist with a spoonful of salt one more time, threw the salt in and covered the pot. A minute later the water was boiling again. Perillo threw in the box of maccheroni. Crisis over.

Nico lifted the paper towel with the grated pecorino and carefully poured the cheese into one of the dry water glasses on the table.

Perillo noticed. "You could have asked for a bowl."

"You don't need your water glass. You're drinking wine."

"Correct. No mold in my intestines. What now for you?"

"My intestines are fine, but the car situation is not. I got a call from the mechanic. The side mirrors are back on the 500, but when he heard about my back and forth to Pitigliano he told me to expect it to break down any day. He urged me to buy a car with balls."

Perillo gave the pasta a stir. "He probably has one to sell you."

"No, he doesn't. You really do think the worst of people, don't you?"

"It prepares me. I do not like surprises. I rejoice when I am wrong. Ivana said the Panda is yours if you still want it. I was going to tell you after lunch. It does not have balls, but it will take you safely to Pitigliano and back for as long as you need. For the price, talk to Ivana. How many more times do you need to go there?"

"Tomorrow for one. Cilia is having a rough time and wants to go home. I'm taking her back for the day. She says she misses her neighbor Paolo Fulci and his dog. I guess if she can't be with her father, Zio Paolo becomes a substitute. While she's with him, I'll try to root out Eddi and have another talk with the beautiful Susanna."

Perillo gave Nico a crooked look.

Nico raised his hands. "What?"

"Do not do anything you will regret."

"I don't intend to."

"Good. Ivana would never forgive you."

"Ivana?"

"Yes. Nelli's reaction is your problem. Ivana's is mine. Enough talk." Perillo plunged the wooden spoon into the water and caught a swirling maccherone. He blew on it, popped it in his mouth and chewed. "Perfetto." With a large cup he picked up pasta water. "Nico, the cheese. Dani, move." He lifted the pot, drained the pasta, shook it into the saucepan with the tomato sauce, threw in half of the cheese and the pasta water and mixed. "In two minutes we eat."

"I found Susanna Necchi on Instagram," Daniele announced as they sat down. "She does publicity for the spa with bathing suit pictures, exercise clothes. With her looks, she should be in a movie."

Perillo dished their large portions of pasta with a warning. "Dani, Stella is the one who is in a movie. Your movie. Do not forget that."

Nico looked at Perillo's frowning face. The maresciallo seemed oddly worried about staying loyal to one's partner. Maybe it had something to do with his upcoming wedding anniversary.

BOWLS WIPED CLEAN WITH bread, in OneWag's case with his tongue, Perillo sat back with a satisfied smile. "Ingesting good food lights up my . . ." He turned to Dani. "What do you call the cells that help you think?"

"Neurons?"

Perillo snapped his fingers. "Neurons! Mine are dancing the tarantella right now."

"Are you sure it wasn't the two glasses of wine you had?" Nico asked. He'd skipped the wine but had eaten two helpings of the irresistible maccheroni and was now ready to take a nap.

"No, good pasta does it. My neurons are saying Eddi is your murderer."

"Maybe, but I'm wondering if not getting along with your father is enough of a motive."

Perillo leaned over the table, his chest almost hitting the empty pasta bowl. "Nico, you do not know how bad was their not getting along." He flung out his arm. "Look, if Lenzi was already dead, why did Eddi not call the police?"

"You have a good point."

"He is very close to his mother, right?" Perillo asked.

"According to Debora, very much so."

"According to Livia's husband, Lenzi was in love with Livia. From what you have told us about Annamaria, that is not something she would tolerate. I say Eddi found out Lenzi was planning to disappear with the money he stole maybe with or without Livia. This would destroy his proud mother, who claims she is a descendent of the Orsini family. She would become gossip fodder. In small towns a great deal of shame comes to a woman who cannot keep her man. Concentrate on Eddi."

He sat back and dropped his hands on his knees. "I need a coffee."

Daniele jumped up. "I will make it." He had been in this kitchen for enough Sunday lunches to know where to find most things.

Perillo nodded his approval. "You are a good man, Dani. I wish I had a son like you."

"Thank you."

"Don't let it go to your head," Perillo said.

Dani shook his head and turned to stare at the still-silent moka on the stove, his cheeks burning.

Perillo leaned across the table and in a low voice asked Nico, "Do you regret not having children?"

"I did, then I moved on." Nico's answer was curt.

"That is what I tell myself also. It mostly works. Was it a choice?"

"They just didn't come."

"Sad, but maybe better that way. We lost three while they were still inside Ivana."

The moka started gurgling.

"Bring it over, Dani," Perillo called out. "We can use the pickup."

BEFORE DRIVING BACK TO Gravigna, Nico called Susanna Necchi. She didn't pick up. He left a message—I NEED TO SEE YOU AGAIN—with his phone number. She was a flirt and he hoped the ambiguity would get her to respond.

His next phone call was to Maria Grazia Fulci, Eddi's Latin teacher.

"Eddi has not contacted you yet?" she asked.

"No. Do you know if he will be at the Institute tomorrow?"

"There are no classes on Saturday, but he is coming for his usual lesson on Monday. I will talk to him again then. I am so sorry. I will give him a very stern talking-to. On a happy subject, you have of course seen my portrait. Is Nelli not an incredible painter?"

Nico felt something like a cold pebble drop into his stomach.

"She brought it over yesterday afternoon," Maria Grazia said. "She has caught my joys, my sadness, anger. They are all there in my face. An ordinary face made interesting. I cried when she presented it to me. Her work should be in museums."

"She is a wonderful painter." Nelli had not shown him the painting. "She'll be glad you are happy with the portrait." He'd asked to see it. *Soon* had been her answer. She had been oddly silent last night after the party at Stella's apartment. No mention of delivering the portrait.

"I am ecstatic," Maria Grazia said. "My husband's teeth would have dropped to the floor at the sight of my portrait lording it over the mantel."

Payback for her husband excluding her, Nico thought. Excluded was what he was feeling. "I need to go now. You will talk to Eddi again?"

"Yes, I will. I will make him see you. Buonasera, Nico."

"Thank you." Nico held on to the phone, tempted to call Nelli.

Why didn't you tell me? I know how important painting is to you. You know how much I love your work, how proud I am for you.

He felt cast aside.

OneWag nudged Nico's elbow with a grunt, his way of saying, *let's get on with it*, whatever the *it* happened to be. "Thanks, buddy. I'll get over it." Nico put the phone on the dashboard holder and pressed his foot on the accelerator.

Once home, Nico went to check on his vegetable garden, a wide rectangle of earth he was proud of. OneWag looked wistful outside the gate, knowing the garden was off-limits. The spinach wasn't ready to pick, but the cabbages looked good, and so did the broccoli. Nico pulled out a carrot. A small scraggly thing. He carefully put it back in the hole, patting it closed in a dubious attempt to let the carrot grow. He picked the largest cabbage head and some broccoli. He hadn't planted celery this year, but he had some upstairs along with a big fat yellow onion.

He was going to be alone tonight. Laura had asked Nelli to have a pizza dinner with her in Panzano, which meant she would sleep at her place.

Just as well. It will give me time to get over feeling sorry for myself.

THIRTEEN

"Are you ready to go?" Nico asked after Cilia finished the last bite of her ciambella.

Cilia licked the sugar off her lips. "Yes, please."

"Away we go."

Livia, Nelli and Gogol followed Nico, Cilia and OneWag out of Bar All'Angolo. Halfway across the piazza, Livia started singing, *"If you are sad and merriment escapes you, come with me . . ."* Nelli and Gogol joined her, *"And I will teach you the happiness song."*

Cilia mouthed the words and hugged her bear.

When they reached Nico's Ford Fiesta, Livia kissed Cilia's forehead. "Give Zio Paolo a big hug for me and a kiss to Cippi. Be a good girl now."

Cilia bobbed her head and slipped into the back seat with OneWag.

Gogol pushed himself in front of Livia and bent down to face Cilia. "'Know you give me joy,' for 'trust and innocence are found only in little children.'"

"Grazie, Gogol." Cilia buckled herself in, then tried to buckle in OneWag who instantly slipped free.

A threesome chorus of "Ciao, have fun" and waves erupted as Nico got into the driver's seat. Silence from Cilia.

"Ciao, everyone. Thanks for the send-off." Nico rested his phone on the dashboard holder and turned on the motor. "Livia, I'll call you when we're on our way back." More hand waves as Nico pulled out.

"Cilia, that was fun, wasn't it?"

"That song is for babies and you should stop. Rocco slipped out of his belt."

"Don't worry. He'll be safe with you."

"And when he is not with me?"

"He lies down and falls asleep."

"Babbo waits to start the car until I am buckled in. Then I can fall asleep. When can he come home?"

"Soon, I hope."

"Stella says hope is a good thing, maybe the best of things, and good things do not die. I am tired of hoping."

"I'm not."

"Good. I am going to read the book Stella gave me now."

"Okay. Happy reading."

Silence followed.

Before entering the autostrada Nico pulled over and tried reaching Susanna Necchi again. In the back seat, Cilia was asleep, one arm hooked over a sleeping OneWag.

Susanna picked up quickly. "Signor Doyle, you have been calling me. I have nothing more to add to what I told you unless you want to share another bottle of Prosecco with me."

"There have been some discrepancies in what you told me that I would like to clear up with you."

"I have only told you the truth."

"I'd like to clarify that truth in your presence."

She answered with a throaty *Aah*.

"I'm on my way to Pitigliano now. I have an errand first and then I could drive over to Sorano and meet you."

Hearing Nico's voice, OneWag woke up and slipped between

the two front seats to drop down on the passenger seat. It was allowed when the car was not in motion.

"Is it me," Susanna asked, "or is it this 'truth' you want?"

"I would like them together." He needed to see how her face reacted to what he'd found out.

"You are tempting me, Nico." She let out a breath. "Monday, one-thirty. Take me to lunch. Meet me at the restaurant La Rocca in Piazza della Repubblica. Look for a bronze statue of a man and a donkey. The restaurant is right there." She shut him off before he could say yes.

Nico was doubly pleased. Susanna had agreed to see him on Monday. Had she said tomorrow, he would have very much regretted cancelling the Perillos' anniversary lunch, where he and Nelli were guaranteed to gain five pounds each and have a great time doing it.

"Who was that?" Cilia asked.

Nico turned to look at her. "Susanna Necchi."

"She is nice."

"You know her?"

Cilia nodded. "Once at Annamaria's house she let me play with her bracelets. She has four! I asked Mamma to buy me one for my birthday, but she said I was too young for jewelry. Susanna promised me she would buy me a silver bracelet when I turn eight. That is in June next year. I better be home by then. I will be, won't I?"

"Yes." It was the only answer she deserved.

"Good, because she can't give me the bracelet if I'm not there."

Nico started the motor. "How old were you when Susanna said this?"

"Five."

"You have a good memory." He started edging out of the shoulder waiting for a break between cars.

"A present is not something I forget. Rocco, come back here. I have to hold you. Come here."

With a quick look at Nico, OneWag obeyed. Cilia wrapped a protective arm around him. Nico got back on the road.

RINGING PAOLO FULCI'S DOORBELL was followed by a torrent of barks from behind the door. "That's Cippi," Cilia announced. "He's very protective." OneWag joined in the ruckus.

The door finally opened. The barking stopped. Cippi jumped up on Cilia and covered her face with licks. She squealed in delight. Paolo slapped his hand against his chest, "Che gioia!"[21] He picked Cilia up and hugged her. The joy on both their faces was palpable. "Ciao, bella mia. I have missed you sooo much."

"How much?"

"As much as there is water in the sea. No, in the ocean."

"That's a lot." Cilia hid her face in his chest. "I missed you too." Fulci kissed the top of her head.

Witnessing the love between Fulci and Cilia, Nico felt a knot of regret for the child he'd been unable to have. "I'll pick her up around four. Is that all right?"

"No, no please," Fulci said. "Forgive me. Come in."

Cilia turned and pointed a hand at Nico, who was still on the landing with OneWag. "Meet Rocco and Nico. Nico is going to bring Babbo home."

"I know. We've met before." Fulci put Cilia down. "Come in. Cippi, get out of the way! Thank you so much for bringing my favorite girl."

"I was happy to bring her." Nico and OneWag stepped inside the small entrance. The two dogs sniffed each other amicably

---

21 What joy!

while Nico unleashed OneWag, took off his down jacket and hung the leash and jacket on the iron tree.

"I want to show Rocco my bedroom," Cilia said. "Can I take him, Nico? Please? I live just over there." She pointed to the door across the landing. "I have lots of dog toys he can play with. Cippi won't mind."

Nico glanced at Fulci to see if he minded. The man was lifting a set of keys off the bird hook. "Here you are, amore. Do not make a mess. I will leave the door open. Cippi stays here so they will not fight over your toys."

"Ciao." She went to the door. "Come on, Rocco."

OneWag looked up at Nico. "Go on. I'll be here."

"Come on, Rocco," Cilia said. "You are going to love my bedroom. I will let you jump up on the bed if you want. Just do not tell Mamma."

Nico and Fulci watched as she unlocked her door and went inside, slowly followed by OneWag.

"I am relieved we have a moment to talk," Fulci said. "I was worried we would not have a chance to be alone. Would you like a coffee, a glass of water?"

"Nothing, thank you." Nico followed Fulci down the short corridor into the living room. The lace curtains on the two windows had been pulled back to let in a bright late morning light that revealed a neater room. Magazines and newspapers were now in two piles on the table. The books were partially hidden behind the sofa. Walking past, Nico caught one title—*La Storia* by Elsa Morante, a famous World War II novel he had struggled through at Rita's insistence.

"Please sit down," Fulci said. "I have made changes." The sofa and the armchair, now covered with bright cotton tablecloths sold at the weekly markets, were empty. "I wanted my home to be welcoming for Cilia. For you too of course."

"Thank you. It looks very nice." Nico sat on the sofa. Fulci dropped down on the armchair. "Please tell me, are you any closer to finding who killed Lenzi?"

"I wish I could say I am. I have discovered strong motives." Cippi jumped in Nico's lap, pushing his small fluffy head against Nico's arm. Nico obliged by stroking his back. "I have not yet found evidence."

"Do you think you will?"

"I'm not giving up."

"Please, please don't." Nico could see the anguish in Fulci's eyes. "What would become of Livia and Cilia if Saverio must keep hiding? Their pain would be unbearable, unthinkable."

"You love them very much, don't you?"

"They have become my family."

Did Fulci see Livia as replacing his wife, Nico wondered. Or was she a sister to him? "Saverio is part of the family?"

"Certainly." Fulci ran his hand over his forehead as if to brush a thought away. "Although, as I am sure you understand, it is different between two men. We respect each other. Sometimes I thought he resented my friendship with Livia, my love of his daughter, but he has never said anything unpleasant to me." Fulci pushed himself to the edge of the armchair. "I call Livia every evening to hear how she and Cilia are managing. La piccola tells me the truth. She cries. I cry with her. Livia is a wall of stone."

"She is a strong woman."

"No, she is not. I know Livia. She is pretending. Inside she is trembling."

From where he sat, Nico could see OneWag padding into the room in bad need of a brush. Cilia followed, a finger over her lips. Cippi jumped off Nico's lap.

Fulci, unaware of his new audience said, "I don't know how to help her."

Cilia peeked from behind the armchair. "I know, Zio Paolo. Rocco and I are hungry." Fulci's dog started jumping on her. "Cippi too." OneWag retreated to Nico's flank.

Fulci stood up. "Of course you are hungry, amore. Nico, you will join us? Cilia's favorite meal. Spinach ravioli in—"

"Burnt butter sauce," Cilia interrupted, "and chicken Milanese with cooked apples. My very favorite meal." She hugged Fulci's legs. "Thank you, Zio."

Now standing, Nico said, "Thank you for the invitation, but the two of you need to catch up without me." It was another clear and mild day. He would get something to eat on his own and then wander through the historic center. Too bad it was Saturday. The synagogue and its museum were closed. "I'll come for Cilia at four."

"So soon?" Fulci asked.

"It is a long trip back."

Cilia looked up at him. "Four-thirty?"

"Not a minute later."

Nico opened the front door of Fulci and Livia's building and walked out on the street with an eager OneWag. A young man covered in black leather stood next to the curb, one booted leg straddling his motorcycle, black helmet propped up on his hip. His strong sculptured face was surrounded by a thick tangle of wavy brown hair.

"Buongiorno, Eddi." An alert OneWag sat down by Nico's feet. "You are a pleasant surprise. How did you find me?"

"The Prof said you were driving Cilia home this morning, told me to show up."

"I will thank her and I thank you now."

"Americano, you are wasting your time and now mine. Saverio killed my father, and if you really made detective in New York, you would know it. Maybe you just want to put some money in your pocket."

"No. I'm glad to see you, though. I am sorry you lost your father."

"That's what everyone says. Some of them even mean it."

"I mean it. Can we sit down somewhere?"

"I can give you three minutes. I have classes to go to. First question?"

Nico leaned against the building. There was little traffic on this side street. "Why did you go to the store the night your father died?"

"Who said I did?"

"A man leaving a party saw you."

"You're making that up."

"He is ready to tell Maresciallo Fabbri he saw you."

"Cazzo!"[22] Eddi sat on the seat of the bike with his lips squeezed together as if to stop himself from saying anything more.

"Why did you go, Eddi? Either you tell me or tell Maresciallo Fabbri."

It took a while for Eddi to relax his lips. "The Prof says I owe you, so I should answer your questions. I guess I do. I got carried away."

"Was knocking off my side-view mirrors necessary?"

Eddi shot his eyes up at the sky, probably with a silent expletive this time. "I just said I got carried away. Besides, a Fiat 500 is no car for an American detective, if that's what you are. Get yourself at least a Giulia."

"I can't afford it."

"Then a motorcycle. Allows you to zoom past all the shit around you."

"What made you go to the store?"

Eddi raised an arm, his face resigned. "Okay, okay. He hadn't

---

22 Vulgar term for "penis"; Italy's equivalent of "fuck."

come home. If he had fallen asleep in the office, the next the day would have been hell. Babbo on less than seven hours of sleep turned into Godzilla."

"He was dead when you got there?"

"He looked dead and not having a pulse confirmed it."

"Why didn't you call the carabinieri right away?"

"What for? They weren't going to give him his life back."

"Come on, Eddi, give me an honest answer."

"I was in shock. Does that satisfy you, Detective? I walk into the office with '*Ehi, GC, wake up. Time to sleep in your bed*,' and there he is slumped over his desk, his face in a pool of blood."

"GC for Giancarlo?"

"What else? That's what I called him. He didn't like it, but he didn't like anything I did. I'm sure you know by now we didn't get along, but seeing him dead, something I wished on him who knows how many times, hit me right between the eyes. Stops you thinking straight."

"I can understand that, but the carabinieri only found out your father was dead after Angela Rossi's phone call hours later."

"I waited for Mamma to wake up to tell her. It felt right to keep it to ourselves for a while. I hope you can understand that too, Detective."

"I can and my name is Nico."

Eddi blew air out of his nose. "Nico Detective."

Nico fought the urge to tell Eddi to quit the attitude, but he had lost his father, loved or not. "Did you have to unlock the door to get into the store?"

"No. That was a surprise. Babbo was not stupid about money. There's a lot of expensive stuff in there."

Interesting, Nico thought. *Now that GC is dead, he turns into Babbo.* "Do you think he opened the door to his killer or did the killer have his own key?"

Eddi bobbed his head. "That's a stupid question. How would I know? Anyway, Saverio has his own key."

"Do you remember if you locked the door when you left?"

"Sure, I locked it. I'm not stupid either."

"I am not saying you are, Eddi." *Angela Rossi had gone into the store that morning, which meant the door was unlocked.*

"You remember locking it?"

"Yes, I think so. Cristo, I just saw Babbo looking like a slaughtered pig. What do you expect me to remember? Did I lock it? I don't know."

"I'm sorry. I'm trying to find out if someone entered the store after you left. You are convinced Saverio killed your father. You have shouted it on social media. You have tried to stop me from asking questions. But your conviction is based on three words of questionable meaning that Saverio shouted in anger."

Nico took two steps to the curb. "So let me ask you this." He locked eyes with Eddi. "When you were in your father's office that night, did you see anything, find anything that could point to the killer?"

Eddi's wary expression was now a rigid mask. He looked down at the handlebars. "No, nothing. I didn't look. Too much blood. The smell of it. I wanted to run, breathe clean air."

"Did you take his phone?"

"I couldn't find it."

He just tripped himself up. "Then you did look around."

"No, just for the phone."

"Why the phone?"

"It was his."

"Maybe you looked for it because you would want your mother to access it before the carabinieri."

His face blanked out for a couple of seconds. "No." His voice was flat.

"Are you certain you didn't find anything that might point to the killer? If not Saverio, someone else?"

"Are you deaf?" Eddi hissed. "All I found was a dead body"— there was a small break in his voice—"a body that happened to be my father."

Nico stopped himself from putting a hand on Eddi's shoulder. The boy would have rightfully shrugged it off. He had always disliked trying to press for the truth when the person was grieving and therefore vulnerable. "I am sorry I have upset you, Eddi. I mean that. But I am trying to find your father's murderer. I have discovered there are a number of possible suspects. Perhaps, for you, Saverio is the less painful choice."

"What the cazzo are you talking about?"

"I'm not sure I know myself," Nico lied. "I am grateful that you agreed to see me and answer my questions. Thank you."

"I had no choice. The Prof—Professor Bertini—threatened to flunk me in Latin if I refused. I am also supposed to apologize to your painter girlfriend, so consider it done."

"Would she really flunk you?"

Eddi seemed to relax. "Absolutely. Mamma's family has given the Institute a lot of money, but that would not stop the Prof. She has balls."

"She's important to you?"

A trace of a smile. "Sure. We get each other."

"You and your mother get each other too, don't you?"

"Leave my mother out of this conversation."

"Does she know you agreed to see me?"

"What my mother and I tell each other is none of your business." Eddi slipped the key in the ignition and turned on the motor. "Goodbye, Nico Detective. Tell the Prof I earned a ten on my next exam." His boot released the kickstand, and with a loud roar Eddi took off.

OneWag pulled on his leash and barked.

"I agree, buddy. He's not going to get a ten for lying. Eddi found something. Lenzi's phone or something else." Nico wondered if Annamaria even knew he'd gone to the store that night. He tugged on OneWag's leash. "Come on, we're leaving the twenty-first century. The Renaissance is more fun."

On the walk over to the historic center, Nico realized fun was going to be hard to come by. Nelli had dropped into his head again. Why hadn't she told him Maria Grazia's portrait was done and gone? Had he done something to annoy her? He was going to bring it up when she joined him at Bar All'Angolo this morning, but by the time she arrived Livia and Cilia were having their breakfast with him.

Nico did a mental headshake. Maybe it was just as well he'd kept his mouth shut. Gogol would have started quoting about Dante's star-crossed lovers, making him feel like an idiot.

At the start of the walkway that led up to the Orsini Palace Museum, OneWag stopped to lift a leg. Nico looked up at the stone animal crouched on top of a pilaster. It had once been a bear, the symbol of that noble family. Someone, who knows when, had replaced the bear's head with a lion's head. The body and the head were clearly mismatched. The head was ugly. Nico felt the urge to knock it off.

Get over it, Nico. We are not mismatched.

OneWag's business over, they walked into Piazza della Repubblica. The leaves of the holm oaks lining one side of the piazza rustled as the wind moved through them. Nico undid OneWag's leash. He wasn't hungry and lunch for OneWag, if any, was only the morsels that fell to the floor by accident.

They took Via Zuccarelli and entered the old ghetto. OneWag kept his nose down to catch the different smells. Nico smelled garlic and tomatoes coming from one of the shuttered windows. The only noise came from Nico's slow footsteps. It was Saturday. It was lunchtime.

Nico stopped once again at the marble plaque memorializing the twenty-two Pitigliano Jews who lost their lives in Nazi concentration camps. Under the double-sided list, a quote from Primo Levi: "Meditate che questo stato." *Reflect that this happened.*

Nico reached for his phone.

After many rings, a soft voice said. "Pronto?"

"Buongiorno, Debora. This is Nico. I hope I'm not disturbing. I just read the names on the memorial plaque in the ghetto and I wanted to let you know how happy I am that you survived."

"That is sweet of you. Have you and your sweet dog any time to pay a visit?"

"We are free from now until four-fifteen."

"Then I expect you in a few minutes. I have already eaten, but if you have not, I can offer mortadella and a local pecorino. If you have eaten I can offer a coffee and the company of a curious old woman."

"Sandwich and company happily accepted."

"Good. There's a key under the third cyclamen pot going up the stairs."

"Please make yourself comfortable," Debora called out as soon as Nico stepped into her large, crowded living room. OneWag cocked his ears. "The blue armchair is best. I am preparing your sandwich."

The dog scooted to the arched passageway that led to the kitchen.

"Can I help?"

"No need." OneWag wiggled. "Yes, yes, something for you too."

Nico crossed the room to take a quick look out of one of the two windows. Nothing had changed since the last time. Only the light was different. The sun, high in the sky, cast a bright light over the thick vegetation on the ridge, making it look like a huge green comforter. Nico heard Debora's footsteps and turned.

"There you are," she said, holding the tray with his lunch.

"Buongiorno!" Nico quickly crossed the room and took the tray from her. The meat and cheese were stacked inside a ciabatta roll. Nico had laughed when Rita had told him what *ciabatta* meant, but the shape of the roll did resemble an old slipper. "Thank you. Just what the doctor ordered."

"You are not well?"

Nico chuckled. "No. It's just an American expression. I'm hungry and your sandwich looks delicious."

"I see." She sounded doubtful. "It is good. I had the same for lunch. I added two escarole leaves over the pecorino slices. Cast them aside if you wish."

Nico looked at the piano bench. The photo albums had multiplied.

"The best place for the tray is your lap. If you sit down, that is."

Nico obeyed, but placed the water goblet on the floor for safety. OneWag had stayed in the passageway, attacking a rawhide bone.

"Should I stay here or should I leave you to eat in sainted peace? I have questions but they can wait until we have coffee together."

"Please stay and ask away. I promise I'll swallow before answering."

"I had no doubt but do take a few bites first."

Nico took two bites, chewing slowly. The bread was warm and crunchy, the thinly sliced mortadella, pecorino and escarole deliciously satisfying. "Very good," he said after swallowing.

"The bread comes from the panetteria where Livia used to work. It's the best in town. Giulia buys it for me. She said she spoke to you."

"I saw her yesterday in Gravigna. I think I was an excuse for her to see Livia." Nico took another bite.

"Not an excuse because she was perfectly willing to help with any information she might have, but I did suggest she go to Gravigna for that conversation."

Nico kept his eyes fixed on Debora's pale, withered face. His mouth worked the sandwich.

Debora looked back at him, a smile in her eyes. "You might think me an interfering old woman, but I feel people sometimes need a nudge in the right direction. Ever since Lenzi's death and Saverio's disappearance, Giulia has wanted to approach Livia but was afraid of being rebuffed. I insisted she try. Now that she has a man of her own there is no reason for Livia to reject her friendship."

"Do you mean she was jealous of Livia and Saverio?"

"According to Giulia—she gave me permission to tell you this—she was in love with Saverio since her hormones kicked in. Sadly and ironically, she was the one who introduced him to her best friend. At a certain point, Livia accused Giulia of being in love with her man. Giulia denied it. Livia did not believe her and shut the door. This morning Giulia's embrace nearly crushed my ribs. There was no need for her to tell me her meeting with Livia went well."

Nico put his half-eaten sandwich back on the plate. "How long has this new man been in Giulia's life?"

"I do not know exactly. She does not tell me everything. Not long, judging by the makeup she now wears. Why do you ask?"

"She must have been consumed with jealousy all these years, seeing Saverio at the store, angry at Livia for pushing her out of her life. Are you sure there is a man in her life now?"

"Please do not let your eagerness to find a culprit cloud your mind." Debora's disappointed face made Nico feel like a reprimanded schoolkid.

"I have to consider all possibilities, far-fetched or not."

"Giulia has a simple heart with simple expectations in life. Yes, she loved Saverio, but she loves Livia equally. She would do nothing to hurt her. You will have to take my word for that. The culprit lies elsewhere."

"Understood."

"Thank you. I will make coffee." Debora stood up and made her way back to the arched passageway. The silence that followed allowed Nico to finish his sandwich and OneWag to tire of gnawing rawhide.

When only a few crumbs were left on his plate, Nico got on his feet and walked to the passageway. "Can I help you?"

"Indeed you can." Debora appeared from a narrow, arched doorway with a tray holding a moka, two delicate cups on saucers and a biscuit. She thrust the tray at Nico. "Take this please. My hands sometimes like to do the tarantella without warning." Behind her Nico saw a modern stove under a large copper hood green with age.

"Have you been able to speak to Eddi?" Debora asked after sitting down.

Not finding a safe place for the tray, Nico sat with the tray on his lap. "I have, thanks to his Latin tutor."

"Good. I am curious to know what he told you about that night."

"Why are you curious?" OneWag sat next to Nico's feet, nose in the air, sniffing.

Debora plucked the biscuit from the tray and gave it to him. "Mimmo came over last night as I was having dinner. He has his own key as my doorbell is as erratic as my hearing. I like him to come whenever he wants. We chitchatted about this and that and then he put his hand on mine, his way of signaling he needed help with something.

"I took both his hands in mine and waited. Tears appeared in the corners of his eyes. He said, '*Babbo was going to leave us. Do you think that's why he died?*'

"I asked him why he thought his babbo was leaving him. Mimmo's room is next to the living room and the night before Giancarlo died, that sweet boy overheard his parents fight. Annamaria wanted to know if Giancarlo had stolen the money from Saverio. With tears streaming down his face, Mimmo remembered every word Giancarlo yelled back. '*I am leaving you, getting as far from here as the money will take me.*' Then the front door slammed. In the morning, his babbo was dead."

Nico sat back. "Poor kid! What did you say to him?"

"I hugged him. What could I say? Lying to children serves no purpose. I told him that I did not know if there was a connection. Then I took out the chessboard and we played for an hour or so."

"Thank you for telling me."

"How could I not? Had you not visited I would have called. Mimmo has given you a possibility that is far from far-fetched. I wish you luck with it." She picked up her small coffee cup. "I am afraid the coffee is cold now." She took a sip. "Still good though."

Nico drank his quickly, trying to stop from grimacing. He hadn't asked for sugar. "Very good." Debora was not a child. Lying was okay.

"Now you know why I was curious about your meeting with Eddi. Did he mention his parents fighting that night?"

"He was at a party that night. Even if he had witnessed or overheard the fight, I doubt he would have told me."

"You are right. Annamaria is his lodestar." Debora put her coffee cup back on the tray still on Nico's lap. "I thank your sturdy lap. Next time you come I will provide a proper side table. I am sure there is one somewhere in the house. Would you mind returning the tray to the kitchen? I am tired."

Nico lifted the tray and stood up. "I'll take my leave then. Thank you, Debora."

She closed her eyes and took a deep breath. "Bring Saverio home. And come again with your sweet dog."

"We will."

HIGH-PITCHED BARKING GREETED NICO and OneWag when they reached Paolo Fulci's door. Cilia opened the door before Nico could ring. "Ciao, Nico." The smile on her face was good news. She picked up the small suitcase at her feet. "I'm ready to go home now."

"Cilia, let them come in first." Paolo was standing a few feet behind her, clutching his barking dog against his chest, trying to calm him. "Please come in, Nico. Cippi will quiet down. What can I offer you? A coffee? Hot chocolate? A glass of water?"

"Thank you, nothing," Nico said. "We do need to get home. The drive is a long one."

"I understand." Fulci looked disappointed. "Thank you so much for bringing her. We had fun together, didn't we?"

Cilia lifted her suitcase, covered in animal stickers. "Zio Paolo gave me a new colored pencil set that will wow Stella and Luciana. And I'm taking all my toys back to Gravigna."

"Good." Nico turned his gaze on Fulci. "Arrivederci."

"Please do come back. I enjoyed talking to you again. Ciao, Cilietta. I'll miss you. Now listen to your Mamma, all right?"

"I always do." Cilia handed the suitcase to Nico. "Come on, Rocco. I'll race you down the stairs."

"Be careful!" Both men yelled, then laughed at each other. Cilia and OneWag made it down the two flights safely.

"I TOLD YOU," PERILLO said over the phone. "Eddi is your killer."

Nico finished what was left of his nightly glass of Pinot

Grigio. He had just filled Perillo in on what he had learned from Debora Costa. "Could be Annamaria."

"No, Eddi," Perillo insisted. "He is the one with the temper, who spread lies about Saverio on the internet and tried to stop you from investigating."

Nelli walked in. "Ciao." OneWag jumped around her while she took off her heavy black down coat. She was wearing a fitted wool dress the same gray color of her hair and black boots that barely reached her knees. "How was your . . . Oh, sorry. You are on the phone." She picked up the dog.

Nico took a quick look behind him, raised his hand in salute, noticed the dressed-up outfit and went back to Perillo. "Eddi wasn't at home then. How would he know what Lenzi threatened?"

"Mimmo must have been scared. He called his brother."

"Maybe."

Walking toward the bedroom with OneWag, Nelli blew him a kiss. *She's not angry with me then.* "Look, Perillo, I have to get some food on the table." *Why the dress up?* "We'll discuss this another time. I'll call you tomorrow."

"No, tomorrow you will come to my house to celebrate Ivana's and my wedding anniversary. Daniele and Stella are also coming. Remember, no presents. And no talk of murder."

"I didn't forget."

"Good. Twelve-thirty. A domani."

Nico went to the stove to heat the soup he'd made yesterday with the cabbage and broccoli he'd picked in the garden. He'd added onions and potatoes.

Nelli walked out of the bedroom in flats and went over to the stove to plant a kiss on Nico's cheek. "Good news on the Lenzi front?"

"Could be. What's missing is proof." Nico turned to look at her. The blue of her eyes, surrounded by gray, looked deeper, inviting. He fought the urge to kiss her by reaching for a hunk of parmigiano.

"I have no doubt that you will find the proof you need. What smells so good apart from the cheese?"

"I hope you're not too hungry. I can only offer soup with croutons and some of Enrico's cold cuts."

"Perfect. I had a heavy lunch with six Querciabella clients."

"That explains the dress up." Nico felt stupid with relief.

"What did you think?"

"Nothing. I just noticed what you were wearing. It's nice." *What the hell was he thinking?* "Could you set the table?"

Nelli studied Nico's face for a moment before saying, "Yes, that's my job." She went over to the table, opened its drawer, picked the necessary cutlery, and decided something was stuck in Nico's throat tonight. She took out soup bowls and plates from a cabinet to the right of Nico and set them next to the stove. "How did it go with Cilia and the neighbor?"

Nico vigorously grated the cheese. "The visit helped her a lot. She came home with a big smile on her face. I hope it lasts."

"She will probably want to go again."

"I'm going back on Monday to meet with Susanna Necchi." He ladled out the soup.

"Ah, the beautiful one." She had overheard him telling Perillo.

"Indeed." He spooned out the parmigiano, covering the surface of the soup. "She is extraordinarily beautiful."

"Why do you need to tell me how '*extraordinarily beautiful*' she is?"

"Because she is and is very aware of it."

"Why shouldn't she be? Are you trying to make me jealous?"

"No." *It would feel good if she was.* "Let's eat."

They picked up their soup bowls on plates, sat down and spooned into the soup. "It's very good," Nelli said.

"Thank you." For ten long minutes the only noise in the

room came from a spoon sometimes hitting the bottom of the bowl and OneWag pushing his empty dish against the wall in hopes of more.

As Nico took the empty soup bowls back to the sink, he said, "I called Maria Grazia last night about Eddi. She told me how happy she is with her portrait. She used the word *ecstatic*. It must be very beautiful."

"I am very happy with it too. Want me to put the cold cuts on a dish?"

"I'll take care of that. I was hoping to see the finished work." He undid the many layers of Enrico's fussy wrapping, keeping his back to Nelli. He knew his hurt feelings were foolish. He knew and yet he felt compelled to add, "I did ask you to show it to me."

Ah, that's what was bothering him. "Nico, I am so sorry. I should have shown it to you. I simply did not stop to think. Work at the vineyard has been crazy. Maria Grazia was begging me to bring it over. I couldn't go before next week and I did not want to send it. I have lost paintings that way. On Thursday one of the Querciabella drivers was taking a van full of wine cases to Orvieto and I took advantage without realizing I hadn't shown it to you first." Nelli got up from the table and went to hug Nico. "Please forgive me."

Nico unclasped her hug and faced her. "Nelli, I care about you, and I care about your art. It's beautiful but even if it were ugly I would care because it's an important part of you. You say you are happy with the portrait."

"I am."

"I may sound like a petulant schoolboy, but I would have liked you to share that happiness with me."

"By showing you the portrait?"

"Yes."

"I am sorry."

"Enough. Over and done." Nico put the cold cuts on a plate, grabbed the basket of bread and walked back to the table. "Come on, let's forget about it and finish dinner."

Nelli obliged but she knew it wasn't over and done. OneWag seemed to know too.

When they went to bed, the dog chose to sleep on the other side of Nico, away from her. Nico fell asleep quickly. Nelli spooned herself against him and kissed a spot between his shoulder blades. *Shoulders that would carry me if I needed.* She slipped out of bed, picked up her phone and walked out of the bedroom. She had some thinking to do.

OneWag, with his back pressed against Nico's leg, heard her and looked up. He didn't follow.

FOURTEEN

Nico, Nelli and OneWag were greeted at the door by an elegant-looking Perillo in gray flannel pants and a navy blue V-neck sweater over a white shirt. Nico had thought about a tie, then ditched the thought. Wool slacks that bagged a little at the knees and a collared red sweater would have to do. Thankfully, unlike Rita, Nelli never commented on his clothes. She believed in freedom of expression.

Nico gave Perillo a thumbs-up and said, "Fico," which meant *fig* but also *cool*.

Perillo shrugged off the comment and cheek-kissed Nelli. "Happy you are here. We can begin the food marathon. Dani and Stella are here. I hope you didn't have breakfast."

"We knew we'd better stick to coffee," Nico answered. He'd woken up feeling stupid about his reaction to Maria Grazia's portrait. Nelli had seemed her usual cheerful morning self.

Nelli took off her coat. She had dressed up for the party in a knit sky blue dress that showed off her slim figure and knee-high tan leather boots. She inhaled deeply. "Ah, we are greeted by the perfume of the gods." OneWag had already headed straight to the kitchen.

"Only one god, Ivana." Perillo took their coats. "I'll put these in the bedroom. Go on without me."

In the kitchen *ciaos* and cheek kisses were followed by Ivana at first protesting, then thanking the two couples for the large bouquet of pink roses Luciana had delivered the day before. She had put them next to the small television. "They belong on the table but there's no room."

"Your setting is so beautiful," Stella said, looking great in wide-leg jeans and a hot-pink floppy turtleneck sweater. The table was covered by a white lace-trimmed tablecloth that held hand-painted terra-cotta dishes from Vietri.

Ivana, wrapped in a large plaid apron that covered most of her wine-red dress, turned away from the stove. "Thank you. The tablecloth belonged to my mother. The dishes were a wedding present from a well-to-do client of our family's fish stand. They come out of the closet only twice a year. Christmas and our anniversary."

Perillo walked into the kitchen. "Ah, yes, the precious Vietri dishes. That man was crazed with love for her."

"Salvatore, stop. You are talking nonsense."

"I only talk sense. I saw the way he looked at you. You were a chocolate he wanted to melt in his mouth, then swallow."

"Are you sure you're not talking about yourself?" Nico teased.

Perillo grinned. "Maybe I am. You should have seen her behind that fish stand in Pozzuoli, looking as pretty as a flower. I wasn't bad myself. Eh, to be young again."

"Oh, do shush, Salvatore, and pour some wine for our guests."

"At your command, Signora. Please, everyone, sit at the table."

Nico, Nelli and Stella did as they were asked. Not used to sitting when a woman was standing, Daniele, wearing a tie with his blue shirt, jacket and corduroy slacks, hesitated. Nico pulled out another chair and tapped the seat. OneWag jumped up on it.

"Not for you, buddy," Nico said while the others laughed.

Daniele gently lifted OneWag and lowered him to the floor, slipping him a treat from the stash he now always kept in one of his pockets.

Perillo took the bottle of Panzanello Riserva from a row of five perched along the window ledge and filled everyone's glass.

Ivana gave Nico a *come here* wave. Nico joined her at the stove.

"I have something for you, Nico."

"I know. A fantastic meal."

"No feast without friends."

"Feast indeed." Every burner held a pot releasing mouthwatering smells.

Ivana smiled. "A special day merits extra work." She lowered her voice. "The car dealer told me what our Panda is worth. I wrote the sum down." She reached into her apron pocket and handed him an envelope. "If you still want it and the price is okay, the car is yours. Salvatore will give you the keys before you leave so you can take it for a ride. The new car is being delivered tomorrow."

Nico read the price. "Very fair." That was one problem solved. "I'll buy it." He slipped the envelope into his pocket. "You're the best."

"Thank you. Remind Salvatore, will you?"

"About the keys?"

"That I am the best."

"He knows that."

Looking unconvinced, Ivana bent down and opened the oven door. Nico handed her a pair of knitted oven mitts. Out came a tray of what looked like small pizzas with mozzarella bubbling on top. "These are our Neapolitan crostini. Crostini because on buttered bread, not dough." She slid the crostini onto a large platter. "Please help yourselves."

Nico took the delicious-smelling crostini to the table.

Perillo spread out his arms to catch everyone's attention. Hands retreated from the platter. "Today, on our wedding anniversary—"

Ivana had turned around to face her husband, arms crossed over her chest, a wary look on her face. "We are celebrating twenty-four years of happiness."

Perillo nodded and dropped his arms. "Today I celebrate our twenty-fourth wedding anniversary with a woman who has changed since our last anniversary. She has become a businesswoman. Although I have grumbled, moped and—"

"Protested loudly," Ivana added.

"Yes, I admit it and Ivana, cara, I could put the blame on you because you have spoiled me from the day you brought me that bowl of fried calamari at the Pozzuoli Carabinieri Station." Perillo picked up a full glass of wine. "I thank you and praise you for always being a wonderful, caring wife and friend. This year I have more to praise. You had the courage to step out of the comfort of our home, join the world of working women and make a great success of it."

He raised his glass. The others did the same. "Brava, Ivana!"

Everyone drank and clapped. Daniele rushed a full glass of wine to Ivana, who took a sip and then protested, "You have embarrassed me now, Salvatore, but you have also always made me happy. No more grumbling?"

His hand came up. "I swear." They hugged each other.

"Let me know if he does," Nico said. "I'll knock it out of him."

"Oh, he will grumble. If you pick a turnip, you cannot expect it to become a potato. Turnip he stays but he is my turnip." Ivana kissed Perillo then gently pushed him away. "I have food to take care of. Please eat those crostini. Much more is coming."

They ate the Neapolitan crostini and drank. Perciatelli Principe di Napoli was next. Thick, spaghetti-like pasta with thin strips of roasted chicken breast, sweet peas, small cubes of moz-zarella, butter and parmigiano tossed with a beef stew sauce and more parmigiano. OneWag got a generous share.

"A dish fit more for kings than princes," Nico said after one taste. OneWag didn't come up for air until his bowl was licked clean.

For vegetarian Daniele butter had substituted the meat sauce. Stella looked at the paler pasta, then at Daniele, her eyes warm with love. "You are the prince, then." This time Daniele's blush came with a smile.

Fried bundles of eggplant stuffed with a pecorino and basil mix followed the pasta, along with a raw artichoke salad.

It was absurd to stay in a bad mood in this room, Nico real-ized after another glass of wine. His friends were having fun, stuffing themselves, drinking too much, showering a tireless Ivana with well-deserved compliments. Nico reached for Nelli's hand. She took it and squeezed. Whatever shards of Nico's bad mood were still there disappeared.

His phone rang. "I apologize." Nico took the cell out of his pants pocket with his free hand. A Pitigliano number he vaguely recognized. He turned the phone off.

"Your extraordinarily beautiful new lady friend?" Nelli asked with a bland expression her face.

"Maybe. I'll call back later. She's not my friend."

"She could become one."

"I seem to recall when we were first getting together that you declared you weren't a jealous woman."

Nelli leaned over and kissed Nico's nose. "That was years ago."

The glow Nico felt from the wine now felt brighter.

"Time for the finale," Perillo announced, taking the spu-mante out of the refrigerator. Ivana sliced the ice cream cake made of layers of chocolate, salted caramel and vanilla, with a strawberry sorbet rose on top. The cork popped. Perillo poured. Ivana sliced. Nico stood up with the others, raised a glass and wished Ivana and Perillo many more years of married happiness.

Half an hour later, the party ended with boozy goodbyes, hugs, *thank-yous* and more good wishes. Perillo slipped Nico the Panda car keys. "If you want to test it now, let Nelli drive. She didn't drink."

"You didn't?" Nico asked her on the way out. He hadn't noticed.

"Someone had to drive us home."

"I want to take the Ford Fiesta back to the rental place now."

Nelli shook her head. "You have time to take it back tomorrow."

"I guess you're right. I am feeling a bit woozy. God, the amount of food I ate!"

"We all did."

"Well, I'm telling you," Nico said as Nelli drove out of the carabinieri station parking lot. "I don't plan to cook or eat for at least a week. If you get hungry, you are on your own."

"No worries. Three days of lemon water for me and plain water for Rocco."

OneWag responded with a snore from the back seat. "Wise dog." Nico leaned his head against the window and closed his eyes.

"WAKE UP, NICO. WE'RE here."

Nico opened his eyes and saw a lamp shedding light over a door surrounded by dark night. He rubbed his eyes and looked again. Not his door. Not his light. "Where are we?"

"In Orvieto. At Maria Grazia's house."

While Nico took a moment to process what Nelli was saying, OneWag squeezed himself between the front seats and gave Nelli a telling nudge. She opened her door and the dog jumped out.

Nico squeezed Nelli's hand. "Amore, you are one crazy woman."

"Now you will see it the way it should be seen. In its proper place."

Nico held out his arms. "Can I hug you?"

"Later, at home, you can hug me all you want and more. Now we go up. She's waiting for us."

Maria Grazia's unframed portrait rested on a white marble mantelpiece in her tastefully adorned living room. Maria Grazia, dressed in wool slacks and a loose black sweater, stood next to Nico. As Nico studied the painting, Nelli took OneWag to the kitchen for some water.

The little Nico knew about painting had come from Rita taking him to museums in New York and Florence. The face gazing back at him moved him. "It is very beautiful," Nico said. Maria Grazia's painted face, looking out at the viewer, was no longer plain. Nelli's brushstrokes had filled it with life. The pale gray eyes looking back at him were brimming with what? Curiosity, Nico decided. Nelli had painted Maria Grazia's face as it looked now. Proud and happy, her wish to have her own portrait center stage.

Maria Grazia turned her gaze to Nico. "Thank you for coming to see it in its home. I hope you and Nelli will come back when it is framed and hanging properly."

"It is very beautiful now. And thank you for convincing Eddi to see me."

"Was it a useful meeting?"

"Very."

"I am glad. I will probably be harshly reprimanded by his mother. She is bound to find out."

"Eddi will tell her?"

"If he doesn't, someone will. Pitigliano is after all a small town. Do not worry about me. Teachers develop immunity to angry or interfering parents. Nelli reminded me that you have a long drive home, therefore, I must not offer you anything." Regret flickered in her eyes. "Perhaps an espresso or a glass of Vin Santo?"

Nico mentally clasped his stomach. "Thank you, no. We came from a Neapolitan wedding anniversary feast."

Regret shifted to a smile. "It must have been wonderful and very filling."

"Yes, it was," Nelli said, joining them with a quenched OneWag. Together they said their goodbyes and left.

Before Nelli could get in the car, Nico grabbed her and hugged her hard. "Thank you. You are a great painter and a fantastic woman."

They kissed and got in the car. Nelli insisted on driving.

As soon as they were on the right road back Nico asked, "Why are you working in a vineyard?"

"I like it."

"You should be painting every day, showing your work to galleries."

"The art world is ruthless, Nico. I don't want to be part of it. Painting gives me joy. I don't want it to become a job. I don't have the necessary ambition. I like my life the way it is. I am willing to consider some changes, but—"

Nico's phone started ringing. "I'll switch it off."

"No. Please answer." She wasn't ready to discuss what those changes might be. "It might be important."

Nico took out his phone. It was the same number as before. He swiped. "Pronto?"

"Ah, buonasera." A string of words followed.

Nico was holding his phone against his right ear, too far, too faint for Nelli to hear whether the voice was female or male, but she decided it didn't matter who was on the other end of the phone. The important thing was he was no longer upset with her.

Nico sat up. "I will be in Pitigliano tomorrow. I would like to go with you."

He sounds surprised. Please, whoever you are, don't ruin our night together, Nelli thought.

"You ask why? I have spent many hours trying to solve Lenzi's murder. I would like to be present when it's resolved."

He's annoyed . . . or angry, maybe?

"Thank you. What time can we meet?"

"Good. I strongly suggest you not share your information with anyone else."

"Thank you. Three-thirty tomorrow." Nico clicked off, dropped his head against the headrest and closed his eyes. He hadn't expected this.

"Who was that?"

"I don't want you to get involved in this mess."

"You can't tell me that after getting upset I didn't show you the painting."

Nico thought a few seconds. "You're right." He sat up. "It seems the Lenzi case is solved."

Nelli gave the car horn a slap. "That is wonderful news!"

"It should be. Livia and Cilia will be happy. Saverio can return home. No more driving for hours back and forth."

"Why isn't it?"

"I don't know. Male pride maybe. Disappointment that I'm not the one who solved it?"

Nelli's hand reached over the gear shift and squeezed Nico's thigh. "No. You are not like that."

"I hope you're right."

"Now tell me. Who is it?"

"Not a word to anyone until the case is officially closed?"

"Nico!" Nelli put her hand back on the steering wheel. "How can you even ask?"

"I'm sorry. Just professional caution." Not wanting to, he told her.

Nelli didn't know who was on Livia's suspect list, so the name meant nothing to her.

"Are you surprised?"

"Yes and no." No, because it was plausible. Yes, because he wasn't convinced. "Look, Nelli, I'd like to forget about it until tomorrow. Tonight, I want to concentrate on us. We have some hugging to do."

"I am all for it, amore."

Hours later, with Nelli's head resting in the crook of his neck and OneWag back on the bed, both fast asleep, Nico's thoughts went back to the nervous voice on the phone confessing to Giancarlo Lenzi's murder.

FIFTEEN

They made love again in the morning, then fell asleep again. OneWag, tired of waiting for breakfast, jumped off the sofa, walked to his empty food dish and knocked it over. The noise did the trick.

Nelli shook Nico's shoulder. "Get up. It's late."

Nico stretched out an arm. "No run. Come here."

"There's no time for that or a run. It's breakfast time. Gogol will show up expecting to see us. And you have to take the rental back."

"Not after last night's phone call."

Nelli's shoulders slumped. "I thought the case was solved."

"I'm going back to make sure it is. Let's have breakfast here." Nico pulled her down on the bed. "I'll make eggs and toast."

Nelli gave him a kiss and snuggled against him. "We don't have any eggs."

OneWag, as if on cue, jumped on the bed and pushed his cold nose in Nico's face. "Okay, I get it. Get off me, you two. I will make coffee and buttered toast."

Nelli slipped into her bathrobe and slippers. "I'll feed Rocco."

Wearing his sleep outfit—shorts and a Giants T-shirt, Nico filled the Bialetti moka and put it on the small burner. He called Sandro.

"Please tell Gogol I'm not coming in. Livia too if she comes in. I hope to see them tomorrow." It was too soon to tell Livia about last night's phone call. He was going to play doubting Thomas and stick his finger in the wound first. With that thought, his mood changed. Away went the desire to bask in the warmth of his home with his woman and his buddy.

"Gogol's already here, protesting," Sandro said. "Are you all right?"

"I'm fine. Just work."

"Off to Little Jerusalem then. Salvatore just walked in. Do you want to talk to him?"

"Sure."

A minute later, Perillo asked, "Why aren't you here? Are you sick?"

"No. Why are you up so early?"

"Indigestion. I heard Sandro say *Little Jerusalem*. What's going on there today?"

"I'm meeting with Susanna Necchi."

"Nelli going with you?"

"No."

"Be wise. Call me afterwards."

"I will to both." Nico clicked off.

Nelli gave Nico's serious face a quick look. The effects of their beautiful lovemaking hadn't lasted long, she thought. He was fully back to the murder now. "Why did you not give him the news?"

"I need answers before I do."

"I hope you find them. I have a light day at work today. If you want, I can keep Rocco with me. The boss is on a selling trip."

"That would be great. Thank you." He took her in his arms, gave her a long kiss. "I love you."

"I love you too."

One Wag looked up at them kissing again and gave one protesting bark.

The bronze statue of Il Villano was at the end of the long
piazza. An almost life-size man in a hat stood beside his saddled
donkey. Behind them the thick greenery of the opposite ridge
wavered in the wind that had risen earlier. The holm oaks lining
the piazza rustled.

"Where is your sweet dog?"

Nico looked up from reading the poem attached to the
statue. Susanna was standing behind the donkey in a silver fur
coat. The wind waved her long hair over her smile.

She really was stunning, he thought guiltily. "Buongiorno,
Susanna. I left him with my girlfriend."

"Too bad," she said in a throaty voice. Whether it was too
bad about the missing dog or the girlfriend wasn't clear.

Feeling awkward, Nico looked down at the poem. "This is a
very nice tribute."

"'Man and donkey express the hard work,' she quoted, 'the suf-
fering, the hope of a better life that today has become a certainty.'"
She tightened the collar of her fur around her neck. "The certainty is wishful thinking. Let's get out of the wind." She turned
around and with a few steps walked into the restaurant.

A woman used to being followed, Nico thought as he followed her.

Once inside, a dark-suited man greeted Susanna. "Welcome
back. Your beautiful presence has been missed." He gave Nico a
once-over that did not produce a welcoming face.

Susanna tossed her hair away from her face and gave the man
a tight smile. "My old table?"

"Certainly." The man led them to a corner table next to a picture window and pulled out a chair. Susanna slipped off the fur
and dropped it on the next chair. She was wearing a one-piece
red outfit that hugged her very toned body.

Nico caught the manager's appreciative look before he walked away. Susanna sat down, her back to the view. Nico sat facing her.

"You come here often?"

"When I was married to Matteo. We used to supply the place with our wines and eat here every Friday. The man who greeted me is the owner. I came here once by myself. It was not a good idea."

"How so?"

"I will just say that the owner had expectations I did not share."

"Was that when you were seeing Giancarlo Lenzi?"

She puffed out her lips. "You have a one-track mind, Nico."

"I'm on a job."

"And here I was hoping that was just an excuse." She handed him a menu. "After we order I will answer all your questions."

A waiter came over with two glasses of Prosecco.

"Thank you." Susanna waited for him to leave. "Forgive me for flirting, but it is your fault. You bring it out in me."

"Why?"

She studied the menu. "I am not used to facing a wall when I am with a man. Even a man on a job."

Nico wondered if he was dealing with an insecure woman. "I can understand that. You are very beautiful, but I'm a man in love with a beautiful and wonderful woman who loves me back."

"I thought so. And you come from Puritan America. Dipping elsewhere is frowned upon." She raised her hand to call the waiter, who came rushing over. "I will have the orata with roasted potatoes and a glass of Gavi. You?"

Nico quickly glanced at the salad list. "L'insalata gentile, please. Nothing else." Ivana's lunch yesterday was still a vivid memory in his stomach.

Susanna picked up her Prosecco flute. "No wine? You *are* serious. I will show you my serious side then. No more flirting."

Nico lifted his flute. "Good." They clicked glasses and drank.

Susanna sat back in her chair. "What nasty things did Giulia say about me?"

"Why are you assuming they are nasty?"

"Because you would not be here if she had been nice. Because she was jealous of my looks. Jealous of my affair with Giancarlo. I suspect he had played with her before I came along. The way she looked at me was creepy. I wanted Giancarlo to fire her. He just laughed."

"You told me the affair with Lenzi lasted two months."

"The intense period two, at most three, months. It is hard to tell right away when you are getting hooked. For a couple of years before that, we just played around. On my part at first to help Matteo and then because I found it fun."

"By intense do you mean you fell in love with him?"

"Maybe a little. Being in love adds an extra dimension to sex."

Their food arrived. Nico wished her "Buon appetito," then dug into a delicious-looking mound of baby spinach, peas, walnuts and baked ricotta.

Susanna kept talking between bites of her grilled orata and sips of Gavi. "We started meeting often. Seeing a lot of Giancarlo made me realize he had nothing to offer except sex. Too much sex can become boring. I told him ciao, ciao."

"When?"

"Just before he left for vacation. We laughed about it. We were both relieved."

"Did you see him again?"

"Ah, Giulia told you, didn't she? The moron wouldn't let me into the store, wouldn't believe I had an appointment with Giancarlo." Susanna's face had become harsh. "The cleaning lady vaunting her miserable little power. She must have loved that moment. Did she tell you?"

"Only that you asked her to call Lenzi at home."

Susanna let out a short laugh of disbelief.

"Why did you have an appointment with Lenzi?"

"He wasn't laughing at our breakup anymore. He wanted me back, calling me every day from Porto Ercole. I kept saying no. When he came back, I finally agreed to meet him at the store. He didn't show up just to demonstrate he was in control. Not the brightest way to convince me to start up again."

"He did meet you, didn't he?"

"Yes, as Giulia told you. I had to bribe her to call him at home. When he showed up, I asked Giancarlo to stop calling, to find someone else to bed. He promised he would leave me alone. I walked away satisfied and that's the last time I saw him."

"Did he keep his promise?"

"Yes, he did." She snapped her fingers. "Just like that. I confess I was a little annoyed. I guess I am stupidly vain. I was relieved too of course. A month and a half later he was dead." Her face paled and she took a long shaky breath.

The waiter came over and took their plates away. "Would you like to see the dessert menu?"

Susanna didn't answer. Her mind was clearly elsewhere.

Nico said, "Un Americano e un espresso, per favore."

Susanna drank some water. "Matteo called to tell me. He was gloating with happiness. I didn't—I couldn't believe him." She drank more water, as though her throat had become a desert. "I called Annamaria. Eddi picked up the phone and before I said a word, he announced, '*Yes. Giancarlo Lenzi is dead,*' and hung up. He did not know who he was talking to."

"He must have been answering many calls," Nico said.

"To my surprise, his death was a heavy stone on my heart. I

could not show my face at the spa for three days. They wouldn't have recognized me."

Vain even in grief, Nico thought.

"I guess I was a little in love with him." Susanna reached across the table for Nico's wrist. "Please find out who killed him." She tightened her hold. "Please."

He retrieved his wrist. "I am trying to."

"Livia has little money. I can pay you more."

"Thank you. I don't need your money."

The waiter came back with the coffees. Nico asked for the bill.

"It is on the house," the waiter said.

Susanna leaned back against the chair, eyes closed, a close-mouthed smile on her face. "How sweet of Luigi. Thank him for me."

"Si, Signora."

"Well, thank you," Nico said once the waiter retreated. "Did you know all along I wouldn't be paying?"

"There's always a next time." She took the small square of chocolate in the saucer, unwrapped it and dropped it in her espresso.

Nico saw no reason for there to be a next time. Susanna was stunning to look at, but not a particularly nice woman. He didn't like not having paid. "Do you think accepting a free meal creates some kind of obligation?" he asked.

"All any gift creates is an expectation on the part of the giver, an expectation that allows him or her to dream."

"I see." Embarrassed, Nico decided she was talking about Luigi's expectations.

They finished their coffees, stood up and wrapped themselves in their coats. On the way out, Nico was surprised the owner did not make an appearance. Nico was glad to leave and be on his way.

Now he had an important meeting ahead of him. One that could put an end to the Lenzi case.

Outside the restaurant, Nico held out his hand. "Thank you for answering all my questions and for lunch. I have another meeting to go to."

Her eyebrows shot up. "No more questions ever?"

"I don't think so."

Susanna threw her arms around him and kissed him on the lips. She laughed at the look of surprise on his face. "Ciao, Nico. If you fall out of love, let me know." She hugged her silver fox coat around herself and walked her high-heeled boots across the piazza.

FULCI OPENED THE DOOR. At his feet the white fluffball barked. "Zitto, Cippi! Forgive him, Nico. Buongiorno. Today he is very nervous. Come in, please."

As nervous as Fulci must be, Nico thought as he stepped inside the narrow hallway. For the occasion Livia's neighbor had put on an old striped suit, the jacket not quite fitting around the middle, over a white shirt and wide striped tie. He had shined his shoes.

"Could I have a coffee and a glass of water please?" Nico didn't want either, but he needed to talk to this man before he went to the carabinieri station. After hanging his down jacket on the cast-iron tree, Nico picked up the barking dog and followed Fulci into the small living room. The magazines, the newspaper and the half-opened books were again spread out over the furniture.

"Sit anywhere you wish." Fulci disappeared into the kitchen a few feet away.

Nico stayed on his feet with the now-quiet dog under his arm. "Have you told anyone else?"

"Only you. I did want to tell Livia. I went as far as picking up the phone, but then I thought she would be upset."

"I'm glad you didn't. I'm not sure she would believe you."

"Why not?" Fulci walked back into the living room holding the coffee cup and the glass of water in his hands. Nico took the glass. "Sorry, but I'm not letting go of Cippi."

"I understand." Fulci put the cup and saucer down on a side table next to a chair. "He does like to be held and he misses Cilia as much as I do."

"But you don't bark." Nico sat down on the sofa, put Cippi on his lap and took a sip of espresso since he had asked for it. The bitterness made him wince.

Fulci sat down in the adjacent chair. "I will bark now."

Nico washed the bitterness away with a long sip of water. He put the glass down. "What are you going to 'bark' to Maresciallo Fabbri?"

"What I told you."

"Over the phone last night, you said you killed Giancarlo Lenzi."

"I did."

"You killed him?"

"That is what I said. I killed him."

"Why?"

Fulci's eyebrows met in a frown. "Don't you believe me?"

"Maresciallo Fabbri is the one who needs to believe you. He has publicly stated that Saverio is the murderer. He will not easily change his mind. You have to convince him. Consider this a rehearsal. I am Fabbri. Why did you kill Giancarlo Lenzi?"

Fulci closed his eyes and took a deep breath. "I love Livia. After Saverio threatened Lenzi, I saw the chance I had been waiting for. With Saverio in jail, Livia and Cilia would lean on me, love me. We would become a real family and Livia would be free of Lenzi's abuse."

"How did you know Lenzi was in the store that night?"

"I take Cippi out for long walks. I saw a light was on. I rang the bell. Lenzi let me in. We went back to his office, and I picked up the hammer and hit him hard."

"Why did he let you in?"

Fulci shifted in his chair. It was clear he was uncomfortable with the questions. "I told him I knew why he faked those invoices."

"Did you?"

"It was obvious." Fulci took a handkerchief from his suit pocket and wiped his mouth. "He needed money to get away with the Necchi woman. Walking with Cippi at night I saw her going in the store or coming out, depending on the hour of our walks. At the same time abusing Livia. I saw him one night on the street, pushing himself against her, pinning her against the wall. Oh, I wanted to hit him then. He was a disgusting man."

"He let you in the store and then what happened?"

"I followed him to his office."

"He let you stay after what you said to him?"

"Yes. Maybe he thought I would leave. He went to his office and I followed. The hammer was on his desk. I saw my chance, picked it up and hit him on the head."

"How many times?"

Fulci sighed loudly. "I do not know, Nico. It is all a confusion now."

"What if the hammer hadn't been there? What would you have done?"

"I don't know. Maybe nothing that night, but it was there."

"Was there a lot of blood?" Nico asked. As far as he knew the press hadn't reported that Lenzi had bled out.

"Basta!" Fulci stood up and jerked down his suit jacket. "I am going to Maresciallo Fabbri. I will go alone because it is clear to me that you do not believe me." He picked up a coat lying on a side table and put it on. "The maresciallo will understand I am telling the truth."

Nico stood up and put the dog down. Cippi ran to Fulci, tail wagging wildly. "Maybe Fabbri will accept your story because it is convenient. He is under great pressure to find a solution to Lenzi's murder."

"Why don't you believe me?" Fulci cried.

"I would like to, but I worry that you are confessing to a murder you didn't commit because you do love Livia and Cilia. They are your family now and you want them to be happy. Saverio can come home and all will be well for them. Will Livia, who has trusted you to take care of Cilia because she believed you are a good man, accept that you killed Lenzi? If she does, she will wonder why you let her, Saverio and Cilia suffer for so long. And what will Cilia think of the man she loves so much she considers him her uncle? That deception will stay with her for a long time."

"Saverio home is what they want. They will forget me. I killed Lenzi. Please, go now."

A sudden thought of what Fulci might do if Fabbri rejected his confession made Nico shudder. "No, I'm coming with you. It's a long walk to the carabinieri station and it's cold. I'll drive you."

"That is kind of you."

Nico said nothing and walked down the corridor with Cippi running ahead. Picking up his down jacket at the front door, Nico asked, "If Fabbri arrests you, what will happen to Cippi?"

"Livia will take him in. Cilia adores him." Fulci unhooked the leash and harness from the iron tree. "Would you have the kindness to take him with you?"

"Of course. I will probably have to bring him back tomorrow."

Fulci shook his head and opened the door. Cippi let out a bark of joy and leapt down the two flights.

NICO PARKED ACROSS THE street from the carabinieri station. "Cippi and I are going to wait for you."

"No! The maresciallo will believe me. Go now. Please." Fulci lifted Cippi from his lap and held him close to his face. "You have to be good, understand?" Cippi responded with a nose lick. Paolo put the dog down and quickly got out of the car.

Nico opened his window and yelled after him, "We're waiting."

An hour went by. Nico leashed Cippi and took him for a walk. The dog was quiet. They went back to the car and Nico called Nelli to tell her he would be late. He passed time scrolling on his phone. Cippi settled on his lap. Nico leaned his head on the headrest.

His phone woke him up.

"Go home, Nico," Fulci said. "Maresciallo Fabbri believes me. Please explain to Livia."

"No way!" Nico shouted. Cippi started barking. Fulci clicked off. Nico called him back. No answer.

Nico started the car and drove away. With the movement of the car, the dog calmed down. Nico kept his eyes on the long trip home and tried to resign himself to Fulci's guilt.

IT WAS ALMOST EIGHT-THIRTY when Nico parked the car below Livia's building. There was no one sitting in the parked cars. *Fabbri must have called off the watch*, Nico thought as he clicked Livia's number.

"Ciao, Livia. I have news."

"Good news?"

"It depends. Is Cilia asleep yet?"

"No, she's playing *Mario Party Superstars*. Come up. We can talk in the kitchen."

"I have Cippi with me." Nico heard her suck in her breath.

"The door will be open."

Livia was standing at the open door in jeans and a sweatshirt. Seeing her, Cippi tried to wiggle out of Nico's grasp. He happily handed him over to Livia. "Why do you have Cip?" The dog was licking her face. "Is Paolo sick?"

He stepped inside. "No. Let's talk in the kitchen."

"The look on your face is scary."

"I'm very tired, Livia."

The kitchen was just to the right of the front door—a narrow room with cabinets and walls painted a strident lemon yellow. Two chairs and a rectangular table covered with a blue oilcloth stood underneath the only window. Livia left the door open and put Cippi down. "Can I offer you anything?"

"No thanks. The dog might need some water."

"Go on, sit down. Tell me."

Nico stayed standing while Livia emptied a plastic bowl containing laundry clips, filled it with water and put it on the floor. Cippi lapped it up noisily.

Tell her straight, Nico asked himself, *or get there slowly by asking about their relationship first?*

Livia pulled out a chair from the table and sat down. "Are you going to deliver your news standing up?"

"No, sorry." Nico sat down opposite her. Straight was the fair way. "Paolo has confessed to killing Lenzi."

Livia stared at him for a moment. "No!"

"He confessed to Maresciallo Fabbri, and Fabbri accepted the confession."

"Paolo is a sweet man. He barely knew Giancarlo. Why would he want to kill him?"

"He says he wanted to have you and Cilia for himself. He told me he was in love with you."

Livia covered her face with her hands. She looked up after a minute or two with a confused expression on her face. "Is it possible? I don't know. I have always thought of Paolo as a gentle man, a little lost after his wife died. He has always been respectful. He has never tried to intrude."

"He has never said he loved you?"

"A lot of times he has told me '*ti voglio bene.*' That is an *I love you* also said to a friend. Never *ti amo.*"

"Has he ever tried to touch you or kiss you?"

"He kissed me once. Years ago. Before Saverio. His wife was in the hospital and I had invited him over for dinner. He looked so sad. I felt sorry for him. I didn't kiss him back, but I didn't protest. I thought it would have been hurtful to push him away. Paolo did become a little possessive when I got together with Saverio. He wanted to check him out first. If Paolo is in love with me, I have done nothing to encourage him except for that one night. He does love Cilia very much. Anyone can see that. Cilia loves him right back."

"Did Saverio ever say anything about your friendship with Paolo?"

"Savi is not a jealous man, but one time when Paolo invited us to dinner to celebrate his birthday, afterward Savi said how sad he was for Paolo, who had to sit there and watch the woman he loved be happy with another. I told him the wine was making him see things that weren't there. We had consumed a great deal of wine."

"Do you believe Paolo could have killed Lenzi?"

"I don't know what to believe. Part of me wants it to be true. This nightmare would be over. Saverio could come home. We could get back to living an almost normal life again."

"And the other part of you?"

"I do not know. What do you think?"

"I don't believe Paolo. I think he confessed to make you and Cilia happy again. On Saturday Cilia spent the day with him. He knew the reason. She was sad and wanted to come home. I think that's when he got the idea. Last night he told me he killed Lenzi and was going to confess to Maresciallo Fabbri. I asked him to wait for me. Today in his home I told him

I didn't believe him, but he was determined. Unfortunately, Fabbri believed him."

"Maybe he is telling the truth. Will they let me talk to him?"

"I don't know what is allowed in this country." Nico picked up his phone. "I'm texting you the station number."

"Thank you."

Nico stood up. "I need to go home now. Nelli is waiting with dinner."

Livia picked up the dog sitting at her feet. "Come and say goodnight to Cilia."

"What if she asks why Paolo's dog is here?"

"I will take care of that."

"Cippiii!" Cilia shouted as soon as the dog ran to her. Many hugs and kisses followed from both.

"Zio Paolo asked Nico to bring Cippi to keep you company. Wasn't that nice of him?"

Cilia nodded. "Can I take him to school with me?"

"No, we will have to find someone to take care of him during the day." Livia glanced at Nico standing at the door of the bedroom mother and daughter shared.

He had had enough of the barking fluffball. "Try Luciana. She dog-sits Rocco." He took a step into the room. "Buonanotte, Cilia."

Cilia looked up surprised. "Oh, ciao. Say 'notte to Rocco."

"I will." Nico let himself out.

AS SOON AS NELLI saw Nico's face, she asked, "What happened?"

Nico went over to the table set for dinner and poured himself a glass of red. "Fabbri accepted Paolo's confession."

She clasped his face with her hands and kissed him lightly. "It is over?"

"I guess it is. Paolo goes to jail for a murder he insists he committed; Saverio, Livia and Cilia will be together again, and I can stop burning gas every day."

"Then why don't you look the least bit relieved?"

He wrapped his arms around Nelli. "Because I'm starved!"

"Sit down then for a Nelli dinner. Minestrone bought frozen from the Coop with Parmigiano-Reggiano Enrico grated in front of my eyes, followed by his caciotta and a round of pane rustico. I didn't know what you wanted for dessert, so I didn't buy any. I hope last week's apples will do."

Nico sat down. "Sounds delicious. I will have you cook for me more often."

"Oh, amore, you really are down."

"It always happens at the end of a chase, whether you're the winner or not."

SIXTEEN

Perillo and Daniele showed up at Bar All'Angolo as Nico was finishing a very late breakfast with Nelli and Gogol. The place had emptied out by then. Livia and Cilia had not shown up. OneWag, at the sight of Daniele, interrupted his crumb reconnaissance to greet him with body wiggles. Perillo walked straight to Nico's table and sat down.

"Buongiorno a tutti."

"Buongiorno." Nelli stood up. She didn't want to listen to the conversation that would follow. "I need to get to work. Gogol, do you want me to walk you home?"

Gogol picked up his last crostino and showed it to her.

"Understood." Ten minutes earlier Gogol had complained the bread was stale. He just wanted to eavesdrop. She kissed the top of his head and Nico's. "Ciao a tutti."

"Ciao," said Jimmy and Sandro; "Arrivederci," said Daniele. OneWag followed Nelli to the door.

"No, you are with Nico today." She closed the door behind her. The dog went back to doing his floor sweep.

"I was waiting for your call last night," Perillo said. He wasn't annoyed, Nico noticed. There even seemed to be a gleam in his eyes. "I expected to see the smile of relief and satisfaction on your face. Instead, your face is heavy with fatigue, perhaps annoyance."

"I am tired."

"'Conquer your weariness with the spirit that wins all battles.'" Gogol dropped his lard crostino on Nico's plate. "This will bring relief."

Daniele brought over a double espresso for his boss, a cappuccino for himself. He sat down next to Gogol, in the chair Nelli had just vacated.

"I heard Fabbri has his murderer." Perillo took a few sips of his espresso. "I don't know how you see it. For the first twenty minutes I did not accept Fulci's confession. I was convinced of Eddi's guilt. Slowly Fulci murdering Lenzi began to make sense. You did tell us how much he loved Livia and Cilia. He must have believed that getting Saverio jailed for murder was his one chance at happiness. Poor man. I almost feel sorry for him."

"'You will see your belief is greatly mistaken,'" Gogol announced.

Perillo narrowed his eyes. "And you know everything?"

"I think what Nico thinks."

Perillo stared at Nico. "You discussed the case with Gogol?"

"I did not. Gogol and I have been friends almost from the day I moved here. He reads me well."

"You think Fulci is lying?"

"My gut says he is, my brain says he could be telling the truth."

"Maybe he is sacrificing himself for love," Daniele offered.

"Yes, Dani," Nico said, "that's where my doubt comes in."

"'A small spark can become a great flame,'" Gogol quoted.

"Yes," Dani agreed. "I admire his courage and the power of his love."

Perillo huffed. "Touch earth, Dani. Fulci is guilty." He turned to face the old man. "Signor Gogol, I admire your knowledge of the great Tuscan poet, but I am not interested in what he has to say about my opinions."

Gogol noisily smacked his lips. "'Opinions formed in haste will oftentimes lead in the wrong direction.'"

Nico put his hand on Gogol's arm, hoping to stop any more quotes. Perillo controlled himself by spooning what was left of the sugar in his cup into his mouth and standing up. Daniele caught Perillo's expression and quickly went to pay the bill.

"I'm taking the rental car back this morning," Nico said to Perillo. "I'd like to pick up the Panda, but I don't have my checkbook with me."

"The Panda is yours. The check goes to Ivana when it pleases you." Perillo zipped up his new shearling jacket, an anniversary present from Ivana. "You should be pleased, Nico. Once Fulci met you he understood you would eventually see his guilt. He just made it a little easier for you. Complimenti. Next time we meet I hope to see on your face the relief and satisfaction that comes with a job well done." Perillo stood up and wished everyone "buona giornata."

"You too," came from Nico. Sandro raised a hand. A burst of steam from the coffee machine drowned out Jimmy's response. Perillo walked out with Daniele following.

Sandro leaned over the counter. "Nico, is it true? Someone confessed to the Pitigliano murder?"

"It is true."

"Good. No more running off to Pitigliano. Now you can stay here and solve our local problems."

Nico's hand was still on Gogol's arm. "And what problems do you have, Sandro?"

"None for now. We enjoy having you around. Gogol, repeat what you quoted yesterday morning when Nico left."

Gogol shook his head. "No more Dante for today. He has been disrespected."

Nico released his hold on Gogol and murmured, "You disrespected the maresciallo, don't you think?"

Gogol's eyes glinted at Nico. "There is no repenting, we smile instead."

A stubborn and irreverent man, Nico thought. *But lovable.* "What did you quote when I left yesterday?"

"My memory is short-lived."

Nico burst out laughing. "That is a good one. Keep smiling. I'll walk you home."

WITH GOGOL SAFE IN the Medici villa, Nico went back to Bar All'Angolo and asked Sandro about Gogol's quote.

"It was something about a lonely old man and a son. I can't do better than that. In school I dreaded Dante. I just saw how much he missed you. Gogol is very attached to you."

"And I to him. Thanks. See you tomorrow."

AFTER HE HAD RETURNED and paid for the Ford Fiesta, Nico drove back to Greve in the Panda with all four windows down. The car was spotless, but Ivana had sprayed it with a cloying, sweet-smelling deodorant that forced him to breathe through his mouth. OneWag rode in the back seat with his snout resting on the open window. Having his whole head hanging out of the car was forbidden.

Luciana was opening her shop when Nico parked the car. "Caro Nico, you have to buy a great many more flowers from me to make up for this." She turned and opened her floor-length red coat to show the barking fluffball strapped to her chest like a newborn. He was fast asleep.

Nico walked over with OneWag. "How clever of you."

"Keeps him quiet. Poor Cilia asked so sweetly I could not

refuse, but you owe me. You are driving Salvatore Perillo's car now?"

"It's mine now."

"Ah. The Ford Fiesta suited you better." She looked down. OneWag was staring up at her, his paw pressing her foot. "Don't worry, Rocco. The cookies are all for you. Come back later." She opened the door. "My plants need some love now. You, Nico, look like you need some love too. Your friend not treating you as you deserve?"

"I am just tired."

"Tell her to make you a tisane of rosemary or mint. It will give you energy." She stepped inside. "The flower truck comes tomorrow. Rita's sunflowers have dropped their heads." Loyalty to a wife, alive or dead, was forever in Luciana's mind.

"Tomorrow then." Nico crossed the piazza, OneWag walking ahead. It was a cloudy day, too cold for Gustavo and his friends to be chatting on one of the benches. Nico would have enjoyed saying hello, exchanging a few words. All he had to do today was shop for dinner. Having a free day was normally something he enjoyed. Today it didn't feel right. He was pretty sure it probably wasn't going to feel right tomorrow either.

Nico entered Salita della Chiesa, the road he climbed and descended several times a day when he worked at Sotto Il Fico during the tourist season. An eager OneWag trotted up the hill ahead of him.

Ten minutes later, Nico found OneWag playing sentinel in front of Enrico's salumeria. Nico opened the door. "Buongiorno."

Enrico looked up from unwrapping the olive loaves from his bakery. "Salve, Nico." He peered at Nico for a moment. "All is well, I hope?"

Do I look that bad? "Everything's fine. I've been doing a lot of driving."

"It is over, I hear."

"Yes, it is. How do you know?"

"Cilia came over last night with the little dog to ask if Luciana could keep him in the shop while she is in school. She told us her babbo was coming home very soon. She was so happy. A different child. Bravo, Nico. You found the murderer."

"A man confessed. It had nothing to do with me."

"I do not believe that. What do you need from me today? I see that Rocco has his nose pressed against the glass of the door. I will cut him a piece of lean prosciutto to chew on. And you?"

"Four olive loaves if they haven't all been reserved and then I don't know. I'm not inspired today."

"That is the fatigue that comes from a job well done. Four loaves are yours." Enrico reached up and unhooked a leg of prosciutto di montagna and placed it in a wooden holder. "How many for dinner?" He tightened the screws on the holder.

"Just me and Nelli."

"Three sausages then. You cannot go wrong with pork sausages." With a thin long knife and using a sawing motion, he carefully cut a half-inch slice from the leg. "Caseless with rigatoni or penne. Sliced in half and grilled. Add roasted potatoes or polenta or beans—anything and you have a good meal." He cut off the fat from the prosciutto slice, then cut the slice into pieces. "That is how I cook them. Without fennel or pepperoncino to keep Luciana happy. For me they are better with fennel, but marriage is compromise." Enrico wrapped the prosciutto, then handed it to Nico over the counter.

"Thank you and add three sausages to the olive loaves. Without fennel or pepperoncino to be on the safe side." Nico had no idea how Nelli liked her sausages.

OneWag pawed the door. Enrico laughed. "I'll wrap quickly. Rocco is in a hurry."

And I have all the time in the world, Nico thought sadly. Once outside he gave OneWag a piece of Enrico's prosciutto and headed farther up the hill.

Sotto Il Fico's door was locked, but Nico could hear Lucio Dalla's gravelly voice singing "Come è profondo il mare."[23] That meant Tilde was there alone. He took out his key and unlocked the door. "It's me, Tilde," he yelled over the music. He followed OneWag through the empty restaurant. The chairs were upside down on the tables; the floor was still damp from being mopped clean. OneWag, aware of the rules, settled down on his pillow in Elvira's corner.

Tilde was in the kitchen, her back to Nico, dressed in jeans and an old sweatshirt with a kitchen towel wrapped around her head. Nico had only seen her wearing dresses. She was singing along, swinging her hips to Dalla's beat, an elbow moving up and down as she scrubbed hard on one of her many copper cooking pots with a cloth.

"Ciao, Tilde."

She looked up. "Oh! You are a surprise."

"So are you."

She lowered the music on the CD player and went back to scrubbing. "When the cat sleeps, the mice dance."

"Where's Enzo?"

"He drove Elvira to the dentist in Greve. No Pitigliano today?"

"Case is over."

"Fantastic!" She dropped the cloth and threw her arms around him. "You did it again."

Nico sniffed, then sneezed. "That is a heavy dose of vinegar you are using."

"Vinegar and fine salt, the best way to clean copper."

___
23 How deep is the sea.

"And a lot of elbow grease." He saw that she had shined three pots and had four more to go. "I'll help."

"No, you should be celebrating."

Nico took off his coat and hung it on the hook just inside the door. "I had nothing to do with the case being closed."

"What do you mean?"

Nico pushed up the sleeves of his sweater and shirt, then grabbed an apron. "I've missed being here. Give me a cloth."

Tilde crossed her arms. "Not until you explain."

He explained. She handed him a cloth, rubber gloves, the salt and vinegar.

In half an hour all the copper pots gleamed. Nico looked at his work and felt much better.

"What are you going to do now?" Tilde asked.

"Let me cook up some lunch for the two of us."

"That's not what I meant."

"I know and I don't know." He opened the refrigerator. "Whether I believe Paolo Fulci is telling the truth or not doesn't matter now. His confession is in the hands of the Italian legal system. There's nothing in here!"

"I cleaned the refrigerator." Tilde started hanging the pots back on the wall. "If you don't think this man is your killer, go back to Pitigliano and find the real one."

"I plan to go back. There's a woman I want to see again."

"What are you waiting for?"

"I don't really know."

"You were caught off guard, Nico. Surprises can make you lose your bearing."

"That's it." *I don't know where to put my feet to keep walking.*

"Siamo i cattivi pensieri,"[24] Dalla sang.

---

24 We are the bad thoughts.

"Thanks, Tilde. You've just given me the startup I needed."

"It's the empty refrigerator that did it."

"That too." He walked out of the kitchen and punched in Debora's number.

She picked up instantly. She must have had the phone on her lap. "Nico, buongiorno. I was hoping to hear from you again."

"I'm glad. I would love to pay you a visit. This afternoon or tomorrow at your convenience."

"I would like that very much. I have heard the unexpected news. I hope you do not mind my asking, were you surprised?"

"I was. Do you know Paolo Fulci?"

"Not in person. Only the little Saverio has told me about him. Can you come this afternoon?"

"Yes. Give me the time to get to you. I'm in Gravigna."

"Waiting comes naturally at my age. Please do drive safely."

"I will." Nico clicked off and glanced at OneWag fast asleep on his pillow. "Wake up, buddy, we're hitting the road again." Back in the kitchen, he put Enrico's package in the empty refrigerator. "I'm going. That's tonight's dinner. I'll pick it up when I get back." He gave Tilde two quick kisses and rushed off.

"Thanks for the cleanup," Tilde called out after him.

AS NICO SAT IN the blue armchair, drinking the sugarless espresso Debora had offered him, the heavy brass clock sitting on Debora's fireplace mantel struck the half hour.

"I am half an hour late," Debora said. "I must not have coffee after two in the afternoon if I want to sleep tonight." She took another sip. OneWag lay on the carpeted floor between them. "I found I needed the boost and rules are meant to be broken as long as they only harm oneself."

"Were you surprised when you heard about Fulci's confession?" Nico asked as his empty stomach protested the coffee.

"It is hard to be surprised when you do not know the person.

I do wonder why he waited so long to come forth. Had you frightened him in some way?"

"I didn't try to. Killing Lenzi to get Saverio in jail seemed far-fetched to me, so I didn't consider him a likely suspect."

"Is that why you are having difficulties accepting his confession?"

"Maybe." *Am I that much of a jerk? Grown vain from my previous successes? She's looking at me with kindness. Makes things worse.*

"It could be that you are not accepting the confession because after years of experience with murderers, your instinct tells you this confession is false."

"Maybe." *That feels better.* "What did Saverio tell you about Livia's neighbor?"

"He said the man was a gentle, humble man. Essentially harmless. That was when he had just moved in with Livia. Sometime later, I do not remember exactly when, Saverio mentioned being uncomfortable with Fulci's evident devotion to Livia and Cilia. We did not speak of him again."

"Have you talked to Saverio?"

"This morning. He already knew from Livia. He sounded very happy and wanted to come back right away. I told him it was too soon."

"You want him to wait until Fulci is found guilty?"

"No. I think more clarity is needed." She put her demitasse and saucer on a stack of books at her elbow. "Have you visited our synagogue yet?"

"No, I haven't. I am sorry."

"No need to be sorry. I would like to take you there now. It is part of the Jewish Ghetto Museum. We can talk there with nothing to remind us that time is passing except the light." As she slowly stood up in her long wool dress, OneWag got on his feet.

She grabbed her cane. "Do not worry, OneWag. You will be welcome. You too are a creature of God."

"Maybe I should carry him."

"Yes, that would be best. I must not upset the women who take such good care of the museum."

Nico took the cups and saucers back to the kitchen while Debora enveloped herself in a floor-length white down coat that had been lying on the sofa. With cane in hand, she slipped an arm in Nico's. With a leashless OneWag leading, they made their way to the entrance and down the many steps to the street.

As the historic town was built on a ridge, the streets were on different levels, often with stairs of varied widths connecting them. It was a slow walk to the synagogue, with Nico holding on to Debora's arm, her cane tapping their progress on the uneven stone pavement. OneWag ran ahead, only to run back to check on their progress.

The synagogue was on the lowest street, on the edge of the tufa ridge. "Our synagogue is not what it once was, unfortunately," Debora said as they made their way down a set of stairs. "Parts of the structure kept collapsing and they finally closed it in 1956." They walked through a high cast-iron gate. "The Jewish community was greatly reduced by then; only less than the fingers on two hands was still here."

"The Nazis," Nico said, remembering the plaque the town had put up to commemorate the victims.

"The Nazis, yes, but many had already spread out over Italy. It took a long time for the town council to rebuild. Let us go in."

Nico swept OneWag up, put him inside his down jacket and zipped it halfway up. "Be good, buddy."

They walked into a plain rectangular room. Near the ceiling, an ochre-colored band ran along the white stucco walls. Underneath the band were a series of sky blue epigraphs written in Hebrew. Two rectangular windows let in the weakening afternoon light. A circle of stronger light came from the large central window above them. Heavy dark wood benches lined the wall on each side. Nico pointed to a curved wooden structure in the center of the room. "Is that the pulpit?"

"Yes, we call it La Tevá," Debora said, trying to catch her breath from the long walk. "It is where the Torah was read when we had one."

She lowered herself on the long bench. "If this were a working synagogue, I would have to sit up there." She pointed to the covered balcony high behind them. "That's where I sat as a very little girl, detesting every second of it."

Nico sat down next to her.

"Is it a long service?"

"I never minded the length. I liked the singing, even tried to sing along. What I hated was being separated from my father and then hidden behind a screen. I felt I was being punished for being a girl."

OneWag had pushed himself half out of Nico's jacket. Debora ruffled the fur on his head, then rested her eyes on Nico's face. "I brought you here because I want you to know something that was told to me in secret. I will be breaking a trust, something I have never done before. Telling you in the house of God makes it somehow feel less terrible."

"Did Fulci's confession make you want to tell me?"

"The thought that this man might be confessing out of the goodness of his heart convinced me you had to know."

"I'm listening."

Debora lifted the Star of David hanging on her chain and kissed it. "Mimmo is a curious little boy and jealous of his brother. Saturday afternoon, he found himself alone in the house and decided to snoop in Eddi's room 'just to do something.'" Debora pressed her hands together.

"What did he find?"

"A bloodied brooch belonging to his mother. Eddi had hidden it in a sock then stuffed the sock in an old soccer cleat."

Nico felt his stomach tighten. *Finally a break.* "Did Mimmo bring you the brooch?"

"No, he put it back right away. Mimmo is frightened, says he does not understand why Eddi has hidden the brooch, why it has blood on it. I am not sure he has connected the blood with his father's death. Or if he has, he's suppressing it."

"Unless he wants to protect his mother even to you."

"Then why bring up the subject?" She shook her head. "Yes, I know. Maybe because he could not help himself. Some release is better than none."

"He is only thirteen."

"Sometimes closer to ten." She bowed her head, her clasped hands resting on her lap. A minute later, with head lifted, she said, "I have done what was needed to be done. I will go home now. I have made the trip here and back by myself many times before, but it would be more pleasant with you and poor OneWag, who will be thrilled to be free to run ahead of us again."

"We would love it." Nico stood and held out his arm. Debora lifted herself up and slipped her arm in his.

ONCE DEBORA WAS SAFELY home, Nico leashed OneWag and walked to the Piazza della Repubblica pharmacy. He was hoping to find Annamaria. Meeting face to face should make it harder for her to shrug him off.

Behind the counter, a white-coated young woman with a pinched face gave him a penetrating look, then glanced down at OneWag. She seemed to stiffen. Nico understood he'd been recognized.

"Buonasera. I am hoping to have a word with Signora Lenzi if she's available."

The woman's nostrils flared. "La dottoressa is not here," she said with emphasis on the title he had not used. "Can I help you?"

He smiled at her. "I wish you could. Thank you though."

"May I know who was looking for her?"

"No need." Nico walked out, took out his phone and pressed Annamaria's number. This time luck was with him.

"Buonasera, Nico here." He got right to the point. "Signora Lenzi, it's important that you and I meet again."

"It is not important to me." Her voice could freeze water. "My husband's murderer has confessed. You are irrelevant to me now."

"Maybe I'm not." Nico mentally crossed his fingers. This was a gamble. "You know that Eddi went to the LenConi store the night your husband was killed."

A sharp intake of breath. A few seconds of silence. "Why are you lying to me?"

"I am not. He was seen and your son admitted it to me. Ask him. The two of you need to talk. And after you have, I hope, in the name of justice for your husband, that you will want to meet with me."

Annamaria clicked off.

Nico pulled on OneWag's leash. "Come on, buddy. The dice are thrown. Let's go home."

NICO WAS THROWING THE drained rigatoni into the bubbling sausage, kale and mascarpone sauce when his phone rang. He dumped the rest of the pasta in the skillet and grabbed the phone off the table to answer.

"Perillo! Your timing stinks. We're about to eat."

Nelli took over stirring.

"You always eat early!"

By the time Nico had driven back to Gravigna, picked up the food he'd left in Sotto Il Fico's refrigerator, gotten home and started cooking dinner, it had been almost nine o'clock. "I had a long afternoon in Pitigliano." Nico walked back to the stove. Nelli gladly handed over the wooden spoon. "I'm too tired to talk about it now." He added parmigiano, flipped the pasta over and under the sauce. "See you in the morning at Bar All'Angolo. I'll have the check for the Panda."

"Okay." Perillo sighed loudly. "Just tell your old friend to save his Dante for when I am not present. Buon appetito."

"Thanks." Nico clicked off, slipped a rigatone in his mouth and chewed. "Done!"

Nelli held out two bowls which Nico filled to the top. "This is it. No other food."

"Wrong, amore. I washed some escarole for a salad. You will have to dress it."

Nico kissed her forehead. They sat down at the table Nelli had set and dug in. Silence followed.

After Nelli had finished her bowl of rigatoni, she looked up at Nico. "Do I have to wait until breakfast with Perillo to find out about your long afternoon?"

"Not now. Murder and good food don't go together. How was your day?"

"Fairly boring. We are bottling the five-year-old vintage. The sauce on the rigatoni was delicious."

"Enrico's idea. Very easy. I just added something to tie it all together."

Nelli wiped her mouth with her napkin and sat back in her chair. Tying it together was what she needed to do. "The new oak barrels from France finally arrived at Querciabella, which reminded me that you haven't finished clearing out Aldo's old barrels from the room downstairs."

Nico said nothing. The downstairs room was a sore subject. He didn't want to deal with it tonight.

Nelli caught on, but if she didn't bring it up now, she might change her mind again. "You were clearing the downstairs to give me more room for my stuff for when I moved in with you."

"I was." He stabbed the last sauce-laden rigatone with his fork and put it in his mouth.

Nelli reached out and rested her hand on Nico's. "Maybe it's time you finished the job."

Nico's head shot up. "What do you mean?"

"I mean we should try living together. See if we both like it."

A wave of heat ran through Nico's body. "No commitment?"

"What is the point of a commitment if one of us ends up being unhappy?"

"I'll make sure you're happy."

The insistence in Nico's voice made OneWag look up from his post on the armchair.

Nelli squeezed Nico's hand. "You might discover you are not happy."

"But I won't—" His phone started ringing in his pocket. "I love you and there's no way—"

"Answer the phone first, please. I will keep."

Nico jerked the phone out of his pocket. "Pronto!"

"Buonasera." Annamaria Lenzi did not bother to give her name. "I spoke to Eddi and I owe you an apology. Signor Fulci did not kill my husband. I will tell you who did. I have proof. Can you come to my home tomorrow at ten o'clock? My shift at the pharmacy starts at eleven. You have my address?"

"Yes. I will be there."

"Good. Your dog is welcome." She clicked off. Nico's head was now a stimulating medley of excitement, possibility, happiness, satisfaction and he didn't know what else. He picked up his glass and downed half of the wine.

"You've had good news."

"Yes, but yours is better. I'll never be unhappy with you next to me."

"I can be trying and there will be times when I will want to retreat back to my two rooms where I have lived for over twenty years."

A nick of disappointment. "You're keeping the apartment."

"For now. I can only take one step at a time. Please understand."

"I love you so I will."

"Thank you. Now tell me the good news."

"After you hand over the salad."

"I'll get the plates."

"Nothing wrong with our cleaned-out bowls."

Nelli handed over the olive wood bowl filled with her salad. "So?"

"I have to dress it first."

"You are impossible!" Laughing, Nelli threw her napkin at the man she had finally decided to live with.

SEVENTEEN

C AN'T MAKE BREAKFAST, Nico texted Perillo before getting in his new car. MEETING ANNAMARIA LENZI AT TEN. FILL YOU IN LATER. The temperature had dropped to three degrees Celsius, but last night's news had given Nico enough internal warmth not to notice. Besides, a pale sun was scaling the sky making promises.

The Lenzi house was directly opposite Debora's smaller place. Only seven stairs, each step flanked by white cyclamens.

Annamaria opened the door and without saying a word led him and OneWag up a short ramp of stone stairs to a large richly furnished room with three windows facing Debora's same view of the verdant ridge with its small waterfall. These windows had dark green velvet drapes, eliminating some of the light. The two adjacent stone walls were covered with flowered tapestries. Opposite the windows a pile of logs crackled and burned in a wide-tiled fireplace.

"Please sit down, Signor Doyle." Annamaria indicated one of the two pale green brocaded sofas on each side of the fireplace. Nico sat on the left one. She sat opposite him, sitting up stiffly in a pinstriped pantsuit, her face deprived of any makeup or expression. She had aged since he had seen her.

"Can I offer you an espresso?" Annamaria asked. OneWag

examined her short-heeled pumps and smelled sugar. "A bri-oche?"

"No, thank you." He didn't want to waste time. "You spoke to Eddi."

She nodded. "I knew nothing about his going to the store that night. I only discovered my husband was dead when the carabinieri called me. Eddi was in shock. He understood right away that his father had been murdered. He wanted to tell me, to prepare me, but he also wanted to protect me from the hideous truth. He chose to let me sleep a few more hours unaware of the tragedy that had befallen us. He meant well. He always does with me. Eddi and I have a very close relationship."

"That is not the reason he didn't tell you, is it?"

Annamaria looked down at her lap.

"You had a big fight with your husband that night."

"One that I will regret for the rest of my life."

"And when Eddi found your husband dead in his office, he also found a bloodied pin. Yours, I believe."

Her head snapped up. "Yes, mine."

Nico kept his eyes fixed on her face, waiting for her to say more.

After what seemed like a minute, Annamaria leaned over and opened an ornate brass box sitting on the glass coffee table between them. She took out a small package and carefully unwrapped several layers of paper towels. She extended her arm. "Giancarlo gave it to me when Eddi was born."

Nico moved to the edge of the sofa and stretched forward. The bloodied pin, resting on the paper towels, was about two and a half inches in width and shaped like a flower—a large central diamond surrounded by five petal-shaped deep blue sapphires. He remembered what Giulia had said about a stolen pin. *Who else but the cleaning lady.*

"Is this the pin you accused Giulia Favelli of stealing?"

"Yes. I was hasty in my judgment."

"When did it go missing?"

"I was certain I had put it with a few other jewels in a safe place when the boys and I left for Forte dei Marmi on the first of August. When we came back the brooch was gone."

"Did Eddi know it had gone missing?"

"No." Pain crossed her face. "That is why he did not tell me or the carabinieri."

"When he saw the bloodied pin near his father's body, he thought you had killed him."

"Yes, and I cannot blame him for thinking it. I was beside myself with fury at Giancarlo that night. He was going to leave us. That is why he falsified those invoices. He needed money. He knew I would cut him off."

"Why didn't you tell Eddi the pin was missing?"

"It would have upset him. He likes Giulia." She pressed her lips together, her face expressing some unpleasant thought. Nico waited.

"For an ugly moment," she finally said, "I wondered, may God forgive me, if Eddi might have taken it. He likes to show off our wealth to his friends. For all his braggadocio he is an insecure boy. His father was not good to him. I tried to love Eddi for both of us."

What about Mimmo? Nico wanted to ask but didn't. "You didn't fire Giulia."

"No. Giancarlo kept insisting she was innocent and that I had somehow misplaced the brooch without realizing it."

"You believed him."

"I accepted it as a possibility. I had been working very hard at the pharmacy and I was extremely tired when we left for vacation. A few weeks later, during a phone call I was not meant to hear, he revealed a truth I had been shunning for too long a time." She stopped and took a long breath. "I am finding this difficult. I prefer to keep my personal life tightly corseted."

"If you want justice for your husband, please go on. You overheard your husband talking on the phone."

She uncrossed her legs and sat up. "I knew he had occasional short-lived dalliances, but I learned to shrug them off. Women make do in these situations. The thought of divorcing him, our family"—her shoulders shuddered—"our name becoming gossip fodder was unthinkable. Besides I loved him.

"I did not know until that overheard call that he was in love—seriously in love—with another woman. That's why he stole the brooch. To give it to her, to Livia." She leaned toward Nico seated across the coffee table from her. "Yes, the woman who hired you."

Nico tried to keep the surprise from showing on his face. "What did he say exactly during the call you overheard?"

"The words are imprinted in my heart." She began to recite, "'I love you, Livia. I need you near me. I cannot stop thinking of you. Please, Livia, give me a chance. I will show you something to prove how much I love you. A gift that proves my love.'" Annamaria twisted her wedding ring, then flattened her hands on her thighs. She turned her gaze back at Nico. "I walked away after that."

"Do you have proof that he gave her the pin?"

"Ask her. Not that she will tell you the truth."

"How much is the pin worth?"

"At least fifteen thousand euros."

"Isn't it more probable that he stole it for the money it would bring?"

"That would have been sensible, but Giancarlo was rarely a sensible man." She stood up. Nico did also. "Goodbye, Signor Doyle."

OneWag, who'd been sleeping at Nico's feet, sat up, alert to the change between the two-leggers.

Nico said, "Please wait until I find proof before going to Maresciallo Fabbri."

"Why should I?"

"Because the bloodied pin, brooch, whatever you call it, found at the murder scene is yours and he might wonder if you aren't the one who killed Giancarlo Lenzi." He saw his words hit Annamaria like a slap in the face. "Think of your children," he added quickly. "Let me find the proof."

"You work for her!"

"Her assignment was to find who killed Giancarlo Lenzi and that is what I will do, no matter who that person is. Do I have your word?"

"You have twenty-four hours."

"Make it forty-eight for the boys. I will keep in touch, Signora." Nico and OneWag found their own way out of the Lenzi home.

In Piazza della Repubblica, Nico went to Caffè Degli Archi and finally had breakfast. The two cornetti didn't compare to Jimmy's. While OneWag slurped a whole plastic bowl of water, Nico called Perillo.

NICO REACHED THE CARABINIERI station in Greve just a few minutes before three. As soon as he entered the maresciallo's office, Daniele stood up at the back of the room. Perillo looked up from behind his desk with arms crossed. "You took your time."

"And buongiorno to you, too, Perillo. Pitigliano isn't exactly next door. Ciao, Dani." Nico sat in the interrogation chair while OneWag headed straight to Daniele.

"You stopped for lunch?" Perillo asked.

"A late breakfast."

"Ah, I understand."

"What do you understand?"

"Why you look like a guillotined mouse." Perillo picked up the phone and pushed a button. "Vince, order a couple of schiacciate, tuna, mortadella, whatever they have left, water, a double espresso . . ." He turned to look at Daniele.

"Nothing for me, Maresciallo."

"I don't need food," Nico protested.

"That's it, Vince. Thanks." Perillo hung up. "That's my lunch. I waited for you."

"Oh, I'm sorry. And the guillotined mouse?"

"You have received information that does not please you. Pull up a chair, Dani."

Daniele obeyed. Seeing the man had no treats for him, OneWag settled at Nico's feet with a loud huff.

"Yesterday Debora Costa gave me information that put a different light on the case." Nico repeated what she had told him in the synagogue. "If Eddi hid the pin, then he never told his mother about finding it in Lenzi's office. He knew that pin belonged to Annamaria, and that night his parents had a ferocious fight. That combination made him think his mother had killed Lenzi. Annamaria didn't know Eddi had gone to the store that night."

Perillo sat back in his armchair with a smirk on his face. "So, it was the wife, eh? Good. Case solved." He raised a finger. "You are a good detective, Nico, but this time you must give the laurels to the Debora lady."

"I will do so happily, but the case is not solved." Nico went on to relate what Annamaria had told him earlier. "Now she was convinced her husband stole it to give to Livia as proof of how much he loved her."

Daniele's eyes widened. "She's covering up by pointing the finger at Livia?"

Perillo dropped his crossed arms on his desk. "What proof did she give you?"

"A phone conversation she overheard in which Lenzi told Livia he would show her something that proved his love for her."

Perillo blew out his lips. "Livia murdered Lenzi? For what reason? That sounds like a fairytale Annamaria tells herself to fall asleep. She overhears her husband declare love to another woman, she becomes a fierce, wounded tiger of a woman. But she is an intelligent woman. She waits for the right opportunity, which Saverio gives her with his public fight with Lenzi."

"And the pin?" Daniele asked.

"Aah, the pin." Perillo sat back in his armchair and thought for a moment. "I'll offer a good probability. She finds it in his office, which could only ignite her anger even more. Maybe, she flings it at him before striking with the hammer. She leaves the pin there since everyone knows it was stolen from her."

"Her children didn't," Nico countered.

"Her children will believe whatever she tells them." Perillo picked up the office phone. "Vince, where the devil are those schiacciate?" He put the handset back with a grin. "They are making fresh ones for me." His elbows dropped down on the desk again. "No one is going to believe that Livia kills Lenzi and when her partner gets blamed hires you to find the real killer."

"Unless that's a ploy?" Daniele asked.

Perillo shook his head with closed eyes. "No, no, no. Annamaria is weaving a story to confuse you, Nico. It is clear you have your killer."

"Looks like it," Nico admitted.

"There's no 'looks' about it," Perillo declared. "It is."

A knock at the door was followed by Vince poking his head into the room. "The schiacciate are here."

Perillo raised both his arms with a loud, "Ah, Vince, come in, come in."

Vince used a shoulder to open the door. Daniele quickly reached the door and took the tray from him. On seeing his friend, OneWag ran to Vince and checked his shoes. They smelled of lick-worthy tomato sauce.

"Ciao, Rocco," Vince said, giving OneWag a quick back rub. He looked over at Nico. "Is it okay?"

At Nico's "Rocco will only be too happy," OneWag was out of the room before Vince. "But go easy on the food," Nico said to a closed door.

"What are you going to do now?" Perillo picked up the tuna schiacciata. "Call Fabbri?"

"I want to talk to Livia first."

"A waste of time." Perillo took a big bite, some of the tuna oozing onto a finger.

Daniele sat back in his chair and rested the empty tray on his lap. "Did you see the pin?"

"Yes." Nico gave Daniele a description and watched him thumb flicking his phone's screen. "What are you looking for?"

"A pin that fits that description." Half a minute later, he added, "Here it is on Instagram." He handed the phone to Nico.

Perillo leaned over his desk to see. What he saw made him frown. "I would have put my hand over the fire I was right."

Nico stared at a picture of a small gathering of well-dressed people with smiles on their faces and flutes in their hands. At the center of the group was Susanna Necchi in a flowing black dress. Pinned to one shoulder of the dress was a sapphire flower with a diamond in the center, looking exactly like the one Annamaria had shown him. He felt his heart pump harder.

"Beauty is wonderful to look at," Perillo said, "but not to be trusted. Stupid of her not to delete that photo."

"She can't," Daniele said. "It's included in a recent brochure the Thermal Baths of Sorano published to mark their anniversary.

They held a fundraiser on the seventeenth of October. There are other photos of her in it, but this one shows off the pin best."

"How did you find it, Dani?" Perillo asked.

"I got curious."

"Aah!" Perillo waived the half-eaten schiacciata in the air. "You wanted to see for yourself la bella di Pitigliano that Nico was interviewing with great interest."

Daniele swallowed and managed not to blush.

Perillo turned his interest to Nico. "Now will you go to Fabbri?"

"No, I want to talk to Annamaria and Eddi first." Nico took out his phone. "Dani, let me take a photo of it." Daniele held out his phone. Nico took the photo. "Thank you, Dani." He pocketed the phone. "You may have just solved Lenzi's murder for me."

"You are taking a leap," Perillo proclaimed after swallowing. "I may still be right."

"Well, I will just have to see." Nico stood and dropped an envelope on Perillo's desk. "Ivana's check for the Panda as promised. I'll keep in touch." Nico crossed the room and closed the office door behind him. Daniele heard him whistle for his dog.

"Finding that woman's picture was a good thing, Dani," Perillo said. "But remember, the woman you love is always la piu' bella."[25] This time Daniele couldn't stop himself from blushing.

AS SOON AS NICO reached the station's parking lot, he called Livia.

"There have been some new developments. It now seems your sweet neighbor made a false confession."

He heard a sharp inhale followed by, "How do you know that?"

---

25 The most beautiful.

"Forgive me, I can't explain right now. There is a lot of new information that needs to be studied and understood. Did Lenzi ever offer you a sapphire pin?"

"He stopped me when I left work one day and showed it to me. He told me it had belonged to his mother, and he was going to sell it so he'd have more money to leave Annamaria and be with me. I told him I would never be with him, no matter how much money he had and walked away."

"When was this?"

"Sometime in early September, I think. Why do you ask?"

"That pin is going to give us the killer. Thank you, Livia. Be patient. It's almost over."

Nico clicked off. His whole body was tense. He was almost there but needed help. He got in the car. OneWag jumped on his lap.

Annamaria answered with, "You work quickly."

"Sometimes luck is on the side of justice. I am going to send you a picture that tells a different story about the destiny of your pin and who the murderer might be. Please call me back when you have seen it."

"WHAT IF SHE DOESN'T call back?" Nelli asked as she smoothed a clean tablecloth over the table. Nico had just filled her in on the latest developments. Four hours had gone by since Nico sent the photo to Annamaria.

"She will get back to me." Nico was heating a cast-iron skillet for pork chops and sautéed baby potatoes. OneWag was by his feet, licking his now-empty food bowl. "Maybe I will have to wait until tomorrow. I gave her quite a shock. She thought she finally had her husband's murder all worked out. I suspect she doesn't like to be wrong. Do you feel like chopping parsley?"

"It is an urge I have had all day." Nelli took the cutting board Nico handed her along with an intimidating knife.

"After dinner I have another job for you."

"Besides cleaning up?"

"I'll clean up while you do a drawing of the downstairs room with everything you're going to want in it. It will be emptied, cleaned and painted by the end of the month."

"That is fast."

She saw the sudden doubt in his eyes. Her doubt.

"Want me to slow down, Nelli?"

"No."

His eyes smiled.

"You get to choose the paint color."

"Even if you hate it?" she asked.

"I can't hate anything about you. You are too wonderful."

Nelli started chopping vigorously to hide her embarrassment. "I think your pan is burning."

It wasn't, Nico saw. She had simply wanted him to stop looking at her. He poured a glass of red wine and placed it next to her. She wasn't used to being loved so much. He needed to remember that.

NELLI WAS CLEARING THE plates and Nico was washing the sauté pan when his phone rang. He answered it with a soapy hand.

"Buonasera, Signor Doyle. I was able to reach Maresciallo Fabbri. He received the photograph you sent me and has already summoned Susanna to his office at eleven o'clock tomorrow morning. I want you to be present for the interrogation. It is unusual, but I insisted. Susanna Necchi is a very manipulative woman, and I fear her beauty will further affect Maresiallo Fabbri's reasoning, which has never been the sharpest. Your presence will annoy him, but it will put pressure on him to ask the right questions. He agreed to allow you to ask Susanna your own questions, should you be dissatisfied with his. I hope that is satisfactory."

"It's perfect. Thank you. You must have waved a magic wand to get him to accept me."

"No magic wand. An important family name does carry weight in a town known for its history, but Fernando Fabbri has been indebted to my family since the day my father saved his mother's life when she was pregnant with him. With your help, I pray my family will finally know the truth. Buonanotte, Signor Doyle."

She clicked off before Nico could respond.

While he was on the phone, Nelli had taken over the washing. A prolonged silence from Nico made her turn to look at him. He was looking at the phone in his hand, a stunned look on his face. "Good news or bad?" she asked.

"The best." He joined her at the kitchen sink and told her what Annamaria had arranged with Fabbri as he took over the washing and she dried. "By tomorrow afternoon we should finally know the who and the why of the Lenzi murder case."

"Are you going to tell Livia?"

"I prefer to wait to give her definitive news. Can you take OneWag with you tomorrow?"

Nelli looked at the dog now curled up on Nico's armchair. "I'll be happy to have him. The boss is away again."

A FEW HOURS LATER, when they were both reading in bed, with OneWag snuggled between them, Nelli put her book down. "I have been thinking about the right paint color for downstairs."

"Good." Nico was reading a recipe for potato pizza.

"I think fuchsia would really light up the room."

Nico swallowed, waited a beat, then said, "It will make your paintings stand out."

Nelli took the cell phone out of his hand and kissed him. "I was kidding, and I love you."

"That's good too." He kissed her back.

OneWag jumped off the bed and made his reluctant way to Nico's armchair in the next room.

EIGHTEEN

"**S**ignor Doyle," the brigadiere announced as he opened the office door. Fabbri was standing in front of one of the two windows in his office, his thin, black-uniformed frame melding with the gray day outside. Somewhere in the room a clock ticked the seconds loudly.

"Buongiorno, Maresciallo," Nico said from the door. Fabbri looked at his watch but did not turn around. Nico stepped further into the room. "Thank you for allowing me to be here while you interrogate Susanna Necchi. It is very kind of you."

"An obligation, not a kindness." Fabbri turned around and walked to his desk. "I find that gazing out of a window helps me gather the questions I need to ask." He sat down behind his metal desk piled with stacks of papers and turned his bony face toward a still-standing Nico. His voice, coming from such a thin, small-boned man, was surprisingly deep. "How does an American detective prepare his questions?"

"I used to make a list."

"No more?"

"No more an American detective. Only an American."

"Who likes to involve himself in other people's business."

"Only when asked."

"Ah yes, the little girl. Take a chair next to the sofa. The left one."

Fabbri waited until Nico had followed his instructions to continue. "As you already know Signora Necchi, when she arrives, please limit yourself to a simple greeting. After I have finished my interrogation, you may ask her a few questions if you feel compelled to do so. I'll let you know when."

"May I ask you a question now?"

Fabbri closed his eyes. Nico took that as a yes. "You have discarded Signor Fulci's confession?"

"I never took it seriously, but I cannot discard it until I have proof he is lying. Making a false statement is against the law. He will have to suffer the consequences."

"Jail?"

"That will be up to the substitute prosecutor." There was a knock on the door. Fabbri shot up from his chair, pulled down his uniform jacket and ran a hand over his gelled hair.

The brigadiere announced, "La Signora Nec—"

The door swung open, and Susanna marched into the room with her high-heeled thigh-high black boots and a thigh-length overstuffed shiny black puffer coat.

"Maresciallo Fabbri, what can I tell you now that I haven't already told you?"

Nico stood up.

Seeing him, Susanna's lips widened into a Julia Roberts smile. "Ciao, Nico, what are you doing here? It is too early for Prosecco. And where's your cute dog?"

"Buongiorno, Susanna. Rocco's at home."

"Too bad."

Fabbri visibly tightened his jaws. "Signor Doyle is here at my asking. He has assisted the carabinieri many times. Having dealt with crime in another country, he can offer a different perspective should one be needed. Please take a seat on the sofa, Signora."

As Susanna walked to the sofa, she slipped off her coat and tossed it to one side of the sofa. Underneath she wore a clingy black turtleneck over her tights. No jewelry, no makeup except for glazed lips.

She's laying it on thick, Nico thought with some admiration. Fabbri's complexion had gone from winter gray to early summer burn.

The brigadiere who had followed her in took a seat at a small table holding a tape recorder.

"Signora, may I offer you some coffee?" Fabbri asked.

"No, thank you." She crossed her legs. "I had to cancel a photo shoot for the Thermal Baths in Sorano to be here." She tossed her hair from one side of her shoulder to the other. "So, tell me, Maresciallo, what can I do for you?"

Fabbri nodded to the brigadiere, who announced the start time of the meeting and the persons present.

Fabbri picked up a brochure from his desk, opened it to a page and showed it to Susanna. "What can you tell me about the pin you are wearing in this photograph?"

"Ah, Annamaria's precious sapphire and diamond pin. Is she asking for it back? If she is, she won't get it."

Fabbri sat down on the right-hand chair. "How do you know it belongs to Signora Lenzi?"

"She loved to show it off at every dinner my husband and I were invited to. Even when she knew Matteo was about to lose the winery and we were begging Giancarlo to give us a loan, her pin sat just above her flat breast, her way of sticking out her tongue at us."

"How did the pin come into your possession?"

Susanna sat back and uncrossed her legs. "That is a good story but if I tell you the truth, Maresciallo, you have to promise not to punish me."

Fabbri grew rigid. "I cannot make any promises. The law is the law."

"If you stand to benefit from the truth, an exception can be made," Susanna said.

"Please answer my question, Signora. How did this pin come into your possession?"

"One night I arrived early to Giancarlo's office for our weekly rendezvous and went through his drawers to pass the time. A small velvet box screamed jewelry, so I opened it. I recognized the pin right away and realized Giancarlo had stolen it."

"Why stolen?" Fabbri asked. "It might have needed repair."

"There was nothing wrong with it. Giancarlo needed money. He wanted to leave Annamaria and start over somewhere else. After we made love, he would sometimes talk about starting a new life. Being in love with him, I thought he was talking about a new life with me. When, a couple of weeks later, he told me we were over, I took the pin and replaced it with the office key he'd given me. My little revenge. I wore it for the first time for the Thermal Bath's party. Have I answered your question?"

Fabbri's *yes* was followed by silence.

Nico took advantage of it. He leaned closer to Susanna. "Giancarlo must have given you a reason for breaking off the affair."

"He said Annamaria was asking too many questions."

"He told you he was in love with Livia?"

Susanna pointed her eyes at Fabbri as if wishing him to interrupt.

Nico leaned even closer to her. He could smell her perfume. "That must have made you very angry. How could he reject a woman as beautiful as you are, a woman who gave herself to him any time he wanted, throw you over for a plain woman who already had a man of her own and his child? It was galling. Unfair."

"Painful!" she whispered to herself.

"Yes, very painful. All the more so because he loved someone who wanted no part of him."

Susanna narrowed her long-lashed eyes at him, the rest of her face frozen. Nico sat back up. There was hate in those eyes.

"The pin you stole, the pin you are wearing in the brochure photo, was found at the murder scene with your ex-lover's blood on it."

Susanna's eyes flashed open. Now they showed surprise. She looked at Fabbri. "Is that true?"

"Yes. There was a great deal of blood at the murder scene. I have a warrant to search your apartment in Sorano."

Susanna waved her hands in front of her face. "No, wait, wait."

"You cannot stop the search!" Fabbri barked.

"No, go ahead. Turn the apartment upside down, but now just give me a moment." She started rocking back and forth, mewling a string of *nos*.

Nico felt a quick pang of regret for his aggression. "What is it?"

"Wait. I never thought . . . Oh God . . ." Susanna searched through her coat pockets for her phone, clicked on photos and flipped through a stream of images. "You have it all wrong. So very wrong." She stopped at one photo and held it out for Nico to see. "I took a selfie after it happened."

Fabbri took the phone away from her before Nico could see what she was trying to show him. He studied the photo with narrowed eyes. "Your dress is torn."

"Ruined. An Armani. Well, an Armani knockoff that still cost more than I can afford. I had no idea he would react like that."

"Who are you talking about?" Nico asked.

Fabbri held out his arm to stop any further questions from Nico.

"One look at Annamaria's pin on my chest and his face turned lava red." Susanna's eyes widened with what looked like shock.

"He demanded that I take it off and was growling like a dog about to attack. A rabid dog. He scared me. I tried to unhook the pin, but the security lock was stuck. He was not going to wait, ripped it right off, taking the shoulder of my dress with it." Susanna inhaled deeply and turned to face Fabbri again with the hint of a smile. "At least the party was fizzling out. I made my exit without being seen. The spa expects me to always look good." The smile widened.

Fabbri handed the phone back to Susanna, his arm still held out like a cop at a traffic stop. "Signora Necchi, are you telling me that you no longer have the pin in your possession?"

Nico groaned in silence.

Susanna slid herself closer to Fabbri's chair. "Yes, Maresciallo, that is exactly what I am telling you. As I just told you, my husband, Matteo Necchi, from whom I have been separated for the past three years, ripped it off me. What he did with it afterward is for you to find out. May I go now?"

"Yes, but you will have to come back to sign the statement once it has been typed." Fabbri nodded to the brigadiere, who looked at the large clock above the door and declared the time and end of the interview.

Susanna stood up, swung her puffer coat over her shoulder and spat, "To think I liked you!" to Nico. Six heavy boot steps later she was gone, followed by the brigadiere.

Fabbri slowly returned to his desk. "Your aggression toward Signora Necchi was uncalled for."

"I was convinced she was guilty. A mistake it seems."

"It seems? You do not believe she told the truth?" Fabbri asked with a lilt of surprise in his voice.

"She may have, but she didn't mention if anyone witnessed what she claims her husband did." *Something I should have asked when you didn't.* "It will be interesting to hear what Matteo Necchi has to say when you question him."

Fabbri lifted the office phone receiver and pressed a button. "Matteo Necchi in my office"—a glance at the clock—"at four this afternoon." He put the handset back in its cradle and sat up straight with a ponderous look on his thin colorless face.

Nico crossed his fingers mentally and waited.

"I suppose your aggressive approach can be useful in some cases. Today it has produced confusion. What was a simple case has become intricate." He picked up a ballpoint pen, clicked it shut. "I do not like intricacies. I have found that the most obvious solution to a crime"—he clicked it open—"is most often the correct one."

"You still think Saverio killed his business partner."

Fabbri kept clicking. "I used to find it indisputable. Now, after your detective work on behalf of Saverio's partner, I find it probable. I am willing to receive new information." He opened a drawer of his desk and dropped the pen inside. "Will you still be in Pitigliano at four this afternoon?" he asked as he seemed to examine the contents of the drawer.

"I would very much like to be here if it would be of any help."

Fabbri's neck seemed to lengthen, his eyes widen. "I do not need your help, Signor Doyle. This morning, I was only extending a courtesy. I may do so again. Please leave your phone number with the brigadiere on your way out."

Nico stood up. "I am very grateful for the courtesy. And I apologize for having spoken out of turn with Signora Necchi."

"This afternoon I will see if it was useful," Fabbri said, "or another waste of my time. Buongiorno."

On his walk back to the old town, Nico called Perillo. "Daniele's photo did the trick. Fabbri let go of his 'Saverio guilty conviction' and met with Susanna Necchi this morning."

"Were you there?"

"Yes, but all the credit goes to Fabbri, remember that. I gave my word that whatever I discovered was his, not mine."

Perillo huffed in annoyance. "You mean, in this instance, also what my excellent brigadiere discovered."

"We are a team, yes?"

"Yes. So?"

Nico told him what Susanna had said about Necchi getting angry and tearing the pin off her dress.

"Ah, good. He takes the pin and gives it back to the rightful owner, Annamaria, who then coldly pays her husband back for his treachery with a hammer blow to his temple. You will also witness the Matteo Necchi interview?"

"I'm waiting to hear."

"Enjoy a good lunch while you wait, and buon appetito. Dani and I are enjoying a tasty polenta alla boscaiola made by Stella in her new kitchen." He lowered his voice to a whisper. "I think she is preparing to be a wife."

"Ciao, Perillo, go back to the Stone Age where you belong."

Nico got the call from the brigadiere while he was sitting at the Caffè Degli Archi in Piazza della Repubblica, after having eaten a toasted schiacciata filled with roasted porcini mushrooms. He was now enjoying a slice of Mariella's apple cake.

"Maresciallo Fabbri asks you to come to the station at four-thirty. Your reason for coming—" The brigadiere stopped. Nico heard the rustle of paper. "Your reason for coming," the brigadiere continued, "is to pay a courtesy visit to report any new information you may have discovered," he was clearly reading, "during your personal investigation of the Lenzi murder."

A clever excuse for his presence, Nico thought. The man could think after all. "Thank you. I will be there."

MATTEO NECCHI, HIS FACE fixed in a scowl, was seated on the sofa when Nico walked into Fabbri's office. He had dressed up for the occasion in a blue suit that might have fitted him better a couple of years ago over a white shirt and a burgundy knitted tie.

Fabbri, still impeccable in his uniform, stood up from his interrogation chair. On his desk were two empty espresso cups sitting in their saucers. "Signor Necchi, I believe you have met Signor Doyle? He is investigating your cousin's murder on behalf of Livia Granchi."

"He asked a lot of questions." Necchi pulled at his tie. "I got him to buy some wine."

"Which I enjoyed very much," Nico said. "Should I come back another time, Maresciallo? I unfortunately have made no progress in my investigation. I was hoping you had news I could refer to Saverio's partner and his daughter. Cilia can't stop crying."

"I hope I will be able to stop her tears any day now," Fabbri said. "This murder case, which I originally thought was straightforward, has revealed itself to be a complicated one. Please take a seat, Signor Doyle." Fabbri pointed to the chair Nico had sat in that morning. "Your client will be relieved to hear that new developments are pointing away from Saverio Bianconi as the murderer. First came a confession that might be false, then the discovery at the murder site of a valuable sapphire pin belonging to the victim's wife, a pin Signor Necchi's estranged wife was photographed wearing at a fundraising party a few weeks before Lenzi's death. And then there is this photo." Fabbri pushed his cell phone, showing Susanna's selfie in front of Necchi's face.

Necchi seemed to sink into the sofa, as if air was leaking out of his body. "I did not hurt her."

"Why did you rip it off her?"

"She had no right to wear that pin. It belongs to Annamaria. It is a special pin, a love token Giancarlo gave her when Eddi was born."

"What did you do with the pin after you ripped it off Signora Necchi's dress?"

"I took it to Giancarlo's office the next day. I had put it in a small box with a note." His body seemed to fill up with air again. "Giancarlo wasn't in. I asked Saverio to give it to him."

Fabbri turned to Nico with a taut smile on his face. Saverio again.

Time to step in, Nico thought. "What did your note say?"

"'*This pin belongs to your wife, not mine.*'"

"You assumed your cousin had given that pin to your wife because you knew they were having an affair together."

"We are separated. What she does with her body no longer concerns me."

"Didn't it concern you when you were still together? Isn't her affair with Giancarlo the reason you are separated?"

"No. I disappointed her when I lost the winery. She was angry and wanted to walk away, go back to Sorano and work at the Thermal Baths."

"According to Susanna, her affair with Giancarlo started because she was trying to bail you out. But then she fell in love and thought Giancarlo loved her back. Your cousin, who had refused to loan you even a euro to save your winery, now had stolen your wife. And one night she invites you to the Thermal Baths fundraiser and you see her in her fancy dress, as beautiful as ever, wearing Giancarlo's pin, a pin you assumed he had given her to show how much he loved her.

"You ripped it from her. What to do with it now? You say you left it with Saverio. You could have returned it to Annamaria and let her share the pain and anger you were feeling. Let her know what a low-life bastard she married. Or face Giancarlo with the pin."

"No, Maresciallo, please," Necchi pleaded. "I gave it to Saverio."

Fabbri said nothing, so Nico continued.

"Weren't you torn, maybe even scared, by the strength of your anger, your pain? Emotions that you had kept under control since losing the winery and your wife. Now you must have felt a fury you could no longer control."

"No." Necchi's voice was impassive. "You are wrong."

"Five days later Saverio discovers Giancarlo's treachery, knocks him down in front of witnesses, and yells, '*You will pay.*' You realize you could make Giancarlo pay for what he has done to you without having to pay for it yourself. Let Giancarlo's devoted friend suffer the consequences."

"No, you are wrong! I gave the pin to Saverio in a box with a note."

"Maybe I am wrong. Maybe Saverio's discovery of Giancarlo's treachery only encouraged you to face your cousin, finally release all your anger at him."

"I was angry, yes," Necchi shouted at Nico. "My anger was justified. I lost my business, my wife because of him, but kill him?" He stomped his foot. "No! No! No!" He turned to Fabbri. "Maresciallo, I have told you the truth. I did not kill Giancarlo."

"I believe you," Fabbri said with a surprising soft voice, "but let us hear what new twist Signor Doyle's imagination has produced."

An insult or encouragement? "Thank you, Maresciallo." Nico bent down, his elbows on his knees, to bring his face closer to Necchi's. "You went to the store with the pin in the early hours of Sunday the twentieth of October to vent your anger, your sense of betrayal. When Giancarlo saw the pin, he told you it had been stolen from him, maybe even thanked you for bringing it back to him.

"He was lying to you as he always had, taking you for a fool. You accused him of giving the pin to Susanna. He must have laughed, told you she had stolen the pin, that Susanna was nothing more than a fling he had ended."

"That's a lie!"

Fabbri stepped in. "No, Signor Necchi. She admitted she stole the pin to me this morning. It will appear in her statement."

Necchi dropped his head in his hands.

The poor man, Nico thought, uncomfortable about pushing Necchi so hard. "Matteo, the Maresciallo needs the truth. So do Annamaria and her sons, Saverio and Livia and Cilia. A long list of people who have done you no harm. Was it after hearing that the woman Giancarlo stole from you meant nothing to him that you noticed the hammer? All you wanted to do was hit him, shut him up. You picked up the hammer, struck his temple with the claw. A crack, a cut, then blood. A lot of blood. You threw the pin at him and ran. You had no key to the store, so the door was left open for Eddi to find a few hours later. If you had hit him with the face of the hammer, Giancarlo would still be alive."

One or two minutes went by, the only sound the seconds clicking by on the wall clock.

Fabbri lost his patience and stood up. "Is there any truth to Signor Doyle's version of events that night?"

Necchi slowly lowered his hands from his face and aimed sorrowful eyes at Nico. "He started drumming his fingers on the desk. He got angry, demanded the pin back. I threw it at him. He said he never spent a cent on Susanna, that she was only good at spreading her legs, that I wasn't smart enough to keep the winery going, no matter how much money he put into it. He was leaving, starting over somewhere else. '*I am going to ride high. I'm not a loser like you.*'

"The pin had fallen next to the hammer. I reached over to take the pin back, picked up the hammer instead." Necchi looked at his hands. "I hit him as hard as I could." His gaze shifted to Fabbri. "Please tell my wife I only wanted to shut him up. She loved him."

Fabbri turned to Nico with a barely perceptible gleam in his gray eyes. "Signor Doyle, on your way out, please tell Brigadiere Villena to bring the tape recorder."

Nico stood up. "Certainly. Your discovery. Not mine." Walking out, he found the brigadiere waiting outside the door, the tape recorder already in his hands.

Nico got back in the car and sat for a while. His aggression toward Necchi left him feeling hollow. He had, in his career as a homicide detective, always tried to coax the truth out of a suspect first, but Fabbri's presence, his possible shift back to Saverio's guilt, had egged him on. He wasn't proud of what he'd done even if it had led to the truth. He felt sorry for Matteo Necchi. No one deserved to be killed but Giancarlo Lenzi came close to it.

Nico picked up his phone. He wanted to spread the good news. No. There was still a slim chance Fabbri would resist believing Necchi's confession as he had supposedly not believed Fulci's. The solution of the Lenzi murder case was now in Fabbri's hands. Best to wait.

Nico put the phone in the dashboard holder and started the car.

LATER THAT NIGHT, NICO was in bed drifting off to sleep, enjoying the warmth of Nelli's foot touching his calf when a text dinged on a nearby phone. "Yours," he mumbled.

"Mine's turned off," she said softly, putting her book down to look at him. He still held the day's tension in his face, a tension he had explained by saying only, "It's just under my nose."

"Something good? Something bad?" she had asked. She got no answer and let it go.

"Want me to check if it's important?" she asked him now.

"Hmm."

Nelli reached over him and picked up the phone from the night table and read.

"Nico, amore"—she shook his shoulder—"wake up. You need to read this."

Nelli's urgent tone prompted OneWag, lying between them, to raise his head.

Nico, eyes closed, asked. "Good or bad?"

Nelli placed the phone in front of his face. "Find out for yourself."

Rubbing his eyes, Nico lifted himself up on one elbow and read:

MARESCIALLO FABBRI WISHES TO INFORM YOU THAT A CELL PHONE ANSWERING TO GIANCARLO LENZI'S TELEPHONE NUMBER WAS FOUND IN THE APARTMENT OWNED BY MATTEO NECCHI. TRUTH OF NECCHI CONFESSION THUS CONFIRMED. DISTINGUISHED SALUTATIONS. BRIGADIERE MAURO VILLENA.

A tidal wave of relief washed over Nico. He fell back on the bed, pulled Nelli down and kissed her forehead. "That is the best of news." He checked the time on his phone. Ten-fifty-three. "What do you think? Wait till morning?"

"Waiting is for bad news."

"Right you are." Nico got out of bed and called Livia.

A sleepy "Pronto?" answered.

"It's Nico. I have good news from the Pitigliano Carabinieri Station. Lenzi's murderer has been found. It is his cousin, Matteo Necchi. Tell Saverio he can come home."

Livia made a strange sound, what sounded like a sob mixed with laughter. "True?"

"Yes. True."

"Thank you." She was openly sobbing now. "Thank you so much."

"Thank Fabbri. I am only the messenger. Buonanotte."

"Not buona, Nico. Stupenda!" Livia clicked off.

Next Nico texted Perillo, Daniele and Debora Costa the good news. Fabbri would be the one to tell Annamaria.

"You told Livia you were the messenger?" Nelli asked when Nico lay back in bed.

"I made a pact with Fabbri. He gets all the credit and Livia won't wonder why I'm not charging her."

Liva turned off the light and spooned herself against Nico. "I am so very lucky I met you, Nico Doyle."

Nico closed his eyes and pushed his nose into his pillow. "Me too," was his sleepy reply.

NINETEEN

Nico stretched one leg, opened an eye. "What time is it?"
"Almost nine. Time for you to get up," Nelli said from the other room. OneWag confirmed by jumping on the bed and nudging Nico's chin with his nose.

Nico swung out of bed and made his way to the bathroom. "Why didn't you wake me? Gogol will think I've forgotten him."

"He knows better. You deserved to sleep. Now hurry up. I have a job to go to."

AS SOON AS NICO walked into Bar All'Angolo with Nelli and OneWag, Cilia ran to him and yelled, "Sorpresa!"

People stood up. Applause broke out. Nico stopped in his tracks. The café was filled with his friends: Gogol, Daniele, Perillo, Luciana, Tilde, Enzo, Elvira, Stella, Laura, Livia holding a mute Cippi, Gustavo, even Laura's new chef, Riccardo. Behind the counter Jimmy and Sandro were also clapping.

"Hey, great to see all of you—"

Luciana interrupted with, "Enrico apologizes but he had to open the store."

"A sensible man," Nico said, emotion clutching his stomach. "Please stop clapping and sit down. Will someone please tell me what's going on?"

Everyone sat, except Luciana. "Happiness is going on. I heard it last night, clapping and laughing so loud it came through my bedroom wall. I complained. Livia explained and asked me to spread the news. I called Gustavo. He did the rest. We are thanking you for Cilia and Livia finding happiness again."

Nico gave Perillo a warning stare before saying, "Maresciallo Fabbri deserves the applause. I only poked around and stirred things up." A chorus of murmured *nos* followed. "Thank you. I am a very lucky man to have you as friends. The applause you gave me rightfully goes to Cilia and Livia for being such strong women."

Everyone stood up again and filled the room with cheers, whistles and applause. Cilia hid behind her mother. Cippi barked. OneWag barked louder.

While Stella, Nelli and Sandro served another round of coffee and pastries, Nico's cell phone dinged the arrival of a text.

THANK YOU FOR THE GOOD NEWS. I HOPE YOU WILL COME AND VISIT AGAIN.

He texted Debora back. NEXT WEDNESDAY? GIULIA'S FRITTATA FOR LUNCH?

I EXPECT YOU AND ONEWAG AT ONE.

Nico sent a thumbs-up emoji, pocketed his phone and went around the room shaking hands and thanking his friends.

"Ehi, what about us?" Perillo waved Nico over to where he was sitting with Gogol and Daniele.

When Nico sat down with them, Perillo turned to Gogol. "What does your poet have to say about this?"

"He says, 'I feel that I rejoice.'"

Nico smiled. "How right he is."

PENNE ALLA NICO

Serves four

INGREDIENTS:

- 500 g. package of ridged penne
- 6 sweet Italian pork sausages
- 4 large garlic cloves—minced
- 1 cup tomato sauce, previously made or from a can
- 1 large bunch of curly kale
- 1 cup freshly grated Parmigiano-Reggiano
- Red pepper flakes
- 3/4 cup of red wine
- Kosher salt

MAKE AHEAD:

1. Remove kale stems and cut leaves into small pieces. Rinse and drain well. Remove casings from sausages and break into small pieces.
2. Heat olive oil in a large cast-iron skillet. Add sausage pieces and cook for five minutes, stirring often. Add red wine and let reduce for two or three minutes. Remove sausage and set aside. Add some oil if skillet is too dry. Add kale and salt. Stir. Add garlic. After two minutes add tomato sauce and sausages, stirring well. Add a few sprinkles of red pepper flakes if desired. Cover skillet and remove from heat to allow kale to wilt and absorb.

WHEN ALMOST READY TO SERVE:

1. Bring large pot of water to a boil. Once water boils add 3 or 4 tablespoons of kosher salt. (The water should taste like seawater). Add penne. Cook one minute less than package directions.
2. Turn heat back on under skillet to medium and uncover. Save a cup of pasta water, drain the penne and add to skillet. Stir well for one minute. Add parmigiano. If mixture seems too dry add some pasta water. If the penne seem too al dente for you add more pasta water and cook a minute or two more. Taste for seasoning. Bring the remaining parmigiano to the table.

Buon appetito!

ACKNOWLEDGMENTS

I thank, first of all, Soho Press for believing in Nico's adventures in Tuscany. Their endorsement has allowed me to discover Gravigna and now Pitigliano, to follow characters that have become a big part of my life. Rachel Kowal, my editor, comes next. She makes sure that my writing is the best it can be. Johnny Nguyen makes sure that everyone who needs to know is aware my new book is out. I am grateful to the copy editor Sarah Lyn Rogers. I admire her patience with my inconsistencies.

Next come the people in Panzano, who, having accepted my yearly intrusion into their lives, still answer my many questions with a smile. Gravigna would never have come to life without the help and patience of Lara Beccatini, vintners Ioletta Como and Andrea Sommaruga, and retired Maresciallo Giovanni Serra. A voi mille grazie!

I ask forgiveness of the Pitigliano maresciallo dei carabinieri. Fabbri is a figment of my imagination. I mean no disrespect.

And last but not least, I thank my readers. I hope you enjoyed Nico and OneWag in Pitigliano.